Adam Kennedy's pre~~~~~~~~~~~~~~~~~~~~~~~~~~~~~~
successful thriller *The* ~~~~~~~~~~~~~~~~~~~~~~~~
the international hit m~~~~~~~~~~ ~~~~ name, to *In a Far Country*, an enthralling family drama set in the 1960s. His most recent titles include the Bradshaw Triology: *No Place to Cry*, *The Fires of Summer* and *All Dreams Denied*; *Love Left Over* – a collection of bitter-sweet love stories; and the first two volumes of the Kincaid Trilogy: *Passion Never Knows* and *Dancing in the Shadows*. He lives in Connecticut with his wife, Susan.

*Also by Adam Kennedy*

*The Bradshaw Trilogy*
No Place to Cry
The Fires of Summer
All Dreams Denied

*The Kincaid Trilogy*
Passion Never Knows
Dancing in the Shadows

*Novels*
Debt of Honour
The Domino Principle
The Domino Vendetta
In a Far Country
The Killing Season
Barlow's Kingdom
The Scaffold
Maggie D.
Somebody Else's Wife
Love Song
Just Like Humphrey Bogart
The Last Decathlon

*Stories*
Love Left Over

# Love, Come No More

## The Kincaid Trilogy
## Volume Three

Adam Kennedy

**HEADLINE**

First published in 1992
by HEADLINE BOOK PUBLISHING PLC

First published in paperback in 1993
by HEADLINE BOOK PUBLISHING PLC

10  9  8  7  6  5  4  3  2

ISBN 0 7472 3961 4

Printed and bound in Great Britain by
HarperCollins Manufacturing, Glasgow

HEADLINE BOOK PUBLISHING PLC
Headline House
79 Great Titchfield Street
London W1P 7FN

For Susan . . .
with my love

One must never understand one's enemy or one's wife. One must never understand anyone for that matter, or one will die of it.

*Jean Anouilh*

# BOOK ONE

# • CHAPTER 1 •

1

Dying is a simple trick. Each of us is able to do it. Those who watch us die, however, have another sort of problem. The effect of death on survivors is bizarre and complex. Although we pretend to be shocked by what we see, we are in fact accustomed to it. Few of us are surprised when a widower, dutifully married for forty years, takes up with a cocktail waitress ten days after his wife's burial, or when a loving son who had promised to cherish and preserve his mother's harpsichord sells it to a greengrocer for thirty pounds. Quite often couples separate or assault each other after one parent or another passes on. Teetotallers discover gin. Widows seduce delivery boys. Once daddy dies, his daughter feels free to leave her husband and children, and disappear to the Isle of Wight.

What does all this mean? Nothing perhaps. On the other hand it may indicate that we're a society of captives defined, at least in part, by our captors. When a captor dies the captive is free to redefine himself. Obligated, perhaps, to do that.

Do such conclusions and perceptions pertain frequently or only seldom? Are they relevant, for example, in the case of Jack Brannigan? He was neither captive nor captor. He had been married to Margaret Cranston for only a few months. Many of her friends and family members had never met him. Why, then, would his death cause such wrenching changes in the lives of the Cranstons, the Taggs, and the

3

Kincaids? Hard to say. But there's no denying that astonishing changes did take place.

Consider Sophie, for example – Sophie Kincaid. Child of benevolence and privilege. She had never questioned that the gods were kindly disposed toward her. Smiling at her birth, watchful ever since. This is not to say that she had seen no hardship. At sixteen she was heart-broken. At twenty she was a widow with two small children. But she never lost her conviction that she was protected somehow, that things would always come right for her.

That feeling was particularly strong in the weeks just preceding Brannigan's death. There were days, many such days, when she awoke in the California morning believing she was the world's most fortunate woman. On those mornings she would ring for her breakfast, stay in bed with the morning paper and her two cats, and lazily list her blessings.

Lifelong patterns resist change, of course. And so it was with Sophie. When the trunk call came through from England, when she was told that her mother's husband was dead and Margaret herself was under a doctor's care, Sophie made plans at once to close the Malibu house and return to Northumberland to her family home. She never doubted that she was needed there.

During that voyage and through the next weeks when she was fully occupied with her mother, with setting right the disruptions that Brannigan's death had caused, Sophie found neither the time nor the energy to study her own state of mind. Her children, Trevor and Sarah, who had followed her home from California, were in her London house now, along with the staff; Kincaid had finished his work in Los Angeles and would be back in England soon; and Margaret, who had been persuaded to leave Clara Causey's house and return home, was in residence again at Wiswell Towers. So Sophie began at last to measure the results of her efforts on Margaret's behalf. By taking a positive approach, by ignoring negative impulses, her conviction that she had a gift for saving situations had pulled her through. And had pulled her mother through. Or so she persuaded herself.

Suddenly, then, when everything seemed in working order, Sophie found she couldn't sleep. Unable to pin-point the cause, unable to identify a particular anxiety that might be keeping her awake, she simply lay inert and dead tired in her bed. When she was finally able to fall asleep, usually at dawn, she awoke to a world of enemies and conspirators, to fits of gloom that were almost unbearable. And they persisted . . . fierce recurring squalls of torment. Flashes of insight told her that the enemies she saw were not true enemies, that the conspiracies were unreal. Still the pain continued, made worse by her unwillingness to tell anyone what she was going through.

In her family it was an accepted truth that Sophie was a Wiswell, that she showed no genetic inheritance from the Cranstons, her father's family. Now, however, she herself began to see reflections of her father in her tortured state. Resisting such a thought, refusing to believe that there could be a resemblance between herself and the hapless retired Major, who polished his rifles and side-arms endlessly while he railed against Whitehall, India, tenant farmers, and his bootmaker. All the same she continued to feel his paranoia taking root in her.

She noticed too, now, that she had begun to take a contrary position to almost any remark, however innocent or trivial, that was said to her. These sharp dissents often went unexpressed but they steamed and bubbled in her mind none the less. Even in people she admired she began to perceive ugly traits and characteristics. She was unloved. Friends became rivals, allies became antagonists. She felt slighted, offended, ignored, and undervalued. Though she didn't lash out at people, she began to feel, very often, a strong urge to do that. These nagging impulses were concealed, of course, behind her familiar veil of tolerance and concern. No one suspected that fire-storms were raging inside her.

5

Kincaid, whose mother was an Aborigine – who in any case *believed* very strongly that this was so – had once said of himself, had said it openly to a journalist who was interviewing him, 'Somewhere inside me there's a wrinkled and ferocious little man with tribal scars on his forehead and a bone piercing his nose.' Sophie had now begun to have such feelings about herself. She came to believe, as she lay awake night after night, that she was inhabited by an unpredictable stunted creature who surfaced without warning whenever it chose to, eager to accuse and condemn, to pillage and burn.

2

In mid December, not long after Sophie had left California to return to England, the following item appeared in Burt Windrow's syndicated column in American newspapers.

Julian Thorne may be having headaches with his Christmas release of *Dillinger*. Rumour has it that his star, Roy Kincaid, could be in trouble with the law. Sources in the prosecutor's office tell us that he may be charged with conspiracy to commit a felony. Kincaid put up thirty thousand dollars in bail money for his friend Homer Tony, who was charged with rape and assault. Tony then disappeared. Authorities who have been reviewing Kincaid's own criminal record believe he may have had a hand in that disappearance. Before he became Thorne's big money-maker, Kincaid was an admitted recidivist.

'What the hell does *that* mean?' Sam Thorne said. 'That's a new one on me. I can't even pronounce it.' He was sitting in his brother's office at the studio.

'Nobody can pronounce it,' Julian said. 'It's a smart-alec word. It means you've been in jail a lot.'

6

Sam shook his head. 'This guy Windrow's a real pain in the ass.'

'I thought you had a conversation with him the last time he took a pot-shot at Kincaid.'

'I did. I explained our point of view and he understood what I was saying. You've seen all the bouquets he's been throwing us in his column.'

'So what happened? This is no bouquet.'

'I guess he's got a bad memory.'

Julian glanced at the press cutting on his desk. 'We're all set to spend a fortune promoting *Dillinger* and now we have to deal with this crap. Have you talked to Sugarman?'

'I called him from home this morning as soon as I read the paper. He says he'll stay on top of it. Says we should do nothing and say nothing till we get some official word from downtown. He says, don't lean on Windrow but make sure that Kincaid stays in California. In case the prosecutor's office wants to talk, it shouldn't look like he ran off to England so he wouldn't have to sit down with them.'

'Kincaid's gonna love that. He's all set to leave.'

'Don't worry. I passed the buck to Sugarman. He'll call him. Tell him what we're up against.'

'I always knew that guy Homer Tony was trouble. He should be in a zoo.'

'Don't let Kincaid hear you say that. He'll lay you out flat. You'd think the guy was his brother or something.'

'The papers just stopped talking about him. Now here it comes again. Everybody in this town thinks he raped that girl . . .'

'I know they do but they're wrong. I told you that. It was a scam. She was lying in her teeth, that little twat.'

'You know that and I know it, but most people don't. Now we've got Kincaid tied up in people's minds with a guy who rapes young girls.'

Sam shook his head. 'Sugarman says they've got no case. They can't prosecute a guy for putting up bond and that's all Kincaid did.'

'Are you sure?'

'Trust me.'

'You're telling me that Kincaid had nothing to do with Homer Tony's disappearance. Is that right?'

'Nothing. Zero.'

'How do you know?'

'Because Sugarman told me and I believe him.'

'You mean Sugarman engineered the whole thing?'

'Not a chance. He's a lawyer. He don't leave his fingerprints anywhere.'

'Then who did?'

Sam shook his head. 'No idea.'

'Do you know where Tony is now?'

Sam shook his head. 'Don't know. Don't want to know. Neither do you.'

'Does Kincaid know?'

'I can't tell you the answer to that. Maybe he got a postcard or something. All I know is that Kincaid didn't engineer the deal.'

'According to you nobody engineered it. Are you telling me that Tony walked out of the Santa Monica jail, caught a bus and went to Tijuana?'

Sam smiled. 'It's possible.'

'Don't cock around with me, Sam. We've got a lot at stake here and I need information.'

'So do I. But I don't know where to get it.'

Julian leaned back in his chair and lit a cigarette. 'All right. Now I understand. Corso took care of things, didn't he?'

Sam held his hands palms up and said, 'Not as far as I know. I can't guarantee you that he didn't help out a little, but if he did, it wasn't through me. John Corso's all over town. You know that. All I can tell you, Julian, is that I'm clean, the studio's clean, and Kincaid's clean.'

Julian smiled. 'You answered my question.'

'No, I didn't. Cause I don't know the answer. But I'll tell you one thing: if John did it, it was done right. Nobody's gonna dig up any link with Kincaid. Kincaid's an innocent

8

friend who blew thirty grand in bail money. End of story.'

Kincaid met with Ralph Sugarman later that same day. After
Sugarman had explained the situation Kincaid said, 'That
fucking Windrow won't be satisfied till I'm either dead or
in prison.'

'That's the price you pay for being famous.'

Kincaid shook his head. 'This is different. This is personal.'

'Maybe so. But our big problem is the prosecutor's office.'

'What can they do to me? Outside of putting up the bond,
I wasn't involved. You insisted on that. Remember? I went
along for the ride when Corso's men took Homer Tony to
San Pedro to get on that freighter, but I never got out of the
car. Nobody saw me.'

'You're right. But the prosecutors have taken a lot of heat
because your friend never went to trial. The newspapers had
decided he was guilty and people wanted blood. So they need
to hang something on somebody. I talked to the District
Attorney about it this morning. He can't bullshit me and
he knows it. He knows they can't pin a conspiracy charge
on you but he has to let his boys play their hand. I don't
even think you'll have to talk to them but we can't take any
chances. They might call you in. If I had to tell them you're
out of the country we'd be in the headlines. No good for
you and no good for the studio. Julian's sweating blood.'

'So am I. I get a cable from my wife in England every day,
asking when I'm coming home. I'm scheduled to leave here
day after tomorrow.'

'I know you are but we can't work that fast.'

'Do you know what kind of a bonfire my wife's sitting on
over there?'

'Sam told me something about it. Her father shot somebody.'

'Not just *somebody*. Her folks are divorced and her mother's married again and that's who's dead . . . the new husband.'

'Sounds like a mess.'

'That's not the word for it. Sophie's father's locked up in a mental hospital and God knows what kind of a state her mother's in. I can't sit here and let her deal with all that by herself.'

'If I were in your shoes I'd feel the same way you do. There's no law that says you have to hang around here waiting for an interview that may never take place. All I'm saying is that anything that puts this case back on the front page is a disservice to Homer Tony, to you, and to the picture you just finished.'

Later that day, Kincaid spent two hours in Julian Thorne's office. That evening he sent a cablegram to Sophie.

DEPARTURE DELAYED. LETTER FOLLOWS. SAILING NEW YORK. SIX JANUARY.

4

On December 8th, Evan Tagg sailed from New York on the *Britannia*. On the 15th he arrived at Southampton. The next day Sophie met him at the railway terminal in Newcastle. 'It's cold and nasty,' she said. 'We can snuggle up in our travel rugs in the back seat and be driven home in style.'

As their car made its way through the narrow streets of Newcastle she told Evan about the cable from Kincaid.

'I know,' Evan said. 'He rang me up in New York the day before I sailed.'

'What is all this crazy business? Can they really prosecute Kincaid because Homer Tony disappeared? Kincaid lost thirty thousand dollars. Do they think he would encourage someone to default when he knew how much it would cost him?'

'I did some research on this. Jumping bail is a felony. Conspiring with someone to help them jump bail and become a fugitive is also a felony . . .'

'But that's what I'm saying. Kincaid could only conspire to do that if he was willing to throw away his money.'

'Nobody thinks they're going to prosecute Kincaid. Nobody wants bad publicity just now.'

'Because of the bloody movie,' she said.

'That's the main reason.'

'But everyone knows Kincaid has a criminal record. He tells anybody who asked him how many times he's been in jail.'

'This is different. There were a lot of newspaper stories in Los Angeles about Homer Tony. The public has already tried him and convicted him. They're convinced he assaulted that girl who worked for you, the one with a face like a cookie. What was her name?'

'Ursula. Last name Martin I believe.'

'People were mad as hell that Tony skipped bail and got away and nobody knows where he went. So anybody who helped him get away is not going to be popular in California.'

'Who cares what those people think?'

'Kincaid cares, I think. And I know damned well Julian cares.'

'Of course he does. Protecting his investment.'

'It's not just that, Sophie. Julian's not a shark. At least not where Kincaid's concerned.'

She smiled. 'I've played the game as far as Julian Thorne is concerned. I think it's lovely that he paid both you and Kincaid a great deal of money . . .'

'Kincaid much more than me, my dear. I'm just a writer.'

'I know. But all the same, in a short space of time, both of you have prospered.'

'No question about that.'

'And no one doubts,' she went on, 'that the key bene-ficiary of your working relationship has been Thorne himself. For all his Savile Row wardrobe and his attempts at Mayfair speech, is he really any different from his crude brother and the rest of their push-cart fraternity?'

'Bitter . . . bitter.'

'I'm not bitter. They've done me no disservice. But I see no need to have illusions about such people. Both you and Kincaid have come to believe that you're dealing with a benevolent gentleman, a man of culture and decency. You even believe he's your friend. Isn't that true?'

'I think you should be having this conversation with Kincaid, not me.'

'Why do you say that? I've known you all my life. We grew up together. Do you think I'm less concerned about your well-being than I am about Kincaid's? You've certainly never hesitated to point out my errors in judgement.'

'Is that what you're doing? What's my latest error?'

'I remember when you were fifteen and just discovering psychology. You used to give me long lectures about the crime of self-deception.'

'And am I guilty of that? Is that it?'

She patted his cheek. 'I'm so glad to see you. And I'm not finding fault with you. I just think you deceive yourself about the magnificence of Julian Thorne.'

'You're probably right.'

'Oh dear. When you agree with me I know I'm in trouble.'

'Not true. In my eyes you're flawless. You know that.'

'I do know that. That's why I'm always eager to see you.'

'Same here,' he said. Then: 'How's Margaret holding up?'

'She's all right, I think. Making good progress. From the way she looks and behaves you'd never guess what she's been through. She's tough, you know. Her life with my father taught her not to feel sorry for herself. I'm sure that was never her instinct in any case. But this whole experience has been more hideous for her than any of us can imagine. After all the pain and the delays of her divorce from the Major there came that whole senseless battle about his leaving the Towers. Mother hated the thought of the constables coming and carrying him away by force but in the end there was no other solution. The thing that made it acceptable to her was the

12

realization that at last her long ugly years with him would be over and she and Brannigan could put together their own sort of life. You know what I'm saying?'

Evan nodded and she went on. 'She didn't want to be away from the Towers that day but Ned and Clara Causey, and the police as well, thought the Major would be easier to handle perhaps if she weren't on the premises as a witness. I know she feels now that things might have turned out differently if she'd been there. I can understand that, because I feel the same way. I think if I'd been there things would have been different.'

'You think she feels guilty?'

'No, I don't. Although it's hard to know precisely how she feels because, as I said, she makes a great effort to act as she always has, to be as she's always been. Margaret's a survivor but she's never had to survive anything like this. She's never had to deal with the kind of hatred she's feeling now. That's all new for her. In a way I think it frightens her but in another way it's her most precious possession. Like a plant someone keeps in their bedroom and carefully nurtures through the winter.'

'That doesn't sound like her.'

'I know. But it's very real. Before I could persuade her to come here from the Causeys she insisted that every single thing that might remind her of the Major be removed. His quarters were completely repainted and refurnished. And she charged me to inspect every inch of the house for any object that might even remotely be connected with him. Beds and chairs and rugs and desks and foot-stools and paintings and photo albums and pipes and decanters and humidors and clothing were carted off to the forest and burned. All his saddles and bridles and boots were destroyed. His roadster and his motorcycle, his billiard table. All his military gear, weapons and swords and uniforms, were carted off to York and disposed of. His horses and dogs were sold in Scotland. Every tiny article . . . ashtrays, toilet things, razors and brushes and tie-pins, pens, pencils,

13

writing-paper, all of it, everything, sought out and destroyed. Mrs Whitson and Trout and I spent a full week checking every nook and cranny, then double-checking each other to be sure that nothing of him would be left. His chair in the dining hall was burned, the chairs and couches in the library and the morning-room and the music-room and the billiard-room, any object he might have used was destroyed.'

'My God. How strange.'

'Naturally, we missed two or three small things. Stuck away in drawers or on high shelves. But Margaret, when she came home at last, went to them like a retriever. She scolded Mrs Whitson and Trout unmercifully because those things hadn't been removed.'

'I don't think I've ever heard her speak sharply to anyone.'

'You would have done if you'd been there that day. As soon as she was inside the house she asked for the staff to be assembled in the great hall. When they were standing before her she said, "I'm a widow now but I'm not a cripple or a helpless old woman. No tiptoeing about or whispers behind my back. And most important . . . mark this clearly . . . I am now going to speak the name of Major William Cranston. But from this moment on I will tolerate no mention of that name. There will be no reference made to the man or the days when he was in residence here. This is the most irrevocable order I will ever give you. Any person who ignores or violates my wishes will be instantly dismissed. No exceptions will be made."'

Near the end of their drive home, when they were only a few miles east of the Towers, Sophie said, 'I've been waiting for a report about my strange and wonderful husband but you haven't said a word.'

'Not much to tell. As I said, we talked on the telephone when I was in New York on the way here. He was bloody annoyed that he had to stay on in California through the Christmas holidays.'

'I'm not surprised. I was damned angry myself when I got his cable. But when I got over being angry, I simply felt

14

rotten that he had to be there all alone in that huge house.'

'He hasn't been living in the house. When we were finishing the film, he moved into his dressing-room at the studio.'

'But where is he now?'

'He's living in Homer Tony's cottage. In the meadow there on your property.'

'You can't be serious. Why on earth would he do that?'

'I don't blame him,' Evan said. 'I went out there with him one day when the actors and crew had just moved back to Los Angeles from Chicago, and your house was a dreary-looking place. Cold and empty inside. All the shutters bolted, the furniture covered with dust-cloths, and that odd caretaker couple lurking about, playing cards in the kitchen with the wireless blasting. And the security guards parked in the driveway day and night. Not an inviting place, Sophie. I don't blame him for moving into the cottage.'

'Well, I do. What an odd decision. I did leave in a great rush because I had no choice. And perhaps the arrangements the staff made when they closed up the house weren't perfect, but good God, I should think he would have stayed in a hotel rather than hole up in that horrid little shack.'

'Have you ever been inside the cottage?'

'Of course not. Why in the world would I?'

Evan smiled. 'You're a dreadful snob, Sophie.'

'Not at all. I saw Homer Tony around the stables and the grounds almost every day. He always looked as though he wanted a good wash. So naturally one draws certain conclusions about the place where he lived.'

'You'd be surprised. He kept it ship-shape. Not a great deal of furniture but everything clean and scrubbed. Painted floors, and curtains at the windows, and the drawings your son made stuck up on all the walls.'

'I know,' she said. 'Trevor was as taken with the place as you seem to be. I decided he liked it because it was as disorderly as his own rooms.'

15

'Not true. Kincaid was snug and cozy there. He said it reminded him of bunk houses he'd known in Australia.'

'Good Lord, what's the world coming to? The man has a house like a castle and he decided to live in a shanty, out beyond the stables. Where did he take his meals?'

'He cooked there in the cottage. That's where he ate.'

'I can't believe it. What's come over him?'

'Nothing. You don't imagine that the way he's lived since the two of you have been married, and since he's been making thousands of dollars a week as an actor, is what he's accustomed to, do you?'

'Whatever he was accustomed to, he's accustomed now to something better, a great deal better. Nobody goes from good to bad by choice. He's not poor any longer. He's not a stable-hand. He's not Homer Tony, thank God.'

'It's not as simple as that. A man like Kincaid doesn't shed his skin like a snake. He is what he is, but he's also what he was before. Of course he's not Homer Tony but he's a lot closer to it than you think.'

'Nonsense. I know they were friends for a long time but . . .'

'It's more than that. They're *connected*. In lots of ways, I expect. When we were on location with *Bushranger*, after Homer Tony was brought up from Australia to play one of the trackers, he and Kincaid were together all the time, laughing and talking in Kincaid's caravan.'

'Talking? Homer Tony can't talk. He's a mute.'

'Of course he is. But he can listen. And he understands. He understands a lot.'

'I know. Trevor told me the same thing. But it's hard for me to believe. The man looks like a savage. He's . . . he's prehistoric.'

'It doesn't matter. He and Kincaid are like brothers.'

'Don't even say that. It upsets me.'

'It's true. Kincaid loves him.'

'Don't be ridiculous. He feels sorry for him. At least he

16

did before it cost him thirty thousand dollars. Now I expect he feels a bit differently.'

'Not at all. He'd do it again. In a minute.'

'It seems you know Kincaid better than I do,' she said. 'I don't recognize this man you're describing.'

He leaned over and kissed her cheek. 'Love is blind. Didn't our nanny ever tell you that?'

5

Still in their dinner-jackets, Evan and his father, Arthur Tagg, sat in Arthur's rooms the night of Evan's return.

'Well, you're back,' Arthur said.

'Yes, indeed. And happy to be.'

'And how do you find us?'

'Pleasant surprise,' Evan said. 'I was expecting a sombre atmosphere. A great deal of sadness. That sort of thing.'

'Yes, I expect you were. But Margaret and I discussed it and we decided that in spite of our inner feelings we must honour the holiday and celebrate the fact that we're all together again.'

'It's a damned shame Kincaid was detained.'

Arthur nodded. 'A disappointment for Sophie certainly. But I hope it won't spoil things for the four of us . . . you and Sophie, Margaret and myself. Like old times, as they say. After all, you and I have spent a great many of our holidays in this old house. And this one should be in that tradition. Much to be thankful for.'

'Not much for Margaret, I expect.'

'Actually I was thinking of Margaret. At last she's free of the Major.'

'But she's lost Jack Brannigan,' Evan said. 'That's another matter altogether.'

'Yes, it is. But the Lord moves in curious ways, doesn't he? Margaret's handling herself very well. And I've never

17

seen her look better. By the way, I assume Sophie told you
. . . Margaret had made it a firm rule that Cranston's name
is never to be mentioned.'

'I assume that doesn't apply to you and me.'

'It applies to everyone,' Arthur said. 'House rule.'

'I've been away, remember? I was assuming you'd tell me
what's gone on. The Major and all that.'

'Sophie didn't tell you?'

'No. We had other matters to discuss. What happened
exactly?'

'How much do you know?'

'In California, Kincaid and I only picked up bits and pieces.
I know the constables had a court order to remove the Major
from the Towers, but when they came to do the job, he
managed somehow to shoot Brannigan.'

Arthur settled back in his chair, placed his fingertips
together like a tiny church tower and said, 'After the divorce
was final, after Margaret had gone to Ireland to marry
Brannigan, when the two of them had returned home here,
the Major, who'd had previous orders from the courts to
leave the Towers, still refused to go. Carried on about his
military record in India and swore that he'd resist by force
any effort to remove him. And sure enough, when the
constables arrived that morning he fired down from that
window over there and shot an officer in the leg.'

Evan got up, walked to the window and looked down on
the broad driveway serving the west entrance. When he turned
back he said, 'These were his rooms, weren't they?'

Arthur nodded. 'Completely refurbished.'

'And they're your quarters now?'

'Yes, they are. Many other changes taking place as well.
Bringing some of the unused rooms up to date. Sophie's in
charge of all that. The entire east wing will be for her and
Kincaid, she says. Larger quarters as well for Sarah and
Trevor. I wouldn't be surprised if there's an apartment in
the planning stage for you. A home for all the family. That's
how she sees it.'

'How does Margaret see it?'

'The same, I expect. Sophie's heir to it all, in any case. There's no quarrel between her and her mother.'

'How do you feel about it?'

'I'm still just a guest in the house. Doing my bit.'

'You didn't answer my question.'

'Nor do I intend to. If I have reservations, they will be voiced sometime in future.'

'Sounds ominous,' Evan said.

'Not at all. I'm a most co-operative man.'

'That's true. But I've never seen you in such a handsome dinner-jacket before. I've never seen you with a moustache. When I arrived this afternoon you were wearing boots and breeches and a hacking-jacket. I'd never seen you in a riding-costume before. So I thought perhaps some other changes had taken place as well.'

'I think not,' Arthur said, 'but time will tell, I suppose.'

Evan returned to his chair. 'You were telling me what happened the day they came for the Major.'

'Yes. As I understand it, the wounded constable was hurried off to hospital and the officer in charge rang his barracks for reinforcements. The Major had barricaded the hall door. So the plan was to send men up ladders on the north wall and at the same time break through the small door there in the corner that leads to the back stairs. Margaret was not here, you know. She'd been persuaded to spend the day at Wingate Fields with Clara Causey.'

'Yes, I did know that.'

'Somehow, when the constables were in place, ready to storm this room from two sides, Brannigan persuaded the chief that he still might be able to reason with the Major, to speak with him from outside the rear door and get him to put down his weapons. The officer agreed to let him try. So Brannigan went up the rear staircase, took a position outside that door, and called to the Major. Immediately a shot-gun blast tore through the door and struck him full in the face. He died instantly.'

19

'My God. The Major's a lunatic.'

Arthur nodded. 'Always has been. But somebody had to die before anyone would admit it.'

'What a rotten thing to happen. Will he be prosecuted or is he . . .'

Arthur tapped his forehead with a forefinger. 'He couldn't be put on trial. Doesn't know who he is or where he is. Like a two-year-old child now. Babbling. Slobbering. No control over his bodily functions. He's locked away for life. A converted military hospital just west of Newcastle.'

'Has anyone seen him?'

'Only Sophie. The authorities told her it was hopeless but she insisted on going none the less when she first came home. Had a notion that there were legal questions, family matters to be discussed. Obligations. Responsibility. All that. Also I think she simply had to see for herself, no matter what anyone said. Sophie's like that, you know. She's a bit like that.'

'So she saw him?'

Arthur nodded. 'She saw something. And the attendants told her it was her father. When she came back here that evening I thought we'd have to put her in hospital. She looked like a poor creature who'd witnessed a beheading. She didn't come right for more than a week. And even then her eyes, when you spoke to her, had a vacant look as though she couldn't see clearly. She didn't mention it to you, eh?'

Evan shook his head. 'Thank God, Margaret didn't see him.'

'Not much chance of that. If the major should have a miraculous recovery, if he came walking through the door downstairs tomorrow, she would pick up a gun, if one was available, and shoot him dead. She wouldn't hesitate.'

They sat with their brandy glasses then for more than an hour, Arthur speaking in great detail about crops and cattle and farm implements, about county rates and local politics and the graft being uncovered in Carlisle. 'The county's changing, the country's changing. There's a new lot of greed about, everywhere you turn. A worker's loyalty to his master, for example. What's become of that? Elliott Good-pastor says it's the fear of war. Not twenty years since the last one ended, but once again people are starting to hoard flour and sugar because they expect rationing. A great lot of cynicism. Not much hope in people's hearts. Dog eat dog. Great estates are being cut up and sold off, daughters are marrying outside the county. Nothing intended against Sophie, but ten or twenty years ago she'd never have married Kincaid. Wouldn't have married anyone who wasn't a county man. And certainly wouldn't have married outside her class even if she chose a lad from Kent or Surrey. And do you think Margaret could have brought Jack Brannigan home if her mother or father were still alive? Never. Not a chance in the world.'

'You didn't like Brannigan, did you?'

'Didn't like him. Didn't dislike him. Didn't know him. I'm not an aristocrat. Not a member of the gentry. But all the same, I've never been on familiar terms with a man like Brannigan. This is not to say that he wasn't a decent enough fellow. I'm sure he was or Margaret wouldn't have been taken with him. But on the other hand there's a certain sort of Irish chap who's able to cast a spell on women. You under-stand what I'm saying? Able to talk and smile, spout poetry, and sing lullabies. Charming rogues. You've met them. You may be one, as far as I know. Even though you're not Irish. In any case, Brannigan, whatever else he was, was one of those hypnotic fellows. I spotted it when he was here for *Country Life* taking photographs, chatting up the staff, and spreading marmalade on all sides. He wasn't a handsome man. Not tall. Gone thick at the middle and a bit thin in the hair department. But in full charge of any situation, able to manage or prevail or whatever was necessary, able to make people chuckle and come round to his way of doing things. No wonder he thought he could stand outside the Major's door and talk him into walking into the corridor and down the great stairs without his gun. Brannigan was a talker. He could talk anybody into anything.'

Evan smiled. 'But you didn't like him.'

'I never thought about it that way. I just didn't think he was good enough for Margaret.'

Just before they said good-night and Evan went back to his room, he said, 'The last word I heard from you was a nasty cablegram. Do you remember that?'

'The last time I heard from you, it was a nasty letter. That I remember.'

'Have we got past all that?'

'I don't know,' Arthur said. 'Let's wait and see.'

'I'm not sure I like the sound of that. Since you've come back here to the Towers now, since everything seems serene between you and Margaret, I thought matters might look different to you.'

'Some matters do. Others don't. As I recall your letter you scolded me at some length because you believed I'd behaved badly.'

'Did I have it wrong? Sophie told me what was in her mother's letter. Margaret said she'd accidentally bumped into you in a bookshop where you were working in London and you'd treated her like a stranger, like any other customer. I simply said in my letter that if it really happened that way I was surprised and disappointed in you.'

'I know exactly what you said. And I know what I said in the cablegram I sent you. I said, "How dare you pass judgement on me?" I still feel the same. That hasn't changed.'

'Did I get it wrong? Was Margaret mistaken about what happened in London that day?'

'That's in the past, Evan. I don't ask you to explain your behaviour and I expect the same courtesy from you.'

'I have the feeling suddenly that I've committed a deadly sin. Am I on probation now? Is this a testing-period? Are you holding me at arm's length till I've proved my worth?'

'Not at all. You have your own standards and I have mine.'

'What does that mean? Jesus, Dad, you're my father. I'm your son. You make it sound as if we're discussing some

business venture, trying to decide if we'd be compatible partners or if we should abandon the whole idea. What's going
on? The last letter I had from you before your angry cable,
that letter was a revelation to me. Things you said about
yourself, about me and our relationship, made me feel that
we had a connection now as two grown-up men, not just
father and son. Do you remember that letter?'

'I remember the gist of it certainly. If I had it in my hands,
I expect I wouldn't disagree with anything I wrote to you
then.'

'Then why do I feel like the enemy now?'

'You're not the enemy, Evan. If there seems to be a change
in me it wasn't inspired by you. Nor is it directed toward
you. I'm fifty-nine years old. Sixty next year. A milestone
in a man's life. A time when one is likely to review what's
gone before and make plans for what's to come. It was a
turning-point for me when I left the Towers some months
ago and went down to London to live by myself. All sorts
of adjustments had to be made. When Sophie came to me
in London after Brannigan's death and convinced me that
I must come back here because Margaret needed me, those
new adjustments I'd made kept me from saying yes. But at
last I agreed, knowing that accommodations and adjustments
had to be made. So if I seem different to you, I admit it freely.
I have changed.'

'Toward me, you mean.'

'No. Toward myself. And perhaps toward everyone else.'

'And what are those changes?'

'Ah, that remains to be seen, doesn't it? I expect you'll
be no more surprised than I will.'

6

An unusual December afternoon in Beverly Hills. A heavy
sky. Rain falling. Kincaid sat in Ralph Sugarman's office on
Wilshire Boulevard with Sugarman and Harold Fenstermaker,

an assistant District Attorney for Los Angeles.

'Now,' Sugarman said, 'before we start this conversation, let's make sure we all understand each other.' He turned to Fenstermaker. 'In my discussions with the District Attorney, when we agreed that this meeting should take place, the following points were made. One: no charges have been made against my client, Mr Kincaid. Two: this meeting was instituted by us to demonstrate our willingness to co-operate with your office. Three: this will not be a discussion of Homer Tony's guilt or innocence in the assault charge. Nor in the secondary charge of fleeing to escape prosecution. Four: since Mr Kincaid is here as a co-operating friend of the prosecution, this meeting will be regarded as a conversation rather than an interrogation. No notes will be taken and no transcript made from memory. Is that your understanding, Mr Fenstermaker?'

'Yes. Those were my instructions.'

'Fine. Let's proceed.' He turned to Kincaid. 'I think it would simplify matters if you began by telling us about your relationship with Homer Tony.'

'We're friends,' Kincaid said. 'He's one of my best friends. I met him in 1923 when I was fifteen years old. We worked together on a cattle run near a town called Glenrowan in Australia. When I was a couple of years older I left Australia. Shipped out on a freighter. I used to mail him picture postcards from wherever I was, but I didn't see him for quite a long time. But two years ago, when I was about to do a picture for Thornwood called *Bushranger*, I asked the studio to bring Homer Tony and three or four of his tribesmen to California to play trackers in the film. That's how he came to be here.'

'And when the picture was finished he stayed on?' Fenstermaker asked.

'That's right. I asked him if he'd like to take care of the horses at my place up above Trancas, and he said yes, he would. So he's been working for me since then.'

'I believe he's handicapped. Is that correct?'

'There's nothing wrong with his brain.' Kincaid said. 'But he can't talk.'

'I'm told the alleged assault took place on your property.'

Kincaid looked at Sugarman, who answered for him. 'It did. That's a matter of record. But Mr Kincaid has no knowledge of those events. He was working in Chicago at the time. And in any case we're not here to discuss those assault allegations.'

'Our case records show that the judge set a high bail amount because he thought Homer Tony was dangerous. Is he a dangerous man in your judgement?'

'Let me put it this way. He's as harmless as your grandmother. He's only dangerous if somebody tries to muscle him.'

'You disagree with the judge's evaluation of him then?'

'That's right,' Kincaid said. 'I know him. The judge doesn't.'

'And that's why you put up bail for him?'

'No. I did that because he's entitled to it, just like anybody else who gets arrested. And I was his only friend in California.'

'Thirty thousand dollars is a lot of money to lose.'

'I didn't expect to lose it,' Kincaid said.

'So you were as surprised as anyone when you found out he'd disappeared.'

'That's right.'

'Were you with him when he left the Santa Monica jail that afternoon? Was that when you saw him last?'

Again Kincaid looked at Sugarman who said, 'Mr Kincaid was unable to go to the jail when Homer Tony was released but I was there. I signed the papers and we walked out to the car-park together. There was a limousine waiting there. The driver told me Mr Kincaid had arranged for him to pick up Homer Tony and take him home. I assumed it was a car from Thornwood Studios.'

'So you put him in the car and he left?' When Sugarman nodded Fenstermaker went on. 'And that's the last you saw of him?'

Sugarman nodded again. 'I watched them pull out of the

car-park and the car turned toward the coast highway. Then I drove back to my office.'

Turning to Kincaid again, Fenstermaker said, 'Did you arrange for the car to pick him up?'

'No. When I found out I couldn't be there, Sugarman said he'd pick him up and drive him to my place.'

'That was the plan,' Sugarman said. 'But when the limousine turned up I thought Kincaid had decided to send him home in style.'

'Was it a studio car?'

'I don't know,' Kincaid said. 'You should ask the studio.'

'We did. They say it wasn't.'

'Then it wasn't. They had no reason to be involved. You asked when I saw him last. I visited him at the jail the day before he was released. And I expected to see him at home the following night. But it was late by the time I got there, there was no light in his cottage so I didn't wake him up.'

'And the next day?' Fenstermaker said.

'Mr Kincaid's new film was on location in Wisconsin at that time,' Sugarman said. 'He'd flown back to Los Angeles for just a few days to try to help out his friend. That morning after Tony's release Kincaid flew back to Chicago.'

'The studio car came to my house at five-thirty to take me to the airport,' Kincaid said. 'I knocked on the cottage door but there was no answer.'

'Didn't that surprise you?'

'No. He's a heavy sleeper. He hibernates. I've seen him sleep thirty hours at a stretch.'

'When did you realize he'd disappeared?'

'He knew it when I knew it,' Sugarman said. 'I called him in Wisconsin.'

'I see,' Fenstermaker said. Then: 'We've had one little piece of information that might mean something. We circulated his picture at the bus stations and railway terminals and at the harbours around LA. We figured if anybody had seen his face they wouldn't forget it. And sure enough a couple of workers on the docks at San Pedro thought they'd seen him one evening. They weren't sure of the day but it seemed to be the day he was released or maybe the day after. There were two or three freighters that pulled out in that time period but the companies when we checked with them had no record of a passenger named Tony.'

'Not much chance a man who can't talk could get himself on a freighter.'

'The dock workers thought there might have been a man with him. But they didn't get a good look at him.'

'If you knew who the men were who picked him up at the jail you might get some answers,' Sugarman said. 'Maybe he didn't run away. Maybe he's dead. He was getting a lot of hate mail when he was in jail.'

'We know that. But till we have a body . . .' he turned to Kincaid. 'I'm sorry. I didn't mean we're hoping to find him dead. But when we're up a blind alley we have to consider everything. We're just wondering . . . if he did get away, if he's out of the country, where do you think he might go?'

'If somebody put him on a boat I guess he'd go as far as the first port,' Kincaid said. 'Then he'd get off, unless ten men were sitting on him. The only place he'd want to go – I mean, if he had a choice – is Australia. If he's managed to get there you can forget about him. He'll disappear in one of his tribes like a drop of rain in a river. Australia's a big country and people don't carry identity cards. In the outback you can work with a man for two years and never know his last name.'

'Don't feel bad about this case, Mr Fenstermaker,' Sugarman said. 'I told the District Attorney that if he brings in that young victim as she calls herself, along with that slippery agent of hers, if you people start asking some creative questions, you'll find out that Homer Tony never should have been arrested in the first place.'

After Fenstermaker left, Kincaid said, 'How did we do?'

'We did fine. We lied a little and told the truth a lot. We did them a favour. We gave them what they needed. John

Corso's friends did all the work, you paid the bail, and that's it. Outside of that your fingerprints aren't on anything. And the District Attorney knows it. The official conclusion will be that you were stupid enough to do a thirty-thousand-dollar favour for a friend and he screwed you, left you holding the bag. I'll settle for that scenario. How about you?'

Kincaid smiled. 'I'll settle for it.'

'Now you can go back to England and herd sheep or whatever people do over there.'

'We do all kinds of naughty things. And I'm leaving tomorrow.'

7

Kincaid went directly from Sugarman's office to Thornwood Studios. When he walked into Julian Thorne's office, Thorne said, 'All your tickets were just sent over from the travel people. Frieda checked the departure times and everything's in order, she says. Sit down. Tell me how it went with Sugarman.'

Kincaid told him in detail about the back-and-forth dialogue with Fenstermaker. Thorne listened carefully. When Kincaid said, 'That's it. That's about the size of it,' Julian said, 'How did Sugarman read it? Plus or minus?'

'He said he'd call you at home this evening. He'll give you a full report. From what he told me, he's got it covered with the District Attorney . . .'

'Carl Moseley,' Julian said.

'Whatever his name is. They've got nothing to hit me with and I think they know it. This meeting today was just to cover their asses. They questioned me, they're satisfied that I had nothing to do with Homer Tony's skipping out of the country, and they can put that in their file. At least, that's Sugarman's scenario and I trust him.'

'So do I. Well, that's good news. Now we can get back to the picture business until your friend Windrow decides to take another pot-shot at you in that bloody column of

28

his. He's really got it in for you. You must have scared hell out of him that day at Lucey's.'

'It looks as if I didn't scare him enough.'

'Sam had a talk with him, you know, a few months ago. I don't know what was said. Sam's got a feel for these situations, so I let him do as he likes. And usually he gets results. We thought he had with Windrow. Since we spiked that rotten whispering campaign about you he's been smooth as butter. No attacks on you and lots of good comments about our product. Quotes we can use in our advertising. Good relations with our publicity people. Now all of a sudden it looks as if he's after you again.'

'Somebody's always trying to make a reputation by smearing somebody. Did Sam tell you what Winchell said? He said, "A columnist should smear everybody. Just be sure they're bigger than you are. Never go after the little guy."'

'Winchell makes his own rules,' Julian said. 'But Windrow is something else. We can pressure people like him. Even Louella will back off if you touch the right button.'

'I don't care what they write. They can say whatever they want to.'

'I know you feel that way. And so far it's worked for you. But I have to look at it differently. It's not enough to turn out a first-rate picture. After it's in the can I have to start selling it. And I have to keep on selling. That's a tough job even when you have no obstacles. But when somebody lays you open to scandal or censorship, when a crowd of dim-wits start carrying posters in front of your theatres, when all of a sudden the Catholic church bars your picture because your leading woman who's not married turns up pregnant – or the American Legion decides you're anti-American, or the City of Boston bans the picture because an actress didn't wear a brassiere under her sweater – then all of a sudden you end up talking to yourself, people stop buying tickets. Some newspaper in Cleveland decides my picture is a dog, and suddenly I'm stuck with five hundred prints of a damned good film that I can't give away. It can happen for no good reason, almost before you know it. That's why a bastard like Windrow can be dangerous. And what's behind it all? You threatened to put him out of commission because of a remark he made about your wife, and he turns it into a vendetta. What do you do with a freak like that?'

'Like I said, Julian. We ignore him.'

'I hope you're right.'

'I'm right. If you try to buck him you just make him more important than he is. And that's what he wants.'

'I'll tell you what I want,' Julian said. 'When we've invested a lot of time and money, when a great deal of thought and sweat by a lot of people has turned out a big money-maker like your first picture, and when the same kind of effort has gone into the one we've just finished, then I don't want anything to get between that product and the audience it deserves. No sabotage, no mistakes, no accidents. This *Dillinger* picture we've just completed has it all. Even Sam likes it and he doesn't like anything.'

'Sure he does. He likes gangster films. Loves the rattle of gun-fire. That's what he told me.'

'That's true. If he was sitting in my chair he'd have only two stars under contract. Mae West and Edward G. Robinson.'

8

At the Los Angeles railway station, when he went early morning to board his train to New York, Kincaid discovered Gloria Westerfield sitting on a bench in the waiting-room. 'Don't tell me you're taking the New York train.'

She shook her head. 'I just got off the train from Chicago and I look awful. I can't sleep on trains. Never could.'

'Come on. I'll buy you a cup of coffee.'

'I'd better not. I'm waiting for a car to pick me up.'

'Don't worry. He'll find you.'

'Don't you have to board your train?' she said.

'Not for twenty minutes. Come on. I'll even buy you an egg sandwich.'

'I hate eggs.'

'Then I'll buy you a bread sandwich.'

When they were sitting in a booth in the station café, he said, 'I haven't seen you for a while.'

'That's right. Since we got together in Chicago.'

'I decided you must have settled there. That was the idea, wasn't it?'

'It wasn't my idea. But I told them I'd think about it. And I did. But finally I convinced everybody at AP that my column only works when I'm based here in California. So that's where I'm going to be. I'm back to stay. And you're heading for England?'

Kincaid nodded. 'After a few delays.'

'I had a note from Sophie, written on the ship when she was going home. What a messy thing that must have been. How's her mother holding up?'

'I don't have all the details but things seem to have got set right. Sophie's good at that.'

'I'm sure she'll be glad to have you home.'

'Who knows?' Kincaid said. 'Maybe she's found a better man there in Northumberland. A tall reckless fellow who shoots little birds with a cannon and chases foxes across the fields.'

'I don't see that as a possibility and neither do you.'

'As I said, one never knows. I'll send you a full report when I'm back in London.'

'And I'll send you a report after I've been to a screening of *Dillinger*. Thorne's promotion people have set up a showing for me tomorrow. They're all excited about it.'

'They get paid to be excited about Julian's pictures.'

'That's true. But since you're not paid to be excited, perhaps I should ask you. You've seen it, I assume.'

Kincaid nodded. 'Saw a rough cut three or four weeks ago and the answer print last Wednesday.'

'So what's the verdict?'

'Not guilty.'

'I'm serious,' she said.

'So am I. I don't make judgements. Couldn't if I wanted to. You know more about films than I do. The verdict's up to you and your colleagues.'

'You're no help.'

'I just bought you a cup of coffee and a sticky bun. How much more help do you want?'

'Hopeless. That's what you are. I must remember to send your wife a sympathy card. Are there special cards for women with hopeless husbands?'

'There must be.'

When they left the café she walked with him to his boarding platform. 'Come see us in England,' he said.

'Maybe I'll do that. When will you be back here?'

'No plans.'

She stood facing him at the platform. 'Are you all right?' she said.

He smiled. 'A sound mind in a sound body.'

'I'm not joking. Are you worried about something?'

'I never worry. I'm a primitive soul. Sleep under a tree, catch a fish when you're hungry. That sort of thing.'

'Sometimes I think you really believe all those things you say.'

'Sometimes I do.'

'Other times, like now for example, I think you're selling yourself a bill of goods. Someday you'll get on a train like this one, but when it arrives where it's going you won't be on it. And no one will know what happened to you.'

'That's an interesting idea but I could never do it. I'm too close with a shilling. I could never climb down from a train before I'd used up my full ticket.'

'Sophie said she told you one time that you were unknowable.'

'I remember she said that. It's wishful thinking on her part, I expect. Trying to make me more mysterious and interesting than I actually am.'

'My sister once told me, "Never try to have a serious conversation with a joker."'

'Good advice,' Kincaid said. 'Somebody told me, "Never cry on a beautiful woman's shoulder."'

She leaned close to him then, kissed him on the cheek and said, 'Goodbye, Dillinger. Why do you have to be killed at the end of all your films?'

'Because I'm bad and the Hays office won't let me stay alive.'

He watched her walk away down the platform. Then he climbed on the train and went to his compartment. When the train pulled out he drew the window shades, leaned back in his chair and closed his eyes.

9

The day after Kincaid left for New York, Ellie Rawson, a stocky woman in her mid fifties, grey streaks in her brown hair, arrived just after five-thirty at the office of Sam Thorne. He came to the outer office to fetch her, then took her back inside with him. 'You look wonderful, Ellie,' he said. 'Life agrees with you, I guess.'

'Can't complain, Sam. You look pretty good yourself.'

'Too fat. Marie keeps after me but I can't seem to take off any weight.'

'Fat and happy,' she said. 'Nothing wrong with that.'

'What's not to be happy about? Never thought I'd like living out here but now I wouldn't trade it for any place else.'

'How about Marie?'

'Still gripes about leaving New York. She thinks Staten Island's the Garden of Eden. But she's got it good here and she knows it. Once she found out the Indians weren't gonna scalp her in her sleep, she felt better. She likes the idea of picking oranges in her garden and having me squeeze them for breakfast. She's lazy and helpless now. Won't do anything for herself. She's a princess, Ellie. You know what I mean?

How about your sister? How's Mona?'

'No better. No worse. I found a nice Mexican woman who looks after her during the day when I'm at work. She really gets a kick out of it when you send her little presents the way you do. Jigsaw puzzles and candy and the like. And every few weeks a box of flowers comes to the house. No card enclosed but she's decided they're from you. That's sweet of you, Sam.'

Sam eased back in his chair. 'My mama always said to me and Julian, "When you give something, you get something back." And I think she's right. That doesn't mean you're looking for a pay-back when you do a kindness for someone. Not at all. I think what Mama meant was, if you're decent to people, they'll be decent to you as well. That's the way I try to operate in any case.'

He sat up straight then and leaned forward, forearms resting on his desk. 'Now, let me tell you why I asked you to come in this afternoon. This may amount to nothing and on the other hand, who knows? What happened was that Julian and I were talking a few days ago and he asked if I'd heard anything from you. He remembers you were on the staff here from the time he started the studio. Then when I came out from New York you got the job of educating me, of being secretary to the fruit-and-vegetable man from Hoboken. No big break for you, I'll bet you told yourself, but you were a God-send to me. Anyway, out of the blue, like I said, Julian brought up your name. He asked me why you'd left us and gone off somewhere else. He'd forgotten the details. So I told him you'd decided to stop working, that you were going to try to do some typing and secretarial work at home so you could be there to take care of Mona. I think I remember it right.'

'That's right. But after a year or so I could see I needed more income so I took on the job I'm doing now.'

'That's what I told my brother but he said, "If she's working again she ought to be working for us." And I agreed. So I told him I'd have a talk with you to see if you're interested.

No rush about it, you understand. We'd want it to be the right job, something that would pay you what you need and not tie you up in the evenings when you want to be with your sister. What do you think?'

'I don't know what to say, Sam. It's sweet of you and Mr Thorne to think of me, and I admit I almost got in touch with you when I decided to take a full-time job again. But I was embarrassed to ask you. You'd been so nice about my quitting before. You know what I mean? I was afraid I'd look like a damned fool telling you I'd changed my mind. I suppose I would have called you sooner or later but then this job with Burt Windrow came up . . . somebody I'd been doing freelance work for recommended me . . . so I took it.'

'Are you happy there, working for him?'

'He pays me well and at five every day I go home.'

'You didn't answer my question.'

'You know me, Sam,' she said. 'I don't like to bad-mouth people. Do you know Windrow?'

Sam nodded. 'I've had some dealings with him.'

'How do you like him?'

'I'd never hire him if that's what you mean. I don't trust him.'

She smoothed her hair with one hand. 'It's hard for me to say how I feel about the situation. Windrow's English, you know. Very polite and well spoken. No foul language. No tantrums if something goes wrong. And he's a hard worker. Gets out five columns a week and a feature piece twice a month. For a man who had no training in journalism, I think he's doing a good job.'

'But . . .'

She smiled. 'But somehow I feel uneasy about him. Whatever the rules are he thinks they don't apply to him. At least that's how it strikes me. For the first time in his life he has a lot of power. He's invited everywhere now. People who didn't know his name a year ago are eager to send gifts and do him favours.'

35

'We had a talk with him earlier this year.'

'I remember,' Ellie said. 'Somebody called our office and said you wanted to see him.'

'Did he tell you what we talked about?'

'No. But whatever it was he wasn't happy about it.'

'We didn't expect him to be. But in any case he listened to reason and we settled our business with him. Ever since then he's been writing some positive things about our films and most of our actors. He even laid off Kincaid for a while. Has he ever talked to you about Kincaid?'

'I know he doesn't like him.'

'Do you know why?'

She shook her head. 'I had the feeling it's something personal.'

'Everything's personal. We're not saying he has to like Kincaid. But when he starts making attacks on him, trying to get him in trouble with the police, making him look bad in front of the public, then that's no good for business and we don't like it. We won't stand for it.'

Ellie smiled again. 'Is that why you called me in today, Sam? You want me to take a message to Windrow?'

'No. I called you in to see if you'd go to work for us again. And we'll get back to that in a minute. I got off on Windrow just because I get steamed any time his name comes up. He may think he's got power but this town is full of people who know how to pull the plug on clowns like him.'

'You know what he'd say if you said that to him. He'd say, nobody's gonna stop him from doing his job.'

'No, he wouldn't,' Sam said. 'I'd have him on his ass on the carpet before he had a chance to get it out.' He poured himself a glass of water, settled back in his chair and said, 'Now, let's talk about you. Here's what I'd like to do. You think over what I've said, I'll get together with Lew Talbot in Personnel, and in a few weeks, whenever you're ready, the three of us can sit down and talk. I want you in a key spot. The casting department maybe. Or co-ordinating with our theatre managers around the country. Something where

36

you can use your brain. And meanwhile, you and I will stay in close touch with each other.'

Late the previous summer, before the filming of *Dillinger* had begun, Julian Thorne scheduled a press conference at the studio. Some months earlier a series of rumours about Kincaid had begun to circulate in California and had spread across the country. It was decided that only a direct response from Kincaid could put a stop to the negative stories.

On the morning he met with reporters and columnists, Kincaid looked as though he hadn't shaved for three days. He was wearing dungarees, dirty tennis-shoes, and a wrinkled sweater. He walked to the front edge of the platform and sat down, directly in front of the journalists sitting in rows of chairs.

'Since I don't give interviews very often I guess I'd better give you an earful this time. The men here at the studio, who care more about my reputation than I do, tell me you have some tough questions to ask me. It seems there are some nasty stories going round. Since I don't hang out at the Cinegrill or the Polo Lounge, and since I never read the junk you people write, I don't know what those stories are. But whatever they are, I guarantee you, the truth is a lot worse.'

A grey-haired man in the first row stood up and said, 'One of the stories we're hearing is that your parents are poor people, not in good health, still living somewhere in Australia. They could use your help but you have nothing to do with them.'

'I hate to destroy my image by telling the truth but this time I'll do it. I have no father and no mother. I'm a bastard twice over. As far as I know, I might have hatched out on a rock. I realize I could never have been born if some man and some woman hadn't got together, but whoever they were,

I've never seen them. If I met them now, I wouldn't recognize them.'

'Who raised you?'

'Nobody. I raised myself. For the first fourteen years of my life the world offered me nothing. I kissed everybody's bum and got nothing in return. So I decided to take what I wanted. Then they gave me something in return. They threw my ass in jail. That was in Port Arthur. In Tasmania. Not far from where I must have been born. By the time I was twenty, I'd been in eight jails in six countries.'

A young woman said, 'Are you willing to tell us why you were in jail so much?'

'Different reasons. Drunk and disorderly. Burglary. Punching a policeman in Long Beach . . .'

Somebody in the back of the room began to laugh.

'. . . armed robbery and aggravated assault. I must have done some other naughty things but I can't remember.'

More laughter from the reporters. A prissy young man stood up and said, 'We all seem to feel guilt for one thing or another. How do you feel about the mistakes you've made?'

'I didn't make mistakes. I did what I had to do at the time. My mistake was getting caught. Let's face it. Everybody's looking to get rich or get laid. Or both at the same time . . .'

A burst of general laughter this time.

'. . . it's a whore's world. Everybody puts out for somebody. I see nothing wrong with robbing people as long as they're not your friends. People have to eat, and everybody's stealing something.'

The young man persisted. 'You're a public figure now. Aren't you concerned that you might be a bad influence on young people?'

'Young people don't give a damn what I say or do.'

An overweight woman with a great feather on her hat said, 'Since you've brought up your prison record, I'll say that one of the rumours we hear concerns that time.'

'Prison's a nasty place,' he said.

'The story is that you were a violent prisoner, that you may have killed another inmate.'

'I'll tell you this. I was as violent as I was able to be. A lot of fighting goes on inside prisons. Sometimes I'd go for a week without a fight. Other times, I'd be in a fight every day. And every fight I was in, I wanted to kill the guy if I could. Because he wanted to kill me. There weren't any rules in those fights. No referees. We fought till somebody couldn't fight any more and the guards carried him off to the infirmary. Sometimes I got carried off. Usually it was the other guy. Two or three times I never saw the guy again. That doesn't mean he was dead but I can't guarantee that he wasn't. If somebody has to be dead I figure it's my job to make sure it's not me.'

'What if everybody felt that way?'

'Everybody doesn't feel that way. Most people are scared of their shadows. I'm not.'

A middle-aged woman with hennaed hair, wearing a low-cut dress, said, 'Some of my readers have written to ask if you're a bigamist. They know you're married but they've heard that you have another wife and child in Argentina.'

'I'm twenty-six years old. My wife and I have been married for almost two years. This is her second marriage but my first. If you want to know if I have a child in Argentina, I can't tell you. I might have half a dozen children in Argentina.'

'Are you saying . . .'

'I'm answering your question. I've been a merchant seaman since I was sixteen years old. You've all heard the stories about sailors . . . well, they're true.'

If the laughter had been tentative before, it was out of control suddenly. Even Julian Thorne, who'd had a serious look on his face, joined in.

'I shipped out on freighters. Rust-buckets. They visited a lot of ports. In every port I went ashore with only one thought in my head. And I was happy to find there was always some young woman there who had the same idea I had. I must have gone ashore five hundred times in those years, so figure it out. It's not likely, but it's possible, that I have five hundred children I've never seen.'

Gloria Westerfield stood up then. When the laughter subsided, she said, 'So much for the lies and rumours. Now maybe you'd be willing to tell us the most important thing you've learned about the motion-picture business.'

'That's easy. Everybody's dumb and everybody's crooked. Here's the first law of Hollywood. If you're on the outside, you're garbage. If you're on the inside, you're *king*. If you need money, all you do is ring up the head of the studio. If the studio needs money, they call up the bank. If the bank needs money, they send a messenger to the mob. If the mob's short of money, we're all in trouble. That means the world's gone broke.'


11


The day after Sophie left the Towers and went down to London to meet Kincaid, her mother sat in her second-floor parlour and wrote a long letter to her friend, Clara Causey.

How remiss I've been. I am so longing to see you and talk to you. Now that I've begun to assert myself again, now that I've established that neither my health nor my mind are damaged, you and I will be able to continue our regular visits. How I look forward to it. I'm surrounded by people who love me and want to care for me, and I'm grateful for that, but you're the only human being on earth to whom I can speak freely. So until we're able to sit down together in your lovely house I will smother you with letters.

How am I? Everyone asks that question. I lie to them and say I'm fine. But I'm not fine. I'm angry. No one guesses how angry I am. They believe that I'm quiescent and accepting and understanding. And sad.

I am sad, of course. If I let myself, I'd be destroyed by the sadness. But mostly I'm angry.

Sophie and Sarah, her daughter, seem to have some residual guilt about the Major. They feel we were all too judgemental and should have behaved differently. They even believe, I suspect, that there's still something that can be done for him. I can't listen to such talk. I won't listen to it. Cranston's a fool, he's always been a fool, and I detest the thought of him. As far as I'm concerned, he can rot in that windowless room they've locked him in. If he has any mind left, I expect he tells himself that he's won at last, triumphed over me, managed to get even. He's right. He did and he has. That's why I'm angry. Why should a miserable creature be allowed to perform one mindless act and thus redirect the lives of any number of innocent people? Thank Heaven, I've never put my faith in God and goodness. If I had, that faith would be totally shattered now.

When I hear Sophie (meaning well, I suppose, and trying to demonstrate her decency), when I hear her say, 'The Major's a poor lost soul', when she says assinine things like that, I want to spring up from my chair and slap her face, bring her somehow to her senses. But I simply nod my head and look down at my lap so she won't see my expression and won't guess what I'm thinking.

My only consolation these days is the knowledge that Brannigan, if he could witness all this, would be proud of me. Jack was a man who knew how to hate and he taught me. But I never had a chance to practise till now.

Are you wondering why I've kept all this to myself? For good reason. Because I want the feeling to stay strong inside me. I don't want to share it with anyone, to dissipate it. I don't want some well-meaning soul to reason with me, to tell me I only hurt myself when

41

I hate so elaborately and fiercely. Sophie says, 'It's a horrible thing but it's over now. It's in the past. You must put it behind you.' Perhaps she truly believes that would make me feel better. She's mistaken. My greatest joy these days is knowing I will never forget. I don't expect ever to see the Major. If I did, it would be for only one purpose, to tell him how much I abhor him. What a blessing it is, what a consolation to me, that we lived apart for most of our married life. It sickens me that I ever touched his body or permitted him to touch mine. Thank God, I have no strong memories of that time.

I'm filled with hatred, you see. I even hate myself, for allowing myself to be driven to your house the day the constables came for the Major. And at times I almost hate Jack for trying to shield me, for forcing me to go. I have no idea what I could have done to change the events of that hideous day. Nothing perhaps. But I can't help thinking that somehow things would have worked out differently if I'd been there.

I keep all these feelings to myself, however. I mourn in private. On the surface I take pains to be what I've always been, a mother, a grandmother, and the mistress of my house. Arthur and I have our daily routine as we always have, and Sophie pretends that neither of us is able to function without her. If I lose my temper and speak sharply to someone, I know they whisper among themselves, staff and family, 'She didn't mean it. It's good for her to strike out like that. Better than suffering in silence. It's a sign she's getting better.' What foolishness. I can't get better. I don't even want to get better. I want to nurture and cherish this divine hatred of mine. I want to live with it and die with it.

Since you have a daughter yourself, since I've been a witness to many of the battles and misunderstandings between you and Nora, I know you'll understand when I speak candidly to you about Sophie. You know

42

how close she and I have always been. But in the past weeks it seems I see everyone objectively, as they really are. Not as I would like them to be, because of a blood relationship or a long friendship, but as they are.

Some wise person once said, 'Objectivity is the enemy of love.' And it's true of course. Though perhaps it's more accurate to say that objectivity kills admiration. Love after all, can survive all sorts of cruelty and deception and disappointment. We both know that, don't we?

So if I seem to see Sophie differently now, just in these weeks since Brannigan died, it doesn't mean that I love her less or admire her less. It simply means that my eyes have been jolted open. I see better now, more clearly. And I can admit to myself what I see. No need to cloud it over, no attempt to redefine it.

Do we all cross a threshold at some point? Do dreams suddenly have less power over us? Does it come at a certain age? At thirty perhaps? Do we say to ourselves, 'I have to be realistic now. I have to consider what's best for me.' It occurs to me that I was just past thirty myself when my mother died. Sophie and I came home from India for the memorial service and we never went back. I believed it was my responsibility, as the only child, to look after the estate, to care for Wiswell Towers. Was I guilty of what I'm about to accuse Sophie of? Perhaps I was.

Sophie was always a generous child. Unselfish. She still is. But now it seems, there's a difference. Her generosities are more carefully selected. As always, she has no hesitation about giving time, money, sympathy, or affection. But now I sense that the action must also serve her, either in a real way or as a kind of reassurance, as public evidence of her private definition of herself. I saw faint signs of it even before she met Kincaid. Since then, this new tendency in her has grown and accelerated.

I am not saying, of course, that she chose Kincaid and married him as an act of charity. It never occurred to her, I'm sure, that she was marrying below her station. Nor did it occur to me. It did, of course, occur to her father. But to Sophie, she simply saw something she wanted and she had the wisdom and the courage to grab it. She may have erred in some people's minds but in mine she didn't. I never doubted her love for Kincaid. I don't question it now.

All the same, whatever the strength of her feelings, she knew that in choosing Kincaid she was also giving him a substantial gift. Of herself, of course, but many other things as well. Her houses, her lands and assets, her place in society. In fairness to Kincaid, I am sure such things mean nothing to him. But Sophie knew their worth. It seemed obvious to her, how could it not, that her holdings, her circumstances, would dictate how and where they would live together. No room for discussion.

Then, quite suddenly and remarkably, Kincaid's own circumstances changed. He was offered choices he'd never had before. Now there *were* matters to be discussed. It was a surprise to Sophie, as it was to all of us, and she didn't know how to handle it. So she handled it badly. In my opinion she's still handling it badly.

Since Toby's death she's had the responsibility of directing her own affairs. And she's good at it. In the past few weeks she's impressed both Arthur and our investment advisors with her ability to make decisions about estate matters. She likes to be consulted. She welcomes responsibilities, just as I always have. I enjoy being informed and decisive. I like to be in charge. But after I married Brannigan, I found I could no longer make solitary decisions and expect him to fall in line. I welcomed that. I suspect that Sophie has had the same experience with Kincaid, but she doesn't welcome it.

However much she appears to relish his success and his ability to make a great deal of money, she secretly believes – I'm convinced of this – that the work he's doing, well paid or not, is trivial and unimportant. And perhaps it is. As we know, Clara, most of the activities our men engage in are trivial and unimportant. But not only must a wife not acknowledge that fact, she must do her best to see that her husband doesn't acknowledge it. My wise and lovely daughter somehow doesn't realize this. She has made an elaborate game of where she will live and where she won't live.

How many wives do we know, my dear friend, whose husbands welcome the chance to get away from them for a few days? Many, many, many. Sophie's husband wants her with him all the time. But that doesn't mean he'll follow after her like a poodle.

So you see, she's taking a big risk. She's setting up a contest she could possibly lose. Worse than that, she might win, then come to wish she hadn't. Men are difficult to manipulate. Men like Kincaid, I suspect, are impossible to manipulate.

Am I being unforgivably critical of my only child? I hope not. You, more than anyone, know how proud I've always been of her. You know how grateful I am that she came here straightaway from California as soon as she knew what had happened to me. And once she was here, she took charge of everything. She went to the hospital where they've confined Cranston and set everything right there. At least in her own mind. Then she went to London and somehow persuaded my vanished Arthur to come back.

She also arranged a glorious Christmas for us, so the children, when they arrived from London, were not confronted by a season of gloom. She's involved herself in the financial decisions and legal matters that either Arthur or I would normally deal with. And of course she's forging ahead with her plans to refurbish the Towers. All that disturbs me a bit, but Sophie says it's been too long put off, and perhaps she's right. I've seen the architect's plans and they seem all right to me. Jock Dunbar is a fine builder. I'm not sure that I'd go as far as Sophie's going in her plans for change, but I suppose she's looking ahead.

In any case, it's her house as well as mine, so there'll be no friction between us unless she proposes to move my bed into the stables.

Two things do disturb me, however. One: she seems to have developed a proprietary attitude that I wasn't aware of before. I see her striding through the corridors in her riding-trousers and boots, with rolled blueprints under her arm, and God help me, I'm reminded of her father when he was a young man and still recognizable as a human being.

I don't say this to be cruel. He is her father, after all. But in my present state of mind about the Major, you can see how disturbing it is to see even faint reminders of him in my daughter.

The second thing that unsettles me is this: from the rustling and whispering in the hallways and the *sotto voce* conversations, I get the impression that I am being defined, by staff and family, as an invalid, someone who must be cradled, coddled, and seldom consulted. Sophie has made remarks about staying on here at the Towers as long as it's necessary, and yesterday, when Rose brought my breakfast, she asked if Sophie would be living here permanently. I told Rose that of course Sophie was welcome to do that if she chose to, but to you I say, I don't need a governess. I'm in excellent health, I have a fine staff, and I expect to live till I'm ninety, as my grandmother did. It would humiliate me if I thought my daughter was planning to redirect her own life somehow, so she could sit at my knee and watch me crochet. I don't plan to crochet in any case. I plan to walk in my garden, play tennis on the lawn, and drive

46

my roadster about the county as I've always done.

If I had the courage to be as candid with Sophie as I'm being with you, I would say to her, 'You have a fine husband, two lovely children, and financial independence. You have an enviable life ahead of you. Don't mar it, I beg you, by attempting to manage everything and everyone. None of us has the power or the wisdom to make a masterplan that will serve the needs of everyone we know. People have roles to play, mistakes to make, and destinies to follow. They must be allowed to follow the paths they've selected even when, in your eyes, they've made the wrong choice. I'm a born activist, as you are, but I've learned that many times I must be a spectator. You have to learn that, too.'

# • CHAPTER 2 •

## 1

'God, how I missed you,' Sophie said. She and Kincaid were in the rear seat of her town car being driven to London from Southampton, where she had met his ship. 'It seems like a year. First you were away from me in Chicago doing your film, and then I had to scurry over here to set things right for Margaret. Do I look like an old crone? I feel as if I've aged twenty years since I saw you last.'

'You're gorgeous,' he said. 'You're always gorgeous.'

'Aren't you a darling? That's the sort of support I've been yearning for. I have so much to tell you. And so many questions to ask. I had a note from Gloria Westerfield. She says your new film is smashing. She loved it.'

'I had a radiogram from Thorne on the ship. He says the picture opened well everywhere. He smells money. Bigger grosses than *Bushranger*, he thinks.'

'My sweet gangster,' she said. She put her hand on his cheek and kissed him. 'What a great vulgar success you've become. But are they going to put you in jail because of Homer Tony?'

'No jail. That's all been settled.'

'If he was innocent, as you say he was, why did he run away? Why didn't he stand trial so he could be exonerated?'

'Because everybody in California had decided he was guilty. They'd seen that girl's baby-face in the papers, and they'd seen photographs of HT, and they'd made up their minds.

48

Even if he'd stood trial and been acquitted, I don't think he'd have been safe in the streets. Not in Los Angeles.'

'But it cost you thirty thousand dollars,' she said.

'He's worth it.'

'Would you pay that much money to keep me from going to jail?'

'I'd have to think about that.'

'You're really a beast, aren't you?'

'Of course. John Dillinger. Public enemy number one.'

'I can't wait to get you home,' she said. She took his hand, put her head against his shoulder and closed her eyes. After a while Kincaid said, 'Are you asleep?'

'No. I was thinking about Homer Tony. I suppose it worked out for the best after all. He's better off, isn't he, being back in Australia?'

'I'm not sure. I hope he is.'

'I'm sure he always felt out of place in California. No one to be with. Being stared at all the while.'

'He liked living with us.'

'And you liked having him there.'

'Yes, I did.'

'Evan says you two are . . . what was the word he used? I think he said, you're *connected*.'

'That's true. We are.'

'Evan says you love him.'

'I do.'

'It all seems so strange to me,' she said.

'Why should it? We're friends. You have friends, don't you?'

'Of course. But it's not the same. My best friends are people I've known all my life. We're the same sort. We resemble each other somehow. But you and Homer Tony seem to be from separate centuries, from different planets.'

'Don't be too sure of that.'

'But I am sure of it. You don't have fierce eyes and a pattern of scar-welts on your forehead and cheek-bones. I know you tell everyone you're an Aborigine, but you're not. You're my sweet dear civilized man, and I love you.'

She told him then in some detail about their Christmas feast and of all the problems she'd had to cope with since her return to England. 'I didn't expect to be praised and glorified for what I've been doing, but I must say I've been surprised at the resistance I've encountered.'

'How do you mean?'

'Resistance may not be the proper word. Perhaps I imagined that everyone would be as keen as I was. I expected a great spirit of empathy and co-operation. People pitching in. Doing their bit. But the attitude seemed to be, "Things will fall into place if given enough time." My experience has been that nothing falls into place. It must be put in place.'

'But it's all working out?'

She nodded. 'I hope so. But it's taken a great deal of persuading. Even Margaret seems unco-operative at times, almost resentful. She told me, of course, how grateful she is, but at the same time I feel that she's saying, "Enough is enough."'

'Maybe it is. Maybe she's ready to manage for herself.'

Sophie shook her head. 'She may think she's ready but she's not. Not by any means. I don't think she realizes yet what a shock she's had. It's changed her.'

'Are you sure you're not imagining some of this?'

'I wish I were, but I'm not. I don't mean to say that people have conspired against me, but it is astonishing that no one seems to see things my way. Even Sarah and Trevor have begun to point out my shortcomings. Among other things they've suddenly discovered in themselves a great affection for their grandfather. They've decided that we all treated the Major badly. When they came up from London before the Christmas holidays, we sent Alfred to drive them home from Newcastle. But when he got there they weren't on the train. He rang me straightaway at the Towers and I rang Mrs O'Haver in London. She told me that Sarah had said I wanted her to take an earlier train so she and Trevor would have time to visit their grandfather at the hospital outside

Newcastle. And of course that's where they were when I rang the office there. Knowing the Major's condition, however, the director, Jennings, had not permitted the children to see him. He told me that Sarah had been very angry and had spoken sharply to him and other members of the staff. And when Alfred picked them up at last and brought them home to the Towers, she was absolutely rude to me. I managed to keep her away from Margaret till she'd simmered down.'

'And Trevor? How did he behave?'

Sophie shook her head. 'He wasn't as abusive as Sarah was, but it was clear that he agreed with his sister.'

'It sounds to me as if it's time for you to pack your valises and come home to London.'

'Not quite yet, I'm afraid. I simply can't believe that what I've done is not appreciated. Thank God for Evan. Many days I've felt as though he was my only ally. That doesn't surprise me, of course. We've always stood by each other, even when we were children. Although we lived in the same house like brother and sister, we never quarrelled and criticized each other as most brothers and sisters do. He's always been a true friend. Someone I can rely on.'

'As I recall, he wasn't too happy about your decision to marry me. We didn't see him for months.'

'That was because of his play. He was locked in his flat working on *The Fatherhouse*.'

'You don't really believe that, do you? Do you think that's the reason we never saw him?'

'Perhaps not. But regardless, it was no reflection on you. He used to say, he didn't think any man was good enough for me.'

'Any other man.'

'Shame on you,' she said. 'You're not jealous of poor Evan, are you? He'd do anything for you.'

'Good. I'll remember that in case there's something I need to have done for me.'

'You're very tough, aren't you? You must stop playing those cruel roles in your films. You're too tough for me.'

51

'No, I'm not. I've always been tough. You told me you liked tough men.'

'Not too tough.'

'Maybe your tastes are changing.'

'Never,' she said. 'I know when I'm lucky. I've got what I want.'

## 2

Sophie's confrontation with Sarah and Trevor had indeed been an unpleasant one. When they arrived home after their failed attempt to see the Major, Sophie met them in the hallway. 'Leave your bags here. Trout will take them up. Let's go into the library. I want to have a talk with you.'

'That's fine with us,' Sarah said. 'We want to have a talk with you.'

As soon as the library doors closed behind them, Sarah said, 'How dare you humiliate us that way? Calling the hospital and telling the director we shouldn't be allowed to see our grandfather.'

'The director made that decision for himself. He wouldn't have given you permission under any circumstances.'

'Not true. We'd almost convinced him. Hadn't we, Trevor?'

Trevor nodded. 'He was about to change his mind before you rang up.'

'Then I'm glad I rang. Do you have any idea what sort of condition your grandfather's in? He's a mental patient. He's not up to having visitors.'

'But we're not visitors,' Sarah said. 'We're his grandchildren and we think he's been treated badly.'

'He's been treated badly? Don't you realize he murdered someone? He shot a constable and then he killed Margaret's husband.'

'That was an awful thing,' Trevor said. 'We didn't say it wasn't. But maybe he reached the breaking-point.'

52

'Trevor, darling, you don't know what you're talking about.'

'Oh, yes, he does,' Sarah said. 'We're not stupid, you know. We've both taken psychology courses. Anyone can go crazy if they're treated in certain ways. We think grandfather just had all he could take, and it pushed him over the edge.'

'Where do you pick up those expressions? No one pushed him anywhere.'

'Oh, yes, they did. How would you expect him to act when his wife divorced him after more than thirty years, then kept him locked away in a separate part of the house.'

'No one locked him away. He chose to live in the west wing. He always lived there by himself, from the time he was discharged from the Army.'

'Then after the divorce, Grandmother married another man, a person nobody knew, and brought him home with her. While the Major was still living in the house.'

'No wonder he acted crazy,' Trevor said.

'I won't have you criticizing Margaret.'

'It's not just Margaret,' Sarah said. 'You're to blame as well. Do you think you treated him the way you should have? Everybody in this house snickered at him or avoided him.'

'That's why we wanted to see him,' Trevor said. 'So he'd know that somebody in the family cared about him. So he'd see that we remembered him.'

Suddenly Sophie had tears in her eyes. She sat looking at her children, simply looking at them, saying nothing. At last she said, 'I don't know what to say. All at once you're both grown-up in many ways and I don't know how to talk to you. But believe me, I'm not treating you as though you were little children. I'm not telling you what you must do or what you cannot do. I'm just trying . . . let's take things one at a time. First of all, I'm the only person in the family who's seen the Major since he's been in that institution. I felt exactly as you do when I went there, that no matter what he's done, he's my father. If he needed things, if I could help him, I felt I had to do my best. The director tried to discourage me but I wouldn't listen to him. Now I wish I had. As soon as I saw the Major, I knew there was nothing I could do for him. I was not allowed to go into the room where he's kept. In spite of his feeble condition the doctors believe he's dangerous. So I could only make contact with him through a wire-grated window. As I say, I was eager to see him, but when they brought me there to the window I was shocked and sickened by what I saw. There was a chair and a bed in his room but he was sitting on the floor in the far corner. He'd removed his trousers and he was slowly tearing a magazine in tiny pieces. When I spoke to him it seemed at first that he didn't hear me. But at last he looked up. He stared at me as though he'd never seen me before, absolutely no sign of recognition in his eyes. Then he went back to tearing up his magazine. I stayed there at the window, continuing to talk to him, trying to get a response, but he never looked at me again.'

'That doesn't mean he wouldn't talk to Trevor and me. He knows you've always been on Margaret's side. Since he's angry at her you shouldn't be surprised that he's angry at you.'

Sophie sat motionless and silent for a long moment. Then: 'I don't know what's come over you two but we must put a stop to it. Now listen to me carefully because we won't be having this discussion again. Your grandfather is not angry, he's sick. He's a desperately ill old man. He's mentally crippled. His mind is gone. Not because of Margaret. Not because of me. His body still functions on a two-year-old level but otherwise he's a dead man. He can't think, he can't speak, he can't feed himself. Do you understand what I'm saying?'

Trevor dropped his eyes. Sarah continued to stare at her mother but she didn't answer. 'No one did anything to put him in the state he's in,' Sophie went on, 'and no one can bring him out of it. If you insist on believing that Margaret and I are responsible for his pitiful condition, I will not try to change your mind. But you must keep those thoughts to yourselves. I insist on that. Surely you would not speak to

Margaret or to anyone else in this house as you've been speaking to me. I hope you're wise enough and kind enough not to do that. But in case you're not, let me tell you this: if I can't be sure that you will do everything in your power to make this a wonderful, peaceful holiday for your grandmother, one that will help her forget all the agony of the past few weeks, then I'll ask Trout to bring your bags downstairs again and Alfred will drive you back to London at once. I'll ring up Mrs O'Haver. She and Oliver will see to it that you have a proper Christmas dinner and I'll send your gifts along with you in the car. It would be very painful for me to do that and it would be difficult to explain to Margaret, but I will not allow you to poison the atmosphere in this house with the kind of remarks you've been making just now. Margaret cannot bear to hear your grandfather's name mentioned. I can't imagine her reaction if she heard you saying what you've been saying to me.'

'What do you expect us to do?' Sarah said.

'That's your decision. If you tell me you'll behave, if you promise to keep your feelings about the Major to yourself, then I'll be very happy that we can all be together. If you insist on airing your opinions to Margaret or to anyone else, then I'm sending you back to London straightaway. Which way is it going to be?'

Trevor looked at Sarah, then back to Sophie. 'It's Christmas, for Pete's sake. I don't want to go back to London. I don't want to do anything to upset Margaret.'

Sophie turned to her daughter. 'How about you, Sarah?'

'You're not giving me much choice, are you?'

'Of course I am. You can stay or go. It's up to you.'

'Are you going to follow me around and listen to every word I say?'

'No,' Sophie said. 'Once you've given me your word, I know you won't break it. You know the conditions. Are you staying or going?'

'I've already told you how I feel about things. I guess I don't have to say it again,' Sarah said.

'Guessing isn't good enough.'

'All right. I know. I won't say anything.'

'I'm a very possessive woman,' Sophie said. 'Do you know that about me? Insanely jealous.' They were lying in bed in their London house, very late. They'd had dinner at La Caprice after their drive up from Southampton.

'That's good,' Kincaid said. 'I'd hate to think you'd turn me over to the highest bidder.'

'I'm serious. It's like a physical pain. I tremble when I think of you lolling about, playing love scenes with all those carnivorous actresses.'

'I don't do love scenes. You know that. I play bad guys. I just shoot people till somebody shoots me.'

'When I think about how I feel about you and realize that thousands of other women feel exactly the same way, it upsets me terribly. The urge to kill.'

'That's because they don't know my flaws. If they knew me as well as you do, they'd lose interest in a hurry.'

'Nonsense. I haven't lost interest.'

'That's because you're remarkably stubborn. Once you've made a choice, you won't admit you've made a mistake.'

'Not exactly. Once I've made a choice, I want to make sure that no one else is choosing what I've already chosen.'

'Ungenerous. Selfish child. Didn't your nanny teach you to share and share alike?'

'I learned that rule but I don't accept it. I wouldn't share you with anyone. Private property. My name on all your tags and collars. Don't pet the doggie. I see the way women look at you but you don't even notice. At least, you pretend not to notice.'

'We've been over this a thousand times,' he said. 'Here's the way it works. First they look at *you*. Then they say to themselves, "Let's see what sort of a chap this lovely woman has picked out for herself." *Then* they look at me and they keep staring. I admit that. But it's only because they don't understand what you see in me. They can't decide if I'm rich or lucky, or if I have some splendid hidden features. So they keep staring.'

'I know you don't believe that. So when you say those things it makes me all the more certain I have something to be jealous about. When I read some of the things you say to reporters I get sick with jealousy.'

'I told you never to read that junk. Besides I never talk about women. I never make myself out to be a lady's man.'

'I don't know what you'd call it then. Don't you remember that press conference at Thornwood when someone asked if you had a child in Argentina? Don't you remember what you said? You said you might have five hundred children scattered about the world.'

'That was a joke, honey. A send-up. Everybody laughed but you.'

'I know that. I know why you did it and why you said the things you said. But it still bothers me. I don't like people to think odd things about you even when I know they're untrue. Do you think I liked it when you were making *Bushranger* and all the papers were printing stories about you and Daisy Bishop?'

'Is this a serious conversation or are we just lying in bed having a few jokes before we turn out the light?'

'It can't be serious because you don't take it seriously. You have a clever answer for everything.'

'Of course I don't take it seriously. You know I'm not bouncing around looking for other women. So if you've decided you're jealous, if you're serious when you say that, then I can only conclude that your mind's not working properly.'

'This has nothing to do with my mind. It's a feeling I have. And feelings don't disappear just because you sit down and talk sense to yourself.'

'All right, let's look at it this way. From now on, whenever

I leave the house, you come with me. If I go to the studio, you come along. If I go on location, you come with me. Every place I go, you'll come along.'

'You'd hate that.'

'No, I wouldn't. I'd like it. And you'd like it, too. Then you'd never have to worry about wild women dragging me into their cars and carrying me off to the hills.'

'I don't mean I don't trust you. But any man can be tempted. Especially in that odd business you're in. I've been on a few movie sets. I've seen all those juicy women hanging about. Not just the actresses. All the women are attractive. With glittery eyes that don't miss anything. If I were a man . . .'

'You're not a man, Sophie . . .'

'Let me finish. If I were a man, and a woman like Daisy Bishop walked into the room, I certainly wouldn't look the other way.'

'Neither would I. I look at everybody. If a chicken walked into the room I'd look at him. Or her. Whatever it was.'

'There you go again. That's what I mean. You can't stay on the subject.'

'I'm not sure what the subject is.'

'Yes, you are. I'm saying it makes me uncomfortable to read stories about you and Daisy Bishop, or anybody else, even if I know they're untrue. And I don't think that's such an abnormal reaction. How would you like it if you found out I was having a romance with another man?'

'Wait a minute. Now you're changing the subject. You weren't talking about me having an affair with Daisy Bishop. You were talking about silly stories in the newspaper.'

'The difference is that nobody would print stories about me, no matter what I did. And they print stories about you even if you don't do anything.'

'Then you're the lucky one.'

'No, I'm not. Because I'm not trying to get away with anything.'

'Neither am I. The only person I'm trying to get into bed

with is you. And now I've got you.' He pulled her close to him. 'So why are we wasting time with Daisy Bishop?'

4

Two days before Christmas, when Sarah came down late to breakfast, Evan was still in the breakfast-room, smoking a cigarette and reading the paper.

'Ah,' she said, 'I've caught you. Why do I feel as if you've been avoiding me?'

'I can't imagine. I've seen you every day since I arrived.'

'Bits and pieces. Faces in the crowd. Ships that pass in the night. That sort of rot.'

'Sophie says you've been spending a lot of time in your room.'

'That's right. I have. I've come to love silence. Solitude. Lovely.'

'Does that mean you've given up an acting career?'

'Don't rag me. I have no career and you know it.'

'I should have asked if you've given up your theatrical studies. The theatre doesn't lend itself to a life of silence and solitude. Unless you're dead or chronically unemployed.'

'I have not given up my studies. More serious than ever. Obsessive. Dedicated. I'll be going to the Churchgate School in Wimbledon right after the holidays. They have an excellent dramatic literature course there. And ten days a month I'll be allowed to go in to London and study at RADA. Kincaid arranged that for me.'

'Sounds good,' Evan said. 'You were doing so well in California, I thought you might be reluctant to leave there.'

'I didn't expect that we'd leave so abruptly, but I knew we'd be back in England before Christmas, so it wasn't a total surprise. I was prepared. And Ethel Richmond had taught me a lot. When I met her the first time, she said, "If you leave here with self-confidence in yourself as a performer,

59

then I'll feel that I've done my job." And she did. At least as far as I'm concerned. I'm very calm now about what I plan to do with my life. I don't mean that I think I know it all. *Au contraire*. The most important thing I learned was that I know very little. I haven't learned to say "Open Sesame" yet but at least now I feel I know the location of the magic gate. Am I making sense?'

'Of course you are. You contradict all the lore about Hollywood. Young women who go there with ambitions usually lose their heads. You seem to have found yours.'

'It just happened,' she said. 'I'm very calm. As I said. I want to settle down and work and make something of myself. You remember, when I was fourteen or fifteen I wanted everyone to think I was twenty. Now I truly feel much older inside but I'm content to be sixteen. No matter how skilful or professional I become as an actress, whatever role I play, the person the audience will see on the stage will always be me. So in addition to my studies, I've decided I need to do a great deal of work on myself. Miss Richmond says, "A true actress never makes her entrance from the wings. She comes from a full and complete world that she's invented for herself."'

'It's the theatre then, is that it? Another contradiction. Once you've been exposed to southern California you're supposed to be permanently hypnotized by the camera and film. Have you avoided that?'

'I'm not saying I'll never work in films. But everything I know now, everything I want now, is in the theatre. That's where an actor can be free. That's where he can do his best work.'

'Does it bother you that a stage actor's best performance may stay alive only in the memories of the few people who saw it. Whereas films reach millions of people, and if they're properly preserved, can be shown for many years to come?'

'Let me ask you that. Are you more proud of your play that ran only a few weeks, or of *Bushranger*, a film that earned millions of dollars and seems to have been seen at least once by the entire world.'

Evan smiled. 'You got me.'

'That's what I thought,' she said. 'Miss Richmond said "the secret of any real achievement – you notice I didn't say success – is to use yourself. When you've learned to do that, you'll do your best work." Do you agree?'

'Yes, I do.'

'There, you see, I've taught you something. Or at least I've demonstrated that I know something. I've also given up trying to seduce you by displaying my body. Now I'm using other devices. Talent. Brains. Wisdom.'

'But you haven't given up trying to seduce me?'

'Oh, my, no.'

'Thank God.'

Sarah smiled. 'I've simply shifted into another gear. You're still the only man I want. I don't expect that to change. But now I'm more patient. I can see that when I'm eighteen or twenty and you're thirty-six or thirty-seven, we'll be much closer in age than we are now. I'll be more experienced and by then I expect you'll have combed Mary Cecil out of your hair.'

'What does Mary Cecil have to do with all this?'

'A great deal. I know you were in love with her. I also know you've broken up now and I know why. I've learned a great deal about Mary Cecil, things even you don't know.'

'You've been reading too many gossip magazines.'

She shook her head and smiled. 'No. My information came to me first-hand. One makes friends in California, you know. I formed an intimate friendship there. I'm sure you must know him. He knows you. And he knows Mary Cecil very well. He once knew her as well as he knows me.'

5

'Have I disappointed you,' Sophie said. 'Haven't I given you a proper homecoming?' It was late afternoon, four days since

Kincaid's return from America. They were dressed for the evening, having cocktails in the library of their London house.

'Very nice,' he said. 'You've been very attentive.'

'Faint praise, it seems to me. We've had lovely dinners, evening walks in Green Park, outrageous breakfasts in bed, champagne chilled at all hours, and tonight I've arranged for us to see the new play at the Haymarket.'

'That's true.'

'And I've certainly given generously of myself.'

'That's also true.'

'But still . . .'

He smiled. 'I have no complaints.'

'Are you quite certain?'

'I admit I had another scenario in mind as I crossed the ocean. I thought we would drive straight to Bournemouth, take the night ferry to St Malo, and go into hibernation in Brittany.'

'Don't be cruel,' she said. 'I would love that. All the way down from Northumberland, I tried to find some way we could go there.'

'It's not too late. We'll go tomorrow. Up early and over to France.'

'Don't tease me. You know we can't do that.'

'Why not?' he said.

'Because we have to get back to the Towers. They're expecting us tomorrow.'

'That's no problem. Ring up and tell them we've been delayed. Tell them you'll be along in ten days or so.'

'I can't, sweetheart. I have a thousand things that must be attended to. Margaret's depending on me.'

'What about the staff? They've been running the estate for years, haven't they?'

'That's true. But they need to be led. And since Margaret's not up to it I have to step in and do my bit.'

'Are you saying that Arthur Tagg can't take charge?'

'Ahhh . . . that's another problem. I don't know what to make of Arthur. Some great change seems to have come over him. He's eager to make decisions about everything. Too eager, I'm afraid. He seems to believe he's the new master of the Towers.'

'What's the difference? Why shouldn't he feel that way? From what you told me he put up with a lot from your father through the years. You can't blame him for putting himself forward a bit.'

'I don't blame him. I just don't want it to go too far. Even if Margaret is ready to put everything in his hands, I'm not.'

'But you came to London and begged him to come back to the Towers. Isn't that what you wrote me in your letters?'

She nodded. 'I told him Margaret needed him, that we all needed him to take on his old duties again. But I did not invite him to take over totally.'

'I don't follow you. You've always said that he and Evan were like members of your family.'

'Being like family is not the same as family.'

'If you want my opinion, I think you're trying to deal with problems that don't exist,' Kincaid said. 'It sounds as though Arthur and your mother are able to manage things as they always have. You've been there for two months. I'm sure they don't expect you to stay much longer.'

'You're right. They don't. Both of them keep urging me to come back here to London.'

'What's wrong with that? That's what you want to do.'

'Of course it is. But I also have to do what's right for Margaret. You see, I think Arthur is influencing her. Putting words in her mouth. So I'm deciding for myself what's best. And I have to see it through.'

'What does that mean exactly?'

'It means I must finish what I've started. If Arthur has grand ideas of his own, then it's critical that I should continue to make my presence known, to put my own plans in motion. That's one reason I've begun the remodelling programme.'

'What's that all about?'

'A great many things have been neglected in the past ten years or so. The plumbing needed to be brought up to the mark. New slates on some of the roofs. So while that work was being done I called in an architect and made plans for other changes. Better quarters for Sarah and Trevor, refurbishing Margaret's apartment, putting in several new bathrooms, and modernizing the staff kitchen.'

'Did Arthur and your mother go along with you?'

'They were quite agreeable at the beginning, but once we'd redone the Major's apartment in the west wing and Arthur had taken it over for himself, both he and Margaret seemed to believe we'd gone far enough. Arthur's disturbed, I think, by my plans to redo the second floor of the east wing as an apartment for us, for you and me. Mother, of course, approves of the idea but hints to me that I shouldn't transform those rooms totally. But I believe that's Arthur's position rather than hers. So I'm going ahead. I want that part of the house to be more like our home here in London. White and gold. More open. More light. You like that, don't you?'

Kincaid nodded. 'I also like the Towers. That's why I duplicated it when I built the California house.'

'I know you liked it as it was. But you'll also like what I've done when it's finished.'

'Here's my next question. You're not planning to pack up and move there, are you?'

'No, darling, but I don't mind if Arthur suspects that's what I'm up to. I think that might be a constraining influence on him.'

'And you think he needs constraints?'

'Yes, I do. It's all very nice that Margaret trusts him and depends on him but he needs to remember that the Towers belongs to me and my children as well as Margaret. And to no one else.' Then: 'I'm sorry, darling. And to you, of course. It's your home, too, as well as mine. I want you to spend time there and get to know it. I expect Evan will be spending more time there as well. It will be nice when everything's all fixed up. You'll see.'

'So you want to go back there tomorrow?'

'I must. The house is full of workmen and the architect's coming down from Carlisle. And some chairs that were reupholstered will be delivered from York.'

'Sounds like a busy place. You'll have your hands full.'

'Yes, I will, but we're close to the end now. Our rooms are almost finished and the reception rooms as well. The remaining work will be in the back of the house. Trevor's quarters. And Sarah's. Everything will be finished by the time they have their next school holiday. You'll be proud of me when you see what I've done.'

When they came home from the theatre that night and were having a brandy in their bedroom, Kincaid said, 'Here's what I think we should do. You go on up to the Towers tomorrow and I'll be along in three or four days.'

'Oh, no, none of that . . .'

'Wait a minute. Let me finish. I wrote a note to Trevor from New York. Before I sailed. I told him I'd stop in St Albans to see him on my way north.'

'That's sweet of you, but I want you to come with me. Everyone's waiting to see you. It's important.'

'A few more days won't matter. This is important, too. I promised Trevor I'd bring him up to date on Homer Tony.'

'Can't that wait a bit?'

'I don't think so. The two of them became good friends when Trevor was doing those drawings of Homer.'

'I know they spent some time together but I don't think I'd call it a friendship.'

'Maybe you're right,' Kincaid said. 'I'm just repeating what Trevor told me. In any case I promised him I'd come to see him as soon as I got back here.'

'I feel like a fool,' she said. 'I came down to London to meet you and bring you back home and now you're not coming.'

'Yes, I am. Three or four days at most.'

'Margaret will be terribly disappointed. What will I tell her?'

'Tell her the truth. She'll understand.'

'Why do you think that? I don't understand.'

'Yes, you do. You may not like it but you understand.'


6


'I remember that girl,' Trevor said. 'Ursula, her name was.'

'That's right,' Kincaid said. 'Ursula Martin.'

They were sitting in a coffee-house on Fishkill Street, mid afternoon, just beside the grounds of Trevor's school. 'She had a pretty face but she didn't know anything. The stable guys used to tease her a lot, make dirty remarks to her, but she didn't mind. She hung around out there in the tack-house whenever she could sneak out of the kitchen. She was on a first-name basis with all the delivery men, too. Every time I saw her, she'd ask me when I was going to get a driver's licence so I could take her for a ride. It was like a standing joke with her. I guess she was really keen for somebody to carry her off somewhere.'

Kincaid told him in detail everything that had happened. How the girl had rushed into the police station at Malibu and told them Homer Tony had attacked her.

'Maybe he really did it,' Trevor said. 'Not rape like she said, but you know. The way she hung around any man she saw . . . she may have taken a shine to Homer and he took her up on it. You can't blame the guy. When a girl like her starts pushing herself at you. Are you sure he didn't?'

'I'm sure.'

'How can you be sure?'

'Because I asked him. Head-to-head, just the two of us. I asked him and he said no. Shook his head.'

'If he was scared maybe he lied to you.'


66

'He didn't lie to me.'

'Why would she make up a story like that?'

'She's not a mean kid,' Kincaid said. 'She's just dumb and ambitious. A bad combination. And she fell in with some ass-hole who's also dumb and ambitious. He told her he could help her be an actress but first of all she had to get some big publicity. So she got her publicity and Homer got stuck in jail.'

'But he got away, didn't he?'

'That's right.'

'How'd he do that?'

'I don't know. Some people helped him.'

'What people? Nobody liked him except you and me.'

'Somebody helped him. That's all I know. He got away and he's out of the country.'

'Where is he?'

'You don't want to know,' Kincaid said.

'Yes, I do.'

'Can you keep a secret?'

'You know me. I don't tell anybody anything.'

'If you tell this, I could be in trouble.'

'I won't tell anybody.'

'He's in Australia. He's back where he came from.'

'That's what I thought. When you said he got away, I said to myself, "I expect he's back there on some cattle run in Australia." I'm glad he didn't have to stay in jail.'

'He wouldn't last a year in jail. If somebody didn't kill him he'd kill himself.'

'If those men hadn't cut him up when he was a kid, if he could talk like other people, I guess a lot of things would have turned out differently for him.'

'I suppose so. But you can't be sure. When you work in a logging camp or on a cattle run you see a lot of men who don't have much to say. Just because they know how to talk doesn't mean they do talk. Most people talk too damned much anyway. I have a hunch Homer wouldn't talk a lot even if he could.'

'Sophie tells me you're considering a new life. As a country squire,' Kincaid said. It was the day after his arrival at the Towers. He and Evan, on a clear cold day, were having a walk across the moors.

'Oh, I don't think so. Although I admit it's an attractive prospect. After all the time I've spent in California these past two years, I'd forgotten how keen I am for this place. I was only eight or nine years old when Dad and I came here to live. I thought it was the grandest spot I'd ever seen. I still think that.'

'So Sophie's right.'

'She's half-right. We've had a bit of time to talk since I came back. I told her I want to start work on a new play and she said what better place to write than up here. So we talked about that for a while. That's all. I didn't come to any decision about it.'

'Does that mean you're turning your back on the movie business? Won't that be a shock to Julian? He thinks he invented you.'

'I don't have a long-range commitment with Julian. I wrote two pictures for him and he paid me a great deal of money. But I'm not planning to sit out there in California twiddling my thumbs and waiting to see what project he comes up with next. As soon as we finished *Bushranger*, I started writing *Dillinger*. But when we wrapped that one early in December, he said nothing about anything coming up. I was relieved in a way. I was more than ready to get out of Los Angeles. You remember, we talked about that before I left.'

'You said you were giving up the beach house.'

'That's right. Burning bridges. I want to flush that whole atmosphere out of my head. Forget about palm trees and camera angles and start thinking in terms of the stage.'

'Good for you. But what if you get a cable from Thorne tomorrow, calling you back to work?'

'I don't expect that to happen, but if it did I'd say no.'

'If you say no to Julian he assumes you want more money, so he sweetens the offer. Now that *Dillinger* looks like a winner he won't want to break up his team. Same actor. Same director. Same writer.'

'Are you saying you know something I don't know? Did he talk to you about a new project before you left Los Angeles?'

Kincaid shook his head. 'All sugar and spice and optimism but no word about what comes next. Julian doesn't fool me. *Dillinger* hadn't opened yet then. He had high hopes but no box-office figures. And he was still nervous about the Homer Tony business. Afraid I might get some bad publicity just when the picture was opening.'

'But that didn't happen.'

'So far so good,' Kincaid said. 'Till Burt Windrow gets another flea in his ear.'

'What's the matter with that guy? He uses that newspaper column like a weapon. What's he got against you?'

'Bloody vengeance. That's his game. I met him the first time Sophie and I went to California. He was trying to work as an actor then and not doing very well. He saw me as a rank amateur married to a rich lady, so the more attention I got from Julian and the other studios, the madder he got. One day I had a drink with him at Lucey's and he made a crack I didn't like about Sophie. So I grabbed him by the neck and shut off his air till he turned seven different colours. I guess he never got over it. Not long afterward he got a job writing his gossip column and he's been trying to shoot me down ever since.'

'Does Julian know that story?'

'I don't know. I may have told him. I can't remember. You see, I don't give a damn what Windrow writes.'

'Maybe you should put your hand on his throat again.'

Kincaid shook his head. 'He's not worth it. I'd rather let Julian worry about him. He can turn it over to Sam. Sam's the one who deals with ass-holes like Windrow.'

'How does he do that?'

'That's what I asked him. He told me he reasons with them.'

8

When she parted from Kincaid in London, he on the local train for St Albans and she on the express to Newcastle, Sophie busied herself with her bags and scarves and books and newspapers as soon as she was settled in her private compartment. It was a habit with her, carried over from childhood. When she didn't trust her emotions she took pains to occupy herself with countless details and distractions and small projects. She had learned through the years to protect herself, to screen herself away from matters that frightened or confused her.

On this day, however, all these techniques and devices failed her. Her guilts and anxieties and self-doubts slingshotted through her consciousness like shards of glass. If she had been able to clarify them and put them in some sort of order in a silent monologue, they might have fallen together something like this:

When I wanted everything to be so perfect, what went wrong? Or is it my imagination? Or do I expect too much?

All my life people have said, 'Don't fret about Sophie. She's got a cool head on her shoulders and steel in her spine. She knows how to manage, how to protect herself, how to deal with the world.' Even when Toby died, when the children were babies, no one who knew me ever imagined that I couldn't prevail and make my way. When I bought the house in London and moved there, I was swamped with all sorts of trepidations and concerns but my family and friends, whether they believed I'd made a wise choice or not, were convinced that I would bring it off. Then when I married Kincaid they felt, I'm certain, 'Ah, well, even if she's chosen the wrong man the gods will favour her as usual. In six months she'll turn him into another sort of chap altogether.'

Now, however, since Brannigan's dead and the Major's gone, I expect there's a different tone. 'Well, then, she's in charge, isn't she? Back at the Towers and taking control. A bit of the Major cropping up in her, don't you think? Sure of her ground, Sophie is, monumentally self-confident. Brought Arthur back, didn't she, when he swore he was gone for good? Dead-set on redoing the old manse so there's a proper place for everyone, and most important, bloody determined to turn Kincaid into a county man and keep him close to home.'

I know what people say about me, how they feel and what they think. If they only guessed how mistaken they are, if they knew how difficult it is for me to make a decision and follow it through. While I'm envied for being a woman in command, I long to be a creature that people want to protect and take care of. But I know that's not to be. I seem to be precisely what I'm not – self-propelled and invulnerable.

Hugh Causey, for example, was a cruel bastard, but he would surely have been less careless about my feelings if he hadn't convinced himself that I was a golden child who could survive anything.

What a tower of self-confidence and capability I must seem to be. God, how I wish that were true. If I told my family about the anxiety and self-doubt that actually characterize me, they would smile and pat my hand and secretly wonder what I was up to. No one would believe how little faith I have in myself as a parent. Nor have I ever felt I've been a rewarding daughter for Margaret. And God knows, I'm tortured by guilt when I think of the poor hapless Major. Did I make enough effort to get through to him, to be a sympathetic grown-up friend as well as his daughter? I know

71

I didn't. I had lined up so squarely behind Margaret that I never allowed myself to consider his needs, never tried to discover why he was compelled to be such a bastard.

And now what? Why do I suddenly feel such a strong pull back to the Towers? Since there's no authority figure now, am I driven to fill that vacuum? And do I see that as a temporary role, or am I looking far ahead and saying, 'At last this home, this domain, this vast enterprise, is my responsibility, *my* legacy.'

There seems, however, to be a consensus that I must not take root here in Northumberland. Once the routines of the estate are stabilized, I must take up my life in London again. But what if I've decided that this *is* my life? Not London but this place, this county. I don't mention that of course. I simply nod my head and smile as people plan my future for me.

Only Evan senses what I'm about. I suspect he feels the pull back here as strongly as I do.

As her thoughts whirled round her head, they began to direct themselves to Kincaid, as though he was sitting opposite her.

Is love enough? I refuse to believe it's not. I have never questioned your feelings for me or mine for you. But then I ask myself, 'Why is it so hard sometimes for us to understand each other? Why can't we make contact? If the work you're doing is important to you why can't it be important to me? And if my sense of place, of domicile, is so critical to me, why can't you sense that and find some way to accommodate it?'

Since you're back from California, you can see that my family situation has changed because of Brannigan's death. But I think you've reached the wrong conclusion. I hope I'm mistaken, but I suspect that you think I'm using these new circumstances to manipulate you, to settle once and for all, perhaps, our differences as

72

to where and how we should live.

If that's what you're thinking, you're mistaken, my darling. I don't make decisions that affect both of us and then announce them to you. That's not my nature and it never has been.

On the other hand I've always been truthful about my feelings. So I'm sure it won't come as a surprise to you when I say that I cannot become an American, a Californian. I tried. I simply can't do it.

As I was coming back to England on the *Aquitania*, tortured by the thoughts of what I might find when I saw Margaret again, trying to anticipate what I might say or do to start some sort of healing process for her, in the midst of my pain and confusion I realized that, as rotten as I felt, I was becoming myself again; that I was ceasing to be the pasteboard creature I'd been in California, and was becoming human tissue.

Also I knew suddenly – there was no doubt in my mind about it – that if I had been in England, Brannigan would not be dead now. I know I could have found some way to reason with my father. He would have moved out peacefully and all of us, especially Margaret, would have been spared the anguish we're going through.

So here we are, up against that same wall again. They say a man with two women loses his soul and a man with two houses loses his head. For a long time I've had two houses, the Towers and my home in London. Now you've built me a lovely new home in California. I know I should adore it, but I don't. I can't live in it, Kincaid. I truly can't. The fact that you made it a replica of the Towers doesn't make it easier. Because it reminds me of England, it only makes it worse.

I'm not saying that California's a dreadful place. I'm saying it's an impossible place for me. The first time we were there I felt uneasy and disoriented. This last time I felt as though I'd lost myself. I felt like an abandoned child in a foreign place where another language was spoken. I simply can't go back there. I know it now.

Am I saying that you must choose between me and your splendid career? Of course not. I could never say that. But I know I can't share that part of your life. I would follow you to New Guinea or to the South Pole. But not to Hollywood. If you forced me to live there, if I forced myself, I would quickly turn into a distorted creature you could neither recognize nor love.

9

Evan's revelation to Kincaid that he had made up his mind to abandon film writing and devote his time to writing a new play was something less than a half-truth. The fact was that he had arrived at the Towers on his return from California feeling disturbingly at odds with himself. No future plans and an uncertain sense of direction. The self-confidence and resolution he had displayed to Kincaid a few weeks later had come to Evan as a gift from Sophie.

The first evening he spent with her at the Towers, they sat up late, drinking brandy in the drawing-room, sitting before the fire and speaking candidly about themselves, delighted to be together and glowing with information and advice and reminiscence. At the tag end of the evening, both of them sleepy and relaxed and warmed by the fire and the brandy, the great house dark and still all around them, Sophie said, 'I felt terrible when I heard about your break-up with Mary Cecil. But for selfish reasons I'm glad you're back in England. And back here where we grew up together. I expect you think of it as just a visit, and so do I. A period of transition where my presence, for the moment, is necessary. But perhaps we're both wrong. Perhaps we're being reminded that this is, after all, our permanent place. I think your father has come to realize that, and maybe some miracle will make Kincaid realize it, too. If Europe's getting ready to explode, if the world's about to go crazy again, then Northumberland looks extremely attractive. At least it does to me. I was surprised to find how quickly I've slipped back into the rhythm here. How clever the Wiswells were to build such a handsome home in such a story-book setting. It makes me wish I were a poet or a painter. What a perfect place for creative work. But alas I have no gift.'

'Talent's just the beginning,' Evan said.

'I know. You've told me that many times. But you have discipline as well. Don't you look round you and think this would be a splendid place to work? No distractions. Freedom to concentrate fully on your plays. You and I must have a serious talk about this.'

'Isn't this a serious talk?'

'I mean about your writing. I hope you haven't forgotten how helpful I was once before. Remember when I told you you needed to put more of yourself and your own experiences into your plays? Isn't that what got you started on *The Fatherhouse*?'

'You're right.'

'So we'll get into that later. After we've decided where you should work, we'll chat about what your next play will be about. I'm sure you know and I'm keen to hear.'

'I don't know at all. I've been totally occupied with camera angles and production problems.'

'Never mind. I'll be your muse. I'll help you get started.' She got up and poked the fire. When she sat down again on the deep couch she said, 'You've seen that I'm refurbishing certain sections of the house. There'll be a complete wing for Kincaid and me, apartments for the children, and certain changes in Margaret's rooms. And . . . I've got a splendid spot picked out for you. The north tower. With a fine sitting-room, a bedroom and bathroom, and on the top level, overlooking the moors, a large, well-lit library and writing-room. A haven. Silence and privacy. A place to think and

75

plan and reflect, a place where you can get back to writing. Serious writing. For the theatre. I know you've had an interesting experience writing for the films, but I'm sure you've never forgotten that the stage is the core of it all. The Americans can twiddle about with their cameras and special effects but we British are theatre folk. Shakespeare and Marlowe and Shaw. That's our tradition. And it's your tradition.'

'I'm not as confident about that as you seem to be.'

'That's because you've been too long in California. You need to get the petrol fumes and seagulls' squawking flushed out of your head. You need to crawl back inside yourself so you can wrestle with a new play. And what better place to do it than right here? You think about it. Think seriously about it. And it wouldn't be all work and solitude. I'm sure of that. I have a feeling the Towers will become a warm and jolly place again. The way it used to be. There's a whole new crop of young women in the county since you went off to Oxford and London. They would be eager to fall into the arms of a splendid chap like you. And you and I could see more of each other as well. I'd love that.'

'Are you saying you expect to take up residence here?'

'It's possible, isn't it? One never knows. Both Trevor and Sarah are away at school now. They're only home on their holidays. I've given them the benefits of growing up in London. So why shouldn't I spend more of my time, or all of my time, here in the country, if it pleases me?'

'What about Kincaid? Will it please him?'

'Why shouldn't it? Remember, he spent most of his life in the outback, on cattle ranches and the like, or on the sea. I mean, he's not a city person. I should think he'd be very happy here.'

'And if he weren't?'

'But I believe he will be. We could all have great times together. Think it over and you'll see that I'm right. But whatever you say, I'm going ahead with your quarters in the north tower. And remember this: "The more you see of the world, the better your home will look." Do you know who said that?'

'I don't believe I do.'

'I said it.'

## 10

'How was your visit with Trevor?' Sophie said. Kincaid had just arrived from London that afternoon. They were alone in the library after dinner. Arthur and Evan were in the billiard-room and Margaret had gone upstairs to her own quarters.

'It was good to see him,' Kincaid said. 'We spent two or three hours together.'

'I haven't heard a word from him since he went back to school. He's as careless about writing letters as you are.'

'I'm illiterate. You know that.'

'No, you're not. And neither is Trevor. You're both spoiled and dilatory. Is he all right?'

'Looks great. Not a kid any more. And he's smart as hell.'

'I know he does well in his classes, but he doesn't go out of his way to show me how intelligent he is.'

'Take my word for it. He's got a good head on his shoulders. He knows what's fake and what's real.'

'Did he learn that from you or are you learning it from him?'

Kincaid smiled. 'He's way ahead of me. Some days I think everything's fake. The next day it all seems real. I don't spend a lot of time trying to separate the two.'

'You're a true primitive. At least that's how you see yourself. You should take up painting. You'd be a sensation. The heart of a lion and the vision of a child. That's what the critics would say.'

'I see myself as an old dog. Following the rubbish lorry.'

'You're impossible. I'm convinced your uncertain self-esteem is just a cover-up for egomania.'

'You're very sexy when you use big words,' he said.

'We'll see about that,' she said. Then: 'Did Trevor tell you all about our Christmas here at the Towers?'

'He said it was quite fancy. Said he had a great time.'

'How did he feel about leaving Los Angeles?'

'He didn't say. You'd know more about that than I would, I expect.'

Sophie shook her head. 'Young men never confide in their mothers. Did he tell you he has a girlfriend out there? A serious romance, it seems.'

'That's news to me.'

'You wouldn't tell me anyway, would you?'

'Probably not,' Kincaid said.

'Well Sarah told me. She managed to weasel some facts out of him when they'd both had a few glasses of champagne on New Year's Eve. It seems he's gone daft over a young woman who posed in his art classes.'

'Good for him. A woman of a certain age?'

'Not really. But a bit older, Sarah says. Seventeen, I guess. Her name is Lucy something. Lucy Street, I think. She's a ballet student. Poses for artists to pay for her classes.'

'Wearing a tutu?'

'Wearing nothing. Trevor showed me his studies from life-drawing class. So I'm sure I've seen a likeness of her. But he never identified her as someone special.'

'That must be a great experience. Keeping company with a girl who was starkers the first time you saw her.'

'I guess I'm getting old. I can't imagine Trevor with a girl. To me he's still a little boy. And he seems dreadfully shy with strangers.'

'Maybe the girl's not shy. That would solve the problem.'

'Well, whatever he's been up to, his sister's disgusted with him. Sarah can't imagine her baby brother being involved with a girl who's a bit older than she is. She likes to believe he still walks about with frogs in his pockets.'

'Did he give Sarah all the details?' Kincaid said.

'He told her almost nothing. That's what she's annoyed about, I think. He just showed her the girl's photograph and said, "What do you think of her? She's my girlfriend."'

'Good for him.'

'I'm not sure I feel that way,' Sophie said. 'He's awfully young for something serious.'

'What makes you think it's serious? He may never see her again. And even if he does, he may have taken a fancy to several other girls in the meantime.'

'I hope you aren't planning to give him the benefit of your experience.'

'Not a chance. And besides I have no experience. Anything I know I've learned from you.'

'I'm sure your fans would be surprised and disappointed to hear that. Did you see the article in the *Telegraph* about you? Two or three days ago.'

'You know I don't read that junk.'

'The title of the article was "Kincaid's Women". It talked about your scenes with Barbara Stanwyck and Daisy Bishop. Said it was plain to see why so many women flock to see your movies. I knew Daisy Bishop was in *Bushranger* but I didn't realize she was in *Dillinger* as well.'

'She's under contract to Julian. He keeps her working all the time. Four or five pictures a year.'

'I knew about Barbara Stanwyck being in the picture. I thought she was to play your girlfriend.'

'Not originally. Daisy Bishop was set to play Lola. Then when we found out about Sally Wick, the girl Dillinger was living with when he was killed, Julian tried to get Stanwyck for that part. But she said no. So Julian made a switch. Gave Stanwyck the Lola part and manoeuvred Daisy into playing Sally Wick.'

'The article also said there were rumours of a real romance going on between you and Daisy. That story again.'

Kincaid nodded. 'But I can only see her on Tuesdays because on the other nights of the week I'm sleeping with Marie Dressler. And Sundays I spend the day in bed with May Robson.'

'You think this is all very funny, don't you?'

'I don't think about it at all. Because I don't know about any of these idiotic rumours unless somebody tells me. Nobody takes this stuff seriously except you.'

'I don't believe that. I expect a lot of people take it seriously.'

'That's their problem. It's not mine and it's not yours.'

'Are you telling me that if these stories were true you'd admit it to me?'

'No. I didn't say that at all. You didn't even ask me that. I thought we were discussing how we should react to lies that are printed in the papers where everyone can read them.'

'We were discussing that but I went a step further. I said I'd never know if they were true or not because you wouldn't tell me.'

'I did tell you. I said they're not true.'

'Then why do the papers keep printing them?'

'Because people like gossip. And most people believe anything they see in print.'

'I don't.'

'Good. Then we don't have to talk about it any more.'

'Why shouldn't we talk about it?'

'Because it's ridiculous and because life is too short.'

'What if the shoe were on the other foot? What if you suspected I was having an affair with someone? What if you'd heard such a story and you asked me if it was true?'

'I wouldn't ask you that.'

'I don't believe you.'

'Why not? If it were true I wouldn't expect you to tell me about it. When somebody has a secret like that it's because they don't want anyone to know. They certainly wouldn't want a husband or wife to know.'

'I wouldn't lie to you if you asked me,' she said.

'But if I didn't ask you I still wouldn't know, would I?'

'I would never deceive you.'

'That's not what we're talking about. We're talking about

80

lying. Whether you'd tell me about it if you did have an adventure with another man. Let's make it more specific. I know you and Evan grew up together. I know you're keen for each other, and I think that's great. But what if I decided it might have been something else some time in the past, what if I asked you point-blank?'

'That's too crazy. You know how things are between me and Evan.'

'That's right. I do. But we're playing *Let's Pretend*. You're pretending there's something between me and Daisy, and I'm pretending there's something between you and Evan. Assuming for the moment that it's true, when would you have told me about it? Before we got married or after we got married? Or would you have to wait and see if I would ever ask you straight out?'

'This is so ridiculous I don't even know how to discuss it. I don't want to discuss it.'

'Neither do I.'

## 11

From his early beginnings in motion pictures, Julian Thorne had learned the importance of press relations, promotion and publicity. When he started his own studio the first person he hired was Dale Biggers. He doubled his salary and stole him from Goldwyn. When Julian's brother, Sam, came from New York a few years later to join him in the business, Julian gave him a rundown of the Thornwood Studios' operation. He went into some detail about Biggers. 'Dale is more important to me than any star or director I have under contract. He managed to make Thornwood an important name out here before I'd finished shooting my first picture. For ten years he was a financial reporter for the *New York Sun*. And he knows politics inside out. He's on good terms with the police. When there's trouble, he knows the right button to push and right person to talk to. People like him and trust him because he's a decent man. And he's good with actors.

Knows when to go to bat for them and when to hold their feet to the fire. Goldwyn had a major leading man who liked to beat up on women. He'd have gone to jail, no doubt about it, if it hadn't been for Biggers. At one time he had a reputation as a booze-fighter, but I've known him for ten years and I've never seen him cock-eyed or even close to it. He's money in the bank for us, Sam, so keep that in mind. He knows where all the bodies are buried but he also knows how to keep his mouth shut. Everybody out here is trying to get a piece of the power. Dale's got a big hunk of it but he doesn't use it as a weapon. He doesn't have to advertise who he is because everybody knows.'

Not long after Kincaid left Los Angeles to go back to England, Biggers met Bert Windrow for lunch at the Ambassador. Through the months since Windrow had begun writing his syndicated column the two men had frequently been in contact. They'd met at screenings, press conferences, sneak previews, and various other business/social occasions. They were friendly but not friends. Although they were not confidants, each of them had managed to learn a great deal about the other.

Biggers knew precisely why they were having lunch together. Windrow had no idea but was not apprehensive. All the same both of them were wary. They proved that to each other by not having a drink before they ordered lunch. After some general conversation about what director's job was in danger, whose career was in jeopardy, which studios were in financial disarray, and whose husband was going to bed with whose wife, Biggers said, 'I've been keeping an eye on your column. You're doing a bang-up job. You must feel good about it.'

'I do, as a matter of fact. It's going well.'

'You made a smart move. I'll bet you don't regret turning your back on acting.'

'Let's not kid ourselves, Dale. Acting turned its back on me. I got off to a good start out here and then the bottom fell out. I could have gone back to the theatre of course.'

'Of course you could. Rathbone told me you were well thought of in London.'

'Surprised to hear that old Basil threw me a rose. We're not exactly chums. He once had a yen for a young lady who had a yen for me.'

'There's always that, isn't there?' Biggers said. 'But now you're free as an eagle. You're in a solid spot. No more competing for jobs. People envy you, I'm sure. Producers who wouldn't return your calls before are now eager to have you over for tennis on Sunday.'

Windrow smiled. 'That's about the size of it. *I* get to call the shots now.'

'A good feeling, eh?'

'Damned right it is.'

Near the end of their luncheon, Biggers said, 'You've been running an item about two of our actors that has Mr Thorne a little upset.'

'That's my business, I'm afraid. I can't turn out a column every day without upsetting somebody.'

'I understand that. But it's my business to protect Thornwood Studios and the people who make our pictures.'

'I've given Thornwood a lot of support,' Windrow said.

'That's right, you have. And we appreciate it. But in the last couple of weeks you've been taking shots at Kincaid. He's an important star in an important picture we've just released.'

'I've seen the grosses. *Dillinger*'s doing great.'

'Yes, it is,' Biggers said, 'and we want that business to continue. We don't want the Legion of Decency or the Baptist mothers of Atlanta carrying posters outside our theatres.'

'I don't follow you.'

'I think you do. You've been writing about a hot romance between Kincaid and Daisy Bishop.'

'I'm not the only one who used that item.'

'I know that. But you were the first one. And that's what counts. Everybody out here plays follow the leader.'

'It's a little gossip item. What's the big deal?'

'There's no big deal. Not yet. That's why I'm doing some flood control. Kincaid's a married man. Daisy's married to Bob Sample. Adultery's a tough item to sell at the box office. That's why we have a morals clause in our contracts.'

'Maybe you should talk to Kincaid and Bishop about it.'

'We have. They say it's a lie and Julian believes them. So do I. That's why I'm talking to you.'

Windrow smiled and made a gesture with his hand. 'Journalism's not a finite science, Dale. You were a news-paperman. You know that. And a column like mine has even more flexibility. I deal with gossip and rumour, the same as Winchell or Louella Parsons.'

'I realize that. But you're also a part of the motion-picture industry. We all help you and you help us. Anything that's bad for business is bad for all of us. When something makes Thorne your enemy, or if you for some reason have a personal vendetta against our studio or one of our stars, then everyone suffers in the long run.'

'Why would I be out to get Thorne or anybody else?'

'I'm not sure. But we've heard from friends of yours that there's no love lost between you and Kincaid.'

'Is that what he said?'

'No. I got my information from someone outside the studio.'

'All right, I guess it's no secret. I'm not a fan of Kincaid. I met him the first time he came to Los Angeles. I didn't like him then and I don't like him now. I don't have time to scurry about trying to dig up dirt about him, but if some-thing comes in that puts him in a bad light I'm happy to put it in my column. But that's between me and Kincaid. Has nothing to do with Thorne.'

Biggers shook his head. 'You're mistaken about that. If Kincaid's damaged, then it hurts business. And if it hurts business, it hurts Thornwood. And if that happens we all have Julian Thorne to deal with.'

'That's not a veiled threat, is it, Mr Biggers?'

'Not at all. This is just a friendly discussion about the problems we both face.'

'You people aren't trying to censor me, are you? Because if you are, that would make a nice lead item for my column.'

'I have a feeling you haven't heard anything I've said.'

'I heard you, but as you said yourself, I'm not walking around with my hat in my hand nowadays. People come to me now and I like it that way. And if Julian Thorne thinks I'm out to hurt his company, you might mention to him that I have information about Sam Thorne and his friends that would really make a hot story.'

Biggers dropped two sugar-cubes in his coffee and carefully stirred it. At last he looked up and said, 'This is a small community, my friend, and you're an outsider. I'd hate to see you screw yourself up.'

Later that afternoon Biggers sat in Julian Thorne's office at the studio. When he'd finished telling the details of his meeting with Windrow, Sam Thorne said, 'That Limey son of a bitch. Who the hell does he think he's dealing with?'

'I thought you two had an understanding, Sam,' Julian said.

'We did. I understood him and he understood me. No doubt about it. He's been kissing our behinds for months. Plugging our pictures like we was paying his salary.'

'So what went wrong?'

'Don't ask me.'

'He's got no love for Kincaid,' Biggers said, 'but there's more to it than that, I think. He's really feeling his oats. He acts like a guy who knows he's holding all the cards. Not scared of anybody or anything. Whatever he knows, or thinks he knows, he feels good about it.'

After a long moment Julian turned to his brother and said, 'What's the situation with Ellie Rawson?'

'I've talked to her a couple times. We'll probably put her in our casting office. She likes that idea.'

'Starting when?'

'First of March. April maybe.'

'So she's still with Windrow?'

'That's right,' Sam said.

'Good. She's his secretary. She must type his columns.'

'Types them. Proof-reads them. Sends them off to the syndication centre.'

'All right. Talk with her tomorrow. Tell her we want a word-by-word report on anything, good or bad, that Windrow writes about Thornwood, our pictures, or any of our people. And we want it as soon as he dictates it.' He turned to Biggers. 'What's his lead-time? When he puts together a column how long from then till it runs in the papers?'

'It has to go to the syndicate, then from there to all the papers who run it. Three days at least, I think. Five maybe. I have a friend at the syndicate office in Kansas City. I can find out exactly as soon as I get her on the telephone.'

'Good. You talk to Kansas City and Sam will talk to Ellie, and we'll find out for sure how much reaction time we'll have if we need to kill something this jackass is planning to write.'

# • CHAPTER 3 •

## 1

The day after Kincaid visited him at St Albans, Trevor wrote a letter to Lucy Street in Los Angeles.

I hope you're getting all the letters I've been sending you. I like to write. It's the next best thing to talking with you. Since I told you not to write me till I was back at school, I'm not surprised I haven't heard from you. I've been here at St Albans just a few days.

I think about you a lot. Especially that last night before I left Los Angeles to come back to England. All those hours are tattooed on my brain and I guess they'll stay there till I'm a hundred. And I don't mean just the time we spent in your bed. That part drives me crazy when I think about it, when I let myself think about it. I wish my eyes didn't have such a good memory. I see you every place I look. Not just the way you are when we're close together or when you were on the model's stand for Grell's drawing classes, but when we were walking along Santa Monica Boulevard together or up Flores Street to your house. Or sitting in a coffee-shop across the table from each other. I remember all the stuff we talked about like it was just this morning.

I know people our age are supposed to be wild and reckless, willing to give up anything so they can be together, and God knows I feel that way and I know you did as well that morning when I had to leave, when the driver came to pick me up. I've been with mobs of people ever since I came home, first for the Christmas holidays at my grandmother's home in Northumberland and now here at school. All the chaps I've known since I came here two years ago and the teachers and the staff people. I'm never by myself but I feel lonesome. I feel old and grown-up, and all the other fellows my age seem very young. I'm sure that statement will give you a good laugh since you're two years older than I am.

I never wrote a love letter in my life. Never had a reason to. So I'm not good at it. 'No *kidding*,' Lucy Street said, as she collapsed on her sofa in a fit of laughter. So what I'm saying, in my tragic poet's manner, is that I miss you. Every day.

It would be great if we could start making plans about when we'll see each other again, but here we are on opposite sides of the world practically with no idea of when I'll be in California again. Is that the way it works sometimes? Can people meet and fall in each other's arms and hang on like they're drowning, the way we did, and then never see each other again? What a rotten idea. The other day I was wishing I was twenty years old, able to cut loose and do as I like, pick you up and carry you off somewhere so we could spend every day together. Am I stupid or cowardly, or something? I know what I want but I know I can't have it. Not now, I can't. You already know what you plan to do with your life, and that won't change no matter what. All I know for sure is that I have to be older and smarter before I can even decide what direction I'm going. But wouldn't it be nice if I could get older and smarter, and still be able to see you every day and every night while the process was going on?

In my other letters I told you about crossing the

country on a train and crossing the ocean. And I told you about the bad things that happened recently in my grandmother's life. Sarah and I have always called her Margaret (she likes it) and we call our mother Sophie (she likes it, too). I was afraid Christmas would be all tears and soft voices but it turned out to be quite jolly. We drank toasts to each other, and to Margaret's second husband who died, as I told you in California, and we said prayers at table and blessed everyone. And then we proceeded to have a proper Christmas celebration.

When I was in California, I could tell that a lot of people I met there are rich. And they are eager to make sure that everybody knows it. And the people who aren't rich are keen to be rich, so they pretend it's already happened. But in our country or in London where my mother has a house, the people with the most land and the most money and the finest homes don't talk about how rich they are. They know they can buy whatever they want and go wherever they like, and they never have to borrow money, but they don't seem to talk about it or think about it much.

You and I talked about that a lot in California. You're a dancer so you have to work and support yourself so you can study and do the things you want to do. I want to be a painter (at least that's what I think I want) and I know I'll have to work at it for many years if I want to be good. But I'll never have to worry about supporting myself. That should make me feel fine but I'm not sure it does. I suspect I may be missing something. I don't mean I want to go hungry or sleep in doorways. My friend Quigley says that only people who have never suffered are convinced that artists must suffer before they can produce good work. But all the same, when I saw you there in California, running from home to work to class and back to work, your eyes shining and your cheeks pink and beautiful, I knew you could see something, or sense something, that I had never seen or sensed. I think I'm capable of making good decisions about my work, of planning ahead, applying myself, and making steady improvement. But I've never been possessed as you seem to be, driven to pursue something you can't see and may never catch up with. I think sometimes that all that chasing after something is its own reward. Quigley told me, 'The process is everything. If you capture the process or if it captures you, you never have to wonder what the result will be. It will be the best work you're capable of.'

What does all this have to do with us? Everything, I think. Remember what we said to each other, that the best way to live and make good use of yourself is to keep things simple. I think about that all the time since I'm back in England. I decided that people like my family who've never had to solve the problems that most people face every day work out an elaborate system of compensation. Because they have money and acceptance and free choice, because their lives are magnificently simple, they keep themselves busy by complicating things, then trying to clear up the mess they've made. You probably figured that out a long time ago but it just dawned on me recently. It's not the way I intend to live. I'm sure of that.

I think you and I will be extraordinary people once we're all the way grown up. So unless Gary Cooper or some smashing chap like him wants to marry you and make you rich and useless, give me some time to get back to California and we'll take up where we left off.

2

When Sophie and Evan were children, when they were being tutored by Arthur Tagg, he encouraged them to keep a daily log, a record of their activities, reading lists, and a candid analysis of their reactions to people and events. 'The hand activates the mind,' he said. 'Also you'll find that many problems and sticky situations are clarified when you write them down in simple language.'

Whereas Sophie was always a vocal, articulate child, unafraid to express her ideas and opinions, Evan, in those early years, was watchful and silent, more at ease with written work than he was with conversation. Consequently he welcomed his father's guidance in the matter of a written record of what he had done, what he proposed to do, and what he thought about particular subjects at particular times.

By the time he went away to Oxford he was no longer shy in conversation. With his full vocabulary and pleasant voice he had no hesitation about speaking his mind on whatever subject might come up. But the habit of keeping a written record of what, when, and how stayed with him. Even in the chaos of Thornwood Studios, surrounded by turbulence, conflict and anxiety, he had started each working day by making an entry in his log. Back in England, at Wiswell Towers, alone in his rooms at night, trying to sort out where he'd been in relation to where he might be going, he continued his process of self-examination.

I don't know what's gone wrong with me. Or perhaps I do know and don't want to face it. As long as I was working on *Dillinger*, when we were on location or in the studio, worrying, arguing, making changes, second-guessing ourselves, I was all right. Working late, drinking myself calm with Garrigus or Kincaid or whoever I could find, then back to the set first thing the next morning. As long as all that was going on I was all right, focused on the work, no thoughts of yesterday or questions about tomorrow. But once we finished the picture, once I'd seen the final cut, I fell apart. I couldn't stand the sight of the Malibu house.

Couldn't be alone there for more than an hour. So I closed up the place, turned the keys back to the estate agent, and moved into a hotel for the last days before I left for New York to board a ship for England.

I expected to feel better when I was in London. But I didn't. I felt worse. The city was decked out for Christmas but it seemed oddly funereal to me. The streets were crowded and it rained every day. So I stayed in my flat. I'd convinced myself that if I ventured outside I'd run into Mary Cecil or her lunatic husband. Or both of them together perhaps. My fear of seeing her alternated with a maddening need to see her. At last I picked up my bags, still packed from the boat trip, went to the railway station and headed north to the Towers.

I have no patience with misguided souls who feel they must make regularly scheduled returns to the womb. Stroke the family dog, sample Mama's trifle, and have a run down the lane on one's old bicycle. But since I've been back here, I've found myself strolling through the halls and public rooms, visiting the nursery and the stables, the dog run, the kitchens, and the great attic, and remembering in detail certain incidents and mishaps and adventures that I associate with those places.

My black-ass depression wasn't instantly cured but it got better. Christmas was the way I remembered it in the years before the Major left the Army and came home to stay. I'd forgotten how good it feels to be inside this great warm fortress of a house, the wind singing outside, snowflakes spitting against the windows, and logs crackling in all the fireplaces.

I took long walks with Sophie and my father, and skated on the pond with Trevor and Sarah. I ate outrageous amounts of food, drank a great deal of wine, and read Fielding and Trollope in my bed at night. California and Chicago, even London, seemed remote and unnecessary. I was splendidly warm, well fed, and half-drunk in the sumptuous house I'd grown up in, and I wondered why anyone would ever leave such a place if they didn't have to.

One late night, one *very* late night, Evan came up to his rooms sober enough to write a legible hand and intoxicated enough not to care about or edit what he wrote. Like a playwright testing dialogue he addressed himself, in direct discourse, to Sophie.

It's a good thing you're married, my dear. If you weren't, when you met me at the station in Newcastle, I'd have hefted you on my shoulder and carried you away to some secret place. I said to myself, 'There's my friend, my oldest friend, the wild young girl I grew up with. How did I ever let her get away?' I exaggerate, of course. At least I think I do. But perhaps I don't. I'm on the rebound, you see, with all that entails. Bleeding from multiple wounds suffered during my unhinged love-war with Mary Cecil. Still . . . quite apart from all that, seeing you again, putting my arms around you, the two of us in your car, the whole crazy quilt of our growing up together wrapped itself round me like an eiderdown coverlet.

Don't misunderstand me, Sophie. I'm not a marriage-wrecker, my experience with Mary Cecil notwithstanding. But even if I were, my ego isn't strong enough to persuade me that I could ever lure you away from a lightning-bolt like Kincaid.

What I really mean, what I'm trying to say, is that our old and intricate and priceless connection, which has burned low these past few years has come marvel-lously to life again. As we chattered away in the back seat of the Daimler, rolling west toward the Towers, I felt idiotic and irresponsible and eighteen years old, and you looked about sixteen. Sense-memory, the actors call it.

So I came to a decision. I decided that no one can know what friendship's all about till he's been in love, or believed he's in love, with somebody who's not his friend. Contradictory and ironic, isn't it? And bloody painful when it happens.

What I'm struggling to say is this: since Kincaid knows full well that I'm not a threat, since I have no intention of doing damage, you and I must make a conscious effort to stay in touch with each other. We share a lifetime of check-points and blunders and wrong choices and misunderstandings that must be remembered from time to time. Exceptional people like us need to be reminded occasionally that they're not totally flawless. Of course, I am flawless but I'll pretend I'm not in order to balance the scale. In short, Miss Sophie, let's take great pains not to misplace each other.

Reading over what he'd written, continuing to warm himself from the brandy decanter by his chair, Evan was vastly pleased with himself. He was fascinated by the direct discourse, a monologue that could be neither heard nor answered. A dramatic scene that need not concern itself with audience reaction because one knew no audience would witness it. Filled with energy and self-confidence, he picked up his pen again and turned his attention to Kincaid.

Everybody thinks you and I are close friends. Loyal supporters of each other. Sickness and health. Thick and thin. All that shit. Do you see us that way? Bosom friends, et cetera. I don't.

You told me once (or maybe she told me) that Sophie said you're unknowable. Interesting description. I've never heard it applied to anyone before. But it fits you.

Perhaps I envy you. I doubt it but I know it's possible. When I first met you I thought you were a likeable chap. Was that only sympathy, because you

94

were destitute, trying to collect a few coins as a busker? I was giving you a leg-up and perhaps that made me feel generous toward you. You were powerless and I was in a position to help. A shilling for the beggar. Crumbs for the birds. So I wrote an article about you in the *Telegraph*, and then I was off to Portugal for a time. When I came back you'd begun to attract attention. You'd been taken up by Rosamund Barwick and the Bloomsbury crowd. I was amused by all that. I had a feeling that my writing about you had triggered it. But to a journalist, most stories last only a day or two. And yours, I felt, would be no exception. An odd Australian chap with an unusual voice and a photographic memory. So much for that.

The next thing I knew you had met Sophie. By chance I introduced you. And not long after that you two flipped off to France and got married. Suddenly I had to redefine you. And I didn't like it. I felt betrayed somehow. By both you and Sophie.

I grew up being told by my father that I wasn't good enough for Sophie. Good enough perhaps, but not in the same social class. I never really accepted those arbitrary standards, but strangely enough (I'm not proud of this), when she married you I began to accept them. I couldn't imagine anyone from your background having the arrogance to marry Sophie. For a long time after your wedding I didn't seek you out, either of you. You may remember that. When we did see each other at last we all got drunk and talked only nonsense together. By that time I was deeply involved with my play and longing to be entangled with Mary Cecil.

When I saw you again, when you two came back from your first trip to California, my play had died after fourteen performances and Mary Cecil had fled to Wales to lick her wounds and visit her daughter.

Then along came *Bushranger*. Your first film, my first job as a screenwriter. I got the job because of you, of course. So there I was. Not only was I working closely with you, I was indebted to you. From a life on the street you were suddenly in a position of power. And once the picture was finished and released, that power seemed infinite. I was stunned by the change in your fortunes and astonished because none of it seemed to matter to you. I expected you to become arrogant and self-important. That would have made it easy to dislike you. Instead you were calm and unchanged. So I had to dislike you for that.

I knew I'd witnessed a small miracle. The beggar become a prince. The mouse devouring a dragon. Soft rain falling on barren ground. Wealth and recognition. All unbidden, it seemed, and scarcely noticed by you. Gifts from all sides in reward for . . . in reward for what? It was a question I couldn't answer and it maddened me. Why you of all unlikely people?

At the beginning I told myself that only a chain of bizarre circumstances had thrust you forward. Benevolent tides outside your control. Once you were tested, I concluded, you would fall like Icarus. But it didn't happen. That straightforward ordinariness (Sarah called you *common*) was your distinction, it seemed. Great masses of people saw something in you that they imagined they saw in themselves, and you were launched. All without planning or training or genius or concentrated effort on your part. No struggle. It all came easily. Just as your conquest of Sophie (or was it her conquest of you) had been smooth and effortless.

You see now what I'm getting at. With no apparent effort you have taken a pivotal position in my life. Even my writing is now connected to you. In Thorne's eyes I'm simply the English chap who writes your screenplays. I am part of the Kincaid team. As you prosper, I prosper. No one sees *Bushranger* or *Dillinger* as Evan Tagg creations.

Do you think I'm tortured by your success? I'm not.

I'm simply astonished, as I've said, by the ease of it all. Pieces falling smoothly into position all round you while you saunter along and make casual choices, each of which, in every case, turns out to be a perfect choice.

As I said (did I say it twice?), I don't begrudge you your good fortune. But it truly pisses me off that all the good fortune in the universe seems to have been marked with your name. You see, I was taught as a boy that rewards come from struggle. I no longer believe that. Until a couple of years ago, your life was one long and hopeless struggle. And nothing came of it. No rainbow. Then, when you stopped struggling, everything came to you. Is there a lesson in all that for me? I expect there is. But I've learned it too late.

3

After Dale Biggers reported the details of his luncheon meeting with Windrow, he and Sam Thorne left Julian's office together. As they walked down the drive toward the executive building where their offices were located, Biggers said, 'I didn't tell Julian everything Windrow said. We can pass it along to him if you say so. But I thought you'd like to hear it first.'

'No reason to keep anything from Julian.'

Biggers nodded. 'Maybe not. I just wanted to tell you first.'

'I've had about enough of this guy Windrow. I'm getting very tired of his crap.'

'Then you won't like what I'm about to tell you. When I was leaning on him, trying to get him to back off from Kincaid, he kept shaking his head and giving me a cute look. Finally he said he had some information about you and your friends that would make a really hot story.'

'He said what?' Sam stopped walking. So did Biggers. They stood facing each other on the tree-lined drive.

'That's exactly what he said. But the way he said it was like a threat. Like if we didn't stop bugging him about the Kincaid knocks he'd give us something serious to worry about.'

'That's all he said? Didn't mention any names?'

Biggers shook his head. 'Just the way I told you.'

'What do you think he was getting at?'

'You got me.'

'Don't jerk me around, Dale. You know everything that goes on in this town.'

'Not a chance. And if I did I wouldn't admit it. I don't like my doorbell to ring at night.' Then: 'Do you want to tell Julian or do you want me to?'

'I'd better handle it,' Sam said. 'There's no rush. Julian's got enough on his mind right now. Besides this Windrow bastard is just blowing smoke. He can't print anything about me. I'm a family man. I go home to my wife every night.'

That evening after dinner Sam drove over to John Corso's house. They sat in the sun-room sipping grappa, looking out across the cello-shaped swimming pool, and Sam told him about his conversation with Dale Biggers.

'What's the matter with this cock-eyed Windrow? Does he think he's playing stick-ball with a bunch of kids?'

'He's a crazy bastard,' Sam said. 'I don't know what he thinks or what he knows.'

'What's to know?'

'He knows we leaned on him once before. It's a cinch he knows that. Made him buy a new car for Evan Tagg and turn over his own car to us. And there's a couple other things he might know.'

'Like what?'

'That we got Dolph Twilly to work over Windrow's friend in London . . .'

Corso shook his head. 'He can't tie us to Twilly. No way.'

'Or maybe he knows we engineered that whole bail-jumping business with Homer Tony. Getting him on that freighter to Australia.'

Corso shook his head again. 'We're clean there. That was passed along to sub-contractors. Nobody knew the whole picture. Just a piece here and a piece there.'

'Well, Windrow's got something in his head. Biggers said it sounded like a threat when he said, "Sam and his friends."'

'So we're friends. That's no news to anybody. We were in business together in Jersey. Trucking produce. Now we're corporate executives and tax-payers in California. Just friends. No business connections.'

'Maybe Windrow knows more about us than we think he does. Maybe he's on to something. We've got Julian to think about too. I don't want him to start getting ideas.'

'Julian's your brother, for Christ's sake.'

'That's right. But he ain't a fool. He's got his eyes and ears open all the time.'

'Does he know what Windrow said about you and your friends?'

'No. Biggers didn't tell him. He just told me.'

'Good. Let's keep it that way. Can we get inside Windrow's head?'

Sam nodded. 'We own his secretary. She used to work for me and she'll be back at the studio again in a couple months.'

'And she's with you now if you need her?'

'Locked in.'

'Good. So let's not get steamed up about this ass-hole Windrow. I know two hundred ways to fix his clock.'

4

One morning, in the group of letters that had been forwarded to him from California, Evan found a Christmas card from his mother. Inside she had written a short note.

I know this card will come to you late because I somehow misplaced the London address you gave me.

So I'm sending this to you at the studio. I just want you to know I'll be thinking about you on Christmas Day. I have a little gift which I'll give you next time we see each other. I hope that will be soon. When will you be back here in California? I went to see *Dillinger* as soon as it opened here in Los Angeles. It's a wonderful movie. The audience loved it. I like gangster pictures. Maybe that's because I'm from Chicago. Congratulations and Happy New Year.

Late that morning, Evan went upstairs to his father's new office and found him sitting at his desk in boots and riding-breeches and a hacking-jacket.

'Looks as if you're going for a gallop.'

'Already done,' Arthur said. 'Long before you were up, I expect. I try to ride a few miles every morning before breakfast. Rain or shine. Gets the blood pumping.'

'All my life I've never seen you ride a horse. Now it turns out you're a cowboy.'

'Not quite.'

'Sophie says you're a damned good rider. She was amazed.'

'I started riding when I was six years old. My father always kept horses. I was jumping in competition by the time I went to university. But when your mother and I were married and living in Chicago I gave it up altogether. Now I'm at it again.'

'How many other talents do you have that I'm not aware of?'

'None, I'm afraid. You've got all the talent in the family.'

'When I saw my mother in Los Angeles she said maybe I got my writing talent, such as it is, from her.'

'I doubt that,' Arthur said.

'She wasn't serious. She was just making a joke, I think. Talking about how much she likes to write letters.' When Arthur didn't answer, Evan went on. 'I just got a Christmas card from her as a matter of fact. I thought you might like to see it.'

'Of course. You must show it to me some time.'

'I have it right here.' Evan took the card out of his jacket pocket and put it on Arthur's desk. His father looked at it without picking it up. 'A nice holly-wreath motif. Very nice.'

'Why don't you read what's inside?'

Arthur shook his head. 'It's a card to you, not me.'

'It's just a note. Nothing personal. She said she's seen the *Dillinger* picture.'

'Good for her. I look forward to seeing it myself.' He pushed the card back across his desk-top to Evan. There was a long silent moment. Then Evan said, 'You don't want to talk about her at all, do you?'

'No. I don't.'

'Any particular reason?'

'No. I simply don't see any reason to discuss her.'

'Even if I want to?'

'I can't imagine why you would want to. The woman I knew as your mother you were too young to remember, and the woman you've met recently in California is a stranger to me.'

'You mean she's not really my mother.'

'I didn't say that. I'm sure it's Amy all right. But she wouldn't be the same person I knew thirty years ago. I'm sure I wouldn't recognize her.'

'I can understand your not wanting to see her. But I'm surprised you can't talk about her.'

'I didn't say I can't talk about her. I simply don't know what there is to say.'

'You remember that last letter you sent me from London after I'd written to tell you I'd been in touch with her?'

'You're not talking about the cable I sent you?'

'No. This was earlier. It was a nice long letter. You weren't angry with me then. Do you remember what you said in that letter?'

'I'm afraid I don't.'

'You said the next time we were together we'd sit down

101

like we're doing now and you'd tell me everything you could remember about my mother.'

After a long pause Arthur said, 'I must say I don't remember that.'

'I still have the letter if you want to see it.'

'I'm not denying I wrote the letter. I just don't remember the contents. Those months I spent in London were unusual. Some of that time I don't remember clearly. A great deal of it I don't remember at all. I hope you won't hold me to a promise I made then. The subject of your mother simply doesn't interest me.'

'But it does interest me. That doesn't surprise you, does it?'

'Of course not. It's normal. But since you've managed to make contact with her after all these years . . .'

'She made contact with me,' Evan said. 'That's the way it happened.'

Arthur nodded, then went on. 'Since you're in contact with her you surely know more about her than I could ever tell you. The woman I knew doesn't exist any longer.'

'Is that what you tell yourself?'

'It's the truth.'

'Does that mean you hate her?'

'Not at all. Hate is an emotion. A powerful one. I have no emotional link with your mother.'

'I'm sure you know your own feelings. But I don't see how you can love someone and have a child with her and pretend she's vanished off the face of the earth.'

'But she did vanish. I used to feel the same as you're feeling now. But finally such feelings wear thin and one's mind takes over. Then there's nothing left but anger. And when the anger goes away there's nothing left at all.'

'Is that how Margaret feels now? Sophie says she hates the Major. Won't allow his name to be spoken.'

'I don't blame her.'

'I don't blame her either. I was just surprised to hear it. It doesn't sound like her.'

'I agree. It doesn't sound like the Margaret we've always known. When we care about someone we're surprised and disappointed when they change. We take it personally. Parents, especially, are not allowed to change. Children won't permit it. Makes them damned angry. They feel it's a personal attack on them. Of course Margaret's not as she was, and God bless her for it. She's spent her entire life giving people the benefit of the doubt. Now she's stopped doing that. And she doesn't feel guilty about it. All through her marriage she persuaded herself that the Major wasn't as worthless and insensitive and paranoid as he seemed to be. Now at last she sees him as he truly was. And she doesn't feel guilty about that. In a way it's quite tribal and primitive. Cranston did his best to destroy her life, now she's destroyed his. To her he doesn't exist. In her mind she's killed him.'

'Consciously or subconsciously?'

'Consciously. That's why she's not shattered. She's not recovered yet. She'll never forget what happened. But she's better and stronger every day.'

'And how about you, Dad?'

'How do you mean?'

'Are you a changed man now? You went off to London and now you're back here. You said that would never happen.'

'I was mistaken, wasn't I?'

5

One day, several weeks after Kincaid's arrival at the Towers, he and Sophie drove the roadster to Hexham and had lunch there.

'Give me a progress report,' Sophie said. They were sitting at a corner table, a fire crackling in the stone fireplace across the room. 'How are you surviving county life?'

'Very pleasant. Eat, drink, go to bed. One treat after another.'

'I don't see you enough. I thought we'd be together every hour of the day and night.'

'No, you didn't. You're busy every moment and I'm not.'

'I'm sorry. Before long all the work on the house should be finished.'

'Then what?'

'Then I can follow you about like a puppy and do whatever you've been doing. I know you go riding every day. What else have you been up to?'

'I've had a few walks with Evan, played billiards a lot, read some books, slept in a chair in the library, slept in a chair in the drawing-room, slept in a chair in the music-room. Exhausting life. Mostly I hang out at the stables swapping lies with the grooms.'

'And at night you're with me.'

'That's right. A little good, a little bad.'

'I'm not sure I like the sound of that. I assume you're saying the days are bad but the nights are splendid.'

'You took the words out of my mouth.'

After they ordered lunch she said, 'We'll have to get you some proper country clothes. Boots and tweeds and jodhpurs and roll-neck sweaters. What have you been wearing to ride in?'

'I borrowed a pair of breeches and some old boots from Jake.'

'Who's Jake?'

'He's the new groom. He's about my size. And Evan has an old suede jacket I can wear.'

'You don't have to borrow clothes. I can call Carlisle and they'll send a man with a lorry full of clothes to choose from.'

'No point to that, is there? My closets are filled in London.'

'But we're not in London.'

'But we will be before long. Then I'll change my shirt four times a day.'

She stirred her drink with care. When she looked up at him she said, 'You're trying to tell me something, aren't you?'

'Am I?'

'Of course you are. You're not happy here.'

He smiled. 'It's a lovely place to visit . . .'

'. . . but you wouldn't want to live here,' she said.

'If I were old and crippled I expect I'd like it fine. Providing I had a room on the ground floor and never had to struggle up the stairs.'

She reached across the table and touched his cheek with her fingertips. 'You're a selfish, obstinate bastard. Have I ever told you that?'

'No. I don't believe you have. I assume you mean that as a compliment.'

'And you're arrogant as well.'

'I don't believe you've told me that either.'

'All the time I was waiting here for you to come from America, busy as I was with a thousand other chores, at the back of my mind I was constantly planning what I could do to make things nice for you once you'd arrived.'

'You've done that all right. If I haven't praised you enough I deserve all those nasty things you just said about me.'

'You certainly do,' she said. 'It seems to me as if you've just arrived here. Now I feel you have one leg out the door heading for London. You've already decided when you plan to leave, haven't you?'

'Not precisely.'

'Yes, you have. When are you leaving?'

'Monday,' he said.

'That's only three days from now.'

'Four actually, counting today.'

'When were you planning to tell me?'

'Just now. I only decided last night.'

'You really are a pill, Kincaid. Just when I think we're settled somewhere, away you go.'

'I'm not going some place to shoot elephants. I'm going home. London. That's where we live.'

'We also live here, don't we?'

'Do we?'

'I feel as if I do. And I want you to feel that way, too. Why do you think I've been remodelling and redecorating and trying to make things nice?'

'Is all that for me?'

'Not all of it, perhaps, but most of it. I want you to feel at home here.'

'I do feel at home. But I'm not at home.'

'God, you're bull-headed.'

'No, I'm not. This is not a contest between you and me. If a stranger asked you if your husband would prefer to live in a big fancy house with a few other people and a swarm of servants, or if he'd prefer to live alone with you in a smaller house where two people *can* live alone, what would you say?'

'I'd say my husband is very fortunate. He doesn't have to make such choices. He can have it both ways. He can live wherever he wants to.'

'I want to live at home.'

'Ahhh . . . then why did you build that mammoth house in California?'

'That's easy. So I wouldn't have to go there by myself whenever I made a picture. And if you're going to ask me why I made it so big, why I duplicated the Towers . . .'

'You did it because you thought I'd like it,' she said.

He smiled. 'You win the cigar.'

She turned slightly and looked across the room at the fire on the hearth. At last she said, 'Are we going to have these discussions for the rest of our lives? We have everything in the world that other people dream of but we can't seem to agree on the simplest matters. We want to be together but we keep finding silly reasons to be apart.'

'I'm not trying to get away from you. I'm going home to London and I assume you'll be coming home as well, once you've set things right here.'

'Of course I will if I can't persuade you to stay on. You've only been here for three weeks.'

'That's a long visit.'

'God, you're maddening. You're not a visitor. This is your

house as much as it's mine. We're sleeping in a new bed that no one's slept in before us. Everything's freshly done and new in our quarters.'

'I'm not talking about furniture or Chinese carpets. I like things plain. You know that. One knife, one fork, one spoon. I don't need a lot of commotion. Doors opening and closing, people on the stairs, in the hallways, servants coming and going. I don't want to move in with somebody. I don't want anyone to move in with us. Just because we're rich doesn't mean we have to live that way. Do you think I spent any time in that grand house in California after you came back here?'

'I know you didn't. Evan told me.'

'I walked around inside the place when I got back from Chicago. It looked like a graveyard to me, one where the monuments had all been draped with grey sheets. A death house. I looked at all that emptiness and I said to myself, "What the hell am *I* doing here?" I felt like a street-cleaner who'd found a fur coat in a dustbin and put it on. I felt like an Airedale in a lion suit.'

Sophie smiled. 'You're no Airedale, sweetheart.'

'Oh, yes, I am. That's exactly what I am. And I like it.'

'I don't know where you get such ideas. You start defending yourself before you've been attacked. I'm not trying to nail you inside a room here at the Towers. I'm not saying we have to move in and stay here for ever. I just think it's a lovely place to be and I hoped you might feel that way too. Have you talked to Evan? Do you know what he's planning to do?'

'He started to tell me but I told him he was crazy.'

'No, he's not. We're building him a beautiful place in the north tower and he plans to spend a great deal of time here so he can work on his plays. In future I expect he'll spend most of his time here. What's crazy about that?'

'Everything. You can't go toddling back to your nanny when you're . . . how old is he?'

'Thirty-three,' she said.

'You can't slip back into your trundle-bed with a stuffed giraffe.'

'That's ridiculous. Evan has no intention of doing those things.'

'Having dinner with daddy every night, pulling the bell-cord when you want a drink of water,' Kincaid went on. 'Leaving your clothes on the floor for somebody to pick up. Back to your childhood. That's what that's all about. Sweet and easy. But it's no way to live if you're a grown-up. And it's sure as hell no way to write a play or a book or anything else. If you've never been dirty or hungry or discarded or disappointed, how can you write about things that are really important?'

'I know what you're saying,' she said, 'and I know why you're saying it. You look at the world through your own eyes. I expect all of us do. But you have to remember that many of us have lived quite different lives. Evan can't pretend that he's had your sort of hardship, that he's lived the sort of life you have. This house, this county, and the people who live here are what Evan knows. He has roots here, he feels secure here, he speaks the language.'

'That doesn't matter. If he tries to come back here now he'll wither up and die like a worm in the sun.'

6

At the end of the following week, after Kincaid had gone back to London, Major Cranston died. When Dr Jennings, the hospital's director, rang Sophie at the Towers, he told her that her father had died quietly in his sleep.

After speaking with her mother and informing the staff, Sophie and Evan drove to Newcastle to handle the form-alities at the hospital. They also visited Reverend Ingram, the Bishop of Newcastle, before driving home. As soon as she was back at the Towers she began making telephone calls to arrange the church service and burial details.

That evening after dinner she went upstairs to Margaret's sitting-room. Her mother was reading a novel with the wireless playing softly beside her chair. 'Shall I turn off the music?' Sophie said before she sat down.

'No, I think not. It's quite lovely, isn't it? They're doing an evening of Brahms. It's not too loud, is it?'

'No. I just thought . . .'

'Let's leave it on then. Arthur recommended this programme to me. It's on every evening at half-seven. Arthur's as keen for Brahms as I am.'

Sophie sat facing her mother and neither of them spoke for a few moments. At last Sophie said, 'I hope you're not terribly upset. We can talk in the morning if you'd prefer.'

'I'm not upset, dear. I won't tell you my true feelings because I don't want to upset you. If you've come to discuss arrangements for burying your father, I'll leave that in your hands.'

'I didn't think you'd be up to it yourself.'

'Oh, I'm up to it, Sophie. I simply don't want to do it.'

'I can understand that. But I must tell you what I've done. Evan went along with me to Newcastle. I signed the necessary papers at the hospital. Then Dr Jennings recommended a first-rate undertaker, so we spoke to him about a proper coffin and the burial details. I had called Reverend Ingram from here as soon as I had the news this morning so we visited him at the cathedral before we drove home. Here's what he proposes, and I've agreed to it. Subject to your approval of course. There will be a viewing in the cathedral annexe on Wednesday evening and the funeral will take place in the cathedral the following morning at nine. The hearse, along with friends and family, will drive to Hexham then, there will be a short prayer service in the chapel and the interment will follow straightaway, in the Wiswell corner of the chapel cemetery. After that, friends and family will come back here for tea.'

Margaret sat silent, as though she were listening to the Brahms. Finally she said, 'As I said, I am very anxious not to upset you. But I'm afraid I must. I truly appreciate all you've done. Under normal circumstances your arrangements would be entirely appropriate, I'm sure. But these are not normal circumstances.'

'I know it will be difficult for you . . .'

'Not in the way you imagine,' Margaret said. 'You see, I don't plan to take part in all this.'

'Of course not. That's why I did the planning myself. No one expects you to . . .'

'You don't understand, Sophie. I don't intend to deck myself in black, to pray or weep or simulate grief. I will not attend the viewing, the funeral, the prayer service or the burial. Nor will I be present at a gathering of mourners in our public rooms.'

'I know how you feel, but . . . it's our duty, isn't it? It's a family responsibility.'

'Not at all. Furthermore, I will not allow your father to be buried in our family plot. He doesn't belong there and I won't have him there. I also think it's a mistake to have a service in Newcastle cathedral. If changing those plans is embarrassing for you I'll ring up Reverend Ingram myself.'

'I can't believe what I'm hearing.'

'Of course you can. This can't be a surprise to you.'

'But it is a surprise. In all my life I've never seen you fail to do whatever had to be done.'

'But that's what I'm doing. I'm doing precisely what I have to do. I refuse to give an obscene performance of grief on an occasion when I feel no grief whatsoever. When you're offering tea to the mourners, I will be at Wingate Fields having a champagne supper with Clara and her husband. And I'll invite Arthur to come along.'

'Do you think you're considering my position? I can't just turn away and pretend he's not my father.'

'Of course you can't. And I don't expect you to. But by the same token you mustn't expect me to go through a charade for the sake of our neighbours. I can't do that, Sophie. I have to live with myself. If I shed one crocodile tear for Bill

Cranston, I'd expect a lightning-bolt to come down and strike
me dead. And I'd deserve it if it did.'


7


Sophie had telephoned Kincaid as soon as she heard the news
about Cranston. When he arrived at the Towers the following
day she told him about the position Margaret had taken.

'I don't blame her,' he said. 'Do you?'

'It has nothing to do with blame. It's a matter of propriety.'

'Hers or yours?'

'You know what I'm saying. We all do things we don't
want to do. When someone dies, when someone in the family
dies, certain behaviour is expected. It doesn't matter if you
liked the person or didn't like him. You put aside your feelings for the moment.'

'Listen, kid. I don't disagree with you. You're in an
awkward position. You did everything that needed to be done.
You made a lot of plans. And now it's hard to find the right
answer. But Margaret's had time to think about this. I doubt
if she'll change her mind.'

'It's just not like her. Or anyone else I know. There was
no love lost between you and the Major but that wouldn't
keep you from going to his funeral. You came back as soon
as I rang you.'

'That's right. But we can't compare Margaret's situation
with mine.'

'I know that. But I still haven't given up. I can't help
thinking she might come round. I have an idea that if
someone made the right argument she might see things
differently.'

'Have you talked to Arthur?'

'No point to that. We all know how he felt about the Major.
But however he felt, he wouldn't go against Margaret. And
in any case I expect he'd reject any suggestions that came
from me.'


111

'What makes you think that?'

'I can't say for sure. It's just something I sense whenever we talk about estate matters or the work that's being done on the house. He says things like, "Let's see what your mother has to say" or "I think that's something we should talk over with Margaret." I've pointed out to him several times that my whole purpose is to free her from the daily decisions she's been accustomed to making. But when I say that he looks at me as if I've failed to complete my geography assignment. And shortly after, I'm sure he bustles along to Margaret to give her a full report of our conversation.'

Kincaid smiled and put his arm round her shoulders. 'It's a lesson all men have to learn. The critical decisions are made by women. The world's a matriarchy and there's no changing that.'

'What nonsense. And especially coming from you. No one makes decisions for you. You don't allow it.'

'Another characteristic of the matriarch. Although she is in command, she insists that she's enslaved by her husband or her father or whatever man happens to be in the room.'

'Listen to me, Kincaid. I fell in love with you because you presented yourself as an unwashed ranch-hand and merchant seaman. If you've suddenly turned into a self-taught psychologist, the deal is off.'

'I'll remember that.'

They were interrupted by a telephone call from the undertaker in Newcastle. When she finished the conversation Sophie replaced the receiver and groaned, 'Events are closing in on me. What, in the name of God, am I going to do?'

'Margaret was no help, I take it. She simply told you what you mustn't do and let it go at that?'

'No. She tried to be helpful. She said the Cranston family have their own burial plot near Salisbury, where the Major grew up. Margaret feels the proper thing would be for the undertaker to arrange for the coffin to be shipped there so he could be buried with his own people.'

'No funeral at the cathedral in Newcastle?'

Sophie shook her head. 'She thinks a memorial service at the chapel in Hexham would mark the occasion and show proper respect. Some of our neighbours here in the county would come, the local vicar would preside, and an announcement would be made that Major Cranston was being buried at Salisbury. And she has no objections to people coming here afterward to pay their respects.'

'Can't you live with those arrangements?'

'I suppose I can if I must, but I would hate to. It all seems cold and needlessly cruel to me. And worst of all, Margaret absolutely refuses to show her face. On that day she insists that she'll be at Wingate Fields with Clara Causey. And Arthur along with her. You and I will represent the family.'

'Trevor and Sarah will be here, won't they?'

Sophie nodded. 'They'll be along tomorrow. But their presence will make Margaret's absence even more noticeable.'

'Maybe people will assume she's too upset. Or that she's ill or something.'

'Impossible. Everyone who's called here or telephoned since Brannigan's death has remarked how well she's held up. And she's insisted to everyone that she feels well. People know how shocked and saddened she was then, but no one believes she'll be huddled in a corner now, feeling sorry for herself. So how can we . . . I'm baffled.'

'I know you don't want to hear this but sometimes there's nothing to be done.'

'I can't accept that. I think there's always a solution. I thought of having the children talk to her when they get here. Sarah would love to do it, I'm sure. But she's so unpredictable and theatrical I don't think I can risk that.'

'I think you're right.'

'Last night after I talked with Margaret, I told Evan what she'd said and I asked him if he would talk to her. He doesn't want to, of course, but finally he said he would if you'd do it with him. Taking the position that she's putting a terrible burden on me by refusing to take any part in the Major's funeral. How do you feel about that?'

'I think it's a rotten idea. There's something more important at stake than what's convenient for us or the bishop or the undertaker. Or what may or may not seem proper to the neighbours. The principal players here are Margaret and the Major. This is the last act of their life together. If Margaret's final word on their marriage and their life is to boycott his funeral, then that's a choice she has a right to make. She's neither demented nor hysterical. She knows damned well what she's doing, doesn't she?'

'She certainly does.'

'Then she has a right to do it. And nobody has a right to try to stop her or change her mind. The rest of us can put on sad faces and tell whatever white lies need to be told but there's no reason for her to do it.'

'But what about me? How am I going to explain? How can I handle all this?'

He put his arms round her. 'That's what you have me for. I will remember everybody's name, I will talk to the vicar, the undertaker, and everybody who comes to the chapel in Hexham. I will explain everything to everyone's satisfaction. I promise I'll make you proud of me.'

8

Late afternoon the day before the memorial service for Major Cranston, Alfred, Margaret's chauffeur, drove her and Arthur Tagg to Wingate Fields where they would be guests of Clara Causey for two or three days.

'Am I being a dreadful fool?' she said, not long after they'd left the Towers and driven down the long tree-lined drive to the public road. 'Am I making a selfish mistake and putting a terrible burden on Sophie?'

'You're asking several questions in one cluster.'

'You mustn't expect me to be totally rational.'

'I don't,' Arthur said. 'I know it's an ugly time for you.'

'Ugly is a good word for it.'

'Let me ask you a question,' he said then. 'Most of us are inclined to be sentimental when someone dies. Never speak unkindly of the dead . . . that sort of thing. From what you've told me, that's how Sophie feels and she's shocked because you don't share her attitude. Is that correct?'

'She thinks I should suspend my true feelings on this occasion and do what's expected of me. Maybe she's right. That's why I asked you if I'm being a fool.'

'Not by my standards,' he said.

Margaret smiled and patted his hand. 'You'd say that in any case, wouldn't you?'

'I might,' he said. 'On the other hand I might not. You've had more than enough sadness these past months. I can understand your reluctance to make a public demonstration of some new sorrow you don't actually feel.'

'I just hope I'm doing the right thing.' Then: 'You were going to ask me a question.'

'I've decided I won't do that. I think it might be difficult for you to answer.'

'That doesn't matter.'

'Also there's a chance I might not like your answer once I've heard it,' he said.

'But you've excited my curiosity. Now you must ask me.'

'Perhaps it's not a question after all. But I've found myself wondering, since we learned of the Major's death, what one does feel when a husband or wife passes away, when suddenly one is aware that, for better or worse, this person you've known for more than thirty years will not be seen again. People describe themselves as lost, empty, or heartbroken. Mourners feel a full range of sorrow and loss. Is it possible that your feelings are so totally opposite the ones we're accustomed to seeing and hearing about?'

'A year ago, if you'd asked me that, perhaps I would have said no. Now the most complete and honest answer I can give you is that I have no feelings at all about William Cranston. No tenderness. No pleasant memories. Nothing.

He had no real existence, you see, for himself or anyone else. He stood for nothing, cared for nothing, accomplished nothing. He had life only in the sense that a cell created in a laboratory has life. No one weeps when that tiny speck of matter is destroyed or poured down the drain, and no one will weep for the Major, I'm sure. Since Sophie was his only achievement perhaps she will mourn for him, but I cannot. I never knew him and, God knows, he never knew me. The things we thought we knew about each other were things we detested. The only sorrow I feel is for the years I lost while I was tied to him. And I'll grieve all my life for what he did to poor Jack Brannigan.'

## 9

When Sarah was told about the simplified funeral arrangements, when she learned that the Major's body was already being prepared for shipment to Salisbury, wary for once, she did not express her disapproval to Sophie. Rather, she cornered Trevor in his room and gave a full performance for his benefit. Tears, indignation, and betrayal. The accumulated anguish and rage of all her sixteen years.

'I'm humiliated. Ashamed to be known as a part of this family. And you must feel the same. Don't we have a voice? Didn't anyone think of consulting us? We're not children. I'm certainly not a child. A pet buried in the kitchen garden would be better treated than Grandfather.'

'Don't yell at me about it. I found out about the plans the same time you did.'

'And you're as astonished by it all as I am. At least you should be. What will people think of us? The Goodpastors and the Cleavers and the Kinsmans? It's a family humiliation. There's no other word for it. Since Kincaid is famous now, since everybody knows who he is and what he looks like, I suppose people in the county have forgiven Sophie for marrying him. But that odd Irishman that Margaret married was a shock to everyone. I'm not saying I forgive the Major for what happened but it must have driven him crazy to see what Margaret was doing with her life.'

'It's none of your business, Sarah.'

'Of course it's my business. I'm part of this family,' she said. 'Cancelling a funeral. I've never heard of such a thing. No one calls the Bishop and says, "Never mind. We've decided to do without the ceremony. We'll say a few prayers in the chapel in Hexham, the Major's body will be shipped off on a train, and that will take care of matters nicely. And by the way, the Major's wife for most of his life will not attend the service and will not welcome friends and neighbours at her home."'

'What are you telling me for? Go wail at Sophie. Or get Margaret in a corner and sort things out with her.'

'You don't give a damn about anything, do you?'

'I don't see any point in screaming and yelling once everything's been settled and people's minds are made up. Will you tell me what good that does?'

'It does me a lot of good. I have feelings. I'm human. When I'm offended or disturbed I need to get it out of my system.'

'You just need a chance to practise your acting lessons. Why don't you wait till we're in the dining hall tonight. Then you'll have a bigger audience.'

'You're disgusting. While most people your age are beginning to mature, you're sliding backwards. Do you realize that?'

'To tell you the truth,' he said, 'I don't examine myself the way you examine yourself. I just go along one day at a time. And wait for you to tell me where I've gone wrong.'

'This isn't amusing, you know. It's serious family business. Be honest with me. Are you telling me it doesn't bother you at all that they're making a farce out of Grandfather's funeral?'

'I don't like any funeral. I don't like it that he died. I didn't like it that he went nutty and they had him locked away in that rotten place outside Newcastle. And I hate it that

117

Sophie's upset and Margaret's upset . . .'

'I don't think she's upset at all. If she were she couldn't be acting the way she is. She's thinking of nobody but herself.'

'I don't blame her,' Trevor said. 'She's got a right to feel however she feels and to do whatever will make her feel better. She's the main person that everything's happened to the last few weeks. She's the one who keeps getting hurt, not us. You can't give other people lessons about how to feel bad. Everybody works that out for themselves.'

'You haven't understood anything I've been saying.'

'Well, don't start again. I've heard enough.'


10


One morning after Kincaid had gone down to London, two days before she learned of her father's death, as she and Evan were sitting in the morning-room after breakfast, Sophie said, 'What about Daisy Bishop?'

'What about her?'

'That's what I'm asking you.'

'You came to the wrong chap. I don't really know her.'

'Of course you do. You've known her for two years at least. She's appeared in both the films you've written.'

'She's an actress. What can I tell you?' he said.

'Since I know nothing about her, you can tell me a lot. What sort of actress is she? Is she good?'

'She is good actually. Julian's keen about her work. He put her in her first film. She was only seventeen, I think. She's been under contract to Thornwood ever since. He keeps her busy.'

'And how old is she now?'

'What's all this sudden interest in Daisy Bishop?'

'I've decided I should take more interest in Kincaid's work. And yours as well. I want to know something about the people you work with and the only way to learn a bit is to ask questions.'

After a long pause Evan said, 'Ever since we started shooting *Bushranger* there have been little items in the California papers about Daisy and Kincaid. Rumours they were having a romance. Is that what we're talking about?'

'Of course not. I don't read that trash and neither does Kincaid. I could just as easily have asked you about Tim Garrigus, the director.'

'There's plenty to tell about him,' Evan said. 'But I'd better let Kincaid pass along those stories. Now . . . where were we?'

'I don't remember. Oh, yes. You said she was seventeen when she started in pictures, and I asked how old she is now.'

'You saw her in *Bushranger*. What would you guess?'

'She looked very young in that part.'

'She's done a lot of work since Thorne signed her. I'd guess she's in her mid twenties. But you're right. She looks even younger than that. She's a big favourite with the university crowd. They stick her picture up on their walls.'

'Did she work on the stage?'

'I don't know. But I doubt it. As I remember, she came from some town in the Midwest. Like many other girls in Hollywood. They win a local beauty contest and the next thing you know they're in California, hoping to be discovered. Most of them go home disappointed. Daisy was one of the lucky ones. Julian found her somehow and got her started. Now he's paying her more money than she ever dreamed of.'

'I've heard that a great many film actresses get started by being somebody's girlfriend.'

'I guess they do. At least some of them do. But Hollywood didn't invent that process. I knew at least three young ladies working at the *Telegraph* in London when I was there who either got their jobs or kept their jobs by doing additional work in the evening.'

'What a graceful way of putting it.'

'But it happens more in the film business because there's

an endless supply of beautiful people. Struggling to be noticed. Trying to make their way.'

'You said you didn't know how Julian Thorne discovered Miss Bishop. Was that a question of what you call evening work?'

'God, no. Not Julian. When he leaves the office he goes straight home to Bella. There's a lot of funny business in all the studios but Julian's not a part of it. Very few people at Thornwood know his wife and I don't know anyone who's ever met his daughter, Rachel. Julian sees himself as a sort of father-figure for everyone who works for him.'

'Including Kincaid?'

'Especially Kincaid.'

'Tell me some more about Daisy Bishop,' Sophie said.

'You're persistent, aren't you?'

'Of course I am. It's my nature. Is she intelligent?'

'Seems to be. No education beyond lower school, I expect, but she's clever and quick and eager to learn. Keen on history. Likes to talk about politics. Something of an expert on American Indians. When we were shooting *Bushranger*, she was reading everything she could find about Australia. Quizzing Kincaid about it every chance she got. And when we were in Chicago doing *Dillinger*, she was all over town when she had free time. At the art museum, the planetarium, the theatres. She's a sweet kid.'

'Don't people swarm all over her as they do Kincaid?'

'I'm sure they do. But she just keeps going. A security man tags along after her in case she gets in a corner she can't wiggle out of, but in most situations she just keeps smiling and goes ahead with whatever she's planned to do.'

'It sounds as if you like her.'

'I do. As I said, I never got to know her well, but she was a pleasure to write for and work with. She does what she's asked to do, she doesn't have tantrums, and she gets on well with the other actors.'

'Will she be very successful?'

'She's successful already. Julian thinks she has a great future.

120

People like her. Audiences like her. It's as simple as that. She's pretty, she has energy, she has a great figure, and she's vulnerable. Big assets for a film actress. Also she has a sense of humour. Not afraid to laugh at herself.'

'Sounds like a good prospect for you.'

'I've been fully occupied for the past couple of years. Remember?'

'Yes, I do.'

'And furthermore, Daisy's not my dish of tea. I go for women my own age. Gloomy types. Women of the world. Shawls and turbans and musky cologne. Clouds of mystery hovering over them. And even if I were desperately keen for Daisy, I'd be out of luck. She's married.'

'Is she? I don't believe I knew that.'

'The studio doesn't feature that fact in her publicity releases but she makes no secret of it. She's been married since she was sixteen, she told me. Since before Julian found her and she made her first picture. A fellow named Bob Sample.'

'Is he an actor as well?'

'I expect he'd like to be, but he's not. He's a stuntman. Mostly in western films. He worked in *Bushranger*. When he and Daisy got married he was a policeman in Burbank. Garrigus has known him for years. They used to get drunk together. Still do, I expect.'

'So she's very successful and her husband is less successful? Is that correct?'

'I think that's a fair way of putting it.'

'I wonder how he feels about it when he reads in the papers that Daisy's carrying on with some actor she's working with?'

'With Kincaid, you mean?'

'With anybody,' Sophie said.

'He probably doesn't like it any more than you do.'

The next time she saw Evan, Sophie said, 'I've been thinking about that talk we had.'

'About Daisy Bishop?'

Sophie nodded. 'I ask you a couple of questions and you

tell me more about the people you work with than Kincaid
has told me in two years.'

'Kincaid's a listener,' Evan said. 'He never talks about
anybody. He listens and answers but he volunteers very
little.'

'Almost nothing,' she said.

'That's right.'

'Why is that?'

'That's the way he is.'

After a moment she said, 'If there was any truth in those
stories about him and Daisy Bishop, would you tell me?'

'No.'

'What kind of a friend are you? Is that your way of saying
the stories are true?'

'No. I'm saying they're not true.'

'You just said you wouldn't tell me,' she said.

'You're not paying attention, I said I wouldn't tell you if
they were true.'

'You're hopeless. I was confused when we started this
conversation this morning and I'm still confused.'

'No, you're not. Use your head.'

11

Julian Thorne's intercom buzzed. When he responded his
secretary said, 'Henry French from Paramount calling you.'
Julian picked up the phone and said, 'Henry . . . how are
you? If you're out of a job I'll hire you.'

'No such luck. I can't be replaced. Nobody else will put
in as many hours as I do. How are things with you?'

'Still in business,' Julian said. 'Stumbling along.'

'Don't give me that. Every time I look at *Film Daily* you've
got a new picture out.'

'That's right. Paramount does quality. I do quantity. Maybe
you should hire me.'

'Maybe we should. We'll have to talk about that some time.

But right now I've got something else on my mind. I had a meeting with Jack Warner and Sam Goldwyn yesterday. We talked about some industry matters that concern us and we all agreed that you should be made aware of our discussion. There's one situation in particular that we'd like to fill you in on. So I hope I can see you as soon as it's convenient. Tomorrow if possible. Either I'll come to your office late in the afternoon or you can come to mine.'

The following day at six Julian's driver took him to Paramount Studios, and a security officer ushered him upstairs to French's office.

'Every time I see you, you've got a bigger desk,' Julian said. 'A thousand scripts bound in leather. Charts and schedules and actors' contracts. All of that with one thought in your mind. To put Julian Thorne out of business.'

'We're not enemies, Julian. It's Thalberg and Mayer we have to keep our eyes on. Have you seen *Midsummer Night's Dream*?'

Julian shook his head. 'Not interested. They'll be lucky to get their money back.'

'All those trips you make to England, I thought you'd be a Shakespeare fanatic.'

'I am. But only in the theatre. Nobody wants to see Cagney and Mickey Rooney in tights.'

'How about *The Informer*?'

'Good picture. But too down-beat for my theatres. Nobody in Ohio gives a damn about Irish politics. Pictures like that one win prizes but they're hard to sell. I'd trade a dozen *Informers* for one *Captain Blood*. I should have grabbed Flynn when I had the chance.'

French nodded. 'It's all about people, Julian. That's our business. If you have the horses, you win the race. You put the right faces up on the screen and the people will lay out their money. We do great business with Colbert and Dietrich and anything De Mille directs. And Cooper and Crosby are going to be big winners for us. But everybody in town would like to steal Kincaid from you.'

'I know you would. I heard about you making a pitch to him in London last year.'

French smiled. 'That's right, Julian. I tried to grab him but I couldn't make the sale.'

'You should have stayed home and guarded the chicken coop. You let Fox steal Shirley Temple from you.'

'Let's not talk about that or I'll do a crying scene.' He got up, walked round his desk and sat down in an armchair facing Thorne. 'Now,' he said, 'let me tell you what's on my mind. As I mentioned on the phone, I had lunch with Warner and Goldwyn at Perino's, and we got into a heavy discussion about John Corso. You know Corso?'

Julian nodded. 'I don't deal with him personally. But we do a lot of business with him. So does every other studio in town.'

'That's the problem. Or it could become a problem. How long has Corso been out here in California? When did he leave New York? Do you remember?'

'Six years ago. Seven maybe.'

'Not so long,' French said. 'That's the point. In a short time he's built a huge business for himself. He started out with the catering. Bought out both the companies that had been furnishing meals to our people on location around Los Angeles. Then he took over the cafeteria operations inside the studios. Promised he could provide better food at lower cost, and he did. Now he's got long-term contracts with everybody, you included. Am I right?'

Julian nodded. 'Allied held out for a while, said they preferred to run their own food operation, but I saw in the *Reporter* last week that they finally signed up with Corso too.'

'All right. The next thing we knew, he was in the laundry and dry-cleaning business,' French went on. 'The people we'd used for years sold out all of a sudden and Corso was there to pick up the marbles. Now he's doing laundry and dry-cleaning for everybody in town. No competition. He's got it all locked up. And here's the topper. This is what I found out from Jack Warner. There are three trucking

124

companies we've all used since we've been in business . . .
Acme, Sullivan's, and Tip-top. Between the three of them
they service the whole industry. Big trucks, little trucks, trac-
tors, portable dressing-rooms, vans, buses, and limousines.
Everything we need, on the lot or on location, to shoot a
picture.'

'That's right.'

'All right. Listen to this. All three of those companies are
now owned by John Corso.' He paused. 'You don't seem
surprised. Did you already know what I just told you?'

Julian shook his head. 'I heard a few months ago that he
might be buying an interest in Acme, but that's all I knew.'

'Well now you have the complete story. And now you can
see what has us worried. Here's a man, one man, who has
us all by the nuts. If he gets a hair cross-wise and decides
to squeeze one of our studios or decides to shut down the
whole industry, all he has to do is keep his trucks in the garage
and we're screwed six ways from Sunday.'

'Why would he want to do that?' Julian said.

'Why does anybody do anything? Either to make money
or to put somebody's ass in the fire. You see what I'm saying?
When we've got suppliers in competition with each other
we can negotiate, make demands, make our best deal.
That's what this business is all about. Spending as little as
possible and earning as much as possible. With stars we can't
negotiate much. We have to pay the going rate. But with
everybody else, from supporting players right down to the
guy who sweeps out the sound stage, we can pay what we
like. But now we're up against a one-man operation. A
monopoly. And I haven't told you the worst. Warner got a
tip from New York that now that Corso's got the truck business all sewed up he plans to put his drivers and everybody
else who works for him in a new labour union that's being
formed in the East. It's called the Committee of Industrial
Organizations, the CIO. When that happens, if it happens,
our production costs will go through the roof. And worse
than that, if anything could be worse than that, we'll have

strike threats staring us in the face three hundred and sixty-five days a year. You know what unions could do to us. We've talked about it before. We've fought back against the actors and the screenwriters, and so far we've kept them from organizing, but the truckers – those guys could murder us. You know what I'm saying?'

Julian nodded. 'So where do matters stand now? What do Goldwyn and Warner think?'

'They don't know what to think. They thought you might have some ideas.'

'It's a tough proposition. There's no law against a man buying out his competitors. No law that I know of. Let me think about it. Maybe we can make some kind of arrangement with Corso. Maybe we can at least steer him away from the union idea. I'll talk to a few people and see what I can find out.'

# • CHAPTER 4 •

## 1

When Sarah was driven back to her school two days after the memorial service for Major Cranston, Evan rode along with her to spend some days at his flat in London.

'Well, it's over,' Evan said. 'I know you weren't satisfied with the arrangements but all the same . . .'

'I thought it was hateful in every way.'

'That wasn't the way your mother wanted it to be. I'm sure you know that.'

'I know she says that,' Sarah said, 'but if she had strong feelings about it why didn't she resist more strongly?'

'No one wants to starts a family war at a time like this.'

'Why not, if something important's at stake? Margaret didn't hesitate to state her views. Or so it seemed to me. She wasn't concerned about creating a conflict.'

'It's not unusual for a widow to have the final say in these matters. She can plan the funeral however she wishes.'

'Are you saying the man's daughter and grandchildren should have no voice in the planning? And besides, Margaret wasn't his widow, was she? She's Brannigan's widow.'

'Well, as I said, it's finished now. And no terminal damage has been done to the family. Sophie certainly has no hard feelings toward Margaret.'

'Don't be so sure of that,' Sarah said. 'I think Mother was as disappointed and humiliated as I was. I can't imagine what people in the county must be saying.'

'I seem to remember your telling me that you're not concerned with other people's opinions.'

'This is different. I think it's senseless to put the family in a bad light. I am willing to take responsibility for my own actions and accept whatever criticism may come my way, but I detest the thought of being condemned for something I had no voice in.'

Evan smiled. 'I'd be very surprised if you're being condemned round the breakfast tables of Northumberland this morning.'

'Now you sound like Sophie. She's able to resign herself to almost anything. But I'm not. I believe in setting things right.'

'A little late for that, I'm afraid. We can't very well dig up the Major's coffin and bury him again.'

'Why can't we? If there were any way to influence Margaret, that's precisely what I think we should do.'

Evan leaned close to her and kissed her cheek. 'If you insist on tilting at windmills, people will think you're much younger than you'd like them to think.'

'What does that mean?'

'You know what it means. You told me yourself that you've begun a serious learning process. Observing people, listening to what they say and how they say it, drawing conclusions from their behaviour. You must have noticed that as people mature, they carefully select the battles they're willing to fight, they conserve energy for those important contests. They don't allow themselves to be upset by every injustice they see or imagine they see. They've learned that some things can be changed and many things cannot. They learn to accept conditions and circumstances that they secretly detest.'

'I'll never be that way,' Sarah said.

'I'm sure you won't. You'll be forever young.'

'Stop saying that. You're the only person I know who continually harps about what a baby I am.'

'Not a baby,' he said. 'Not at all. You're a lovely young woman, full of energy and indignation. Everyone I know wants to be young. Except you.'

'I know I'm young and I'm delighted about that. I just don't want to be thought of as young.'

'What's my alternative?'

'You have no alternative. You have a closed mind. But as I told you at Christmas-time, there are a great many people who see me as fully grown up and who treat me accordingly.'

Evan nodded. 'I remember your saying that. You cited one person in particular, a chap in California who knows all sorts of secrets about me.'

'Did I say that?'

'Words to that effect.'

'I thought I said he knew a great deal about Mary Cecil.'

'Perhaps you did. Who is this wise person?'

She laughed. 'You don't think I'd trust you with privileged information, do you? You'd run straight to Sophie with anything I might say. And even if you didn't she'd weasel it out of you somehow.'

'You're mistaken about that and you know it. But still, I can understand your position. If you've created a make-believe romance for yourself, the fewer details you have to create, the less chance that your story will fall apart.'

'You're trying to trick me.'

'No, I'm not. I'm applauding you. That's the first rule for someone who's decided to lie about something: keep it simple.'

'I'm not lying. Why would I lie to you?'

'All sorts of reasons, I suppose. Since you're trying to persuade me that you're a grown-up experienced woman, it makes sense to invent a phantom lover.'

'He's not invented and he's not a phantom. I should know.'

'Are you telling me you're in love?'

'I didn't say that. A woman can have a lover without being in love. I'm in love with you, you know that. I have been for years. But until you're willing to accept that, I'll have to educate myself with other people. And Burt, you see, isn't the sort of man . . .'

'Burt . . . ahhh, he does have a name.'

'That just slipped out. But all right, his name is Burt. What

I started to say is that he's not a man to marry or even fall in love with, but thousands of women are attracted to him.'

'Thousands of women?'

'You know what I mean. Jean Harlow's a sexy woman and Burt's a sexy man. He let me read some of the letters he gets from women. You wouldn't believe the things they write to him.'

'Sounds like a classy chap. Sharing his love letters.'

She shook her head. 'He's not classy at all. He's dreadfully handsome and he's a great talker and he knows everything there is to know about women, but he's not to be trusted. I knew that the first day I met him.'

'But he plied you with champagne and seduced you.'

'He didn't have to seduce me and we didn't need champagne. I was available and he knew it.'

'You're not going to give me all the details, are you?'

'No. I'm not.'

'Good. Those are harder to invent, I expect.'

'Are you playing dumb or do you really not believe me?'

He took her hand in his and echoed her voice. 'I really do not believe you.'

'All right,' she said. She opened her shoulder-bag, took out a photograph the size of a file-card, and said, 'Here's his photograph. I didn't invent that.'

The face that Evan saw was that of a truly striking man. Blond, sun-tanned, wearing a tennis sweater. Across the bottom, he'd written, 'Love and kisses to my divine Sarah . . . Burt.' Evan felt a sudden emptiness in his stomach. 'I think I know this chap. Is he an actor?'

'He used to be but not now. Do you still think I've invented him? Do you know who he is? Do you know what he does?'

'I don't believe I do. But his face is familiar.' As he said those words he suddenly remembered where he'd seen him, and the circumstances, and how he connected him with Mary Cecil. 'Where did you meet him?'

'If I told you all that you'd know who he is.'

'I already know what he looks like and I know his name's Burt. I'm sure I could find out if I asked some questions here and there.'

'I don't care if you find out. I'd like you to know. Otherwise I wouldn't have told you as much as I have. But I'd be in serious trouble if my mother found out. I know she knows him and so does Kincaid.'

'If you think I'm going to run to Sophie and tell her everything you and I talk about, then you shouldn't tell me. You shouldn't talk to me at all if you believe that.'

'Do you promise?' she said.

'I don't have to promise. You've told me all sorts of things in the past two or three years. Do you think I passed them to Sophie?'

'I guess not. Otherwise she'd have murdered me.' She looked out the car window for a long moment. Finally she said, 'His name's Burt Windrow. You know that name, don't you?'

'Of course I do. But I never connected it with . . . I didn't know what he looked like.' He handed her back the picture while the pieces of an old puzzle began to lock together in his mind. 'He hates Kincaid. Did you know that?'

She nodded. 'He told me. He doesn't like you much either.'

'Did he tell you why?'

'No. I didn't want to know. But I guess it's because of Mary Cecil. But I don't think I should talk about her. I know you were wild about her.'

'That's right. But that's ancient history. So I'd like to talk about it. It might answer some questions I couldn't figure out before.'

'I don't know the gory details. I just know she and Burt had a flaming affair a few years ago.'

'Before she was married?'

She shook her head. 'While she was married. When they were both acting in London. Her husband never knew about it, Burt says.'

'You said you read some letters.'

131

'I shouldn't have mentioned that. I don't think . . .'

'Were some of the letters from her?'

'I think so,' she said.

'Either they were or they weren't.'

'They were. But I didn't memorize them. They were love letters. I told you, a lot of women have been crazy about him. And they told him about it, in detail, in their letters. Her letters were pretty much like the others. But as you said, all that's ancient history.'

'That's true.'

## 2

'Too damned busy this past year,' Geoff Bingham said. 'Pushing the machinery too hard. Tempting the bloody fates. Dorothy tells me I'll be an old man before my time, but by God, we're all in chancy trades. One minute you're God's greatest creation and every producer in the West End is keen to have you in his play. Dependent on you, they say. If you don't say yes, they'll shelve the project. "It's a role that only Geoffie can do." All lying bastards, of course, but all the same I hear that plea over and over. "Put on the putty nose, Bingham, and a bit of crêpe hair, and save us from perdition and bankruptcy." Damned nonsense, all of it, but music to my ears. Insincerity works wonders with my arthritis. And only great dollops of praise put a bit of spring in my arches. "Be a warhorse," I tell myself every morning when I trim my moustache. "Eat your fill while the table's heavy-laden." So I did three plays this past year, full houses every time we raised the curtain, and I'm deep in rehearsals for *The Wild Duck* right now.'

'I also see your name in the film adverts every day,' Evan said. They were sitting in the lounge at the Savile Club, late afternoon, two days after Evan had come down to London.

'Yes, God help us, those poofs and pirates at Pinewood think the old man can still sell a few tickets in the cinema palaces, and it must be true or they wouldn't be dishing up benevolent contracts and sending Italian limousines to carry me to and fro. One likes to believe that one is loved and pursued for the quality of one's work but the voice of truth tells you it's all a matter of commerce. As long as the shillings rattle in, you're everybody's love-song, but if two films in a row produce a foul odour at the ticket window, you have all the appeal of a piece of cod that's gone off.'

When he signalled for refills, the waiter, stiff and pale and severe in his livery, collected their glasses, silent and unsmiling, and walked away stiff-legged to the service bar. 'Stuffy bastard, isn't he,' Bingham said, 'but he's just what's wanted in a funereal atmosphere like this. It's a cardinal rule of a gentleman's club. All the waiters and attendants must be snobs of the first order. Absolutely necessary that they feel superior to the membership and that they totally shun invited guests like yourself. Only in that way can a club set the proper tone. The members must fear the staff, never the other way round. Thus an atmosphere is set up that absolutely stultifies any impulse for joy or hilarity. Only the chaps who dig drains and drive lorries are meant to enjoy themselves when they drink. They shout and sing and fondle the barmaids and swill down their lager by the pint. But a true gentleman, such as the members of this establishment, drinks in silence. Serious business, you see. Seldom speaking to their fellows, they gradually become mute and immobile. Staff members then trundle them upstairs to bed or load them into automobiles to be driven home to their pale wives, who sleep soundly behind the bolted doors of their celibate bed-chambers.'

The waiter returned with their drinks then. Bingham lifted his whisky glass and said, 'Enough about me. Let's talk about you for a while.' He took a deep drink, set his glass down and said, 'Conquered those California cretins, haven't you? Two enormous successes in a row. Damned good work, Tagg. Commendable. You and Kincaid are a pair. Sky's the limit, I predict. You've proved you can deal with the world of cow-men on the one hand and with safe-crackers and car thieves on the other. Since these are staples of that bastard art-form they've stuck together out there among the orange groves and pussy parlours, I expect that no impediment will be put in your way, now or in future. Nirvana, old fellow. Milk and honey. Pleasant days at the writing machine and carefree strolls to the bank. Oysters and champagne and succulent women. Speaking of that, Dorothy tells me that you and sweet Mary have parted, as the saying goes.'

'That's true.'

'Should I be sorry to hear it? Or should I salute you?'

'No blood was shed, if that's what you mean. It was a primitive love affair with a civilized ending. No effort to maim or kill from either side. But perhaps you heard it differently.'

Bingham shook his head. 'No details were reported to me. If Dorothy got a fuller report from Mary she failed to share it. That would be unusual, however, since my wife knows that gossip is mother's milk to me. You're as close-mouthed as our friend, Kincaid, so I know I'll get no bedroom titbits from you. Now, where were we? Future work. What's your next project for Julian Thorne and his elves?'

'Nothing specified. As a matter of fact, I'm planning to stay in England for at least a year. Perhaps longer. I have an itch to start a new play.'

'You do, eh? That surprises me. I've always felt that once a gifted writer like yourself falls into the rhythm of film-making, where you're actually paid for what you do, where the money comes before the first scene is photographed, when you've had that happy experience as I say, it must require a special sort of patience and dedication to return to the lonely trade of writing for the theatre. Months going by without a shilling to show for your work, a small payment usually when the play is accepted for production, and unless the play is a formidable success, very little income thereafter. Damned discouraging, I expect. Is that an accurate picture?'

'I'm afraid it is. But a playwright's job is to write plays, just as an actor's job is to act.'

'Oh, yes, the artist's credo,' Bingham said. 'One hears it in every dressing-room and on every rehearsal stage. When I was your age I believed it fervently. Now I have a different view. I believe an artist's job is to survive. In the theatre and in films, where theatre managers and producers make great amounts of money because they concentrate all their energies on making great amounts of money, those furtive fellows are very happy to hear clowns like you and me refer to themselves as artists. To a producer's ears this means one thing: that we are dedicated to the process, to the work itself, and that any thought of financial reward comes second. So when we work and struggle to create a play and bring it to life, when it opens and closes and we've seen little or no financial reward for our labours, producers feel neither guilt, compassion nor responsibility. Their rationale being that, since we've all had such a bloody good and creative time together, it doesn't matter if we're penniless when it's over. I'm a man of the theatre. Everyone knows that. But I have learned to be a businessman first and an actor second. Once I'm assured that my lady wife and I will profit from a venture, then I am able to forget about commerce and be a complete actor. If someone asks me to perform for the sake of art, I stun them by saying I perform only for the sake of Bingham. So when you tell me that you're keen to devote a year of your creative life to the writing of a play, one side of my brain applauds you. The other side says, "Consider very carefully what you're about, old cock." After a year of work, maybe more, you'll find yourself in the coils of a rogue like Hale Gossett, hypnotized by his charming cynicism and seduced by his feigned love for the theatre and all its components.'

Evan laughed. 'I thought you liked old Hale. When we were rehearsing *The Fatherhouse*, you two were quite thick. All sorts of whispered conferences in the wings, secret jokes. Old companions. Fast friends working together.'

'Ah, well, that's the politics of our business, isn't it? As long as Hale is giving me a packet of pounds each Friday, he is indeed my bosom friend. Absent that condition, I find him contemptible, unreliable, and off the mark in his personal habits. His cavalier treatment of your wonderful play was only further evidence to me that he's a man without qualities. If he'd given us a few weeks' run, if he and Applegate had strapped that little fruit, Donald Rugger, to a chair, and told him he'd be ceremonially castrated if he didn't stick to the performance we'd rehearsed, if little Mary had been allowed to settle into her role, if the audience that has followed me through the years had been given time to book seats and show up with their friends, it would have been a different story. We'd have made our way, we'd have been in profit, and your first play would have been a success. But Gossett lost his balls and folded our bloody tent for us, and all the good work, yours and ours, went for naught. The only positive thing that came of it is that Fail Gossett, as the chaps at the Garrick bar call him, hasn't mounted a play in the West End since the day we closed, and Donald Rugger has left London and is living in Crete with an international assortment of lavender creatures.'

'And what about Mary Cecil?'

'Of course, I'd forgotten for the moment. You two are no longer in close communication. Did you know she was in Novello's new play?'

'I knew it had been offered to her.'

Bingham nodded. 'And they approached me as well. But I was scheduled for an evening of Chekhov at Her Majesty's just then. Mary and I discussed it, in fact. Over a pot of tea at Browns. She was more taken with the play than I was, and had agreed to do it. But there were certain elements in the piece that baffled her. I think it consoled her to learn that I was as much in the dark as she was. Did I tell you the title? *Butterfly Land*. Perhaps it was the title that threw me off. In any case, Mary went ahead with it but I didn't. They got Cedric to do my part and Bobby Newton joined them as well.'

'Did you see it?'

'Oh, no. I never see a play I've turned down. Too bloody agonizing if it's turned out well and dreadfully boring if it hasn't. As you'll see in the theatre listings, it's still limping along but the rumours are that it will shut down soon. The men at *The Times* and the *Observer* said nice things about it, but the *Daily Mail* thought it was obscure and the *Telegraph* found it silly. Dorothy, however, who follows such things closely, said that all the critics had lovely things to say about our Mary. That little sadness she shows behind her happy face is a great asset in almost any role. Draws the audience to her. Tickles them with a bit of mystery that never gets solved. Something to wonder about after they've stumbled out of the theatre.' He drained his glass, set it down and said, 'Perhaps it's of no interest to you but my lady wife, when I told her I'd be seeing you today, instructed me to tell you that Mary has taken a flat of her own. She's fled from her bed and board arrangement with Alec Maple and made a solitary nest for herself.'

After a moment Evan said, 'That no longer affects me but I expect it's a blessing for her.'

'That's the word for it. No question. She's wasted too many years on that worthless hyena.'

After he said goodbye to Bingham and left the Savile, Evan walked slowly along Brook Street to Claridge's. He took a table in the bar lounge, ordered a drink, asked the waiter for some writing-paper, and wrote a note to Mary Cecil.

I'm sure you haven't expected to hear from me, and when I returned to England I had no plans to contact you. Your last letter to me and my last letter to you did not seem to require additional explanations. Either from you to me or from me to you.

I expect that's why I'm writing to you now. There must be a more humane and civilized way for two people to end a love affair. I'm not suggesting that we kiss and forgive, that we try to take up somehow from where we were before everything fell apart. I know that's impossible. We've already said goodbye to each other in no uncertain terms. But don't we owe it to ourselves to do it properly, in a more civilized manner, face to face?

Three days later a note came to his flat by messenger.

You're right of course. Meet me at the theatre after Thursday's performance. I'll buy you a drink in some low bar and we'll say goodbye like proper cannibals.

3

A week after she returned to school at Wimbledon, Sarah wrote a letter to Ethel Richmond, who had been the drama teacher at her school in Ojai.

Well, here I am, back home in England. Everyone expects me to be happy about it but I'm not. I don't mean to say that I miss California or America as places to be, but I very much miss the person I was when I was there. Also I miss your classes terribly. And the talks you and I had together outside of school.

Picasso says he felt as if he was born the day he arrived in Paris from Barcelona. He was eighteen or nineteen then, not much older than I am. At any rate, that's the way I'm feeling now about the time I spent in Ojai, as Picasso did when he discovered Paris. I'm certain you'll know what I mean. You're the only person I can think of who would know.

You may remember when we said goodbye, you told me I could write to you. About anything, you said. So that's what I'm doing. And what I'll continue to do unless you tell me to stop.

I have a nice family. My mother and my grandmother are unusual women. I complain about my brother,

138

Trevor, but I know that he's at least as good as anyone else's brother. And better than most. Kincaid, as you know, is my stepfather. At least that's his official title because he's married to my mother. But he doesn't try to pretend he's my parent. Doesn't tell me how to behave or expect me to do the things that daughters are meant to do. He doesn't ignore me, however. I feel as if I could go to him if I were in trouble and he wouldn't give me a lecture. Still, I don't know him well enough to sit down and talk about my feelings. And if I did I don't think my mother would like it much. She likes to know what's happening inside the family. She's not keen for my having secrets she doesn't know about. I mean, she has some secrets, I'm sure of that, but I'm not meant to.

So here I am, not feeling sorry for myself, surrounded by relatives and friends and schoolmates but constantly aware that there's no one to whom I can really talk. Or weep with.

Don't be frightened. I don't intend to use you as a confessional device or babble on to you as though you were a psychiatrist. But I know from all the talks we had together in Ojai that you're an understanding woman and that you remember what it was like being the age that I am now.

That's the problem I seem to have to deal with daily. The age question. There's my true age, measured in days and months and years since I was born. There's the somewhat older person that I like to pretend I am. And there's the impossible twelve-year-old category where my family seems determined to keep me.

Here's the crazy part. Sometimes I feel much younger than twelve, keen to dissolve back through the years to age six or eight, when nothing much was expected of me and I expected nothing of myself. And many times when I'm in my classes with girls my own age, I feel perfectly placed there, being a regular

139

sixteen-year-old, accepted as that and accepting myself as that. Then, of course, there are the other times, either with strangers or with my family, when I'm determined to convince everyone that I'm twenty. Why do I do that? All sorts of reasons, I suppose. For one thing it separates me from Trevor. He's just one year younger than me but I've always been humiliated when people assumed we were the same age. Another reason, of course, is that I want to be free of the rules and regulations and disciplines that I feel I've outgrown. As you know from my work with you, I am capable of taking on demanding tasks. Eager to do it. Hungry for instruction and guidance when responding to a wise adult like you, using myself as an adult.

In addition to my work here at school I'm allowed to go into London for two afternoons a week at RADA. Totally exhausting and indescribably thrilling. Just as the work was with you. You told me to use myself fully, and that's what I'm doing in my acting classes. It's what I want to do with all the areas of my life but I'm not able to. Not just because of outside restrictions but because of restrictions I continue to put on myself. Some of the problem, of course, is simply not knowing what to do with myself. I have no experience to guide me. Only my life with my family and my life as a schoolgirl. So when I try to encourage myself to break loose, I'm not sure what that means. Keeping a bottle of gin hidden in my room is not the answer. Not for me. And I think it's assinine to chain-smoke cigarettes in the loo. Although I'm aching to have a grown-up relationship with a man (one man in particular), I have no intention of dropping my knickers for anyone who asks me, just to prove I'm old enough. Am I shocking you? I'm sure I'm not.

All those quandaries and confusions and indecisions come out, when I'm with my family, as anger and resentment. I say to myself, 'Why can't they see that I'm a woman with a woman's feelings, and treat me accordingly?' In the process of proving my adulthood, I throw fits that brand me as a child. I feel so desperate sometimes that I'm completely vulnerable to anyone who treats me as a grown-up. That happened to me just before I left California. After it was over I told myself it was just a rite of passage, but I was terribly frightened at the time. And when I think of it now, I'm even more frightened. And cautious. I never imagined a man could be something to fear. Now I know better.

Am I boring you to death? I hope not because it's very good for me to be able to write down things I'm thinking and send them along to someone I trust, someone who knows me and doesn't expect me to be something I can't be. Please don't think I'm falling apart. I'm not. I'm just trying very hard to sort things out for myself. At the same time I'm trying to show everyone that I have an answer for everything. Tick-tock . . . crazy person.

You'll hear from me again soon unless you write and tell me to spare you.

4

'I seem to recall we sat in these same chairs, was it a year ago?' Rosamund Barwick said. 'I was bemoaning the fact that all my old friends had died or were dying. It's still going on. I gave up looking at the obituary page months ago but the telephone rings and the post continues to bring the dreadful news. England was hit hard last year. Pinero left us. And Elgar. Dear Gerald du Maurier. And Roger Fry and John Collier. And this year seems to be the turn of the French. They've lost two already. Signac and Gaston Lachaise. And soon, I predict, we'll be counting the dead in thousands. The men with tiny brains, our leaders, are signing peace treaties with the other tiny brains who are preparing for war.

Who will you be fighting for, Kincaid? Whose uniform will you be wearing?'

He smiled. 'Whoever grabs me first, I expect. And how about you? When I saw you last October in Chicago you were off to North Carolina or somewhere, with Willy Maugham.'

'Exactly. He'd persuaded me that I should sit out the war on the plantation of one of his admirers.'

'What happened?'

'Second thoughts. I persuaded myself that I should return to England and die, if I must, in my own bed. Three score and ten, the Bible promises us. I'm already three years on the far side of that figure. So I'll make no appointment in Samarra only to be done in by a falling magnolia tree or a roving alligator.

'So how do you assess yourself these days?' she said then. 'If I'm to believe the newspapers, the Gods have smiled on you again.'

'It looks that way.'

'Julian sent me a great bundle of press-cuttings a week or so ago. I confess I don't go through all that material.'

'Neither do I,' Kincaid said.

'Good for you. I did see enough, however, to convince me that you're having another grand success.'

'All the blood's on Julian's hands. And most of the money, too.'

She smiled. 'You know the story about the young girl in the bordello who was there for a year before she realized the other girls were being paid?'

Kincaid laughed. 'That's not my problem. Julian takes good care of me.'

'He should. It appears that your two movies have taken very good care of him. I was right about you, wasn't I? Do you remember the first time we ever talked? When they'd released you from jail into my custody. I said you had something that was saleable and unique but I wasn't quite sure what it was.'

'Are you sure now?'

'I'm still not certain what it is but it's clear to me that it's saleable. You must know what it is.'

'Now I've got a story for you,' he said. 'A man walked up to a centipede and said, "You must have at least a hundred legs. It's amazing to see you walk. How do you do it? Do you move half your legs and then the other half, or do they all move at once? You have to explain it to me." The centipede was very polite so he said, "It's simple. First these legs move, then . . . no, that's not right. Actually the front legs on the left side move together. Then the rear legs on the right side . . ." He rolled over then and found himself on his back unable to walk at all. The man who'd questioned him flipped him upright again onto his legs and said, "Now . . . what were you saying?" The centipede didn't answer. He quickly moved away.'

'I get your point,' she said. 'There's a lesson in that for all of us. Hindemith once said to me, "Musicologists will be the death of music. They think everything can be explained. The fact is, the brain has almost nothing to do with writing music or performing it. And it has nothing to do with listening to it.'

'Heresy,' Kincaid said.

'Of course. But it's true.' Then: 'If you can't tell me how a centipede walks, then tell me about your next project.'

'I don't have one.'

'Then tell me what Julian has in mind,' she said.

'I expect he'll be over here pretty soon. You'll have to ask him. I don't know the answer.'

'I was talking to Herbert Marshall about you not long ago. Have you met him?'

'Once in California, I believe. Before we stopped going to parties out there.'

'In any case he knows who you are,' she said. 'He said he's heard that you're the most reluctant actor in Hollywood.'

'I'm not sure what that means but I guess he knows.'

'It means you don't give a damn whether you work or not.'

'That's right, I don't.'

'Why don't you stop then?'

'Maybe I will.'

'What does your wife think about that?'

'We haven't talked about it. We don't have to. She'd want me to make up my own mind.'

'As I recall she doesn't like being in California.'

'Not much. She likes to live in England.'

'So if you give up the films it will make everybody happy?'

'That might be true. On the other hand it might not. In any case I haven't decided if that's what I want to do.'

'You don't care where you live, do you?'

'No. But that's not what we're talking about. We're talking about whether I work or don't work, not where I want to live.'

'You once told me you could live in a haybarn or in the back of a truck. Could you really do that?'

He nodded. 'Of course I could. I've done it.'

'But that was another life. Everything's changed for you since then.'

He shook his head. 'Not so much as you think. You see, I don't want everything to change. I don't want to depend on things I might not be able to hang on to. I never had dreams when I was a little kid. I still don't. I don't want to fasten on to something that could melt in my hands. I want to be able to be what I've always been.'

'You can do that without living in a haybarn.'

'I didn't say I wanted to live in a haybarn. I just don't want to forget how things used to be for me. I want to be able to go back there if I need to.'

'From what you've told me it wasn't a pleasant life.'

'Maybe it wasn't. But it was the life I had. I'm not one of those lizards that changes colour depending on what he's perched on. I'm the same colour all the time and I expect I'll stay that way.'

She smiled. 'It's a good thing I didn't meet you when I was young. We'd have ended up living in a cave somewhere.'

'Haybarns are better. Not so damp.'

'What does Sophie say when you talk like this?'
'I don't talk like this to Sophie.'

'I don't know what I expected,' Mary Cecil said, 'but I didn't expect this. I feel very strange.'

She and Evan were sitting in a late-night wine-bar just round the corner from her theatre. 'Do you feel strange?' she went on.

'Disorientated,' he said. 'I'd forgotten how formal everything is in London. I've become accustomed to beach life.'

'So had I when I returned. I couldn't get warm for days. I'm chilled now, sitting in this warm room. Maybe this isn't such a wonderful idea after all. As I said I feel very strange.'

'I didn't imagine that we'd sit down and start chatting as if I'd just come home from the studio. Did you?'

'I didn't let myself think about it,' she said. Then: 'I'll start again.' She took a deep breath. 'Congratulations, Mr Tagg. The picture's a big hit, isn't it?'

'Seems to be. Have you seen it?'

She shook her head. 'Don't think I'm quite ready for that yet. I may never be. You can understand that, I'm sure.'

'Yes, I guess so. So shall we talk about your play? I understand the papers wrote nice things about you.'

'Yes, they did. The critics are always kind to me. I think they mistake my confusion and ineptitude for some private and mysterious performance-level. They're not sure what I'm doing, any more than I am, but they seem to think it merits praise.'

'If you're presenting yourself as an inept actress, I reject that. We did a play together, remember?'

'Oh, I know my craft all right. I should by now. I feel as though I've been at it for a hundred years. But I've never felt that I came close to exploring all the corners of a role, never believed that I've truly brought a character to life the way the author intended. Not ever. In any play I've done, whether I played it for a month or for two years, I've always had a moment, two weeks or two years after the last performance, when I said to myself, "Ah . . . that's what you missed, that choice, that colour, that reaction." So you see, I'm not simply being modest. I'm always floating about in a fog, trying to find my way. And the play I'm doing now is no exception. We'll be closing soon and I still feel as though I haven't mastered Arabella, haven't found the key to her. Of course, there is something mysterious about her. Ivor's written her that way. And the critics, God bless them, believed they discovered that elusive, misty quality in my performance. But I assure you, it's bewilderment they're watching. Not perception or technique. Sheer glassy-eyed bewilderment.'

'I'm anxious to see it. Novello's done some fine work.'

'Indeed he has. Although some of the critics were not so kind to him in this instance. I expect he thinks the actors didn't serve him well. He hasn't been seen at the theatre since the night we opened. Very naughty.'

'I agree.'

'So much for my latest triumph. I'll be glad when we close.'

'Then what?'

'Straightaway to Cardiff to see my daughter.' She sipped her drink and let her eyes wander round the room. It was starting to be crowded now with people just out of the theatres. 'I may not act again,' she said then. 'Does that surprise you?'

'If I believed you it would surprise me.'

'But you don't believe me?'

'Not for a moment.'

'In March, I'll be forty years old. I've always felt sorry for actresses who hang on for too long, worrying about their weight, trying to cover up with make-up things that can't be covered up.'

'You're one of the loveliest women in London. You're ageless and you know it.'

'I did know it. I don't know it any longer. I've felt very old these past few months. The way things came apart for

146

us and the rotten business with Alec. It was almost as if I could feel some vital fluid draining out of me. I used to be up early every morning, afraid I'd miss something. Now I lie in bed till noon, awake with my eyes closed. Sometimes I don't get up till it's time to go to the theatre.'

'I can't believe what I'm hearing.'

'It's true, Evan. I feel like a shock victim.' She sipped from her glass again. 'Don't misunderstand me. I don't blame you. I don't blame anyone. Not even poor crazy Alec. I blame myself. Architect of my own downfall.'

After a moment he said, 'Is this making things worse for you, sitting here with me?'

'I feel rotten, if that's what you're asking me. But if you got up and left, I'd still feel rotten.'

'Do you want to talk or shall we just sit and drink claret?'

'I thought we came here to say goodbye. That's what you said in your note.'

'We already said goodbye. Several months ago. I'm sure you remember those letters we wrote.'

She nodded. 'I remember.'

'It was stronger than goodbye. We more or less told each other to go to hell.'

'That's right,' she said, 'and that's where I went.'

'I couldn't understand why you left California so suddenly to come back to London. I still don't understand. When you accused me in your letter of sending three men to Alec's apartment, to bully him into giving information about who set fire to my car, I didn't know what you were talking about. I still don't.'

'I believed the story Alec told me. Maybe I shouldn't have. Maybe he was lying. I don't know the answer to that. I don't know the answer to anything.'

'You must know why you left California so suddenly. It wasn't because Novello's play was going into rehearsal, was it?'

'No. But I had to go all the same. Someone forced me to.' Before he could answer she went on. 'But I don't want to talk about that. There's no point to it now.'

After she'd left him in the Los Angeles railway station several months earlier, after she'd crossed the country, then crossed the ocean to England, Mary had posted a letter to him from Southampton.

God, but it was a miserable crossing. I never left my stateroom. Took all my meals there. Never went on deck. I thought if I isolated myself I could find a way to sort through the tangle we seem to have got ourselves in. That terrible drive to the railroad station haunts me. How could two people who love each other as we do find themselves in such a turmoil? Each time I remember the hurt look on your face I begin to weep. I want you to know that whatever went wrong I'm sure it was my fault. I'm not certain just what I did or what you think I did, but I'm convinced that I said or did something stupid. It all started with the things Alec told you when you saw him here in London and it went on from there. The business about the car upset you terribly, I know, just as it did me. But we let those things go all out of proportion.

I won't write more now. I have to get some things settled first. Then I'll send you a long letter. I know you're busy at the studio, so I hope you haven't been as tortured as I've been. I promise you, all this foolishness we've been going through will soon be settled once and for all and we'll be together again the way we were. Nothing matters except us. I cannot be estranged from you.

Please don't think bad thoughts about me. Just be patient for a bit longer and I promise I will deliver myself to you, all bright and smiling and gift-wrapped. I love you and I miss you terribly.

As soon as he'd finished reading her note he'd sent her a cable.

He believed those words. And the more he thought about
it, the more he thought about her, the more he believed them.
Her absence, he concluded, had put things in perspective.
He told himself, the things that had disturbed him could be
put aside, must be put aside. Looking forward to the long
letter she'd promised, he began one of his own to her. Before
he could finish it, however, and post it, he heard from her
again.

I can't believe the ugly things that are in my head just
now. No one could ever have convinced me that I could
have such sickening thoughts about you. I was so upset
at first that I couldn't write to you. I decided simply
to forget that you exist, to put every thought and
memory of you out of my mind. But at last I knew I
had to tell you what I know. I couldn't bear the
thought of your going smoothly along, thinking you'd
got away with something dreadful.

What kind of man are you, Evan? That question has
been ringing through my brain ever since I found out
what you've done. What sort of secretive, manipulative,
merciless bastard are you?

In my note from Southampton I told you I had some
things to settle here in London. I was talking about
Alec, nothing else. I knew I had to thrash out the divorce
situation with him so I could come back to you free
and unencumbered.

I lied to you when I said I'd insisted on a divorce
from Alec before I came to you in California. I also
lied about the letters I said I was sending to him. I hate
to lie but I thought in this case it was justified. I was
so happy being there in Malibu with you, so drugged
with contentment, so sensitized to every nuance and

149

every moment. That sort of total abandonment, losing myself in you, was a new experience for me. I didn't want it to end and I didn't want to risk diminishing it or altering it in any way. I didn't want our lovely evenings to be spoiled by discussions of Alec and his unpredictability. So I nailed him up in a closet and forgot about him. He was no longer a problem, no longer my husband, he didn't exist. Childish behaviour? Of course. But I'd never been a child in love before. So I continued to tell you white lies about the divorce and I continued to forgive myself. I rationalized that the longer I was away from Alec, living openly with you, the easier it would be to convince him at last that you and I are permanently together, that there was nothing to be gained by his playing dog-in-a-manger, that divorce was inevitable.

If you believe there's never a defence for lying, then what I'm saying will mean nothing to you. But the central point is this: when I arrived in England I had only one objective, to go at once to Alec and tell him that somehow, as quickly as possible, I planned to divorce him. With his co-operation or without it.

And that's what I set out to do. The first full day I was back in London. Alec normally sleeps late but I went at nine in the morning so I'd be sure not to miss him. As it turned out it wouldn't have mattered when I arrived because he doesn't go out now. He hasn't been outside his flat for days. When I saw him, when he told me why he's afraid to go out, I was physically ill. As I write about it now, I feel nauseous.

Perhaps you know everything I'm about to tell you. I'm certain, since you arranged it all, that you know some of the details. But there's no way you could know it all without hearing it from Alec and seeing what's become of him.

You've met Alec. Two or three times. You've talked

with him. You've seen what he's like. I should say what he used to be like.

Alec is a vain man. He never concealed it. He celebrated it. It was his armature. His friends accepted it, as I did, and his enemies detested him for it. But it was a fact, a hateful but central characteristic. His hair, his teeth, his nails, their care and public presentation, were of vital importance to him. He would spend three days in a dozen stores selecting a shirt. His long scarves were knitted or crocheted to his finicky specifications. When he bought new boots he deliberately aged and tortured them, then applied thirty coats of shoe crême so they looked old but beautifully preserved. Each article of clothing had a history. Each outfit was a careful combination of old and new, army surplus and Bond Street, a patched suede jacket, faded corduroys, a sweater that cost sixty pounds and handmade boots from Jermyn Street. And the silk kerchief in his breastpocket once belonged to John Barrymore. That sort of thing. A hopeless dandy and peacock. That was Alec Maple. But I never realized until I saw him yesterday that those ridiculous vanities, that self-absorption, were the glue that held him together. If you and your horrid friends set out to destroy him, I assure you, you've succeeded. If you saw him as he is now you wouldn't recognize him.

There was no answer when I knocked on the door of his flat. At last I tried the knob and the door opened. There was an ugly stench in the place as if the windows had not been opened nor the loo flushed for days. The window-shades were drawn and only one small lamp in the far corner was lit. Just before I switched on the ceiling light I heard him say, in a hoarse whisper, 'They ruined me, Moo. Look what they did to me.' He had called me *Moo* when we first met, but not for more than twenty years now.

He was sitting in a wing-chair just opposite the hall

151

door. He hadn't shaved for ten days or two weeks, however long it had been since they left him there. His precious hair which had been shampooed once a day through all the years I'd known him was matted and thick and stringy, clotted, it seemed. His face looked grey and stained, he smelled of urine and sweat, and his lips were badly infected by the surgical tape they'd plastered across his mouth. Those twisted strips of tape were still lying on the floor by his chair. And his little dog whined by his feet.

My stomach turned over at the sight of him and from the stink in the room. I went past him to the water closet and was sick.

When I came back to the sitting-room I opened the drapes and the windows. By daylight the flat looked even worse. Scraps of food and cartons and soda bottles scattered across the floor. I gathered up a great bagful and put it in the kitchen in the dustbin. Then I forced myself to sit down in the chair facing him. He told me then about the men you'd sent there and what they'd done to him.

Good God, Evan, what kind of a mind do you have? What sort of conscience? And how do you have connections with such men? You know how I feel about Alec. He's a worthless person. I have nothing but contempt for him. But when I saw him sitting there like a broken toy, like the victim of a street accident, I thought to myself, 'For the love of God, this is a human being.'

Was it all about that bloody car? Was that it? Was it just because your car was destroyed? Or was it some sort of vengeance because of me? Whatever it was, what good did it do? What was in your mind? Did you know what those men would do to him?

I'm not saying they beat him or strangled him or tortured him physically. Apart from taping his mouth and his wrists I don't think they injured him. They did something worse. They frightened him almost to death. They humiliated him, destroyed his dignity, caused him not to recognize himself. He hasn't lost his mind. I don't mean that. He's simply lost himself. The bravado and guile and sly tricks he's always used, his image of himself as a reckless freebooter, all those crutches for his self-esteem were kicked out from under him. He said, 'I wet myself,' like a numb and defeated old man in a rest-home.

And it was all so senseless, Evan. He knew nothing about your car being burned. He wasn't able to tell them anything. Finally, when he was afraid of what they might do to his dog, he says he made up a name to give them, a name he'd never heard of. And that seemed to satisfy them. After they'd flushed his tropical fish down the toilet, opened the window and turned his parrot loose and almost driven Alec out of his mind, all they got was a fake name of somebody who might have poured gasoline on your car and burned it up. What good did that do them? What good did it do you? I assume they sent the name along to you since you're the one who hired them. They told Alec how much money you were paying them.

I'm sure he'll pull himself together after a while. He'll start to clean himself up. He'll go outside again and visit his pubs. But he'll never be the same as he was. Some people might say that's good. God knows, he's never been a paragon of virtue or honesty or anything valuable. But Jesus, he deserves better than this, to be tied to a chair and treated like an animal.

I thought I knew you. If someone had told me you could be responsible for something like this, I'd have said they were crazy. But now I could believe anything. I can't tell you what this has done to me. I had turned myself over to you completely. Now I feel lost. And suddenly I'm afraid. Will I come home some night and find strange men waiting there for me? It's a thought that haunts me.

You won't hear from me again. And please don't send me any of the things I left in Malibu. I don't want to be reminded.

Evan had found Mary's letter when he came home one afternoon from the studio. He read it as soon as he was inside the house. He slowly read it through again. Then he sat down at his desk and wrote out a cable message.

STUNNED BY YOUR LETTER. DON'T KNOW WHAT YOU'RE TALKING ABOUT. LETTER FOLLOWS. I LOVE YOU.

That night he stayed up very late, sitting in his chair by the sea-side window listening to the gulls and the night-birds and the sound of the rain outside and the onshore wind rustling the fronds on the date palms just beside the house. When he went to bed at last, the wind had picked up and the rain was slashing against the windows.

When he woke up the next morning he rang the studio and told his secretary he'd be working at home all day. Then he sat down at the kitchen table and began a letter to Mary. He wrote without pausing. All the thoughts he wanted to put down had crystallized in his mind as he lay in the dark the night before.

I knew when I came back to California from London, when you met me in the railroad station in Los Angeles, that something had gone wrong for us. I understood, of course, that you were upset by what had happened to my car. And so was I. But there was something else disturbing you. I didn't want to question you. I thought it would all come out when we'd had time to settle in a bit. But the tension, whatever was behind it, stayed with us.

You seemed angry when I told you about my meeting with your husband. Not angry with him, I felt, but angry with me, as though you didn't believe what

I was telling you. As though you thought I was lying. Now, of course, in the letter I've just had from you, you tell me you were lying. And the reasons you gave were understandable. But still I wonder why that would make you so angry or impatient or ill-at-ease with me.

Then there was the matter of the fire investigation. I couldn't help thinking that you knew something about it that you hadn't told me. And when I suggested that the police should be told about Alec's penchant for setting fires, you were adamantly opposed to any mention of him. I honestly didn't believe that he had made a long secret journey from England to America to destroy my car, but all the same, the force of your opposition surprised me. It made me wonder if he had indeed been here and you knew it.

But let's get back to what was happening from the time I returned from England till the day you left to go there. Suddenly there was a climate between us, an atmosphere, that seemed new to me. You were loving and affectionate as you've always been but something was changed. Was it your concentration, something as subtle as that? Did it mean something that you often seemed totally inside yourself, that your eyes wandered off sometimes in mid sentence, that you began to misplace your keys, your lipstick, your hairbrush almost every day and that such tiny unimportant incidents seemed to make you angry or unduly critical of yourself?

Admittedly, I may have been sensitized by the change in our life together, something gone off, gone awry. And you, perhaps, were also confused by the way things were going. But, however one describes it, we seemed to be surprising each other.

Then came your abrupt departure. And your apparent unwillingness even to discuss the reasons for it. And the rotten time we had on the way to the station the morning you left. After you left I kept asking myself if I really knew you, if we really knew each other. Then, just a few days ago, the note you sent from Southampton arrived. And all our problems, whatever they had been, seemed to be solved. I wanted to believe that. You know from the cable I sent that I was eager to put the difficulties and misunderstandings behind us.

Then came your strange letter – your last letter to me, as you made clear in the final paragraph. That letter is as foreign and incomprehensible to me as if I had picked it up on the street with no knowledge of who sent it or to whom it was addressed. And the more I studied it, the more peculiar it became. At last, however, as I lay in bed last night thinking about it, as I began to place it alongside all the things I've just outlined here, it began to make sense to me. I concluded that you had decided to leave me long before I knew anything about it, perhaps when I was away in London. When you used the Novello play as your excuse, did you assume that I would see through that at once and conclude that you had another reason for going? I did have that impulse and you sensed it of course that last morning, but I wanted very much to believe you so I told myself I did believe you. But always those words I'd heard from Alec, that you would never leave him, that you could never leave him, kept coming back to me. And he was right, wasn't he? That's what this letter of yours, in its convoluted, comic-strip fashion is trying to say, isn't it? But why did you feel you had to invent a damaged, wounded, possibly deranged Alec? And where in God's name did that idiotic story come from, that I hired some shadowy characters to question him, tie him up, and drown his goldfish? Are you trying to convince me that such a thing really happened? Or has Alec just made you believe it took place? He is an actor, you know, and a borderline psychopath as well. You must know that such a thing never happened, or that if something remotely like that did happen I could not possibly have been involved in it. I would swear that you know these things. So I'm left with my original conclusion, that you needed some sort of crutch, some sort of device, to justify your kissing me goodbye. And the alleged suffering of poor Alec, allegedly caused by me, gives you, at least in your own mind, that justification. What outrageous poppycock, Mary. If we're going to give each other up, can't we have a little class about it? Do I have to conclude that you never felt any attachment to me beyond a temporary one? Do you have to pretend that I caused some psychological cruelty to be practised on your husband? And all this because some California nut burned up my car? Let's use our heads. You asked in your letter how it is that I have connections with such men. The answer is that I don't.

I hate the thought of our breaking up, Mary. I particularly detest the idea of its happening in this idiotic way. Don't you realize that all these trappings and stage dressings aren't necessary? I'm a grown-up. I knew you were married from the start. You'd never given me gilt-edged guarantees. Don't you know that all you had to say was, 'I'm sorry. It's not going to work.' I wouldn't have liked to hear that but I would have accepted it. Just as I accept the charade that's taking place now even though it disgusts me. When you loved me I didn't have to be a saint or a god. Now that you've decided not to love me any longer, why is it necessary to turn me into a comic-book felon?

Since you've decided that all this is a melodrama about a destroyed automobile, I feel obligated to provide you with the final scene. But it's not a fantasy like your story about my cruelty to Alec. This actually took place. The physical evidence exists. One evening a week or so ago, two men came to my door. One was a tall blond fellow, the other one shorter, heavier, Italian-looking. I'd never seen either one of them before. The tall one handed me a set of car keys and said, 'I'm sorry for what I did to your car. I've just replaced it with a new one.' They turned and walked away then, up the steps to the highway. When I went out to the car-port a few minutes later, there was a new Packard sitting there, still smelling of the showroom. Just like the one that was burned. In every detail.

There's a missing piece to the story that you don't know about. When I'd just come home to California from England I answered our phone one night and a man's voice said, 'Oh, it's you. You're back then. Well . . . welcome home.' It was a British voice. A trained voice. Like an actor. When you asked me who it was, I said it was a misdial. Do you remember that? In any case the man who gave me the car keys to the new Packard was the same chap. The same voice. Unmistakable. So the mystery of who burned the car and why he did it may be more complicated than we thought. Maybe you're the only one who knows the answer. Also the guy came down to the side door, the way we always do. He didn't come to the upstairs door, the way people do who haven't been here before.

You asked me not to send you your things but I'm sending them anyway. I don't want to be reminded either.

6

'I can't have another drop of wine,' Mary said. 'I have a matinée tomorrow. And the smoke in here is choking me.'

'I'll find you a taxi and bundle you off home.'

'Yes, I expect that's best.'

'Does that mean you want to go home,' Evan said, 'or you don't want to?'

She smiled. 'It means I don't know what I want.'

Evan signalled for the bill and paid it. Then they made their way through the crowded room to the pavement outside.

'Blessed air,' she said. 'I used to light up thirty or forty cigarettes a day. Since I've stopped I can't stand the stink of tobacco smoke.'

There was a taxi rank just down the way from where they were standing. 'Taxi or no taxi?' Evan said.

'I told you I can't make up my mind about anything. You'll have to decide.'

He took her arm and they walked toward the taxis. Suddenly she said, 'What I really need is a cup of coffee. Something to clear my head. There's a little place just round the next corner. Never crowded because the proprietor discourages smoking.'

When she'd had her first taste of coffee she said, 'Ahh, that's better then, isn't it?'

'Where are we now?' Evan said. 'Do we small-talk our way through the coffee or do we try to sort out the mess we've made?'

'Too late for that, isn't it?'

'Perhaps. But if we're going to hate each other, let's do it for the right reasons.'

'I don't hate you, Evan.'

'You hated me when you wrote that last letter. You remember that letter, don't you?'

'Of course I do. I also remember the one you wrote in return.'

'So do I.'

'I was upset,' she said. 'I was very upset. And I know you were, too.'

'That's right, I was. I still am. I hate unfinished things. I hate to be misunderstood. I want to tell you what I know that I didn't know before or that you didn't know I knew.'

'Don't do it. Please. I don't want to go over everything again.'

'Perhaps you don't. But I do. If it's too much for you, you can walk away, go out the door, and I won't try to stop you.' He looked at her. She didn't say anything. She traced small circles on the table-top with her spoon. 'Don't interrupt me,' he said then. 'When I finish talking, if you're still here, you can ask as many questions as you like, call me a liar or say anything else you want to.'

Again she was silent and he went on. 'I told you in my last letter that I had nothing whatsoever to do with Alec's night visitors. If they said I hired them, they were lying. On the other hand his story that people came to him for information may be true. And if that happened I'm not surprised that they were unpleasant to him. But who they were and who sent them is a mystery to me. I didn't know then and I don't know now. But here's what I do know. As I told you in my letter, two men came to the house in Malibu and brought me a new Packard, exactly like the one that had been burned. That was after you'd gone and it could have been close to the time when Alec says he was questioned by those men. So there may be a connection there.

'I also told you that one of the men who brought the new car apologized for what had happened to my other car. He was a tall fellow with blond hair. I recognized his voice as the same voice that had called our house on the beach late one night when you were asleep.'

'But what does that mean? Why should . . .'

'Just a minute. Let me finish. I had no idea who that blond chap was. I knew he was English because of his speech and I'd decided he was someone who knew you. And then a few days ago, since I've been back in London, someone showed me his photograph and told me his name. The man is Burt Windrow. I'm sure that sounds familiar to you.'

'Why should it? I only know he writes a column but I've never seen his picture.'

'That's my line, Mary. I knew about his column but I'd never met him or seen his picture. But in my case I'm telling the truth.'

'So am I.'

'I'm afraid not. The person who showed me his photograph told me Windrow's known you for years. He told her he was in love with you at one time and showed her some love letters you had written to him.'

'Who told you all this?'

'A young woman I know. Her name would mean nothing to you. But I assure you she was on intimate terms with Windrow.'

'Well, I wasn't. And I don't want to discuss this any longer. I guess I should have known better than to respond to the note you sent me. I thought it would be nice to see you but it's not nice at all. Why are you trying to manipulate me? What possible reason can you have?' She pulled her coat round her shoulders, got up from the table, and walked to the door. Evan stayed in his chair, eyes straight ahead. He called for the waiter then, ordered another coffee and remained at the table, his back to the door, facing an old-fashioned clock.

Almost fifteen minutes later she came back, pulled out her chair, and sat down across the table from him. Each of them seemed to be waiting for the other to speak. At last she said, 'I started to walk home. My head was whirling. Finally I said to myself, "Why should I lie to him? Why not brush the cobwebs away and tell the truth?" So here I am.'

When he didn't answer she went on. 'It's true, I once had an idiotic affair with Windrow. It seems as if it was a hundred years ago and I've hated myself ever since. Some time later I knew he'd gone to Johannesburg, and still later I heard that he'd gone to California. I thought I'd never see him again. I certainly didn't want to. But last year, when you came back to London and I stayed behind at the house on the beach, he got in touch with me. He pretended he wanted to return some foolish letters I'd written him, but when I saw him it turned out that he was looking for items for his column, things I might have heard from you about Thorne or Tim Garrigus or anybody else you might be working with. But mostly he was looking for dirt about Kincaid. He'd like to wreck his career if he can.'

'I know that.'

'He had no intention of giving me back those damned letters,' she said. 'He knew that as long as he had them, as long as I knew he could send them to you at any time, I was vulnerable. Still, I tried to tough it out with him. I told him I'd never pass on any stories I'd heard from you, and I told him I'd tell you about the letters myself.'

'I wish you had.'

'Maybe I should have. But I was afraid you'd think . . . I didn't know what you'd think. I was afraid of anything that might wreck what we had together. Also I knew, or at least I thought, I was on safe ground as long as you were in England. Then, just before you came back, somebody set fire to your car. And that really put me in a panic.'

'Did you connect that with Windrow?'

She shook her head. 'I couldn't think of any way he might benefit from that.'

'Does he know your husband?'

'Very well. They're two of a kind. They were in repertory together when they were very young. Actors who knew them then said they were in competition with each other to see which one could acquire the nastiest reputation. They always had some sort of scheme going. But I still can't imagine them conspiring to destroy your car.'

'Well, let's look at it this way,' Evan said. 'Windrow admitted to me that he was responsible. And whoever sent those men to question Alec must have assumed he was involved. So it certainly seems possible that they were both involved.'

'Alec swore to me he knew nothing about it.'

'Does he always tell you the truth? I already know the answer to that. And when he told you he just made up a name to give to them, I'll wager you a great deal of money the name he made up was Burt Windrow. For once he did tell the truth. Why wouldn't he? You said he was scared to death. And besides you were on your way back to England

162

by then, so he had no more need for Windrow.'

'Are you guessing or do you know?' she said.

'Call it an educated guess. If Alec could put enough pressure on Windrow to involve him in the arson business, if he could force him to engineer that, then it stands to reason that he could convince him to use those letters you'd written to persuade you to come back to England. Did Alec know about you and Windrow?'

'I never thought he did but now I'm not certain. They're a strange pair. It sickens me to think of it but Burt may even have showed him the letters. If he's passing them round to his new girlfriends anything is possible.' She pushed her hair back with one hand. 'I still can't figure out who would have sent those men to Alec's flat.'

'It was somebody who had something at stake. The insurance company maybe. Or somebody else who doesn't like to see their property destroyed.'

'Who else? Who are you talking about?'

'I can't tell you, because I'm just guessing. And if I knew for certain, I couldn't tell you then either.'

7

By chance – it could have been nothing other than chance – the evening of the day before he was to have a rare confrontation with his brother, Sam Thorne's wife, Marie, gave an unusual performance as they were having supper in their kitchen.

'I'm getting sick and tired of Julian and the way he treats you,' she said.

'I don't know what you're talking about,' Sam said. 'Don't start up something tonight.'

'You know what I'm talking about, all right. Your mother, God bless her, said the same thing before she died. Said it more than once in my company. Said it often, Sammy. Trust me.'

'Don't drag my mother into anything. She worshipped

Julian. Thought the sun rose and set in his navel. Never a bad word from Mama about Julie.'

'That's all you know. Would I make it up? I'm your wife, Sam. I tell you the truth. I'm not like those tootsies at the studio, wiggling through the hallways and telling you whatever you want to hear. I only tell you what's actual and what's right. And when I say that your dear mother, closer to me than my own people, when I tell you that she said many times what I'm saying now, you can believe it.'

'Give it a rest, Marie. I'm trying to eat my brisket here and you're breaking my chops. Enjoy yourself. Have a good meal.'

'I can eat and talk. I'm not some animal that growls when she eats.'

Sam put down his fork and took a sip of seltzer. 'Nobody called you an animal, Marie. Nobody called you anything. You've got nice table manners and you're a kind woman. Clean about yourself. And you pick out pretty clothes to wear, without putting me in the poor-house. And you're quiet. A nice soft voice, and not trying to take over every conversation the way some women do. Many times I've told you – correct me if I'm wrong – many times I've said you should speak up more. You know what's going on in the world and you can express yourself without screaming or getting into a cat-fight. You're a gentle person by nature. Many times I've been told by my friends that you're the perfect wife. And I don't disagree. But God damn it, sometimes you get on a subject and you can't let up. Out of the blue. We'll be sitting here alone, having a quiet meal, all by ourselves, and whammo, you'll be off to the races. Rolling your eyes, waving your hands, and your mouth going a mile a minute.'

'Am I rolling my eyes and waving my hands? Look at me. I'm sitting across from you in my nice chair, serving you food, filling your glass when it's empty and keeping an eye on the oven so the banana cream pie don't get too brown on the bottom. But I am also telling you something important. Reminding you of a few things you have a tendency to forget.'

'Then let me forget those things. And you forget them, too. At least till we have our cream pie. Then we'll take our coffee into the parlour and you can talk yourself blue in the face.'

'Don't expect me to fall for that,' she said. 'On the couch or in your Morris chair, and you'll be dead to the world. Snoring loud enough to set off the burglar alarm. The room shakes when you get going. Do you remember that? Anyway, I don't plan to talk to a corpse. I'll say what I have to say right here at the table, while we're having our meal like civilized people.'

Sam picked up his knife and fork and began to work on his third slice of brisket.

'I'm not Julian's enemy and you can't say I am,' she said. 'I always went out of my way to honour your relatives. You and him are brothers. I've got respect for that. You're the older brother in fact. May I point that out to you? In my family that means something. To the Gingriches that means a lot. My brother, Louis, was like a god to us other children. Held in high esteem. We listened to him. Hung on his every word.'

'Louis is a shoe clerk, for God's sake. He'll always be a shoe clerk.'

'What does that matter? He's an important man.'

'What's important about him? Does he own his home? Does he have money earning interest? Do his sons attend Fordham or Brooklyn College?'

'It doesn't matter. He's Louis Gingrich, the eldest son. That makes him important. In our family he's respected and valuable. In your family it's another matter altogether. The Thornes make their own rules. The truth is that Julian makes the rules. Always has since you were boys together. Your mama told me that. He's decided that he's the eldest son. And you accept that.'

'Where am I? In Temple? Are you giving me the lesson

165

of the day? Elder schmelder. Who cares? I'm supposed to be in a pissing contest with my brother every day? Is that what you want?'

'Don't talk smut. This is our home. You're not in your office or the steam bath now. Smoking cigars and talking dirty about Clara Bow and Jean Harlow.'

'You're really wound up tonight, aren't you? Don't you think you should look in the oven and see how the pie's doing?'

'Do I ever serve you burned pie? Name one time when I've put a piece of dried-out, burned-up pie in front of you. Why do you think I run this house by myself with only a Mexican cleaning-woman twice a week? I know we can afford to have cooks and butlers and maids in tight uniforms prancing around, and I know you'd like that. A house like a movie set and a dozen servants underfoot day and night. But I won't have it. I made you a good home in Staten Island and I make you a good home here. If your mother was alive she'd like to come here to visit. She'd be comfortable here. She wouldn't be fooled by those old pieces of furniture at Julian's . . .'

'They're antiques, Marie. French antiques. Worth a fortune.'

'Not to me. Old furniture is old furniture. Chinese rugs and ugly paintings from Europe that cost thousands of dollars don't impress me either. Does all that stuff he buys in England and ships home in crates make him important? Does it make him better than you? I'm asking you.'

'What's got into you all of a sudden? Why now? Should I look at a calendar? Is this some special day set aside to crucify Julian?'

'Do I want to do harm to your brother? Did I say that? His wife is like a sister to me. Outside of my own family nobody could be closer to me than Bella Thorne and Arloa Corso. No day goes by that Bella and I don't talk on the telephone or visit together here in my kitchen. She likes to come here. I'll tell you the truth. She doesn't like those ugly pictures and that old-fashioned furniture Julian buys any better

166

than I do. And you think she likes those crazy tight suits he has made for him by some nutso tailor in London? Julian's a nice-looking man. A good head of hair still and no belly sticking out. He should leave himself alone. I could feed a family of five all year for what he spends on a suit. And that high-toned way of talking he's got now. Like Ronald Coleman or Leslie Howard or somebody. Julian never used to talk like that. He even does it at home. You think Bella likes it? Not a chance. She says those things to me. I mean, she's a loyal wife like I am, but she's not deaf, dumb, and blind. She sees how Julian treats you and she doesn't like it any better than I do.'

'You've got too much time on your hands, you women. Nothing to do but analyse and criticize. I'll tell you how Julian treats me. He brought me out here eight years ago and made me a partner in his film company.'

'Some partner. Julian's got no partners. He's the only boss and everybody knows it.'

'Who's this everybody you're talking about? You're an expert all of a sudden on how to run a business? Maybe you should write a letter to Henry Ford and tell him how to build cars.'

'You know I'm right. I know you like I know my pocket, Sam. When you start to get steamed it's because you know I've made a correct statement.'

'I know you're meshuggenah, that's what I know. To hear you tell it, a person would think I'm mopping floors or cleaning out toilets. I'm vice-president of a major film company.'

'You're a book-keeper, Sam. You're a whiz with numbers and figures. Everybody knows that. That's why Julian wanted you out here in California. Admit it. That's why you turned him down when he first asked you. You've got a short memory, Bubba. We sat in our kitchen in Staten Island, just like we're sitting here now, and you said, "I've got my own business, me and Johnny Corso, why do I need to tag after Julian just to look after his books?" You remember saying that? Those were your exact words. And you were right. I was proud of you.'

'I wasn't right. When I thought it over I decided Julian was offering me a good deal.'

'This is Marie you're talking to. I was there. You didn't reconsider. You didn't change your mind. You talked to Vincent Corso and he changed your mind. Johnny's Uncle Vinnie, that's who leaned on you to come out here. You and Johnny both.'

'Nobody leaned on me. Vincent thought it was a good move. That's what he said. "I think it's a good move, Sam." And he was right. I'm making more money in a year than I used to make in ten, and Johnny Corso's gonna own this town before he's through.'

'What's to own? Who wants it? So the two of you didn't make a fortune with your business in Jersey. You made all we needed. More than we needed. And we *lived* somewhere. With people we knew all around us. Families that had lived in the same neighbourhood for fifty years. A rabbi we all knew since we were kids. Out here I read in the paper the other day, sixty per cent of the people buy a house and live in it for only two years. Then they sell it and buy another one. Sixty per cent! What kind of a crazy place is this? And the rabbi at our temple here . . . he looks like Rudolph Valentino come back from the grave and he doesn't know from straight up about what's kosher and what ain't.' She got up from the table, took her pie out of the oven, carefully removed it from the tin and put it on a china plate. 'Is that a pie? I ask you. A banana custard to win a trophy with. Just right the crust, and the meringue a perfect light brown but not too brown. This kind of a pie I used to take to my sister Eleanor's when we went there to eat on Thursdays.' She cut the pie carefully like a surgeon, put a large piece on each of their dessert plates and handed Sam's across the table to him. 'This is real life, Sammy. A nice piece of brisket from the butcher on Fairfax and a pie like you can get only in New York. Or in Jersey if you know exactly where to go.'

168

They ate in silence until they finished. 'Another piece?' she said. 'One for the road, as they say.'

Sam patted his stomach and said, 'I'd better not.'

'Better not, better not,' she said. She took his plate, put another wedge of pie on it and handed it back to him. 'Who says, "better not"? You're not an adagio dancer or Gary Cooper on a horse. My father used to say, "A man without a belly is no man at all." You want to look like a grasshopper like Julian, you have to eat lettuce leaves like a rabbit and wear a rubber girdle under your pants.'

'Don't start on Julian again. We've got a good life here, Marie. And we've got Julian to thank for it.'

'That's what I mean,' she said. 'That's what he wants you to think. That's what I've been talking about. So you've got a big office and money rolling in. So people call you on the phone and make you feel important. You think this is real? It's not real, Sam. You're Julian's brother. That's the way people think of you. You know I'm right. He doesn't have respect for you the way he should, and other people out here don't either. The only real friend you have in this nut-house city came from New York when you did. Johnny Corso. He's a friend. He knows about respect. He knows what you're worth. I know and Johnny Corso knows. Nobody else. Not even you, Sam.'

# BOOK TWO

# • CHAPTER 5 •

## 1

The following day, at the beginning of his regular morning meeting with Sam to review theatre grosses and reports from exchanges across the country, Julian said, 'Let's not go into the numbers today. Leave the sheets with me and I'll look them over this afternoon before I go home.' He buzzed his intercom and said, 'Hold all my calls, Freida, till Sam and I finish our meeting. If Benjamin calls from New York tell him we'll get back to him.'

'What's up?' Sam said. 'We got a problem?'

'I'm not sure. That's what I'm trying to work out. Two days ago I had a meeting with Henry French. He called me and said he wanted to tell me about a talk he'd had with Goldwyn and Jack Warner. So I went over to Paramount to see what he had to say. As it turned out he wanted to talk about one subject only. John Corso.'

Julian described in detail his discussion with French. When he finished Sam said, 'It sounds like you memorized every word he said.'

Julian nodded. 'As soon as I left him I came back here to my office and dictated a memo to myself. As much as I could remember of what was said. I wanted something I could refer to later on.'

'You seem to think this is serious business. I'm not sure I see what the shouting's all about.'

'That's what I want to know. How it looks to you. Maybe

I picked up on French's feelings. According to him there's no question that Goldwyn and Warner think they're about to see a lightning-bolt aimed at their studios. If they're right we'd be in the same fix.'

'Let's look at this one piece at a time, Julian. Johnny Corso's done himself a lot of good out here. And it didn't take long. No question about that. Part of that's because he was in the right place at the right time. But most of it's because he's a hard-nosed little guinea. He knows how to operate, you know what I mean? I know lots of guys like Corso in New York and Jersey. Street-smart bozos. They know how to handle themselves. Know how to get what they want. But those birds are few and far between out here. That's what I mean when I say Johnny got here at the right time. Bobby Scardino from Baltimore was the only sharp operator out here when Johnny came. Bobby had his eye on the truck business too. But Johnny aced him out, did it clean and clever like a gentleman, so Scardino didn't look like an ass-hole to his family. Bobby decided he had a better future in Reno. You see what I'm saying? Johnny's a fact of life out here now, and if it wasn't him it would have been somebody else, somebody not so patient, some torpedo from Detroit or New Orleans who made up his mind that muscle was faster and cheaper than negotiation. I don't mean Corso's an easy man to do business with. He's not. He and I didn't build our produce business by kissing anybody's ass. You know the process. You know what I'm talking about. But here in Los Angeles, Johnny's operated like an altar-boy. He's got more lawyers than I've got neckties. Hasn't made a move without clearing it with those creeps. It cost him money but he did it clean. No skeletons in the closet.'

'What are you saying?'

'I'm saying he's a legitimate businessman and he's put together a hell of a business, all legal and proper. People may not like it but they'll have to live with it. You think French wouldn't gobble up Republic or Monogram or even Columbia if he got a chance? Damned right he would. And so would we. Movies are big business now. Important money to be made. Guys like Corso will be thick as thieves in this town before long. Mark my word.'

'You don't think it's dangerous for one man to have that much power over the studios?'

'It could be expensive but I don't think it has to be dangerous. If I have to knock heads with suppliers I'd rather square off with one guy than have half a dozen of them snapping at my heels. Production costs may go up. They're bound to. Everybody's screaming for a bigger piece of the pie and sooner or later they'll get it. But just remember that all these people, Corso included, want business to go on. If things grind to a halt, no matter what the reason, nobody gets rich.'

'What about the CIO thing?'

'I hate unions,' Sam said. 'And Corso used to hate them when we were back in Jersey. Nobody wants some union bastard to tell him how to run his business. When you hire a man and pay him wages, you want to make the rules. You don't want the guy who begged you for a job to come around six months later flashing a union card and telling you you're working him too hard or the toilet in the men's can don't flush. But I been watching this CIO bunch and they're tough monkeys. They won't roll over and play dead for anybody. You put strike-breakers up against those bozos, you'd better pass out shot-guns first.'

'What are you saying, that the studios can't do anything but watch? We've kept the actors from organizing. And the writers. Times are tough. People don't want to risk losing their jobs.'

'You got it. That's it right there. That's the biggest appeal these union organizers have in their pockets. "Join the union and you won't lose your job. The union will go to bat for you. They'll protect you." People are scared. So when the union promises them something that sounds good, when they think somebody's gonna help them put meat on their plates, they sign up in a minute. Most guys feel that joining the union is like taking out an insurance policy. Maybe they're right and maybe they're wrong, but either way unions are here to stay. Getting stronger every day. And I'll tell you something else. If we get dragged into that crappy war that's heating up over in Europe, there'll be more work and more jobs than anybody ever dreamed of. The plants will start pulling in the money and they'll stop fighting labour. They'll be looking for people to hire. Men, women, and cripples. If we get into that war, every working stiff in this country will carry a union card.'

'So you're saying there's nothing we can do except watch and wait?'

'No. We can do what we've always done. Talk tough, threaten to fire everybody, threaten to close the studio if they try to organize. But they know we don't want to lose any production time. We got theatre schedules to fill. So we can't go head to head with the people that work for us and still turn out sixty or seventy pictures a year.'

'You sound like you're making a case for Corso,' Julian said.

'I'm not making a case for anybody. You just asked me what I thought and I'm telling you. Maybe I'm wrong. Maybe you've got a different idea. But I've been dealing with truckers and guys that sweat for a living all my life and I think I know how they operate.'

'With the writers and actors they've been trying to start their own operations, organize from the inside,' Julian said. 'So we've been able to lean on key people and break up every initiative they come up with. But if Corso makes a deal for his truckers with the CIO, that's another situation altogether. Then we either negotiate or stop production. If Corso hates unions like you say, why does he want to invite them in?'

'I don't know what's in his head. I mean, he hasn't discussed it with me. But it's not hard to figure out. If all his people are organized, it's gonna cost him more money. In wages and benefits. But he'll just pass those costs along to us and the other studios. That's no problem for him. The big thing he gets out of it is leverage. He knows the studios are scared of strikes and that's a threat we have to live with. But here's Corso, sitting in the middle. If he can handle the union and the studios, and keep everybody working, he'll be a hero to his men, to the CIO, and to us, too. Everybody will be happy to pay a little more to keep the cameras turning.'

'You make it sound pretty simple but I don't know a studio head in town who'd buy that philosophy. These guys like Mayer and Goldwyn are rug merchants. They want big profits; they want to keep costs as low as they can as a hedge against pictures that make a small profit. Or no profit. They see every dollar they spend as a dollar they'll never get back. Corso may think he has leverage but he'll have to prove it to these people. They'll scramble and fight and scratch and gouge in every way they can think of. Most of these men are from the New York streets. They didn't get where they are by being philosophers. I'm not sure how much they know about Corso's background, but if he tries to push this union thing down their throats I guarantee you they'll find out every move he's made since he was two years old.'

'Johnny's clean as a whistle,' Sam said. 'He's got nothing to hide.'

'Don't kid yourself, Sam. Everybody's got something to hide. And Corso's got plenty. His dad was the biggest bootlegger in Jersey City, his brother, Joey, went to the pen for extortion, and Vincent Corso's his uncle. It doesn't matter if he's clean as a whistle, as you say. If the newspapers start moaning that the eastern mob guys are moving in on the picture business, things could get very complicated out here. Police inquiries. Legal stuff.'

'I wouldn't blow the whistle on him, would you?'

'Nobody has to blow the whistle. When one guy ties up all the truckers in Los Angeles that's big news. Half the newspaper people out here came from New York. Do you think they never heard the name Corso?'

'Johnny's on his own here. He's not connected to any of his uncle's operations.'

'I don't believe that for a minute, Sam, and neither do

you. But even if we did we'd have a hard time convincing Jack Warner and his crowd. Especially if they decide they want to make trouble for Corso.'

'They can say anything they want to but they can't take his business away from him. And so what if he's got an uncle who's connected? Nobody can link him to Vincent.'

'Can they link him to you?' Julian asked.

'How do you mean? What's that supposed to mean?'

'It means you and Johnny were in business together for twenty-five years.'

'So what? That was then and now is now. You think we're still hustling produce here in Los Angeles? Johnny's got his own fish to fry now and so do I.'

'I'm talking about appearances. The way things look. You're still friends, aren't you?'

'Are you serious? He's my best friend. You know that. I see him two, three times a week. We hit the track together, go to the baseball game on Sunday. We know each other since first grade. He's like my older brother. He likes to boss me around and I let him. It's a game we play.'

'You can play any games you want to, Sam. But not if it hurts my studio.'

'What are you talking about? I'm gonna hurt the business here by going to the ball game with Johnny Corso?'

'There's more to it than that. A lot more. Let me lay out a scenario for you. Corso's locked up the truckers and the laundries and the caterers. Let's say he makes it clear he's going to lead all his people into the CIO. It won't happen overnight because the CIO is just getting itself organized for a big push. Am I right?'

'That's the way it looks.'

'All right. So there's still some time to manoeuvre. Let's assume the studio heads will agree on something for once and decide to do some organizing of their own. What do you think they'd do?'

'You tell me.'

'They'd call in their lawyers and publicity people and start planning a counterattack. First of all they have high-level meetings with all the newspaper owners and explain the situation. They tell them what they want to see reported and what they don't want to see. The publishers hate unions more than anybody. And they know that anything that hurts the movie studios will hurt them as well. You see what I'm saying? The lines are drawn. Both sides know it's a war. Knockdown and drag-out. What if the studios tell Corso they'll set up their own trucking operation? Buy the equipment, bring in new drivers? Then what?'

'Johnny's no dummy. They try to lock out his truckers he'll find a dozen ways to fight them.'

'Exactly. The battle starts. Meanwhile business goes on as usual but everybody's shaky. Looking over their shoulders. It's us against them. Every studio in town lined up against Corso's people. You think that might happen?'

'I wouldn't be surprised. But they won't out manoeuvre Johnny. I guarantee it. They can push and holler all they want to but he'll win in the end.'

'I know you believe that. That's what worries me.'

'What's to worry about? You asked me my opinion and I told you.'

'Let me take my scenario a bit further. What if my phone rings some morning and it's Warner or French and they say to me, "What's this about Sam and Corso? We're breaking our chops trying to bury this guy and your brother is seen with him all over town. Does that mean Thornwood is playing its own game with Corso? Are you with us or against us?" How do you think I should handle a call like that?'

'Tell them to go screw.'

Julian shook his head. 'I can't do that, Sam. And you know I can't. If that ever happened, if this thing came to a head with Corso and word got around that we were in bed with him, that Thornwood Studios had a relationship or a secret agreement or an understanding with him, I'd be dead in this town.'

179

'What are you talking about? You're not in business with those other studios. You call your own shots.'

'That's where you're wrong. In a labour situation we're all together. Against the actors, the directors, the writers, wherever the threat comes from. We're competitors but we all play by the same rules. There's a thousand ways to cripple a studio that decides to go it alone.'

'I give up,' Sam said. 'What am I supposed to say?'

'I hope you'll nod your head so I can be sure you know what's at stake here. I'm saying you may have to distance yourself from Corso.'

'What are you talking about? I've known him since we were kids. Like I said.'

'That's right,' Julian said. 'But then was then and now is now. You said that, too.'

'What are you telling me, Julie? You want me to call up his house and say, "Listen, Johnny, something's come up. I can't go to the track with you on Wednesday. And you and Arloa can't come to the house for dinner Sunday. Matter of fact you better not call me up for a while. And don't come to see me at the studio." Is that what I'm supposed to do?'

'You think this is all a joke?'

'You don't see me laughing, do you? I think it's fucking ridiculous. I can't believe what you're saying to me.'

'You have to believe it and I have to believe it. We can't wait till the storm starts before we patch the roof. We have to take care of it now.'

'What's happened to you? All of a sudden you're nervous as a cat. I've never seen a problem you couldn't solve. You're the guy who makes the rain stop. That's what the crews say about you.'

'This is different. This is family.'

'I don't like the sound of that. You're not about to ship me back to Staten Island, are you?'

'No. But I intend to keep talking till I'm sure you know what I'm talking about. Let me ask you a question. When you and Corso gave up your business in Jersey what happened to your partnership?'

'We sold the business to Allie Stern and his brother-in-law. End of story.'

'But what happened to your corporation or limited partnership or whatever it was?'

'We made a five-year pay-out deal with Stern. So we had to keep our little corporation on the books cause that's where the payments went.'

'What about now?'

'Stern paid everything on schedule.'

'I don't mean that. I mean, are you and Johnny still in business together?'

'You mean is that one-horse corporation still on the books in New Jersey? I don't remember. It might be.'

Julian got up and walked to the wide window behind his desk, looking out across the saw-tooth roofs of his sound stages. When he turned back he said, 'Now I have to ask you a tough question, Sam.' He came back to his chair and sat down again. 'It's eight years since you came out here to work with me. Corso came not long after. Have you two had any financial dealings since then?'

'Every day. You know that. We use his trucks, his food wagons and his laundry service. We send him big cheques every month.'

'That's Thornwood business. I'm not talking about that.'

'You'd better tell me what you are talking about.'

'I want to know if Corso's ever asked you to participate in his business ventures?'

'Why would he do that?' Sam said.

'Why wouldn't he? You like each other. You worked with him for years. You know how the studios operate. You'd be an asset to him.'

Sam lit a cigar. He took his time doing it. Finally he said, 'Am I on trial here or something? Because if I am I don't like it. I feel like you're about to smack my hand with a ruler. I'm not some office boy you caught stealing paper-clips. Why do I have to sit here and answer questions?'

'You don't.'

'Yes, I do.' He puffed his cigar. 'The answer to your question is no. Corso and I are not in business together. Now let me ask you a question. What if I'd answered yes?'

Julian studied him carefully. 'You didn't answer yes, so let's drop it. You know we're talking about critical matters here, so when you tell me you're not in business with Corso, I know you're telling the truth.'

2

'I don't know if I was cut out to be a mother,' Sophie said. 'I was so young when Sarah and Trevor were born I never had a chance to consider such things.'

'Most of us don't,' Margaret said. 'Except for exceptional, far-sighted people, the odd young persons whose only mission in life is to reproduce themselves. Except for those unusual cases, most people don't really think much about parenthood till there's a baby in their arms. From then on, for the next eighteen or twenty years, it's a matter of catching-up.'

'There is no real preparation for it, is there? It's training in the work-place. Learning on the job. And just when you begin to believe you've got the hang of it, it's all over.'

'You're talking like a woman who's begun to suspect her children no longer need her.'

Sophie smiled. 'I've suspected that for quite a long time. Now it's something more than a suspicion. I feel as if I'm destined for the dustbin.'

'There are no dustbins for discarded mothers. No such facility has every been designed or funded.'

'I always overscrutinized myself, like a job applicant filling out employment forms. I was so keen to be a perfect mother that I questioned every decision I made. You remember, I'm sure. I tried to anticipate all their needs, protect them from germs and injuries and anxieties. That was my instinct even when Toby was still alive. When he died I felt as if I had to be even more protective. I didn't want them to be blindly dependent on me, I knew there was a danger to that, but I had a firm conviction that I could plan and provide in such a way that they would never be able to look back when they were grown and say, "Why didn't she do this? Or why didn't she prepare me for that?" Latter-day wisdom, of course, tells me that such planning is senseless and doomed to failure. I mean, one can't hope to shield a child from everything ugly or unpleasant or uncomfortable. And one shouldn't do it even if it were possible.'

'That's true,' Margaret said, 'but all the same, when you care for someone it's human nature to want to protect them. Reason has very little to do with it.' They were sitting in her second-floor rooms, long after dinner, one late night, the great house dark and silent all round them.

'My taking them to London was all part of the master-plan,' Sophie went on. 'As much as I'd loved living here at the Towers, bringing them up where you brought me up, all warm and safe and attended to, by the time Sarah was nine and Trevor eight, I felt it was important for them to be exposed to something other than country life. So I bought my house in London and took them there. I remember that the Major thought it was a dreadful idea and I believe you had reservations as well.'

'I was being selfish, I expect. I'd become accustomed to having you and the children on hand. You'd never been away from me except for short periods of time and neither had Sarah and Trevor. I imagine I was experiencing some of the feelings you're having now.'

'I still believe I made the right choice, for myself as well as them. In fact, until recently, I felt that I'd done as well as any parent could possibly have done for her children. "You're not only their mother," I told myself, "You must be their friend as well." And I was. We had smashing times together, the three of us. But I was careful also to spend time with each of them alone. I tried to expose them to everything that London has to offer. Museums and picture galleries, libraries and monuments and historic sites. Car trips, boat trips, strolls through the parks and gardens. By the time they were ten or eleven they were familiar with opera and ballet, and they'd been to the theatre hundreds of times. They swam well and played tennis, Sarah played the cello and Trevor the piano, and we saw all the important rugby and soccer matches. I wanted them to be exposed to all sorts of things, cultural and otherwise. We visited sections of London where people live who are less fortunate than we are and we discussed the ways that all people resemble each other and the ways in which they differ.'

'Sounds to me as if you have a record to be proud of,' Margaret said.

'One would think so. I certainly was confident as they were growing up that I was being a responsible parent. I also believed that they were aware of the efforts I was making and the guidance I was trying to provide. I never imagined that I could be both mother and father to them, but the fact that I am a single parent made me more keenly aware, I'm sure, that care and concern were required.'

'Do you realize,' Margaret said, 'that you're speaking in the past tense as though Sarah and Trevor were fully grown and had gone off to live in Canada or Australia? They're still at home and they're still in their teens.'

'Of course. I never forget that. But I feel that they have forgotten it altogether. It's not just that they're away at school. That's a normal development, something all young people in their circumstances expect to do when the time comes. And their parents expect it as well. It's a part of growing up, isn't it? Living away from home and being educated in a formal way in structured surroundings. I repeated that to myself many times each day when they'd gone off to school for the first time and my house in London seemed as empty as a winter field.'

'I think I know what you're about to say. The real problem is not that they're away from you so many weeks each year, but that when you do see them they seem to be centred somewhere else.'

'That's exactly what I mean. Why are you so clever?'

Margaret smiled. 'It's not cleverness. Simply a good memory. When you were just a bit older than Sarah is now, you were married and expecting a child. I was excited for you and pleased that you had plunged ahead and found an adult life of your own, but some tiny voice inside me kept saying, "It's too soon. She's too young. She's not ready yet. I'm not ready yet." And of course that final point was the critical one. I wasn't ready to let you go. Mothers are never ready. Perhaps you'll be surprised to hear this, but when you married the second time I wasn't ready then either. Because your father was being such an ass about it I tried to be totally supportive, but something inside me held back. Not because of Kincaid. I didn't know him, of course, but I was genuinely pleased to know that you'd found someone you cared about. All the same I felt as though I was giving you up again. Does it surprise you to hear this? I expect not. As I said, I think what I felt is close to what you're feeling now. At the time, however, I felt guilty about it. Just as I'm sure you feel some guilt now. We're supposed to prepare our children for their own lives, not keep them nearby for ever as a part of ours, but since we're imperfect creatures we're not always able to follow the rules and behave as we should.'

Sophie sat silent. At last she said, 'Sometimes I tell myself that I made a mistake by marrying again. Not because of whom I married but just because I got married. I find myself wondering if Sarah and Trevor felt disenfranchised somehow. Perhaps they felt there was some deficiency in my life that they were unable to fill.'

'I'm sure that's correct,' Margaret said. 'Just as they are developing spaces in their lives that you can't fill.'

'I know that. At least when I'm thinking clearly I know

185

it. But many times when I'm lying awake at night and the goblins are after me, I don't think clearly. I don't think at all. I just agonize about things I can't accept or understand. Even though I know that these changes in my children began to manifest themselves before I even met Kincaid, I fret about how my marriage might have altered their feelings toward me. Or about themselves. When I'm with them now, either one of them, their minds seem to be elsewhere. They put on their very best listening faces but their eyes tend to wander off.'

Margaret smiled again. 'You've simply forgotten, as all of us do, what it's like to be sixteen years old.'

'I hope it's that simple. But I can't help thinking there's something that wants fixing and I don't know how to fix it.'

Margaret reached over and patted her daughter on the knee. 'I prescribe a bit of brandy and a good night's sleep. Tomorrow the goblins will have gone off to bother someone else.'

'I think not. These are my resident goblins. I read much more than I sleep these days.'

'You're not letting yourself get into a state, are you?'

'I'm not ill if that's what you mean. I'm just trying to solve equations that resist solution.'

After a long moment Margaret said, 'How about this equation: why aren't you in London with Kincaid?'

'I'm surprised you don't ask why he isn't here with me.'

'Sophie darling, you're not still playing that game, are you?'

'It's not a game. At least it's not my game. But there does seem to be a subtle contest of wills going on.'

'Nonsense. We had this silly conversation in Portugal more than a year ago. I'm surprised at you. Everything's in order here now. Arthur and I are perfectly capable of coping. There's no reason in the world why you can't leave for London tomorrow.'

'But I can't possibly do that. I need to finish what I've begun here with the builders and decorators. We've discussed this before. I want to spend more time here from now on.

I want Kincaid to feel that this is his home as well as mine. So rather than run back to London I'm trying to lure him back up here.' She smiled. 'And I think I'm making good progress.'

## 3

After his first film, *Bushranger*, had been released more than a year earlier, when he was unable to move freely about London or dine in a restaurant without being recognized or pursued, Kincaid had received some wise counsel from Geoff Bingham.

'Damned annoying,' he'd said, 'not being able to stroll about and live your everyday life without having some over-heated shop-girl and her friends descend on you like a swarm of spiders. Bobby Newton used to handle it well. Brutal but effective. "Hands off, you lot," he would shout, coughing and wheezing and thrashing the air with a battered umbrella he always carried. "Back to your harlot's house," he'd scream. "Practise your trade and let me be," or "Take your stench to the public bath or I'll ring the Minister of Health and have you sprayed." I've had good luck myself at keeping the gad-flies at arm's length although I confess they don't beleaguer me as they do some of you younger chaps. I scowl a lot when I'm in public spots, hat pulled low and a furrowed brow. Try to look like a wicked old sod, and I succeed, I think, to some degree. Some defence must be found, some combat technique, or by God, a man will find himself a captive in his own water closet. During one of my buccaneer trips to Hollywood (the purpose being to grab as much money as fast as I could and leave), I met Jim Cagney one day in a tiresome bar that was attempting, with no success what-soever, to pass itself off as a Dublin pub. He was drinking a tedious brand of American ale, along with two actor chaps named McHugh and Montgomery. Their reason for coming to this particular place, they told me, was because they could drink and talk there in peace. The owner watched like an eagle from behind the bar and anyone who approached his customers was summarily collared and dumped outside on the pavement.

'Cagney was a down-to-earth chap if I ever met one. Devoted to his craft, I believe, capable of first-rate film work, but not at all impressed by the fame his films have brought him. He was born and raised in New York, you know, in a section they call Hell's Kitchen. But it's almost impossible for him to visit there now. Swarmed over everywhere he goes. He said if he and his wife check into the most exclusive hotel in the city, using an assumed name and going upstairs by the freight elevator, his telephone will begin to ring as soon as he's closed the door of his suite. And in a few minutes strangers will begin knocking on his door. So when he goes to New York now, for a business meeting or to see a play, his wife stays at the Sherry-Netherland and he goes to a little bedroom on the top floor of the Players' Club on Gramercy Park. "Like visiting your old aunt in the country," he said.'

'So there you are, a gifted man held captive by his own notoriety. Because that's what it is, you know. Not fame but bloody notoriety. Those cretins who stumble after us in the streets usually don't know who we are or what we've done. God knows, they've never sat in a theatre stall. They're like a pack of dogs who've picked up a scent of some hairy but edible creature, and they're bent on pursuing it till it drops or climbs a tree.

'But . . .' he went on, 'there are ways to handle them. Jimmy Mason was a master of it. He'd just done two successful pictures, and his photograph was everywhere you looked. He'd played a cruel bastard in both films and as a result every woman in England had fallen in love with him. But he had a perfect formula. He said, "I will not be a captive in my own home. I go wherever I wish as I've always done. But before I leave my house I tell myself that I'm unrecognizable and unassailable and to a large degree invisible. My manner is such that no one dares approach me. If someone does, I simply don't see them. I keep moving ahead at my regular pace. By pretending I'm alone I am left alone." And he was, by God. I've walked with him along Shaftesbury Avenue, where the heaviest concentration of touchers and droolers and autograph-collectors are wont to gather, and no one bothered him. One could see glints of recognition and hear voices murmuring as we passed by but not a single alien form approached us.'

Kincaid profited from that conversation with Bingham. He had always ventured out to Green Park, usually early in the morning, hat pulled low on his forehead and wearing smoked glasses. Now, using the James Mason formula but still wearing hat and glasses, he went farther afield. Many afternoons, he put on the seaman's togs that had been his complete wardrobe when he'd come to London three years earlier, positioned his watch-cap square on his head, and took the underground from Green Park station to Leicester Square, from there to Embankment, then east to Monument. From there he walked past the Customs House on Lower Thames Street to a pub called Fore and Aft, where the crewmen from the riverboats gathered, some of them just arrived from Kew or Richmond, others preparing to cast off for Greenwich. In this company, Kincaid spoke with a marked Australian accent. He drank and talked with the crewmen two or three times a week but he volunteered no information about himself and they asked for none. He occasionally rode along on an up-river or down-river trip, standing at the railing of the bow or the fantail watching the swirl of current he'd become familiar with during his years as a seaman.

Other days he stayed at home, inside the house on Queen's Walk, sat by the great bow-window in the library, Green Park stretching out before him, and read leather-bound volumes that Sophie had shipped down from the Towers when she bought her London house. Most often he read books that detailed the events of English history. Or biographies of soldiers and government leaders.

189

When he went out for a meal he went to a small pub on King Street, or to the Caprice just a few steps from his door. And occasionally he joined Sophie's Uncle Howard for luncheon or drinks at the Reform Club. In all these places he had guaranteed privacy.

At the Garrick, where he dropped in from time to time for a late-afternoon drink, where in the company of actors, writers, and miscellaneous theatre people his face and name were well known already and where the general atmosphere was one of camaraderie rather than privacy, of shared opinions and gossip and oft-told tales, where Kincaid had been identified from his first visits there as a loner, one who preferred to sit in a corner with his drink, he was, to a large degree, allowed to do that. 'A solitary chap,' the barman said to the waiter, 'pleasant when he talks to you but not full of himself like some of our strutting peacocks, not in love with the sound and timbre of his own voice. Kincaid's a private fellow, I'd say. Damned rare type for an actor.'

This is not to say that when he sat in his chosen corner the invisible wall that seemed to surround him was never breached. Theatre folk, by and large, are gregarious and the Garrick, as indicated, was a gathering-place, quite unlike Geoff Bingham's description of the atmosphere of the Savile Club.

Actors, whatever their rivalries and insecurities and professional envies, are comrades when they meet, thinking themselves members, even when unemployed and out of pocket, of a select group, blessed with the power to persuade, enlighten, and entertain. And speaking, for the most part, a private language, rich with terms and references and expressions which are fully understood only by their fellow performers. The rich rewards of their profession fall to very few, but the rejections and frustrations and disappointments are common currency to all. Not only do they display their talent in the marketplace for potential employers, they display themselves, and when the purchaser turns away it's that personal self that has been rejected. 'It's a degrading trade,' one veteran actor was overheard to say, 'but by God, when it's just right, when everything comes together, when you know you're functioning at full power and subtlety, and you sense that the dreadful blighters out front know it too, when that electric current crackles and flows back and forth across the footlights, when no one cares or remembers what's taking place in the dreary outside world, what the fools and dental surgeons smugly call "the real world", when total suspension of disbelief has taken place, when the life on one particular stage at one particular moment is the only life there is, then by God, when those moments happen, we know why we've chosen such a chancy and ill-paid route, why we cater to our inferiors, are shunned by cretins, and destroyed a thousand times each year by the disdain of strangers. Once one has experienced flight on one's own wings, once one knows for certain that such exhilaration and fulfilment are available, all other earth-bound activities are hateful and meaningless. An actor can nourish himself for his lifetime on one truly triumphant moment. One great roar of laughter, one memory of a smiling audience standing and shouting approval, can conquer an actor's self-doubt and define him as King for ever.'

All this to say that the bond of a shared activity draws performers together, makes them feel, in the company of their fellows, that all is clear and understood and accepted, that one may approach even an aloof comrade and commend him for his work, offer him congratulations and good wishes and perhaps come away with a bit of his good fortune dusted across one's own shoulders. So members of the Garrick enclave, Kincaid's comrades-in-work, did speak to him occasionally at his half-hidden table. When they came away they felt, as the barman did, that he was a decent and approachable chap, not at all set up by his extra- ordinary and swiftly achieved success in films.

Kincaid was not surprised, therefore, when Alec Maple approached his table one late afternoon, rakishly cadaver- ous and handsome in his tweed lounge-suit and suede boots, a tumbler of gin in his hand, and the sweet scent of juniper floating round him.

'You don't remember, I expect, but we did have a conversation together some months ago. Called on you at your home. Without an invitation. Damned cheeky of me but I was trying to do you a service.' He held out his right hand, 'I'm Alec Maple.'

'Yes, I remember. How are you?'

Maple smiled. 'Not crippled at the moment. Or dogged by symptoms of depression. But not at my peak either.' As he sat down he said, 'Mind if I sit for a moment? There's a chap I detest at the bar just now. I'm hoping he'll claim his hat from the porter soon and toddle off. But I mustn't disturb you. Don't want to interrupt anything. Shall I shout you up a drink?'

'Not just yet,' Kincaid said.

'That's the phrase you Aussies use, isn't it? Did I get it right?'

'Close enough.'

'One doesn't have a sharp ear for argot and vernacular. Not my strong point. You're not offended by my calling you an Aussie, I hope.'

Kincaid shook his head. 'That's what I am.'

'One never knows how a man will react to national labels. Liable to be a hidden perjorative lurking about. I've been known to insult people, rather dreadfully sometimes, but I hate to do it accidentally.' He turned in his chair and made a silent signal to the waiter who moved at once toward the bar.

'This isn't just an aimless visit,' Maple went on. 'Any more than our last meeting at your home on Queen's Walk was aimless. I'm not just bouncing about my club here looking for a drinking companion. *En principe*, I'm rather a solitary drinker myself. I don't drink for effect. Don't believe I've ever set out to get pissed. My instinct always is to sharpen my senses, not to numb them. You know what I'm saying? I drink for pleasure. Things that don't excite my taste-buds,

192

I avoid. Calvados, Jamaican rum, Slivovitz, Drambuie. When only those drinks are offered to me, I abstain. Gin and cognac speak softly to me and I respond. What I'm struggling to say is this: a man who drinks for the pleasure of his palate requires neither companionship nor encouragement. Like a love affair, drink properly appreciated is its own reason for being. So much for that. As I said, I sat down here with you for two reasons. Ahhh . . . here are our drinks.'

The waiter bent toward Kincaid and said, 'I thought you'd be wanting a drink as well, Mr Kincaid.'

'Of course. Thank you.'

As the waiter turned away, Maple said, 'First off, as one actor to another, I want to salute you for the success of your new film.'

'You've seen it then?'

'Indeed I have. And you're doing fine work. Those of us who learned our craft through years of repertory are theatrical snobs for the most part. We were taught in those tender years, had it drilled into our skulls, in fact, that the path we'd chosen was the only path. One must do the classics, play the great roles, or more often, play the tiny roles while watching some older actor wrestle with the mighty scenes and speeches. Only through those years of experience and observation and self-discovery could we hope to come at last to something approaching our best capabilities. The hard road. The long road. Drudgery and self-sacrifice. As you may know, as I may have told you before, I turned away from the theatre, perhaps unwisely, because I came to believe that once I had explored and exposed and developed myself to my full potential I would still be far short of the personal goals I had set. It was a matter of ego perhaps. If I couldn't reach some Olympian heights of performance, some new reading of the great roles that no one before me had ever achieved, if I was to be merely competent or successful or even splendid, that was not enough. The successes I had as a young performer only served to underscore, at least in my own mind, my inadequacies and shortcomings. So, as I've told you just now, and perhaps when we met before, I tipped my hat and slowly walked away.'

'No regrets?'

'Good question. It's been asked a thousand times by one's old comrades, one's wife, and the odd lady of the evening. But I seldom give an honest answer. A flippant reply suffices usually. Or feigned anger. One is never keen to reveal one's true motivations. And of course there may not be a solid and definitive answer. The word *regret* itself springs more from poesy than from logic. I will say this, however. As I've followed the careers of my young comrades, chaps I appeared on stage with in my green years, when I see the heights of acclaim and reward that their meagre talents have taken them to, it's difficult not to woolgather a bit about the triumphs I might have enjoyed if I'd stuck with it.'

'You've not been tempted to take it up again?'

'Tempted perhaps but never persuaded. The fact that I've continued to resist any impulse to return to acting further convinces me that my decision to give it up was a correct one. The theatre is for those who can't live without it. All others should stand aside. Or so I tell myself.'

He signalled to the waiter again, then turned back to Kincaid. 'When I sat down I believe I said I had two matters to bring up with you. The second, I'm afraid, is more complex and less appetizing than the first. So I'll make it brief. I have an old acquaintance, not quite a friend, who lives in California. I believe you know him as well. Burt Windrow.'

'I've met him but we're not friends.'

'I realize that,' Maple said. 'I think Windrow would put it even more strongly than you have.'

Kincaid smiled. 'I know how he feels about me.'

'Does that bother you?'

'Why should it? I don't spend my time trying to make people love me. And even if I did, I expect I'd draw the line at Windrow.'

'Can't he do you a great deal of damage by writing

negative things about you in his column?' Maple asked.

'I'm sure he thinks he can. But I don't give a damn what he writes.'

'Perhaps you'll feel differently when you see this.' Maple took an envelope out of his jacket pocket. 'I've just had this letter from him a few days ago. He sent it to me in strict confidence, but once I'd read it I felt I had to make sure you knew about it.' He slipped a page of folded letter-paper out of the envelope and placed it on the table between himself and Kincaid. 'I think you should read it.'

Kincaid glanced at the piece of paper but made no move to pick it up. Finally he said, 'Since it was sent to you in strict confidence, as you say, why don't we leave it that way? As I said, I'm not really interested in what he has to say about me.'

'Perhaps I need to explain what my instructions were. In case Windrow should have a fatal accident, if he should suddenly turn up dead, I'm to send this letter to the District Attorney's office in Los Angeles.'

'What does that have to do with me?'

'If you read the letter, you'll understand.'

'Look, Mr Maple. I don't know what you're up to and I don't want to know. If Windrow sent you a letter to send to the courts in Los Angeles, then why don't you follow his instructions. Why are you coming to me with it?'

'Because it implicates you,' Maple said. 'He says you and your studio are the only ones who might benefit from his death. He says if they make a thorough investigation of his death they'll find that you're responsible.'

'Oh, for Christ's sake. That's the most idiotic story I've ever heard. What makes him think he's so important that somebody would want to kill him? Did he tell you to show me this letter?'

'God, no. He'd be furious if he knew I'd even mentioned it to you.'

'Then why are you mentioning it to me? And why did you come to me before with that story about a whispering campaign that was about to start that might ruin my career? Did Windrow prompt you to do that as well?'

'No, he didn't. It was a story I'd heard and I thought you should be told about it.' Maple picked up the letter and put it back in the envelope. 'Just as I thought you should be told about this letter.'

'If you've appointed yourself as my benefactor I appreciate your efforts but I don't entirely trust them. To be blunt about it I don't trust anyone who's involved with Windrow.'

Maple put the envelope back in his pocket. 'You have an odd way of responding to a kindness.'

'Let me put it this way. If I find out some time in the future that you've done me a kindness, I promise I will respond with the proper gratitude. In the meantime I can only connect you with your friend Windrow, and that leaves an ugly taste in my mouth.'

4

Until her father's death, Sophie never realised – or perhaps she never admitted to herself – how much the Major and her childhood impressions of him had dictated her reactions to Arthur Tagg.

The two men, other than the fact that they were both male human beings, resembled each other in no way. One was soft-spoken, the other bombastic and self-assertive. One was slender and undangerous in appearance, the other massive in girth and heavy-footed, with thick wrists and cruel hands. One was thoughtful, the other merely vocal. The Major defined himself by his contacts with guns and horses, Arthur with books and music. Whereas her father had always presented himself as a booted and uniformed absolute, Arthur Tagg, from his first interview with Sophie and her mother, had seemed accessible and tolerant. And he was Evan's father, of course. Sophie contrasted their child-father relationship, from the beginning, with that of herself and the Major.

It was to be expected, then, that in the Major's absence, during those years when he was still posted to India and she and Margaret were in residence at Wiswell Towers, during that scrambling and experimental and formative time, she would see Arthur, not as her father, but as a solid, kind, and dependable male presence, the sort of creature fathers are purported to be. As he instructed her, advised and counselled her, encouraged her to do her best work, she constantly reminded herself that he was Evan's father, not hers. But when the Major came home on leave and she was able to measure the two men side by side, still not permitting herself to reject her true father, she could not ignore the scales that tipped in favour of Arthur Tagg.

Her determination that she would not go the final step and say to herself, 'Although he's not truly my father, in my eyes he is', that resolve was made easier to maintain because of Arthur's behaviour toward her. It was as if he wore a placard that read, "I am your tutor and your friend and I help your mother, who is my employer, to manage her estate. I am those things and nothing more." Once he felt that message was clear, once the rules of attitude and behaviour were laid down, then their daily contacts were allowed to be warm and easy, as long as all those concerned understood that some were family members and others were not. 'Why can't I hug him and kiss him?' she sometimes said to Margaret. 'That's what I want to do.'

'So do I, darling,' her mother always replied, 'but we mustn't. Arthur would be dreadfully embarrassed. I expect he'd think we were quite silly.'

During her marriage to Toby Black, when Sarah and Trevor were babies, and later on after Toby died, Arthur had begun, she felt then, to pull down some of the barriers he had constructed during his years at the Towers. His manners remained totally correct and he never inserted himself into family situations, but at the same time, where her children were concerned, he never declined to function as a quondam family member when the occasion demanded a man of his generation to be present. Because infants know no rules, the grown-up rules also seemed to become less rigid in those months before the war ended and the Major came home to stay.

Then, of course, the house with the Major inside it became a different place. Movement seemed less fluid, voices more subdued (except for the Major's voice) and all roles, staff and family, more clearly and rigidly defined. And Arthur retreated from what he had begun to be and became a man who did precisely what he was hired to do. When Evan went away to Oxford, when Arthur's father-function, at least the day-to-day manifestations of it, had come to a close, he dissolved even further into his role as a senior staff member.

Later, however, when Sophie had moved to London with her children, when their visits to the Towers were infrequent and Arthur's visits to London occurred almost never, she was free to think of him as she had when she was a girl, free to remember the best moments, and to invent whatever other memories were needed to mould Arthur and make him into the warm responsive fellow she wanted him to be.

The continuing strife her father had caused, his repeated efforts to dismiss Arthur, his accusations that Margaret and Arthur were lovers, his threats to sue for divorce, naming Arthur as co-respondent, had been as painful for Sophie as they had been for her mother. Each of them knew that Arthur was the principal victim of the Major's lunacy, but they also knew that their sympathy would not be welcome. At least Sophie knew this. Even Margaret, who was able to defy Cranston and defend and reassure Arthur, could not assess the full amount of damage that was being done to him.

None of the discomfort and frustration the Major engendered, however, was in any way comparable to what Arthur must have felt when he learned of Margaret's decision to marry Jack Brannigan. Or so Sophie believed. She and Evan, since they were children, knowing nothing of the mysterious mechanics of adulthood, had firmly believed – and thoroughly discussed those beliefs – that somehow, some day, by a miraculous alteration of circumstances, her mother and his father would be married in the lovely summer garden. They believed that, they told each other, not just because it was something they wanted to happen, but because they were convinced that Arthur and Margaret wanted it. And had always wanted it.

So Brannigan was a surprise. And in spite of herself, Sophie thought less of her mother when she heard the news. Not only had Margaret decided to remarry as soon as she was divorced from Cranston, she was hopelessly, girlishly, sexually in love. Sophie was stunned by all this. A mother's shock when she realizes that her seventeen-year-old daughter takes off her clothing and enthusiastically submits to the passions of an untidy neighbour boy with bad skin is nothing compared to the dismay a daughter feels if she discovers her middle-aged mother is doing the same things with her husband and enjoying it just as much as the daughter does. Each generation fervently believes that sexual joy did not exist till they invented it.

Both Sophie and Evan, when they learned about Brannigan and Margaret, had said to themselves, 'What about Arthur?' Arthur, it seemed, had asked himself the same question and not long thereafter had left Northumberland and moved to London. Although Sophie was in California with Kincaid, just then, and Evan was there as well, she was heartbroken at the thought of Arthur's boarding a train in Newcastle and heading south to London, ending, it seemed, the period of more than twenty years that he'd spent at the Towers.

During the weeks she spent in their California house while Kincaid was working at the studio or on location in Chicago, Sophie thought very often of Arthur. Sometimes sadly. Sometimes in anger. Whatever had taken place between him and Margaret, however he felt about her now, Sophie was bewildered and hurt that he should have cut himself off from her as well. One moment she was determined to contact him and tell him that she was in no way responsible for Margaret's actions, to tell him she was absolutely unwilling to abandon him after so many years or allow him to abandon her. The next moment she told herself that if she meant so little to him, then she would not allow him to mean anything to her. If he could pretend that she no longer existed she would find a way to turn that same card.

Whatever conclusions she had reached, however, they all lost significance when she learned about Brannigan's death and her father's pitiful state. As she planned what she would do to set things right, Arthur's name was always in her mind. As she crossed the ocean every scenario she contrived featured him in some important way. And when she was inside the Towers again, when she was aware of her mother's state of mind, when she'd seen her father in his locked room, she felt more surely than ever that if she was to be the armature of everything that needed to be done, Arthur must be her armature.

When she went down to London to fetch him, to play on his conscience, his sense of decency, his debt to Margaret for her loyalty to him through all the years, as she listed those appeals and many others, she concluded that determination was her greatest weapon. 'I simply will not be denied,' she told herself. 'I will not let him say no.'

As she headed north from London two days later, she felt triumphant. Arthur was in the twin compartment with her, his valises in the overhead rack, his crates and cartons in the baggage car behind. 'Coming back to stay,' she told herself. Feeling proud of her accomplishment, of her powers of persuasion, she told herself also that he truly wanted to come, that while he'd played a game of resistance he was as convinced as she that his place was not in London but in Northumberland.

If he seemed silent and self-absorbed during their train trip, she reasoned that he had always been that way. If he was detached and reserved, that too was a familiar mode for him. She knew that when he was back in his regular routine at the Towers he would quickly become the complete and contented man that circumstances had prevented him from being before.

It happened as she had hoped. Starting, it seemed, from the moment he stepped into the great hall. John Trout and Mrs Whitson had assembled the entire staff to greet Arthur. As he moved along the line, speaking a few words to each person, he bore little resemblance to the silent gentleman who had shared Sophie's compartment on the train up from London. There was nothing military about his reunion with the staff, no hint of the commander returning in triumph to rejoin his division, but there was, all the same, an unmistakable scent of authority in his manner. It was clear that the staff regarded him as the new master and he gave no indication that he rejected that assumption.

When she described the homecoming to Margaret, who at that time was still at Wingate Fields, where she'd been since the day of Brannigan's death, Sophie said, 'What a thrill it was to see him at the Towers again. It was as though the place had come suddenly to life. And it seemed that Arthur came back to life as well. You'll see for yourself as soon as you're home again.'

That feeling of exhilaration was short-lived for Sophie. Little more than a week later she would write in her journal:

I can't imagine what has come over Arthur. Has he undergone a total personality change? Or is it just that he has an attitude toward me that is unlike anything he's felt before? His eyes seem to glaze over when I speak to him. I feel as if he's passing judgement on me, or has already passed it and doesn't want me to know what he's concluded. Does he resent my persuading him to come back here? What is it?

Later on, in a letter to Kincaid in London, she wrote:

Is it possible that Arthur sees me now not as the young woman he's known for more than twenty years but as his employer, someone he must obey and cater to? I can't imagine his feeling that way but there must be some explanation. When I try to consult with him about estate affairs or ask his advice about the restoration and decorating plans I've started, he goes mute or nearly so. But even when he's silent, especially then perhaps, I sense an antipathy that baffles me. Does he now consider himself the true master of Wiswell Towers? Was his decision to use the Major's old rooms as his quarters symbolic as well as utilitarian? Has that gentle unassuming man become suddenly power-crazed?

I've tried in a subtle way to sound out members of the staff, Trout and Mrs Whitson particularly. But they seem to have nothing but praise and affection for him. And respect of course. When I asked Margaret in an elliptical way if she saw any change in Arthur since he's back she said, 'He's not a changeable man. We all know that. That's his strength. Sometimes he comes slowly to his decisions, but once he's weighed the alternatives and made a choice, you can be sure that he'll stick to his guns. He's the sort one can count on.'

Sophie had pursued the question of Arthur more specifically with her mother. 'Does he seem dissatisfied to be back here?'

'Not at all,' Margaret said. 'I've seen no hint of anything that would make me suspect that. Has he said something to make you believe that?'

'It's nothing he's said. He says very little to me. It's just a feeling I have. Perhaps I've offended him somehow. Has he mentioned anything of that sort?'

Margaret smiled. 'Of course not. He has nothing but praise for you. He thinks you were incredibly kind and loyal to me when I needed you. He admires you. And though he would never let himself say the word, I'm sure he loves you just as he loves Evan.'

'Let's be honest with each other, Mother. Even if he were put out with me about something or other he would never let on, would he? And he certainly wouldn't mention it to you.'

'I can't imagine what you're getting at, dear. It isn't like you to be scurrying about examining people's motives, and trying to determine who's displeased with you and who isn't.'

'Perhaps that's so. But in this instance I'm not imagining things. I know what I see and hear and what I sense. And there's no doubt in my mind that Arthur's attitude toward me has undergone a remarkable change. Does he resent my being here? Is that it? Would he prefer to have me pack up and go back to London?'

'Of course not. Why would he wish for such a thing? He knows this is your home just as it's my home.' She paused. 'He may be surprised that you haven't gone back to London now that Kincaid's there. But Arthur would never presume to make any such suggestion to you.'

'I'm not so sure of that. Sometimes I feel as though he's just on the brink of blurting out something that would be a total surprise to me. I see something in his expression that looks like resentment. There's a contentious note in his voice when he speaks to me, as though he's mustering his defences against some sort of attack that I'm about to make on him.'

'Sophie, Sophie, Sophie . . . What's come over you?'

'Nothing's come over me. I'm simply saying . . .'

'But when you talk about Arthur, you're describing a man I don't recognize.'

'That's what upsets me,' Sophie said. 'I don't recognize him either. I torture myself trying to decide what I could have done to turn him against me. Sometimes I think he resents the work I'm having done on the house, the changes I'm making. Has he said anything about that?'

'We've discussed it, of course. Arthur and I discuss everything. When I first came back here after Jack's death, I didn't want to concern myself with anything involving the estate or the staff. You know that. But little by little Arthur's brought me round and now we're dealing with the details together as we always have.'

'But don't you see? That's an example of what I'm talking about. When I brought him back here from London we had an understanding that he and I would handle everything, that you wouldn't be burdened with any of the investment details or operational problems.'

'I realize that and I appreciate the way you handled it. But now there is no burden. I'm able to do my share and quite happy to do it.'

'Of course you are. But I didn't want you to be saddled with all that, and Arthur agreed. Now, without a word to me he's taken a separate course on his own. And that annoys me.'

'I'm sure he believes he's relieving you of the burden, just as the two of you were relieving me.'

'I wish it were that simple but I know it's not. There's some sort of contest going on and I hate it.'

After a long moment Margaret said, 'Why don't you go back to London, Sophie? You're getting yourself into a state over nothing. Everything's in order here now.'

'I'm afraid not. I feel as if I'm being manipulated and I need to know why. For some reason that neither of us seems to understand, Arthur is keen to have me out of here and back in London. Well, I'm just as keen to stay till I find out what he's up to.'

'He's up to nothing, Sophie. He's simply doing his job.'

'I'm beginning to think he doesn't understand what his job is. Does he imagine he's a Wiswell now?'

'Oh, Sophie, for heaven's sake.'

'I'm serious. Did moving into the Major's rooms cause him to redefine himself? Is that why he behaves so peculiarly toward me? There has to be an explanation, Mother. Everything isn't all honey and sweet cream, as it appears to you.'

'Do you want me to say something to Arthur? Is that what you're getting at?'

'Not at all. This is a private discussion, between you and me. I'll deal with Arthur in my own way.'

'I certainly don't like the sound of that.'

'You needn't worry. I won't do anything foolish. I'm not angry with him. I'm simply bewildered. I need to sort things out so I'll know what's on his mind. The building plans, for example. I want to see if that whole programme has upset him.'

'It hasn't upset him,' Margaret said. 'I told you a moment ago that he and I have discussed it.'

'And what does he say?'

'Nothing dramatic. But Arthur's a conservative man, you know. I am also conservative in certain areas. He loves the Towers just as I do. While he recognizes that a place this size needs constant attention and maintenance and restoration, he believes that the original appearance and spirit of the interior should be preserved. I believe that, too.'

'So do I,' Sophie said. 'In principle. But on the other hand times change and requirements change. Our needs change. It's foolish for us to tie ourselves to circumstances and facilities of the eighteenth century. Many changes have been made in the Towers since it was first built and many more alterations will be made in future. I've had to make choices and compromises in my work with the architects but they've all been made with one purpose in mind, to make the Towers a living place, not a monument to the past, to make it a warm and comfortable home for all of us, for my children and their children to come, to have splendid private quarters so all of us can feel this is our home, a place where we can keep our most precious possessions, a place we can always return to or live in permanently as we choose.'

'I certainly don't disagree with your objectives. My mother used to express it in much the same way. But when the details of construction and decoration are discussed it's natural that people will have different tastes and different views.'

'Of course,' Sophie said. 'That's to be expected. But those are family matters. Choices that you and I and Kincaid must make. And later on Trevor and Sarah. Arthur, as valuable as he's always been to us, should not concern himself with such details.'

5

'I'm not sure I understand what you're saying,' Ellie Rawson said. She was sitting in Sam Thorne's office, late afternoon, a steady rain falling outside.

'That's because I didn't finish explaining it,' Sam said. 'It's an unusual arrangement, I agree, but it's one that will be very beneficial for you. Since you and I met last there's been a great deal of discussion about you here on the lot. I probably shouldn't tell you this but every department head I talked to would like to have you on his payroll. But I remembered you said you wanted the casting department if we could work it out. So that's what I concentrated on. It's a big department, as you know. Fifteen or twenty people we've got there. But I wanted to make sure you were in the right slot. And we got lucky. For fifteen years Leon Barkin and Sonia Biltz have headed up that operation, Leon running the administrative end of it and supervising independent casting and Sonia handling our contract people, keeping them happy. Arranging for loan-out to other studios and working out the deal when we want to borrow a contract player from somebody else. That's the job I see you in but we didn't know how to handle Sonia. Then we got lucky. I remembered she used to work for Selznick so I had somebody whisper in his ear that she was unhappy with us and the next thing I knew she was in my office crying because Selznick had offered her an associate producer's job. She wants to take it but she doesn't want to leave me and Barkin in the lurch. So I told her we'd have a tough time getting along without her but she was free to leave whenever it suited her. So that spot's open now and it's yours. You'll be making twice what you're making working for Windrow and three times what we paid you when

206

you worked for Thornwood before.'

'Sounds wonderful,' Ellie said. 'When do I start?'

'You're on salary now. You'll get your first cheque Saturday. But for the time being we want you to stay with Windrow.'

'For how long?'

'Two or three months maybe.'

'I don't get it,' she said. 'Why are you starting to pay me before I come to work?'

Sam smiled and lit a cigar. 'Because we like you.'

'Don't kid me, Sam. Nothing's for nothing. What's going on?'

'I'll answer that in a minute. First I want you to answer some questions for me. Maybe we discussed this before but I've got a bad memory, so let's sing it again. Tell me how Windrow's operation works. How does he put his column together?'

'We do three columns a week now and a Sunday piece for the *Kansas City Star*. They're the syndicators. I wire them a column Monday, Wednesday, and Friday. The Sunday feature, usually an interview, goes out on Tuesday.'

'Who actually puts the column together?'

'It's a mish-mash. A flood of stuff comes in the mail every day from press agents and studio publicity departments. And the phone rings all morning from people with still more items. Everything gets typed up on file cards for Windrow to look through and shuffle together along with the items he's picked up at parties or night-clubs or from his private spies. As soon as he gets it all in sequence with his transition remarks added, he gives it to me, I type it up, he corrects it, and it's ready to go out on the wire.'

'How soon after it's put together in final form does it hit the wire?'

'The column we finish Monday goes to Kansas City Wednesday. Wednesday's column goes out Friday, and Friday's column goes Monday.'

'And you put it on the wire yourself?'

207

She nodded. 'Windrow never sees it after he's corrected the typescript.'

'Good. That means there's a little breathing-room between the time the column's written and the day it's published.'

'That's right. Not much but a little.'

'All right, here's the situation,' Sam said. 'There's some serious stuff going on. I can't tell you the details because I don't know them yet. No one does. But there are some danger signals we're looking out for. We're not just monitoring Windrow, we've got our regular sources alerted in offices all over town. What we need from you is this. We have to know, as soon as *you* know, about any item that concerns Kincaid, Thornwood Studios, Julian or myself. Or John Corso. Also, any rumour about problems between the studios and the truckers, or any mention of efforts by union people to organize some branch of our industry. We have messengers coming to you all the time from our publicity people so all you have to do is call my office, not Julian, and not our publicity people, and I'll have somebody over there in twenty minutes to pick up whatever you have for me.'

'Then what? It's hard for me to hold items back from Windrow. And once it's in a column, even if I cut it out, he'd know it as soon as the column ran.'

'I'm not asking you to do that. That's not your job. We just need to know what to expect. If there's something we have to kill we'll do that in Kansas City.' He squared himself in his chair and leaned forward on his desk. 'You have a funny look on your face. Am I asking too much?'

'You know me, Sam. I'm a straight arrow.'

'I know you are. And I wouldn't ask you to do this if it wasn't necessary. If it makes you feel better I promise you that what we're doing won't hurt anybody. Not Windrow or anybody else. When I tell you this is critical business, that's exactly what I mean. For the whole industry. So we all have to do what we can. And by the way, nobody knows about

208

this conversation but you and me. I'm asking you to trust me as much as I trust you.'

Since her conversation with her daughter about Arthur, Margaret had thought of little else. After a close relationship that had been characterized through all of Sophie's life by openness and warmth and total honesty, she felt now that screens and walls had somehow been erected between them. Usually able to think clearly about any problem that presented itself to her, Margaret now found herself adrift, unable to find a solution or even to clearly understand the problem.

She fussed and floundered about in her second-floor sitting-room, stared out the window at her gardens, and tried desperately to make one plus two add up to three. At last, in an effort to channel her thinking somehow, to stop her mind from skipping about from one uncertain spot to another, she sat down at her writing-table and wrote a letter to Kincaid.

How sorry I am that we know each other so little. We've had very few opportunities to talk and listen and discover common ground. But my instincts tell me you're an unusual man. And certainly a gifted one.

I also know that my daughter loves you, in a way that's new to her. And therefore a bit frightening, I suspect. Does she also see you as an invincible adversary? I think she does. And that would attract her, of course. But I expect it's also a challenge to her. Since she has never had to compete for money or recognition or position, all her competitive instincts have been channelled into her personal relations. She'd be shocked to hear me say this, and it's something I could never say to her directly, but it's none the less true.

Having never been dominated by another person

or by any circumstances, I believe she has come to accept that as her legacy: to be in gentle benevolent control of her own life and all its elements. Although she is not careless or cruel or manipulative by nature, although her protected life has seldom put her in direct conflict with anyone, one gets an impression, all the same, that she is constantly prepared for conflict. Eager for it perhaps. And determined to prevail when it occurs.

I wonder sometimes if this is a characteristic she's inherited from her father, some dilute solution of his paranoia. I prefer to think not, but in any case the characteristic I'm describing, that hunger to prevail, is very much a part of my charming and valuable daughter. None of this will come as a surprise to you, I'm sure. Does she continually baffle you as she does me? Since I've known her longer than anyone, I should be able to guide you a bit, to advise. But I cannot. I would only suggest that you hold your ground. Sophie is surely not eager to learn the gentle arts of compromise and gracious surrender but it's vital, for her and for you, that she does learn these things.

As she slowly reread what she'd written, Margaret said to herself. 'I really must send this letter.' But she knew she wouldn't.

# • CHAPTER 6 •

## 1

'What the hell has come over you?' Alan Winkler said. He was sitting across the table from Evan, in a wine-bar in Chancery Lane.

'Nothing,' Evan said. 'You asked me how things are going for me and I told you.'

'No, you didn't. You told me some dismal story about a man who's come to the end of his rope. If that's your true state of mind you're in trouble, my friend. You're committing the eighth deadly sin. You're feeling bloody sorry for yourself.'

'No, I'm not. You must have heard something I didn't say.'

'You said it all right and I heard it. That's what I get paid for, to listen and remember. And even if you'd said nothing I'd still get the message. You've got all the joy of a pall-bearer about you, the last man through the cemetery gate.'

'You're drunk, Alan. We're both pissed to the gills and you're not making sense.'

'I may be pissed but I'm not deaf and I'm not crazy. In any case tomorrow I'll be sober but you'll still be feeling sorry for yourself.'

'You don't know what you're talking about.'

'You. That's what I'm talking about. And that's a subject I'm an expert on. I've known you since you left Oxford and came toddling down to London ten years ago. Good times and bad we've known each other. Think it over. Who knows you better than I do? Did I give you a job on the *Telegraph* two months after you hit town? Damned right I did. And I never regretted it. You did some fine work for us. You'd be top of the mark in the journalism field if that's what you wanted. But you were straight with me from the start. Play-writing . . . that was it, you said. Shaw, Ibsen, Chekhov – those were your gods, you told me. Better to fail at something worthwhile than to get rich as an estate agent. That was your credo and I admired you for it. So I talked to my editor-in-chief and we rigged a schedule that would leave you time for your own work. Feature assignments. Interviews. That sort of thing. Happy as a dog, you were. Earning your keep and hammering out a new play every month or so. Remember those days?'

'You set me up just right, Al, no doubt about it.'

'Happy I could do it. Had faith in you. I used to tell my wife, "Evan's a worker. He doesn't sit around and dream about work. He gets right to it and turns out the pages." And you did. I ought to know. I read every scene of every play you wrote, didn't I?'

Evan nodded. 'That's right.'

'And remember what I said when you gave me the first one, the one about the woman with a hundred canaries in her sitting-room?'

'*The Bird Woman.*'

'That's the one. When you gave it to me that morning in my office, I said, "Don't ask me my opinion if you don't want me to tell you the truth." Remember that?'

Evan smiled. 'And that's what you did.'

'Exactly,' Winkler said, 'and that's what I'm doing now. I'm telling you, you're feeling bloody sorry for yourself, and worse than that, you're enjoying it.'

'Let's get off this subject before we start throwing chairs at each other.'

'I don't want to get off it. You've been moaning and wailing all evening, and now it's my turn. I look at you and I see a damned good writer who's also been damned lucky. All right, your play wasn't a howling success but it got you noticed. It had a good production in an important theatre and people were saying, "There's a young chap to keep your eye on." Am I right?'

'You're half-right.'

'I'm right,' Winkler said. 'Off to a good start. Establishing yourself. Up-and-coming. Then the bluebird swooped down and stuck a rose in your ear. Julian Thorne waved his wand and money started to fall in your hat. "Write me a movie," he said, "and I'll take you where the oranges grow and make you rich." Not once but twice he said it. So it's two big films to your credit. Your name on the screen and in the adverts. Evan Tagg, a name to reckon with. A money name. Talent and money and a house by the sea. And naked young women floating up to your door with every wave. It's all true. You know damned well it's true. The golden days of young Mr Tagg.'

'Sounds great,' Evan said, 'but that's not the whole story.'

'Of course not. It never is. It's always raining somewhere. But unless a man is crazy he tries to keep dry. That's why roofs and umbrellas were invented. Only a fool goes looking for trouble when good things are happening to him.'

'I'm not looking for trouble.'

'You're not, eh? I don't know what you'd call it then. Let me give you a synopsis of the pain and woe you've been pouring on me for the last . . .' he looked at his watch . . . 'for the last three hours. To start off with, although you've accumulated a cozy amount of money which gives you the freedom to tackle a new play, or half a dozen plays if you like, you're not certain that you really want to write a play just now. The time may not be right. Maybe it's too soon. People may remember that *The Fatherhouse* was not a big success. Or perhaps you've waited too long. People who were impressed by that play may have forgotten all about you by now. You're also troubled by the fact that the perfect producer might not be available, or if available might not

213

be interested.' Winkler lit a cigarette and offered one to Evan.

'Another factor disturbs you,' he said then. 'Perhaps you should continue to strike while the iron is hot in California. Merchandise yourself and your recent success. Write as many scenarios as possible and squirrel away the money till the bubble bursts. But you see a downside here as well. Why squander your talent and your energies on a superficial medium? Why write on water when you can craft something enlightening and significant for the theatre?'

'Makes sense, doesn't it?'

'Of course. Mindless anxiety always makes sense to the person who searches for it.'

'You're trying to make me angry, you bastard.'

'I'm willing to but I'm not trying to. I'm trying to let a bit of light in through that cloud of fog round your head.' He drained his glass and signalled for the waiter. 'Why shouldn't you do a play now? No one would object to that. No one except you. You have any number of ideas, you say, but the problem lies in selecting the correct one, the most timely and profound one, the one that is serious and provocative but also accessible and entertaining, an intellectually demanding play that will also appeal to kitchen workers and shop-girls. Having once told me that only writing, not planning or dreaming, produces worthwhile work, you have now concluded, it seems, that a play can be conceived, developed, and abandoned without putting one word on paper. "A man who decides to sustain himself on a diet of caviar, truffles, and champagne will not be well nourished and may soon be dead." You know who made that statement? Neither do I.'

The waiter returned then with glasses of claret. 'Let's concede the point,' Winkler went on, 'that although you were once capable of writing several plays per year, you are now on a new rhythm whereby the decision to start a play, the choice of material, could take two or three years or even longer. Having made that concession you come up against another thorny problem. How does one sustain oneself, both

214

financially and as a craftsman, during such long arid periods? Why shouldn't the theatre function like the motion-picture industry, you ask? When you are engaged to write a film scenario you are paid throughout the work process. If the film is not a success or if for some reason it's never even made, you are still rewarded for your services. Now we begin to see the price you've paid for your Hollywood adventure. From the dedicated playwright who's willing to make whatever sacrifice is necessary to get his work done, you have become the Chinese laundryman who says, "No tickee, no washee." If no coins are dropped in the writing machine, no writing will be done.'

'Everybody likes to be paid for what they do,' Evan said. 'You wouldn't work for nothing, would you?'

'Of course not. But I'm not an artist. I'm a wage slave.'

'Maybe I'm not an artist either.'

'Maybe you're not. Time will tell, won't it? Or have you already decided?' Evan didn't answer, so Winkler went on. 'No decision. That's good. There's still some hope then. But first we have to deal with another hurdle you're facing. Putting aside for the moment the difficulties of selecting a project, let's focus on the problems of the work-place. Where is the ideal spot for you to write a play once you've chosen a play that deserves to be written? One who's known you as long as I have might say that since you always used your flat here in London as a work-place, since you've written all your previous plays there, that would be the simple solution to your problem. But you say no.'

Evan shook his head. 'I didn't say it was out of the question. I could work there, I suppose, but it's not ideal.'

'Ah, yes, ideal. That's the operative word, isn't it? Think what great works Rembrandt and Chaucer might have done if they'd had central heating and indoor plumbing.'

'Go to hell, Winkler.'

'Abuse of one's opponent is no argument.'

'We're not opponents, for Christ's sake.'

'Exactly. We're working together, reasoning together, in

an attempt to solve your creative problems. I'm sure there are distractions in your flat. Memories of other days, old associations, familiar frustrations come back to haunt you. And although you like the climate in California and the house that's available to you by the sea there, too, if I heard you correctly, there would be hurdles to get over. Even in isolation, alone in the house, the telephone switched off, no contact with your associates in the film community, you anticipate that it would be difficult to sit down each morning and put in a solid day's work.'

'In the case of California,' Evan said, 'at least the place where I was living, it's almost too quiet and peaceful, too much isolation. You can hear yourself breathe, hear the cat moving about the house, monitor your own heart-beat without a stethoscope.'

'Too ideal,' Winkler said, nodding his head.

'I'm serious. A certain kind of stillness has a presence of its own, one that starts to ring in your ears.'

'I see. So California, unless one could find a less sheltered area, would be out of the question. To say nothing of the cultural deprivation. No theatre, no libraries or museums, no concerts or picture galleries. Just sunshine, the waves lapping gently on the sand, no sounds of human congress. Only a spinster verse-writer would envision such surroundings as a proper atmosphere for creative work.'

'You're a sarcastic rat, Winkler. And you've a great red spot of claret on your necktie.'

'If you admire it, it will arrive at your door suitably gift-wrapped next Christmas. Meanwhile, let's continue our search for a place where you can function. Quiet but not too quiet, remote but not isolated, and familiar but not disturbingly so. Your last available choice, it seems, is Wiswell Towers, scene of your boyhood follies and triumphs. If I'm not mistaken, you said earlier this evening that rooms are being prepared for you there. A work-room with library, a sitting-room, bedroom and bathroom. All this high in a corner tower with a view across the moors. Ideal, one would think, but here again you hold back. The family, although they can be neither seen nor heard from your eyrie, are none the less present and you would be constantly aware of them. Also, the schedule of meals, while convenient, might prove to be restrictive. Just as the carefully conceived view from your desk could become a distraction.

'You've told me, too, and you seemed quite serious about it so I will be serious as well, you mentioned a drawback that would never have occurred to me: you said that being a writer in a house where there were no other artists or writers, where everyone else had known you since childhood and had drawn all sorts of conclusions about you through the years, this familiarity with your old self and total lack of familiarity with the person you've become and the work you'd be struggling each day to do, these contradictions, you said, could create a sort of silent conflict. I believe you told me you would be carefully examined each time you entered the dining hall to see if the day's writing experience had made any visible change in you. Did I get it right?'

'It sounds preposterous, of course, coming from someone else's mouth but it's true it can be a pain in the neck when you're trying to work and live a family life all at the same time. One feels a stronger than normal responsibility toward the household and its activities.'

'Everything you say has the ring of truth. So I conclude, as you obviously have, that serious work will have to wait until the clouds part one day and some magic haven reveals itself to you.'

'I may be drunk but I'm not stupid. You think I don't know what you're saying, in your assinine city-editor fashion? You're saying I don't really want to write. Or I can't write. So all this searching about for a place where I can work is just a camouflage of that fact. I hate to send you off in a fit of triumphant laughter but I think you may be right.'

Winkler finished the wine in his glass. 'No triumph here,' he said. 'If that's what it's all about, it doesn't make me feel like laughing. It makes me feel rotten.'

Lew Ethridge had been Julian Thorne's book-keeper from
his first ventures with store-front nickelodeons. When Julian
went to California and established Thornwood Studios, Lew
was the first man he hired, some time before he persuaded
his brother, Sam, to come west to join him in the business.

Ethridge and Julian had been born in the same neighbourhood in New York and in the same year but they had
little else, other than intelligence, in common. Lew was an
only son who had been raised and trained in book-keeping.
He quit school when he was sixteen and worked with his
father, going to the stores and shops of their clients and
bringing their account books up to date once or twice a month.
When his father collapsed and died on the street one sultry
August day in 1914, Lew continued the business by himself.

He stayed on in the apartment he'd shared with his father,
cleaned and scrubbed it every Saturday, and cooked supper
for himself each evening. He never married and, as far as
his neighbours or anyone who knew him could tell, never
went dancing or walking or to the neighbourhood brothel
where Diamond Jim Brady was reputed to have paid occasional visits.

His neighbours seemed to take no notice of Ethridge's
celibate life. Occasionally, however, someone's aunt or
sister came to visit from the Bronx or Newark and seeing
Lew on the sidewalk, would remark about his lean figure,
his pleasant smile, or his thick auburn hair. The reply was
always the same. 'Oh, that's just Lew, the book-keeper. Lives
by himself. Goes to Temple on Fridays but the rest of the
time he's upstairs in his flat, working on his books. Or sitting
on the fire-escape on summer evenings.'

Before he would agree to come to work in California,
Ethridge made the long trip across the country by train. Julian
sent a car to meet him at the station and bring him to the
studio. As soon as he came into Julian's office he said, 'I

can't live out here. It's like Egypt to me. I hate the sun burning down every day. And outside of the Mexicans, I see nothing but yellow hair and green eyes. I haven't seen a Jew since I left Pennsylvania station.'

Julian put his arms round his shoulders and said, 'You come with me tomorrow. We'll go to the old part of the city. Then we'll walk along Fairfax Avenue and you'll believe you're in Sheepshead. We'll find you a place to stay. You'll think you're in the old neighbourhood. Except for the sun. We can't stop that and we don't want to. That's why we're out here so we can shoot pretty pictures without paying a big electric bill.'

'I hate the sun.'

'So you'll have an office on the shady side of the building. And I'll buy you a fifty-dollar panama hat first thing tomorrow.'

At the end of the following day, wearing his panama hat, Lew had agreed to give it a try. 'Two or three months. Then we'll see what happens.' After he saw the stores and shops on Fairfax and heard New York accents all round him, he and Julian walked together along the nearby side-streets. Just a half-block off Fairfax in Winston Street they found a walk-up apartment to let on the top floor of a three-storey building. 'I guess this will do me for a few months,' Lew said. Fifteen years later he was still living there, duplicating the life he'd lived in Brooklyn. Taking the bus to the studio six mornings a week and attending the Wilshire Boulevard synagogue every Friday evening.

If Julian was the grand architect of Thornwood's financial affairs, Sam was his general contractor. But Ethridge was the structural engineer. Even Sam, who prided himself on his skill with figures, acknowledged that he was a novice alongside Ethridge. 'Nobody has to look over Lew's shoulder. When he says a job's done it's done. He gets it right. He's a wizard.'

Two weeks after his meeting with Henry French and his subsequent meeting with his brother, Julian asked Ethridge to come see him in his office. When they were sitting across from each other Julian said, 'We're here on the same lot six days a week and I never see you. Why is that?'

'You're a busy man, Julian, and I'm busy, too.'

'We're not overworking you, are we?'

Lew shook his head. 'I know my job. I keep ahead of it. My papa told me – first thing he taught me when I started in his business – "Ours is a business of details. Either we handle those details or they'll handle us."'

'Good advice. I think I'll have that printed on cards and hand one to all my producers.' He studied Ethridge carefully. 'I know you don't wear make-up, Lew, and I know you stay out of the sun so where'd you get that nice sun-tan?'

'You remember Mrs Gold, the lady who owns the building where I live. She put a swimming–pool in the back yard a year or so ago. I take a dip there every evening when I'm home from work, and then we sit out there and drink a Cuba Libre and watch the sun go down.'

'You and Mrs Gold?'

Ethridge nodded. 'We're the regulars. But there are two other tenants – Ruth Harley, who does window displays for the May Company, and Emma Donald, who teaches art at Fairfax High School . . . they use the pool, too.'

'Quite a harem you've got there,' Julian said. 'You're drinking rum, getting a sun-tan, and living with three women.'

'Mrs Gold has a special kind of sun-lotion. Even with my red hair and fair skin I never get a burn.'

'Well, you look good. I think I did you a favour when I lured you out here from New York.'

'It's a different life, Julian. There's no doubt about that.'

Julian rolled his chair closer to the desk and said, 'There's something I want you to do for me, a confidential matter. My brother doesn't know I'm talking to you about this and I don't want him to know. I assume that's no problem for you.'

'Not if it's what you want.'

'It's what I want. Strictly a matter between you and me. Understood?'

'Right.'

'All right. Here's what I need. According to my calendar you're just about winding up your report on last year's figures. What we spent and what we took in.'

Ethridge nodded. 'Should finish all that in a week or ten days. Then it goes to the printer and you should have it on your desk a week later.'

'Good. We've had a good year. I'm anxious to see how the figures play out.'

'Biggest year we've ever had. And this next one looks even better.'

'Let's hope so. But the information I need won't be in that final report. It's in your work-sheets. I want to see a detailed list of every payment we made for trucking, catering, laundry and dry-cleaning. Three separate corporations, all of them owned by John Corso. Any problem with that?'

'No problem. I'll put it together myself.'

'Good. I also want to see the invoices that correspond with those payments. And a list of all cash deposits my brother made to Thornwood accounts as well as withdrawals. And any cheques he may have written or authorized to John Corso other than direct payment for billed services.' When Ethridge didn't answer, Julian said, 'Am I going too fast for you? Am I asking for records you don't have?'

'No, it's not that.'

'What is it?'

'Am I going to get somebody in trouble?'

'Of course not,' Julian said. 'Why would you think that?'

'I don't know. I'm just in the habit of reporting every-thing to Sam..Now it looks like I'm checking up on him and he doesn't know it.'

'That's right. He doesn't know it and I don't want him to. I trust Sam completely, just as I trust you. But Thorn-wood is my company and I have a responsibility to take a close look from time to time at every component part of that company. Normally I don't second-guess Sam and I'm not doing that now. I just need to see certain records and I felt confident you could help me.'

'I'll do my best,' Lew said. 'I'll get back to you as soon as I've pulled everything together.'

Later that day Julian called Henry French at Paramount. 'I've been giving some serious thought to the things we talked about in your office. I suggest you set up a meeting with Goldwyn and Jack Warner and one of Mayer's key people. Best to do it in your office, I think, and make it in about ten days. That will give me time for a fast trip to New York. I may have to fly in next week.'

'What shall I tell them we're meeting about?'

'General discussion of the Corso problem,' Julian said. 'Between you and me, I think we have to do some under-cover exploration of what we discussed before. Buying our own trucks, running our own cafeterias and food wagons, setting up an industry-operated laundry and cleaning operation if necessary.'

'You're talking about laying out a lot of capital, Julian.'

'I know that. But we'd be buying control with it. Everybody on salary paid by the studios. That's money in the bank in the long run'

3

Although she saw her mother several times each day and the hours they spent together were as easy and warm and rewarding as they had always been, Sophie held in her mind constantly the earlier conversation they'd had about Arthur Tagg. It buzzed about her ears like a persistent mosquito, annoyed and unsettled her. As she sat in the dining hall each evening with her mother and Arthur, Arthur at table's head, Margaret on his right and Sophie on his left, she felt resentment simmering inside her. She felt like a guest in her own home, a maiden aunt who'd stayed on after the Christmas holidays.

Arthur, who always dressed for dinner now, sat easily in his great carved chair, his stiff-bosomed shirt crisp and white in the candle-light, his tie like a black satin butterfly nestled under his chin. He was talkative now in a way she had never known him to be. Quips and anecdotes, well-composed toasts for special occasions, long conversations with Margaret about the tenant farmers, the price of land in York or Durham, the shortcomings of Richard Brattle, the young veterinary surgeon who had taken over the practice of retiring Dr Gallop.

Arthur had become amusing now, in a way that was new to him, using impersonation and mimicry and ridicule for comic effect. Sophie couldn't remember seeing her mother laugh so heartily, and she herself pretended that she was enormously amused. But in truth she was offended by Arthur's relaxed grace at the table, his manner with the staff as they served, his studied tasting of the wine and the port and the brandy, his kind but firm rejection of a portion of mutton that was not cooked to his liking. Once his habits and his stories began to annoy her, she found she was annoyed by everything he did or said. His very presence unsettled her, his increasing identification as the central figure, the decisive voice, at Wiswell Towers.

Equally disturbing was the fact that she seemed to have become invisible to him. She rarely saw him now during the day. He was often away, handling estate affairs, meeting with solicitors and accountants, or lunching at clubs he'd joined in Carlisle or Newcastle. And he had become remarkably authoritative in the area of Northumberland politics. He mentioned one evening that he had been suggested as a possible candidate for the House of Commons.

'What a fine idea,' Margaret said. 'What did you say?'

Deftly touching the corners of his mouth with a napkin,

he said, 'Good Lord, no. That's what I said. I told them I'm a poor but honest man with none of the skills necessary for public life.'

The following morning Sophie asked her mother if she believed that Arthur had been approached to become a candidate for Parliament. 'You've known Arthur as long as I have. Have you ever heard him say something that wasn't true?'

'I didn't mean he was lying exactly. I felt he might have exaggerated a bit. Or perhaps he misunderstood what was being said to him.'

'Arthur's the most honest man I've ever met. I would never question anything he said.'

Such dialogues with her mother only fuelled Sophie's discontent in the matter of Arthur. She considered having a frank discussion with him. Candid questions and honest answers. If it became a confrontation, so be it. Perhaps discomfort or anger would clarify a situation which she now saw as hopelessly muddled. It was hard to imagine Arthur's losing control, saying anything he hadn't carefully considered, difficult to imagine his revealing even the smallest facet of his private self. But it was worth a try, she told herself. When a situation nagged at her during all her waking hours and kept her from sleeping properly at night, unusual means were justified to bring it to some satisfactory conclusion, to clarify attitudes, to correct misunderstandings, to put a long-valued relationship on course again.

All her conclusions seemed reasonable to her. Each night as she sat at dinner watching Margaret and Arthur chatting amiably together, seeing her mother's rapt attention when he spoke of grain prices, the wool market, or the falling value of shares because of the military threat from Germany, or hearing her delighted laughter when he impersonated Neville Chamberlain, Sophie felt smaller and smaller, like a neighbour child in a high-chair who'd been taken in for a meal but would be driven home just after the trifle was served.

This is not to say that she took no part in the dinner conversations. It was chemically impossible for her to have no opinions. And she never hesitated to voice them. Both her mother and Arthur seemed to listen attentively when she spoke. But when the conversation between the two of them resumed it was as though Sophie's comments had in no way influenced their private dialogue. She spoke to them but they spoke only to each other. Trying to describe the situation in a letter to Kincaid she wrote:

> One evening I will come down to dinner in my loveliest silk negligee, slip it off as I enter the dining hall, take my seat at table, and enjoy my dinner totally nude. I'm sure they would notice but I don't believe any comment would be made.

Such slivers of humour were rare in the dead-serious frustration she felt as she plodded through each day, consulting with the architect and the construction supervisor, and religiously overseeing the workmen and decorators, pointing out their errors of taste or execution. The prospect of a serious down-to-earth discussion with Arthur seemed more and more inevitable to her, whatever the consequences might be. In the end, however, that word *consequences* frightened her off. She couldn't promise herself that she'd be able to control the anger that had been building inside her for weeks. A lifetime's observation of her father, Major Cranston, had taught her the folly of words spoken in anger, the permanent damage, the wounds that couldn't be healed. Also, there was no way of knowing what reactions might come from Arthur. It was hard to imagine him truly angry, particularly with a woman, with her, impossible to think of him turning mean and vindictive. But what if he did, how would that affect Margaret? Would the house come tumbling down? Could a rift open between Sophie and her mother? After all their years together was it possible that one of them might say, 'How dare you?' to the other? The thought caused Sophie to hesitate.

At last, unable to face a confrontation with Arthur but also unable to live with what she considered an intolerable situation, she decided to sheathe her weapons and attack with honey and sweet cream. She decided to write him a letter. She wrote and rewrote and edited it over a period of three days. At last she concluded that it was a civilized but clear expression of her feelings. She put it into an envelope, rang for Trout and asked him to deliver it straightaway to Arthur.

My dear Arthur,

In all the activity and commotion since my return home from America, I'm afraid I've failed to convey the great admiration I feel for you. Along with the old affection from my childhood. But mostly there's simply a sense of warm gratitude because of your presence here, because of your ability to put behind you the events and the memories that caused you to leave in the first place.

Margaret, despite all she's been through, is not a helpless, shattered woman. I thank God for that. It seems like a miracle to me. And you are certainly a part of that miracle. Seeing you here at the Towers, calm and solid and capable, was a tonic for her, I'm sure. Seeing Trout and Mrs Whitson and the staff assembled the day I brought her home from Wingate Fields, and you there beside them, did a great deal, I expect, to carry her back to the way things were before that ugly day last autumn.

It's clear to me, clear to everyone, I suppose, that you're a different man now, that you feel differently now that the Major's gone. Your appearance is different and your manner is different. You're also different in your attitude toward me and that disturbs me. I know you resisted some of the improvements in the Towers that I've put in motion. Now, however, I believe I've made my position clear on those changes. Or perhaps I haven't.

One other thing disturbs me. I have the feeling that you expect my presence here to be a temporary thing, just till we're sure that Margaret's solid again. That is not the case, Arthur. I plan to spend a great deal of time here. Perhaps all my time. Kincaid will also be here as much as he's able, and I'm hoping that Evan will make the Towers his home again.

This estate is called Wiswell Towers because it's our family home. After Margaret's gone it will belong to me, just as it belonged to her after her mother died. When I'm gone it will belong to Kincaid, then to Trevor and Sarah. This does not mean that you are excluded. Quite the contrary. I promise there will always be a place here for you and Evan.

That evening, when Sophie went down to dinner there was only one place set. When she came into the dining hall Trout said, 'Your mother ate early in her rooms. She asked me to tell you she's taken a sleeping-powder and she'll see you at breakfast.'

'I'll just run up to say good-night before I have my dinner.'

'She asked me to say that she didn't want to be disturbed tonight.'

'I see,' Sophie said. She looked toward the table. 'And Mr Tagg won't be dining either?'

'Mrs Whitson said he drove over to the inn late this afternoon. Meeting some gentlemen there, I expect.'

'Thank you, Trout.' When she walked to the table she said, 'Since I'm dining alone, please set my place at the head of the table.'

Trout quickly changed the place setting and seated her in the great carved chair. 'Will you have a glass of champagne?' he asked.

'Yes, I will. I may have a great deal of champagne.'

She slept late the next morning. When she woke at last, she rang for breakfast to be brought to her room. When the tray arrived there was a note from Margaret.

> Please come to see me after you've finished your
> breakfast.

After breakfast, Sophie's maid shampooed her hair and she
had a long soak in the tub. It was midday when she walked
along the corridor to her mother's rooms. Margaret was sitting
in an armchair near the fireplace. Arthur sat in a matching
chair just opposite her.

'Come sit by the fire,' Margaret said. 'Shall we have some
tea?'

'None for me, thank you. I had a late breakfast.'

Sophie sat in a straight chair facing the fireplace, Margaret
to her left, Arthur to her right. There was a heavy silence,
only the sound of the fire hissing and humming. At last
Margaret indicated an envelope on the table by her chair.
'I think we should talk about this note you sent along to Arthur
yesterday.'

'Am I on trial?' Sophie said. She glanced at Arthur whose
eyes were fixed on Margaret. 'Your note said you wanted
to talk with me. If I'm to be attacked or grilled from both
the right and the left, I think I'll excuse myself.'

'I hope you're not going to be rude about this,' Margaret
said.

'I make no promises, Mother. I'm afraid I'll have to wait
and see what sort of meeting this is meant to be.'

'I was baffled by your note. I thought maybe you might
be willing to explain it to us.'

'As I remember, it was all quite clear. If you hand it to
me, I'll read it aloud. Beyond that, I have no explanation
to offer.'

'You're really very angry, aren't you?'

'I'm damned surprised at what you're doing. I'm not a
schoolgirl who slipped out of her room to have a cigarette
in the lavatory. How did you expect me to react to this minia-
ture kangaroo-court?' She looked at Arthur, then back to

Margaret. 'Will Arthur be making a speech later or are you carrying the entire burden for the prosecution?'

'Arthur didn't want to be here. I insisted that he stay.'

'Did you insist that he run to you with my note as soon as he got it?'

'I'm glad he came to me. Arthur was confused and hurt by what you wrote.'

'Then why didn't he tell me that?'

'As I said, he was hurt.'

'As I recall, I used words like admiration and affection and gratitude.'

'Why couldn't you have stopped there?' Margaret said.

'Because I had other things to say.'

Arthur stood up suddenly. He took a step toward Margaret and said, 'I'll leave you two alone now. I'm afraid it was a mistake for me to be here.' He turned and left the room.

'Oh, dear,' Margaret said. 'Now what?' When Sophie didn't reply she said, 'I'm afraid you've put me in a dreadfully awkward position.'

'I don't see how. If you're in an uncomfortable spot, it's Arthur who's put you there. He chose to include you in a private matter between him and myself. What did he expect you to do, scold me?'

'I'm sure he thought you might explain why you wrote to him in that way.'

'Oh, for the love of God, Mother. You can't be surprised. I've tried several times to talk to you about it, to explain how uncomfortable Arthur makes me feel, but you haven't been willing to discuss it. So I chose to go directly to him, to let him know what's on my mind.'

'You certainly did that. In no uncertain terms.'

'Why shouldn't I let him know how I feel? I'm not a potted plant. Are you saying that Arthur's feelings must be protected at all costs?'

'No. I'm saying that none of us should say cruel things to each other.'

'I said nothing I'm ashamed of in that note. Sometimes

it's more unkind to say nothing. If Arthur feels offended why doesn't he speak up and say how I've offended him? Why did he stomp out of the room like a child?'

'I expect he felt uncomfortable.'

'I feel uncomfortable. So do you. Why is Arthur the only one who must never be uncomfortable?' When Margaret didn't answer she went on. 'Does he think I'm someone whose views can simply be dismissed? Do you feel that way as well? I can't believe you do, but when I'm summoned here like a naughty child, what am I to think?'

After a long moment Margaret said, 'We know each other very well, Sophie. We always have. Not only are you my only child, you're my closest friend. We've always understood each other. Now . . . all at once, I don't know what's happening. I've never seen you in a state like this.'

'I'm not in a state at all. I'm quite calm. You see, this is a matter to be settled between Arthur and me. There's no reason for you to be involved.'

'How can I not be? When two people who are dear to me are at odds with each other how can I stand aside and pretend not to notice?'

'But that's precisely how I feel. How can I pretend not to notice? Did you read my note carefully? Didn't I make clear what troubles me?'

'Of course I read your note. Several times. And yes, you did express yourself clearly. But you must realize that what you said was less important than the way you said it. There was an attitude expressed that astonished me. It was like a warning note to a servant. Not a threat of dismissal but a reminder that such action might be taken.'

'Nonsense. I was the one who persuaded Arthur to come back here. Begged him to come back.'

'Exactly. All the more reason he should be confused by what you wrote in your letter.'

'How could I have been more clear? If you read again what I wrote you'll see that I said both Arthur and Evan would always have a home here.'

Margaret nodded. 'Yes, you were clear about that. If you'd been addressing an old nanny who no longer could function in the household, or a stable-hand who'd been crippled by a horse, it would have been a generous gesture. But it's condescending and offensive to say such a thing to Arthur. He's not a servant and never has been and he must not be treated as one. Not for a moment.'

'I am being scolded after all,' Sophie said.

'I never scolded you as a child and I'm not scolding you now. But I feel obliged to express my views just as you do. You've created a situation and I'm trying to find a way to make it better.'

'If there's a situation it wasn't *my* doing.'

Margaret shook her head. 'Have it your way, dear. Let me put it another way. Whatever the cause, a situation does exist. And since it seems unlikely that either you or Arthur can resolve it, it's up to me to do whatever I can.'

'Why do I feel that I'm the errant servant who's about to be dismissed?'

'I have no idea why you would feel that or say that. This is your home. You're a Wiswell. You made that very clear in your letter to Arthur. And it's true. If this foolishness that's developed between you and Arthur can't be dispelled somehow, if the two of you can't put it aside, I will not be put in the position of taking sides in your quarrel. Nor will I see this wonderful home turned into a house of strangers as it was when the Major was alive. So if you and Arthur have declared war against each other it mustn't be fought here. If someone must leave, then Arthur will go. He may have already decided to go. When the smoke settles, we'll see.'

'But we mustn't allow him to go,' Sophie said. 'That was never my intention. I wouldn't want to be responsible for that.'

'But you are responsible. Surely you realize that. The reason I didn't involve myself when you complained to me before about Arthur was because I didn't want to enlarge on the question. I hoped it would solve itself. But it hasn't. Now it's crystallized and become worse.'

'Why don't I go to Arthur and sit down and have a talk with him? Just the two of us. Would you like that?'

'It's not a question of what I might like. I would like it if the situation didn't exist. I would like it if you hadn't felt the need to write this letter.'

'But the situation does exist and I did write the letter. Now it's a question of whether Arthur and I should talk.'

'I can't answer that. I suppose it depends a great deal on what you plan to say. I assume you don't intend to be apologetic in any way.'

'Of course not. I have nothing to apologize for.'

'In that case I think it would be pointless to talk. As you said earlier your letter was very clear. If that still represents your feelings, then I think there's no benefit that will come from repeating those feelings to Arthur.'

'I disagree. When two people are reasonable . . .'

'But two people at odds with each other are never reasonable. When one's shortcomings are being pointed out the reaction is usually quite unreasonable. You are firmly convinced you're in no way at fault, so your only recourse is to convince Arthur that he's at fault. I assure you, the chances are slim that he would be convinced.'

'Then that proves my point about him.'

'Does it?'

'Yes, I believe it does.'

'Well, whether it does or not, I don't see further discussion as a solution just now. I think matters should be allowed to simmer down and cool off. My best suggestion would be for you to go down to London for a while. When you come back in a few weeks perhaps you'll discover that the situation, as we call it, has taken a turn for the better.'

'Running away is never an answer, is it?'

'Going away, going home to London, is not quite the same as running away.'

'It seems the same to me. And besides, even if I wanted to go, I can't go just now. This is a critical period in the renovation. I must be here to watch over things.'

'There's nothing that wants doing that I can't do. The structural work is finished. You told me so yourself. Now it's largely a matter of plaster and paint and fixtures to be mounted. Doors and shutters to be hung. Carpets laid. That sort of thing.'

'But I must be here for all that. I need to finish what I've started.'

'I hope you're not saying you must finish what you've started with Arthur.'

'I'll admit I don't like to run away from problems. You know that.'

'Trust me when I say your best move is to go home to London for a bit.'

'I trust you, Margaret, but I can't go. Not just now.'

4

Two days before Julian Thorne was scheduled to fly to New York, he arranged for Daisy Bishop to meet with him in his office. When she was sitting across from him, facing his desk, he said, 'Are you feeling all right?'

'I'm OK, I guess. Why? Do I look funny?'

'You never look funny. You're a beautiful girl. Young and healthy. Twenty-five years old in March. The twenty-first.'

'Boy, you remember everything, don't you? Sometimes I feel like I can't remember my own name but you've got all the facts and figures right there in your head.'

Julian smiled, 'Your name was Florence Early till I changed it to Daisy Bishop. You come from Elkhart, Indiana, you've got two brothers and a sister named Eileen and your dad works in a hardware shop.'

'There you go. What did I tell you?'

'Wait a minute,' he said, 'I'm not finished. Since you've

233

been under contract to Thornwood you've done nine pictures for us and four on loan-out. You scored big in *Bushranger* and *Dillinger*, two of our strongest hits . . .'

'And now I get to do a picture with Joel McCrea.'

'That's right. Name above the title. Just like I promised. The first day you came on the lot I told you you could do important things in this business.'

'I remember,' she said. 'I almost peed my pants when you said that.'

'And it's all happening. Just like I said.'

'I pinch myself every day. I know it's real, what's happening to me, but I still can't believe it.'

'It's real, Daisy. The camera loves you, audiences love you, and everybody here at Thornwood loves you. If we don't make mistakes you'll have an important career.'

'I work hard,' she said. 'I try to do every scene in two or three takes at most. I don't make any mistakes if I can help it.'

'We all know that,' Julian said. 'But we can make mistakes, too, you know. Putting you in roles that don't suit you, casting the wrong men opposite you, not marketing your films the way we should. We have to be careful with everything. Things can backfire. Bad publicity. Silly rumours.'

'I don't fool around,' she said. 'No scandal in my life. I'm married and that's it. There's nothing bad for anybody to write about me.'

'I'm sure of that. But sometimes reporters get wild ideas. If they can't find a good story they make one up. Look at the fairy-tales they print about Kincaid.'

'I know. I've seen some of that stuff. It's awful. They even keep saying there's something up between him and me.'

'I know. They're stuck on that story. It started when we were on location with *Bushranger*. There's nothing to it, is there?'

'What do you mean? Gosh, no.'

'I'm not trying to run your private life but on the other hand I've got a big stake in it. We used to be able to get

234

away with a lot out here. We could do the stories we wanted to do and our actors could sleep with anybody they liked, snort a little cocaine and drink gin by the barrel. But things have tightened up. That's why all our stars have morals clauses in their contracts now. We've got Church groups to deal with, the American Legion, the City of Boston, all kinds of people looking over our shoulders. Barrymore or Errol Flynn can get as drunk as they want and screw anybody they take a shine to. But a young girl like you, especially if people know she's married, has to watch her step. You know what I'm saying?'

'Sure I do. I mean, I guess I do. But like I just told you, I don't mess around.'

'And I believe you. But tell me again. You see our publicity people can do all kinds of miracles if they know the truth. What's hard to deal with are surprises. So if I seem to be prying into your business it's for your good as well as mine.'

'I know what you're saying. But what am I supposed to tell you?'

'I'm concerned about the Kincaid stories. When something like that keeps popping up, pretty soon people believe it's true just because they've heard it for so long. And next thing you know people are saying, "That's Daisy Bishop. She's married to Bob Sample but she's sleeping with Kincaid."'

'Did somebody say that to you?'

'No. But that doesn't mean it's not being said.'

'That makes me feel awful. If anybody ever said that to Bob, he'd kill me.'

'What's he say when he sees stories about you in the paper?'

'About me and Kincaid? He gets mad as hell. He thinks every guy in pants is after me and he says what you do. If there's nothing going on with me and Kincaid, why do the papers keep writing about it? He says half the women in town have a crush on Kincaid, so why should I be the exception? I told Bob I've never been alone with him in my life, not even for a cup of coffee. But I don't think he believes me.

I've talked with Kincaid on the set, like I would with anybody else. But that's all.'

'All right. That's good to know. I'm going to New York this week and we'll be talking about the publicity campaign for your picture with McCrea. I'll tell them that they should spike any rumours about you and Kincaid because I give my personal guarantee they're not true. Can I say that?'

'Sure you can. It's the truth.'

'Good. Now let me ask you a couple more things.'

'You're making me awful nervous. All this time I've worked for you, you never asked me stuff like this.'

'It's business, Daisy, nothing else. Dollars and cents. Up till now you didn't have dollar signs around your head. Now you do. From now on, your pictures will either lose a lot of money or make a lot of money depending on what you do or don't do.'

'That's scary. It makes my hands sweat.'

'Nothing to fret about. It just means you're important enough to worry about now. That should make you feel good.'

'I do feel good but it's still scary. What else did you want to ask me?'

'We've had reports from the make-up department that they've had some problems. They say your eyes have been swollen when you showed up in the morning for make-up. They also report bruises on your face and arms. I want you to tell me about that.'

'Oh . . . well . . . sometimes if I'm nervous about a scene I don't sleep so good the night before. And the bruises . . . I don't know. I guess I'm just clumsy. I bump into things a lot.'

'Tell me the truth, Daisy. Gene Clymer in make-up said your eyes looked as if you'd been crying. And nobody gets bruises on their neck by bumping into things.'

'I don't know what to say.'

'Are you having trouble at home?'

'No . . . I mean . . . no, there's nothing wrong.'

'Yes, there is.'

236

'I mean, it's nobody's fault. If it's anybody's fault, it's me. Bob's not mean or anything but it's hard on him seeing me do so well. I mean, when I met him, when we got married, I was only sixteen and he was getting a good start in westerns at Monogram. People told him he was gonna be another Buck Jones. But he had some bad luck. Things just didn't break right for him. When you took me on here, we really needed the money. By then Bob was stuck with extra work, stand-in stuff, and an occasional stunt job. Nobody offered him speaking parts any more, not even under-fives. So like I said, it was driving him crazy. It still is. He's a big good-looking guy and he's a crackerjack with horses and guns. So he just can't understand why the whole business gave up on him. I don't understand it either. Then when things started happening for me, when any time the phone rang he knew it was somebody calling me, and then a little later when you found us our big house on Rossmore and there was a car and driver waiting for me any time I wanted to go some place, it really got his goat. Bob studied one summer at the Pasadena Playhouse. Did you know that? I mean, he knows a lot about acting. So when he sees me, a dumb kid from Indiana who didn't finish high school . . . when he sees my picture in the papers and on bill-boards, you can imagine how it makes him feel. He doesn't mean to hurt me. But after he's had a few drinks, he gets mad at the world and he has to take it out on somebody. Like I say, it's usually my fault. I say something dumb or I don't understand something he's trying to explain to me, and he flies clear off the handle. He can't help it. That's just the way he is. You know how it is with some guys . . .'

'No, I don't know how it is. I just know how it is with me. I'm running a business here. Millions of dollars involved. Hundreds of people on the payroll and sheds full of equipment. If somebody damages any of our lights or our cameras we make a great effort to see that the person responsible pays for the damage. If they steal from us we try to get them put in jail. It's not because we're mean or vindictive. It's because if we lose one day's work, if we lose one hour, it costs us a

237

great deal of money. And if an actor can't work, if one of our key people can't be photographed for some reason, can't do his scheduled scenes in front of the camera, then we're really in trouble. You understand what I'm saying?'

'Yes.'

'It doesn't matter to me how angry Bob Sample gets or what he's angry about. He must be made to understand that if you can't work because of something he's done to you, then he's taking money out of my pocket. And I won't let him do that. Someone has to give him that message. Do you want to do it or shall I have my brother Sam talk to him?'

'I couldn't tell him,' she said. 'I can't tell him anything. If he even knew I'm talking to you like this, he'd kill me.'

Julian shook his head. 'No, he's not going to kill you or frighten you or put bruises on you. We will explain the situation to him, and if he can't accept our point of view we'll move you into one of our dressing-room apartments the week before we start shooting the McCrea picture. You'll stay there till we wrap. And your husband won't be allowed on the lot.'

'I can't do that, can I? How can I do that? What will I tell Bob?'

'You don't have to tell him anything. Sam will tell him.'

'Gee . . . I don't know . . .'

'You have to know, Daisy. As I told you before, I don't want to run your life or your husband's life, but I'm damned determined to run this studio. If your first loyalty is to your husband I won't try to change that. But my first loyalty is to my production schedule. If you're not willing to do this film with McCrea the way it must be done, I can pick up that telephone and have a deal with Frances Dee or Jean Parker in ten minutes.'

'Wait a minute. You told me you bought this story for me. You borrowed Joel McCrea because I asked you to. I'm gonna be above the title. You said so yourself just a little while ago.'

'That's right. I did. This picture was planned for you and

written for you. It's a perfect part for you. But only if I can depend on you, only if you do what I say. I want you on this lot from the first set-up till we wrap. Just say yes or no.'

'Yes,' she said. Julian got up, came around his desk, and kissed her on the forehead. 'You won't be sorry, Daisy. We're going to make a great film together.'

When she stood up to leave she said, 'I never saw you like this. I feel like I was run over by a truck.'

'Don't worry about it. That truck has a picture of you on both sides. And a loud-speaker inside blasting your name.'


## 5


If Evan had felt at odds with himself before his drunken evening with Alan Winkler, that condition was much intensified afterward. The self-deception he'd been practising, his conviction that his only problem was to find a proper place to do his work, was no longer possible after Winkler's sharp diagnosis. He was forced to admit to himself that the work itself was the problem. No subject seemed profound enough or sufficiently provocative. Whereas before his adventure in Hollywood he had made long lists of subjects and characters and situations he wanted to explore in his plays, now, as Alan had pointed out, he sat staring out the window waiting for lightning to strike. He realized he was behaving like a mindless and pragmatic film producer, playing results, trying to flush out a sure-fire, audience-pleasing idea for a story that would guarantee production, distribution, and profit long before the first page of dialogue had been written.

All his instincts and experience told him that a true starting-point must be human pain, not a car crash, a flood, or a building on fire. Still, every situation that came into his mind quickly turned into a series of pictures and camera angles.

One afternoon he went to a cinema palace in Charing Cross

Road where *Dillinger* was being shown and sat through three showings, examining every scene critically, surgically isolating each piece of action, each line of dialogue, each emotional moment. When he left the theatre he realized he'd been watching a Kincaid film, a Tim Garrigus film, a Julian Thorne film. No visible or audible evidence of Evan Tagg. Or so it seemed. No evidence of the writer in the work. Even the dialogue which he had slaved and suffered over seemed secondary, or slightly altered by the actors, or inconsequential. This experience, which one might have expected to send him straight to his typewriter to reassert and redefine himself, had, in fact, no such effect. He simply returned to the chair in his flat and continued to look out of the window. Instead of asking himself, 'What must I do now?' he asked himself, 'What have I done?' And even for that empty question he could find no definitive answer.

If Evan had expected that his claret-stimulated dialogue with Winkler would somehow ease the situation he found himself in with regard to his writing, he would have been disappointed. One purpose was served, however. His attempts to grapple with that situation forced him into areas which he thought were less dangerous but which, when explored, were more tangled and complex than his quandaries about where he should work and what he should write. Once he allowed himself to dwell on Mary Cecil, and Sophie, and Sarah, he began to see the true colours and dimensions of the emotional williwaw in which he found himself.

When he had contacted Mary, he knew the risk he was taking. Although he had concluded, when they broke up, that, painful as it was, it was the only solution to their problems, he realized that making fresh contact, being together, being alone together, even in a public place, could possibly bring to life again something they both believed was finished. But he chose to take that risk, looked forward to it in a way, not because he was certain he could resist a new entanglement but because he sensed that some reckless illogical part of him might welcome it.

The time they'd spent together, first in the wine-bar, then in the coffee-shop nearby, had not been the wrung-out, anxious meeting of separated lovers. Each of them wanted information from the other and that searching process, the careful listening and slow absorption of answers, had characterized the hour-and-a-half, two hours perhaps, they'd spent together. More research than rendezvous. More curiosity than passion. When they parted, no wistful looks were exchanged, no suggestions made about future meetings, no reference to what once was or what might have been.

As Evan walked home after putting her in a taxi he felt a sense of completeness because of the new information he'd received. He had a better understanding now of what had taken place between them. And he was relieved that there had been no tears or recriminations. 'It had to be done,' he said to himself. 'We did it and now it's over.'

When he was alone in his flat, however, as he sat with one dim lamp lit and sipped brandy, he felt drained suddenly, dry and empty. How could they have been so matter-of-fact toward each other? How could those days and nights of touch and taste and smell be so quickly forgotten? Or if not forgotten, somehow discounted. To her he was simply something from the past now. Just as Burt Windrow was. It wasn't a matter of speaking well of the dead. The credo seemed to be, 'Let's not speak of them at all.' We were together . . . now we're apart . . . fiddle-dee-dee and let's get on with it.

He had an impulse toward anger but he couldn't fan it to flame because he knew that her feelings, or apparent lack of feeling, were matched by his. He told himself that after an angry separation one grows cold because one must. First line of defence: 'I won't be hurt because I won't let it matter to me.'

But he had been hurt. It was a clear and jagged memory. But it was just that. No warm breath. No blood pumping. It seemed as distant now as the cottage in Malibu, as though Mary had been provided to him by Thornwood Studios,

241

as house and car had been provided.

Any blame he tried to put on her began to turn back on him. How could the passage of a few months totally obliterate a person, a relationship, a life, that he had believed was the centre of his work, his pleasure, his very existence? Even if wisdom and experience told him they were lovers ill-met, that other people and other tangled lives stood between them, even if he had managed to accept fully the fact of their separation, shouldn't he have some residual feeling, shouldn't he regret that parting and her absence? Sitting across the table from her, shouldn't the last nights they'd spent together in California be bursting like festival rockets in his brain? Shouldn't he be longing for her, for every soft and familiar part of her? Since the body has no conscience, no reason, no caution, why was his body not yearning for hers?

For all his questions he found no answers. For an instant he tried to make some correlation between the conversation with Winkler about his work and his feelings, or lack of feeling, toward Mary. He quickly sensed, however, that he was on chancy ground and allowed the two elements to wrench themselves apart.

Evan was disturbed in quite another way by Sarah. Was it the Windrow connection? He told himself no. But all the same it seemed strange that a man he had never met and had seen only once had slipped into his life as an intimate of two women, neither of whom knew each other but both of whom knew Evan. If it had given Evan's stomach a jolt when he learned that the excerpts from letters he'd received anonymously at the studio were actually passionate valentines from Mary to Windrow, his knowledge that the man who had inspired such letters had also practised sexual voodoo on Sarah's sixteen-year-old body produced a reaction in Evan that he was unable to deal with or classify. He told himself that it was like a father's reaction to the end of a daughter's innocence, but that explanation didn't satisfy him. Nor was he satisfied by any other explanation he came up with. Although he told himself repeatedly that it was not his business, and resolved to put it out of his mind, he was unable to do that.

Evan's new preoccupation with Sophie was another matter altogether. The hours he'd spent with her at the Towers since coming home from California till after the holidays when Kincaid returned, that time had stirred memories in each of them of the years when they had grown up together, studied together, and played together. And fought with each other as well.

Until they were there in Northumberland, until they were together every day, they hadn't realized how seldom they'd seen each other in the past two or three years. When Sophie mentioned this one afternoon, Evan said, 'What did you expect? You're a married woman. Busy with her husband and children. Shopping and lunching and popping into the theatre whenever the mood strikes you. No time for old friends.'

'Don't pass it off on me. You're the most unavailable chap in Britain. Even in California I never saw you. Our houses were no more than six miles apart but you were never to be found. Closeted day and night with your actress friend, Miss Dolly Drop-drawers.'

The afternoon he came up from London after his arrival in Southampton, she trailed along after him when the porter took his bag upstairs. As soon as they were alone in his rooms she said, 'These are the ground rules. Your job is to entertain me and make me smile. This has been a gloomy place these past weeks and I have been as serious and responsible and dour as the next person. Even Sarah and Trevor are silent and long-faced for some adolescent reasons that escape me. I expect they're not mourning for Brannigan since they didn't really know him, and God knows, they were never closely bound to the Major. But all the same, Sarah, as she will undoubtedly tell you at great length, put on an overwrought performance when she first arrived. Her grandfather had been shamefully mistreated by his family, principally Margaret and me. That was her thesis. It was never clear to

243

me what she planned to do to set things right but I allowed
her to sob and rail at me and flounce about for a few days,
and at last she lost interest in her cause and returned to
normal, if there is such a state in Sarah's case. Your father,
too, who was never a bundle of laughs, has been more
restrained than usual. Margaret, thank God, who has
suffered the most, seems less eager than others to wear grief
on her sleeve. As for me, I feel as though I'm held captive
here, like the only flesh-and-blood exhibit at Madame
Tussaud's. So I welcome you, old friend, and I charge you,
as I've said, to bring a bit of joy into my days. Amusing anecdotes will be appropriate, outrageous plays on words, and
little songs of the season. If you require a cap and bell I'm
sure we can find those things for you.'

Evan was delighted and relieved to fall into the rhythm
Sophie proposed. Without showing disrespect for the general
unhappiness at the Towers, they discreetly and in private
enjoyed themselves. When they referred to the past they edited
out all unpleasantness. No references to her first marriage
or to the strain and frustration of life with the Major.

No mention either of the period, much more recent, when,
after her marriage to Kincaid, Evan, under the pretence that
he was totally occupied with his play, didn't see either of
them for months. When he referred one day to his break-
up with Mary Cecil, Sophie said, 'I don't want to hear about
her. If you promise not to tell me about your life with an
actress, I promise not to tell you about my life with an actor.'

Not a serious statement. Evan knew that. They both
laughed when she said it. Occasionally, however, in the days
that followed, he thought of what she'd said. But after Kincaid
arrived from America that statement by Sophie became again
what it had been originally, simply a clever remark without
meaning.

The only times they sat down and talked seriously was
when they discussed Evan's work. That work, in Sophie's
mind, did not include writing for the screen. 'You're a playwright. You can be a wonderful playwright. That's what you

should be doing. That's what you must do.'

She was eloquent on the subject of the theatre. Since childhood she'd been captivated by plays, reading them and seeing them performed. Evan had always suspected that one of the reasons she'd moved to London after Toby's death was so she could be within walking distance of the West End theatres. Sophie was the only person, apart from Alan Winkler, who had read every play Evan had written. She remembered the story of each one and the names of the characters, long after they'd become muddled in his mind, mixed in with the people and the events of the piece he had worked on most recently. When *The Fatherhouse* had been produced she'd been in America, so she'd never seen it performed. 'But I read it again every few months,' she told him. 'It's a lovely play.'

She always insisted that *The Fatherhouse* was her play. 'I got you started on that one. I remember very clearly the day I told you that you'd never do your best work till you put more of yourself into it, till you dealt with people you know doing things you understand. That's when you wrote *The Fatherhouse*. Am I right?'

'That's right.'

'So I deserve all the credit,' she said. 'Hooray for me.'

'The play wasn't successful. Do you take credit for that, too?'

'No matter. It will be done again some day and everyone will see what a heavenly piece of work it is and what a wonderful writer you are.'

Evan had learned early on that careless criticism can be very destructive to a writer. He had concluded also that praise can do the same sort of damage. 'Consider the source,' he always told himself. 'When it's a friend who's speaking, neither praise nor criticism has value. It's like kissing your aunt. You can't take it seriously.'

None the less, when Sophie spoke at length about his work, when she expressed so clearly what he had attempted to do, when she told him how splendidly he had done it, it was an exhilarating experience for him. But when he tried to toss it off, when he said, 'You're the best possible audience. You're easy to please', she came back at him. 'No, I'm not. I'm damned hard to please. Sometimes I think I'm impossible to please. Don't be an ass, Evan. Just because I say you're good doesn't make you worthless. You think you're good, or you wouldn't be a writer. And I know you're good.'

When she showed him the rooms she was having prepared for him in the north tower, he knew that was all a part of her encouragement, of her urging him to go ahead with his work. And when he admired what she'd done and told her the rooms were indeed a perfect place to live and write, he meant just that, nothing more. It never occurred to him that when she was at the Towers she liked him to be there also. If it did occur to him he refused to admit it to himself.

6

The day after Julian flew to New York, Sam Thorne called Leon Barkin in the casting department and asked him to bring in Bob Sample.

'What picture are we talking about, Sam?'

'I don't know. What westerns we got coming up?'

'*Comanche Trail* starts shooting next week at Red Rock and five weeks later the Tim McCoy picture starts at Lone Pine. What do you want to offer him?'

'Nothing yet. Just tell him I want to talk to him.'

The next day, late in the afternoon, Sample sat in Sam's office. He was a tall man. Wide shoulders. Deep chest. Weathered skin and strong features except for a softness around his mouth. Like the other men who made their living by working in western films, from Tom Mix and Ken Maynard down to worst-paid wrangler or atmosphere extra, Sample always wore western clothes. At home, on the street, in his car, everywhere he went, even to the Grove or La Boheme or the Embassy Club, every shirt or jacket, even his dinner-clothes, were cut western style and worn with hand-made boots. The actors who liked him often said, 'Old Bobby sits a horse better than Cooper, handles a gun better than the best of them, and the women go for him, ain't no doubt about that. It's a mystery he's never turned into a big star.' On the other hand, the men who detested him, who'd make an excuse to walk out of a bar if he walked in, had a different opinion. 'Sample ain't worth a shit. Livin' off his wife and beatin' up on guys half his size. That's his speed. And it's all right there on his face. You get a close-up shot of him and he ain't good for nothing except to play the part of a dirty heavy. Nobody wants to hire him any more but he struts around like he's Hoot Gibson or somebody big.'

Sam Thorne had his own double definition of Sample. On the one hand he was an out-of-work cowboy type with a bad reputation – Leon Barkin wouldn't have recommended him for any Thornwood picture, and no film executive would have had a reason to talk to him. On the other hand Sample was married to Daisy Bishop, one of Thornwood's valuable people. So, as her husband, Sample had special entrée. Certain exceptions were made. But all the same, this was the first time he'd ever been asked to meet with Sam in his office.

'I haven't seen you for a while,' Sam said. 'When was the last time?'

'The *Dillinger* wrap party. When was that, early December?'

'December fifth. And we had prints in all our theatres in time for Christmas. You must have been proud of Daisy. She did a hell of a job.'

A killer grin from Sample. 'She's starting to get the hang of it. When I met her she was working behind the counter in a hash-house on Ventura Boulevard. I'm not saying I taught her everything she knows, but she'd be the first one to admit she didn't know nothing before I took hold of her.'

'Well, she certainly knows something now. So I guess you deserve a lot of credit.'

'She's still a kid but she's coming along.'

247

'What's happening with you these days? Everybody in town's shooting westerns. You must have more work than you can handle.'

'I would if I took everything that was offered to me but I stopped doing that a couple of years back. Monogram wants to tie me up in a long-term deal and Bill Farley over at Universal's been after me for six months. But I've been around for a while, you know that, and I'm not gonna lock myself in for seven years without some control over what I'll be doing. No more Saturday serials and that kind of crap. I mean if you're willing to tie yourself up with second-raters, that's where you'll end up. Am I right?'

Sam nodded. 'You're right, Bob. If they want you bad enough, they'll bend a little.'

'That's the way I see it. And if they won't, I'd rather spend my afternoons down at Agua Caliente.'

'You're smart. Most actors won't make a tough stand like that. They're scared the studios will get down on them and they won't work at all.'

'That's the way I used to be. I was a sucker. Some casting guy would call me up and say, "It's a week's work. We need a savvy guy like you to do some horse falls and a saloon fight. No lines this time but we won't forget it if you do us a favour. Next time it'll be a different story." So I'd be a good guy and go along with it. Did that for three or four years. But I never got what I was promised. Just more of the same. So I laid the law down. I said I wanted second leads, good character-parts, or nothing. A year of that, I promised myself, then I'd be ready to play leads. I mean how many western stars can do the riding and fighting and physical stuff that I can do? Not very many. Nobody I can think of. Except Tom Tyler maybe.'

'Well, it sounds to me as if you've got things pretty well in hand. I had an idea that maybe we could talk a little business but you're way ahead of me. Two years from now, if things work out for you the way you've got them planned, we might be standing in line, willing to offer you any kind of a deal you want, but until things start to happen for you, till you get two or three good parts under your belt, I'm afraid all we could offer you is the sort of work you don't want to do. Now that I know how you feel about your career I'd advise you to sweat it out. Stick to your guns. It's like you say . . . if you don't think you're important, no one else will either.'

'I appreciate that,' Sample said. 'I'm glad you agree with me.' Then: 'Just out of curiosity, what kind of business did you want to talk to me about?'

Sam shook his head. 'Nothing that would interest you. I'm sure of that. It never became all that concrete. It was just a conversation I had with Julian a little while ago. Your name came up and I decided it might not be a bad idea to call you in and have a talk. I wanted to get some reaction from you. You know what I'm saying? I mean, it's a waste of everybody's time if you go too far and then find out your man isn't interested.'

'Who says I'm not interested?'

'You did. At least that's the way I heard it. As I said a minute ago, if you're going after leads or second leads we can't offer you anything like that.' Then: 'Look, why don't I tell you about the conversation I had with Julian? Then you'll see what I've been talking about. But when I'm finished, I guarantee you'll be pissed off and tell me I'm wasting your time. You want a cigar?' He held a humidor out to Sample and they both selected cigars and lit them. 'A week ago, maybe ten days, Julian and I were screening a print of *Bushranger*. You did some good work for us on that. It wasn't the kind of a part you're after. I guess you wouldn't call it a part at all, but you did some great riding stunts, you were on the screen a lot, and Garrigus gave you three or four tight close-ups. So you had a chance to register. When we came out of the screening-room Julian said, 'Bobby Sample's got a good look. We should be able to do something with him.' So later on I had a conversation with Barkin and he talked to a couple of our western directors,

Billy Watts and Fred Veach, and we sketched out a little plan. Then I decided I'd better sit down with you before we went any further. And I'm glad I did because I can see now that you're way ahead of us. I mean, what we're able to offer is not what you're looking for. You're talking about career roles and Julian is talking about making you a member of the Thornwood team, keeping you busy, bringing you along, with an eye to building you up gradually to the point where he could make you an important player in our western films.'

'And you think that wouldn't interest me?'

'Not from what you said. Watts and Veach know your work. Both of them said they'd want you to do some stunt work and help them choreograph fights and maybe double for the star. But you'd have a part in each picture, you'd have some lines, and they promised to beef your parts up as shooting goes along. When the pictures are finished, Julian wants to see a lot of your face on the screen.' Sam took a long puff on his cigar and squinted at Sample through the screen of smoke. 'I think you should mull it over for a couple of days, talk with Daisy about it. She might not want you to be away for so long. We're doing three westerns, back to back, one at Red Rock, one at Kanab, and one at Lone Pine. You'd be locked into all of them. You'd be away for almost three months. So think it over carefully and let me know how you feel. Then maybe we can get Barkin to put it down on paper and we'll have a deal. But don't sweat it. If it's not good for you, it's not good for us.'

250

# • CHAPTER 7 •

## 1

The previous October, when Kincaid had said goodbye to Homer Tony on the freighter wharf in San Pedro, when he'd watched him walk away from the black limousine, climb the gangway, and disappear on the deck of the *Rio de la Plata*, Kincaid had known it would be a long while before they would see each other again. He would send occasional picture postcards as he'd done when he'd left Australia as a boy, but he expected no reply from Homer Tony or anyone else at the Glenrowan cattle run unless Brig McBride, the top-kick, took a moment to scrawl a note on the back of an order form.

Although he had learned as a boy to read and write, Homer Tony seemed to have lost interest in communication after his voice was destroyed. He liked to listen, he was an attentive audience to the lies and whore-house tales that studded the dialogues of his bunk-mates and he had always concentrated fully on anything that Kincaid might say. But it was a one-way street. With Homer Tony, Kincaid only knew what his senses told him.

After Homer Tony's return to Australia from California, Kincaid had indeed sent him occasional postcards but he had received no replies except for a Christmas card sent to the studio with a message scrawled on it in HT's schoolboy hand: 'Keep your pecker up.'

Since he'd been back in London, however, with time on his hands, Kincaid had promised himself that he would write

251

a letter to Australia. At last he did it. One late night in his bedroom in the silent house in Queen's Walk.

I got your Christmas card, you ugly bastard. You must have sent it by donkey mail. It didn't get to me till February. I felt bad when I opened it because I could see how much time you'd spent composing the message. But at least you didn't tell me any bad news. So I guess you must be all right.

I'm back in London. Been here since early January. Sophie's old man died, plus some other troubles at her home place in Northumberland, so she's been spending a lot of time up there. Having some work done on the house. And God knows what else she's up to. Solving problems, I guess. That's what she likes to do.

Mostly I've been hanging around the house here, reading some good books and killing time. But I've also found a way to move around London without having some freak tugging at my sleeve to tell me he saw me in a movie. I don't shave for three or four days, put on rough clothes like I wore when I was shipping out on freighters, pull my watch-cap down to my eyebrows, and wear a pair of wire-rim spectacles I bought at a street market. Like that I can go wherever I like. Hands in my pockets and a scowl on my face, I can get on the tube and go.

You've never been to London and you'd hate it if you were here. It's the biggest city in the world. Too big for blokes like you and me. But there are lots of parks where a man can sit and watch the squirrels and the swans, a public house on every corner, and a big wide river running through the centre of everything. That's where I hang out mostly, down at the docks by a place called Tower Pier, where ships pull in from the channel to tie up, and where local boats leave for trips up and down the river. There's a pub there called the Fore and Aft. Sailors from all over spend their dock

time there and sleep in the seaman's lodge just down
the way. I've seen a few roughnecks I used to ship out
with, guys who never knew my name and don't give
a damn. If I told them I was working in movies now,
they'd either think I was lying or it wouldn't mean much
to them. They don't go to movie theatres. But they all
know who Clara Bow is. Still, any guy I recognize I
steer clear of. Just in case.

I've spent a lot of time with a crazy Irishman named
Donleavy. He's first mate on a timber-carrying freighter
that plies between London and New Zealand. His ship's
so old it's in dry-dock more than it's in the water. But
he's due to sail for Auckland again pretty soon and he
wants me to come along. Just for the ride. What do
you think of that? I asked him if he ever goes on to
Sydney and he says sometimes he does. So who knows?
You might see me stumbling into McBride's one of
these days.

Before he finished, he'd written a four-page letter, reminding
Homer Tony of things that had happened when they were
working together at Glenrowan, asking questions he knew
would never be answered, about the work and the weather
and the rainfall, and sending greetings to McBride and the
other men who remembered him from ten years before.

After he'd put the letter in an envelope, addressed it and
stamped it, he sat quietly in his chair by the window, just
his reading lamp turned on and a soft light above Sophie's
dressing-table on the far wall. He studied the details of the
large gold-and-white room, its four tall windows looking out
across Green Park, its carved doors leading to separate bathrooms and dressing quarters and to the second-floor hallway.
All the pictures, the pieces of furniture, the hangings, the
carpets, the mammoth bed, the clusters of bottles and
flasks, tiny vases and brushes and jars on the dressing-table,
spoke softly of Sophie. The scent in the room was hers. All
the patterns and textures were reflections of her stubbornly

eccentric tastes. It was her room. It would always be her room, her creation and her habitat, filled with her presence.

Sitting there quietly, as he was doing that particular night, he felt like a trespasser. Not permitting himself to long for her, as his eyes wandered about the room and his nostrils marked her scent, he longed for her all the same. His senses told him she had just stepped out of the room for a moment, reason reminded him that she was miles away. The first message made him feel dreamily content, the second made him angry. Since his last return to London from Northumberland this sharp internal conflict had become familiar to him. It lessened when he left the house, returned again when he came home, and was most difficult to deal with late at night before he went to bed, or still later when he lay awake in the darkness unable to sleep.

On this night, triggered perhaps by the letter he'd written to Homer Tony, he lay unquiet and wide awake at three in the morning. And at four. When it was nearly dawn, when light had begun to bleed through the slats of the window-shutters and early traffic had begun in the street outside, he got up, sat in a chair in his robe, and wrote a short note to Sophie. He shaved and bathed then, got dressed and left the house, wearing his seaman's clothes and his wire-rim glasses. He walked to the corner of Arlington and Piccadilly, dropped the two letters in a post-box there, then took the underground from Green Park station to Charing Cross, on to Embankment, and from there to Monument.

2

Whatever anxieties and frustrations she felt in the matter of Arthur Tagg, the change she perceived in his attitude toward her, toward himself, and his duties and responsibilities at Wiswell Towers, however clearly she expressed those concerns to Margaret and to Arthur himself in the note she wrote to him, Sophie was scrupulously careful to keep such matters within that tight triangle, her mother, Arthur, and herself. No discontent or antipathy was allowed to show itself to the staff, not to John Trout or Mrs Whitson or to the most transient kitchen worker or stable-boy. At table, when she and her mother and Arthur met for breakfast or luncheon, or for dinner in the evening, all was civility and charm. Even after the highly charged meeting in Margaret's sitting-room, after Sophie's note to Arthur was discussed, when he excused himself and both Sophie and her mother seemed blind to the other's point of view, even after that unpleasant and unresolved encounter, none of them, at their next meeting in the dining hall, seemed to remember it or harbour ill feelings.

It was all distorted *politesse*, of course, learned by each of them at their nanny's knee, a special sort of refined cruelty. Never shed a tear in anger, never honour an opponent by showing pain. Get on with it, carry on, and plan for the day when you can claim total victory. Stay inside yourself. Never lose composure.

For Sophie, member of a more emotional generation than Margaret and Arthur, more aware of her privileges, her powers, and her entitlements, more convinced of the purity of her convictions and the almost divine power of her resolve, absolutely secure in her belief that right was on her side, that any clear-minded and objective person would recognize her position as a correct one, burdened in this way by the almost unbearable weight of self-righteous indignation, for her it was especially difficult and painful to sit quietly at table waiting to be exonerated. But she managed it.

While some highwayman's instinct bubbled in her blood, some throw-back to a cut-pocket rogue named Wiswell, while she hungered to strike out, draw blood, and claim unquestioned victory, she followed her daily routine, never indicating by her expression or her voice that she was quietly preparing for a future battle she was certain to win.

The failure of her note to Arthur had been a set-back. She had miscalculated. It had not occurred to her that he would go straightaway to Margaret. And even if she had anticipated such a move she would not have guessed that her mother would come down so sharply on the side of Arthur.

As she reviewed that meeting, and she thought of it almost constantly in the days that followed, she concluded that the flaw had been in her. Her first instinct had been the correct one. She should have gone directly to Arthur, persuaded him to sit down in a room with her, calmly discuss their differences and define their roles, clarify where his authority began and where it ended.

Such a meeting, she believed, was still possible and necessary. She convinced herself that, in their previous three-way conversation about the contents of her note, nothing had been said that couldn't be modified or finessed somehow. As she had told Margaret, she didn't feel that apologies were appropriate, certainly not from her, but she had no objection to an appearance of flexibility as long as every-one came at last to understand that she would make no concessions. In her mind it was a matter of establishing her position rather than altering it.

Seeing everything clearly, she saw no reason why she shouldn't plunge ahead. Or perhaps, she decided, it should be matter of gliding rather than plunging. Avoiding obstacles rather than attempting to dislodge or destroy them. Each passing day made her stronger and more sure of her ground. Or so she told herself. Having imagined every argument, every position that Arthur might take and having carefully honed her counter-arguments, she felt battle-ready, prepared to speak calmly and reasonably, without rancour or condemnation, a rapier rather than a broad-sword in hand, not trying to persuade Arthur but skilfully helping him to convince himself that he had misjudged and misread her. She was fearless, calm, and prepared. Unassailable, impregnable, and keen to enter the lists. All that was needed was to approach Arthur and propose a meeting. But she didn't do it. Days went by and she didn't ask him.

Then one morning he came to her in the morning-room

and said, 'If you have a few minutes, I think we should have a chat.'

After all her planning and scheming as to how she would approach him, she was stunned to see him taking the initiative. It never occurred to her that it might simply be a routine estate matter that required her attention. She knew as soon as she saw him walking toward her that the discussion she had so carefully rehearsed in her mind was about to take place. When she didn't answer at once he spoke to her as he had when she was the pupil and he the tutor. 'Cat got your tongue, Sophie?'

She felt the colour in her cheeks suddenly. 'No, of course not,' she said. She forced a smile. 'Sit down.'

As soon as he sat down in the chair he said, 'I want to apologize to you. This won't be a long speech but since I'm not a skilled speaker perhaps you'll be kind enough to let me get through it before you . . .'

'I won't interrupt you.'

'Thank you.' He repositioned himself in his chair. 'In all the years I've known you, that we've known each other, I can't remember an angry word passing between us. Can't remember a misunderstanding of any sort. But now . . . since you sent me that note and since we had that short meeting with Margaret it's clear to me that I've done something to upset you or offend you. It seems I've even made you angry. Although I'm not sure what it is I've done, I don't mean to imply that I think I've done nothing. I know you well enough to realize that you'd react as you have only if something had brought on that reaction. So I want to tell you how sorry I am. I must admit I was bewildered by certain things you wrote in the note you sent me. That bewilderment was what made me go to Margaret. But she was as baffled as I was. The fact that you would write to me when we're living here in the same house and taking our meals together was as puzzling to Margaret as it was to me. It was not my impulse, however, to have you sit down and explain yourself to your mother and me. But Margaret thought that was the best solution. As it turned out . . . I'm sure you'll agree it was quite unsatisfactory.'

'Yes, it was.'

Arthur nodded. 'I have no wish to repeat that experience. Nor do you, I'm certain. But I do want to tell you, as simply and clearly as I can, that my feelings toward you are as warm and kind as they have always been. I have no antagonism toward you, no wish to quarrel with any of your decisions, past or future. Margaret has always treated me as if I were a member of the family, but I'm not, of course. I have tried to do a responsible job of managing certain affairs of the estate and I will continue to do that as long as I'm needed, but all critical decisions must be made by you or your mother. No one could be more conscious of that than I am. Family decisions must be made by the family. And however kind you and Margaret have been to me and my son, we are not family members. Your mother engaged me years ago because there was a need for my services. When there's no longer such a need, I will move on.'

Sophie sensed that she was being wrapped in a soft web. On the one hand she felt she had misjudged this quiet, kind man who had been a solid cornerstone for much of her life. On the other hand she could not stifle an instinct that told her she was being manipulated. 'Of course you won't move on,' she said then. 'I think I made that clear when I wrote to you. You must think of the Towers as your home. Margaret insists on that and so do I. Quite apart from the work you do, you belong here. And so does Evan.'

After he left her she felt jangled. She tried to remember the precise words she had used in the note she'd sent him. Was this short talk she'd just had with Arthur the solution to her problems? Had her concerns been dealt with? Without going into detail he seemed to have said what she needed to hear, that she and her mother were the final authority, the only authority, that he had no pretensions and no illusions. But why then did she feel there was a message behind the message? What did she hope might come out of a meeting with Arthur that had not come out of this one? She had no answers for those questions. After she'd discussed the matter with Margaret later in the morning she still had no answers. When she said to Margaret, 'I had a visit from Arthur this morning,' Margaret said, 'Oh, dear, are you bringing me dreadful news?'

Sophie shook her head and smiled.

'No war drums?' Margaret said.

'Not at all. It was pleasant and civilized. He was very sweet.'

'And were you very sweet?'

'Mostly I was mute. Arthur did the talking.'

'And did he say what you wanted to hear?'

'Yes, I believe he did.'

'How lovely,' Margaret said. 'I can't tell you how good that makes me feel.'

'Do you want to know what he said?'

'No. I think not. That's between you and Arthur, isn't it? If you're satisfied, I'm satisfied.'

Again Sophie felt, as she walked along the corridor from Margaret's rooms to her own, that some essential piece of the puzzle was missing. There was something incomplete about her mother's reaction. Had she discussed the matter with Arthur before he came to Sophie in the morning-room? Had he gone to Margaret as soon as he and Sophie had finished their conversation? Was that why she had no interest in a complete report of what was said?

Sophie had no answers to those questions as she went into her sitting-room and found the morning post on her writing table. Sorting through it, she found a letter from Kincaid. When she slit open the envelope there was a short note written on a white card.

Made a decision yesterday. I'm off to New Zealand on a freighter. Mixed cargo going down. Lumber coming back. I'm going as a chum of the first mate, not as a seaman. It's a long trip. I'll be back in about three months, God willing. I'll leave London in a week

259

or ten days. Come see me for a farewell dinner if you can manage. Hope all goes well for you on the moors.

As soon as she finished reading the note she turned to the telephone and rang her home in London. When the butler answered she said, 'Good morning, Oliver. Would you call Mr Kincaid to the telephone, please?'

'I'm sorry, Madam. Mr Kincaid went out quite early. Just after his breakfast.'

'Do you know where I can ring him?'

'I don't believe he left any word.'

'Perhaps I can reach him at his club.'

'I think not.'

'Why do you say that?'

'When I saw him last in the breakfast-room he was dressed quite informally. He was wearing what he calls his seaman's togs when he went out.'

'I see,' Sophie said. Then: 'Will you tell Mrs O'Haver that I'm on the line and I need to talk with her.'

As soon as Mrs O'Haver came on the phone, Sophie said, 'Is Oliver still there in the room with you?'

'No, he's just gone out.'

'Good. I want you to tell me what's going on there.'

'I don't understand.'

'There seems to be some mystery that I'm not being told about. Whenever I ring up for my husband, he seems to be out or asleep or otherwise engaged. I don't understand.'

'It's not a mystery, Madam. Mr Kincaid is out of the house quite a lot these past weeks. Seldom takes his meals at home except for breakfast. And when he's at home he often tells us he'd prefer not to take telephone calls.'

'That means business calls, Ruth. He doesn't like annoying calls from the press people or from America. It doesn't mean that he won't take calls from me.'

'I explained that to Oliver. But he says Mr Kincaid leaves explicit instructions. No calls at all.'

'What nonsense. Very well. As soon as you see Mr Kincaid

or hear from him ask him to ring me up here.'

'It could be quite late, I'm afraid. As I said we usually see him only in the breakfast-room.'

'I see,' Sophie said. 'Very well. Just leave a message in his bedroom that Albert will be driving me down to London. I'll be there midday tomorrow.'

3

At eleven the following evening, when Kincaid came home, Oliver met him in the foyer.

'Did you have a pleasant journey, sir?'

'Very nice. A bit of a squall near Oxford but lovely weather once we passed that. Sunny and clear in Bristol.'

'Mrs Kincaid is waiting for you in her sitting-room.'

'Oh, good, she's here.' Then: 'I'm hungry as a dog, Oliver. Could you bring up some food and a bottle of claret?'

Oliver nodded. 'A cold supper's been prepared. I'll send it up from the kitchen as soon as you ring.'

'Now, Oliver. I'm starving to death.'

When he walked into their second-floor sitting-room, Sophie got up from her chair and came to meet him. He put his arms round her and kissed her. 'Welcome home,' she said, steering him to the couch by her chair. 'We have champagne. Lovely fizzy champagne.' When he sat down she poured him a glass. He took it from her and said, 'Here's to us, kiddo.' As she sat down facing him she said, 'I love your outfit but you shouldn't have gone to such trouble. We're quite informal here.'

He patted the leg of his canvas trousers and said, 'This is my London wardrobe now. Sturdy but not pretentious. Nothing to attract attention.'

'Depends where you are. I expect those clothes would attract a great deal of attention at Caprice.'

'None at all. They'd never let me inside the front door.'

'Yet here you sit in a lady's boudoir.'

'That's right. Here I sit.'

She rang for Oliver then and almost at once trays of food and china and wine and crystal and silver came up from the kitchen. While the table was being prepared Kincaid went into his dressing quarters and put on pyjamas and slippers and a silk robe. As the servants left the room he sat down at the table, where Sophie was waiting.

'Am I a new man?' he said.

'You still want a shave but your wardrobe is improved.'

As he poured the claret he said, 'I'm thinking about growing a full beard. I had one in *Bushranger*. Remember?'

'I saw it in the movie and I hated it. Thank God, you'd shaved it off before you came home to England.'

'You didn't like it, eh? Pity. A common thing for a seaman, you know. Warms the face. Attracts the ladies.'

'You're not a seaman any longer.'

'No, but I used to be.'

'You used to work for a butcher as well, but you don't do it any longer.'

'Still able to whack off a first-rate chop. No question about that. Give me a sharp cleaver and a proper knife and I can lay waste to a side of beef in no time. I'd need a saw as well but a good saw's not hard to come by.'

'Are you longing back to your childhood? Nostalgia for the old life, is that it?'

He shook his head. 'Nothing like that. Just whiling away the hours. Killing time. Keeping my feet on the ground.'

'You're keeping a full schedule it seems to me. Whenever I ring up you seem to be out of the house, sound asleep, or taking no phone calls.'

'I hate the bloody telephone. You know that. A threat to health, those instruments. Encourage people to talk whether they've anything to say or not. Some smart chap should invent an apparatus that discourages talk. Like every time you make a stupid pointless remark you get a sharp head-pain.'

'You've been left alone too long. You're on the way to becoming a misanthrope.'

'No such thing. Although my best friends are dogs and horses, I also have a few choice mates who are human beings. But none of them have much to say.'

'That means you can do all the talking.'

'Not me. Some days I have no conversation at all from the time I get up till I roll into bed. You'd be surprised how well I sleep on those nights. A clear head. Like your brain's been cleaned with steam. I met an old black man when I was in jail in Massachusetts. He used to say, "Almost anything a man says, he'd be better off if he hadn't said it." What do you think of that?'

'I don't know what to think,' she said. 'That means nothing to me.'

He told her then, in greater detail, what he had told Homer Tony in his letter, about the hours he'd been spending at the Fore and Aft. 'Hard to describe it. Hard to believe you're in London. Hong Kong, Panama, Buenos Aires, Marseilles, any place the ships pull in, you can find a saloon by the docks that's just like the Fore and Aft. The same sailors, the same whores and bartenders and bouncers. Every language you can think of bouncing off the walls. Cigar smoke, cigarette smoke, pipe smoke. Sweat and hair-oil and the stink carried out of a ship's hold that doesn't smell like anything else.'

'Sounds as if you've been having a splendid time. Returning to your roots and all that.'

'Not exactly. It's not all good stuff. It's not like a family reunion. Nobody's singing sea shanties or dancing the horn-pipe. Going to sea doesn't make anybody happy. Not the ones who do it for a living. I've never seen a seaman standing at the rail admiring the sunset. They're scrambling to stay alive and put some bread and a bit of meat in their guts, like everybody else. It's a hard life. Boring. You work and sleep and eat bad food, and if you're lucky you have a good fist fight every now and then. Or you're two days drunk in port. Or you spend twenty minutes in a doorway with some sad whore. If you're lucky she'll give you lice or crabs. If you're unlucky she'll give you something worse.'

'So that's it, eh? You've been spending your time, at this place called the Fore and Aft? And you like it?'

'I didn't say I like it. I just mean, it's what I know.'

'You just like being there because you know you don't have to live that life any longer. You've put it behind you.'

He didn't answer. At last he said, 'You're right.'

They sat quietly then, eating their chops and cheeses and finishing the bottle of claret. At last she said, 'I thought you'd be surprised to see me.'

'I'm glad to see you but I'm not surprised. When I came home last night I found a note from Mrs O'Haver saying you were coming down to London today.'

'Mrs O'Haver thought you hadn't found the note.'

'Why did she think that?'

'I expect she thought you'd wait for me instead of going out right after breakfast and not coming home till just an hour or so ago.'

'No connection. I'd made a promise to Tom Donleavy, this new friend of mine. He had to drive out to Bristol to see his sister and I told him I'd go with him. We made an early start and we just got back to London a while ago. Matter of fact he dropped me off. Right at the door.'

'So I came to London and you went off to Bristol.'

'Couldn't be helped,' he said. 'But it does seem as if that happens to us a lot. You know what I mean?'

'I'm not sure. I'm trying to decide what you're up to. Are you trying to make me angry? Is that it?'

'Why would I do that? I told you, I'm glad to see you.'

'And I needed to see you. That's why I came to London. And all day I've been sitting here waiting for you to wander home from wherever you'd gone.'

'Bristol,' he said.

'I know that now. But I didn't know it till a few minutes ago.'

'I didn't think you'd be sitting here waiting for me. I thought you probably had a full day scheduled. Dressmakers, solicitors, hairdressers, all that lot.'

'You're playing some sort of game, aren't you? I see that now. How long are we going to sit here pretending you didn't send me that strange note about your travel plans?'

'Oh, good. You received that before you came down here, then. When you didn't say anything about it, I figured it hadn't been delivered by the time you left.'

'Was that supposed to be some sort of joke?' she said.

'What do you mean?'

'I mean, I'm not supposed to take you seriously, am I, when you say you're going off to New Zealand of all Godforsaken places?'

'Have you ever been there?'

'Of course not.'

'I've been there a dozen times. It's a great place. On the South Island you can drive all day and never meet another car. Thousands of sheep. Not many people.'

'What in the world has come over you? I know you're sober, and you act as though you're serious, but you're not making sense.'

His tone was slightly different when he answered her. 'What is it you don't understand, Sophie?'

'I don't understand why we're having this bizarre conversation. I don't understand why you've made up this story about a trip to New Zealand.'

'There's nothing strange about it. I'm going. Donleavy's ship will be ready in a week or ten days, and when she sails I'll be on board. Nice quarters of my own and free run of the ship.'

'I can't believe it but I think you're serious.'

'I am serious. I mean, there's nothing important about the voyage. Just a routine freighter trip. But for me it will be a lark. I'm looking forward to it.'

'Let me be absolutely certain I'm getting this straight. In a few days you're going to sail off into the sunset and I won't see you for three months.'

'Give or take a few weeks. You never know with a freighter.'

She put her fork down on her plate with a clatter. 'God, you are an exasperating man. I'm trying very hard not to get angry but it seems that's what you want me to do. Did you really imagine that when you gave me this ridiculous news I'd just smile and nod my head?'

'I didn't imagine anything. Why are you trying so hard not to get angry?'

'Because I can't believe what I'm hearing. I can't believe that you'd make a plan like this and never even mention it to me. I can't believe you'd consider going off and leaving me for three months. I'm astonished. I really am. You're as casual about it as if you'd decided to pop round the corner for a box of cigarettes. People simply don't do such things. I'm your wife, for God's sake. We're civilized people. People don't just make separate plans and then announce what they're going to do. People don't get married and then start figuring out schemes to keep them apart. They get married so they can be together. That's what it's all about. That's what it means when you love somebody. That's the way . . .'

'Bullshit, Sophie.'

'What did you say?'

'I said bullshit.'

'Don't talk to me like that. No one has ever talked that way to me.'

'Now somebody has.'

'I've never seen you like this. And I don't like it.'

'That's too bad, Sophie. That's too damned bad.'

She stood up suddenly. 'I'm not going to listen to abusive language.'

'Suit yourself.'

'Now you're the one who's angry.'

'You're damned right, I'm angry.'

She moved to the back of her chair. When she spoke her voice was calmer, in control. 'Let's not talk while we're angry.'

'Why not?'

'We may say things we're sorry for, things we can't take back.'

'We may say what we mean. I'd like that.'

'I always say what I mean,' she said.

'You always mean what you say. It's not the same thing.'

'We're not drunk, are we?'

'You may be but I'm not. I don't get drunk sharing a bottle of wine. And don't use that condescending tone with me. I've never had a nanny and I sure as hell don't need one now.'

'I don't know you when you're like this. I don't recognize you.'

'You recognize me all right and I recognize you.'

'This isn't getting us anywhere. I think the best idea would be for you to sleep in the blue bedroom at the end of the corridor tonight. Then tomorrow . . .'

'I'm sleeping right here,' Kincaid said. 'Where I always sleep.'

'Then I'll sleep down the hall. And we'll talk in the morning.' She moved over to the fireplace and stood with her back to the fire.

'I've got a better idea,' he said. 'You sleep wherever you damned please and we'll talk when I come back from New Zealand.'

'You're not fooling me, you know. You never intended to go to New Zealand. You're angry with me about something and you're just trying to upset me.'

'Good-night,' he said. 'Go to bed. Go to hell.'

She slowly came back to the table. 'I can't imagine what's come over you.'

'You said that before,' he said. 'That's the trouble. The fact that you don't know, that you can't even imagine what's come over me . . . that's the problem.'

'What is it?'

'Don't talk to me like I'm one of your children with an upset stomach. I'm not suffering. I'm not in pain. I'm fed up. Let me tell you something. I've lived alone most of my

267

life. That's no hardship for me. I know how to survive. I can get along. I know how to take care of myself. I don't need to be cuddled or tucked up or fed with a spoon. I don't need to be married.'

'That's a rotten thing to say.'

'No, it's not. I got married because I wanted to, not because I had to. I can live by myself or not by myself. But I'll tell you one thing for certain. I didn't get married to you so I could live by myself.'

'Ah . . . now I see what's got into you.'

'No, you don't. Because I haven't told you yet. And we're not talking about whether something's got into me. We're talking about something that's been in you for a long time. I'm not asking you to please come home so I won't have to sleep by myself. I'm not counting up the months we've been separated in the three years we've been married . . .'

'I hope not. None of those separations were my fault. Your friend, Julian Thorne . . .'

'Nonsense, Sophie. I've never been any place, since the day we were married, that you couldn't have been with me. So why weren't you? That's what we're talking about. There was always an excuse, at least in your mind, but there was never a reason.'

'I have responsibilities too, you know. I have a life, a family, things that must be done. I can't simply become a mirror-image of you, even if I'd like to . . .'

'Go on,' he said. Very quietly.

'Maybe it's because I'm a few years older than you. Maybe Trevor and Sarah have something to do with it. Almost any woman who falls in love wishes she'd known the man all her life, that he'd known her. She wants the rest of the world to go away. But the world won't do that. At least my world won't. I had commitments before we met and I still have them. I can't make them disappear. I don't want them to. They're part of me. A small part compared with you but something I can't ignore.'

'All right,' he said. 'That's your thesis. I've heard it before.

And nobody but an idiot would quarrel with what you're saying. But it's not as simple as that. Not in your case. Everybody has obligations, things they have to do whether they want to or not. But here's where it gets tricky. If I'm obliged to be on a sound stage all day Thursday and somebody invites me to go to a horse show I want to see, the obligation makes the choice for me. I'm obliged to work. At that moment the obligation owns me. On the other hand, same scenario, I have to work on Thursday and somebody asks me to take his aunt to lunch, I use the obligation as an excuse not to do it. You see what I'm getting at?'

'No.'

'Yes, you do. You've got a wall built round you. Lots of gates in that wall, people coming and going. But not without an invitation. And nobody strays inside after closing time. You pass out hundreds of pieces of yourself but nobody gets the whole cake. Not your first husband, not me, not anybody. Everybody finds a way to survive. You keep yourself together by what you hold back. Sometimes that can work. Sometimes it doesn't. When things get out of balance and you hold back more than you give, it gets to be a problem.'

'Is that your problem? Is that what you're saying?'

'No. It's your problem. But it affects me as well.'

'If that's me you're describing, you must be a miserably unhappy man.'

He shook his head. 'I'm not miserable. I love you and I'm trying to fix something that isn't working very well.'

'I feel like someone hit me in the stomach,' she said.

'So do I.'

'She'd stood behind her chair while he talked as if she were anchored there. Now she sat down. 'Do you know what you're saying to me?'

He nodded. 'I've had a lot of time to think about it.'

'You're saying I'm some sort of synthetic superficial creature, that I don't truly love anyone, that I can't love anyone. Do you really believe I can't love you, that I don't love you? Are you leaving me? Is that what you're saying? Is the story about going to New Zealand real after all? What on God's earth am I meant to believe?'

She started to cry then. Silently. Tears slipped out of her eyes like a child's tears. She sat there looking at him, making no effort to wipe the tears away. 'I hate myself,' she said then. 'I've never felt this way before.'

She got up from the table then, crossed to the hall door, and left the room. Far down the corridor he heard a door open and close.

It was nearly dawn when his bedroom door opened and closed again. She slipped into the bed, lay close against him, and put her arms round him. 'Don't wake up,' she whispered. 'Go back to sleep.'

## 4

'When I left you the other night and went off down the hallway to sleep in a bed by myself, I felt as if I'd been prepared for surgery. Partially anaesthetized but still feeling the pain.'

They were lying together beside the fireplace in her cottage near Dinard. They had come there from London the previous day by train, Channel steamer, and hired car. The fog was heavy, a cold misty rain was falling and the clouds seemed as low as the tree-tops. When they were inside the cottage at last, Sophie opened the shutters and looked out the window at the grey wall of moisture outside. 'What a beautiful day,' she said. 'Have you ever seen such a gorgeous day?'

The previous morning, once they'd had breakfast in bed and decided to go to Brittany, it was as though they'd taken a vow of silence. They were touching and very much together but they spoke hardly at all, no review or dissection of the painful scene of the night before, no attempt to resolve the threads that had been left dangling. They seemed determined now to do no damage to themselves, with words, with theories or accusations or recriminations or conclusions; no analysis, no blame, no guilt.

When they'd come there the first time, three years before, Sophie had made a small sign and propped it on the mantel above the fireplace – *Only Wine and Sensuality are Welcome Here*. The sign had disappeared long since but they clearly remembered the message.

On the second night, however, it seemed safe and appropriate to Sophie to weave some connecting strands between their present state of *luxe* and indolence, and the near-explosive confrontation they'd had in their London bedroom. 'I was angry and hurt and confused. I can't remember having felt that way, so totally destroyed, since I was eight or nine years old, when even a frown from an adult could turn me to jelly. I was still weeping when I crawled into bed, expecting to lie there all night, sobbing and staring into the darkness. But I must have cried myself to sleep. Because suddenly I woke and it was almost four in the morning. If I'd been a dreadful muddle before, everything seemed quite clear to me then. I could hear your voice and the words you'd said to me as though they'd been recorded on a wax record. If indeed there was a wall round me as you'd said, it began to crumble as I lay there with my thoughts racing and bubbling. The things you'd said that I'd rejected so forcefully seemed suddenly to make sense. I found I was able to say *mea culpa* without falling apart. If before I had felt some need to be flawless in my own eyes, I began to feel that certain warts and wens and inadequacies were not only acceptable but beautifully human. I'm still struggling with some of the things you said, still protecting myself in some areas, but I really am going to stop trying to fix everything for everybody. Also, I'm not going to leave you alone in future if I can possibly help it. And I'll fight like a cat if you try to leave me alone. You frightened me terribly the other night. I was scared silly. No one's ever done that to me before. It's not something I'd like to go through again.' She moved closer to him and kissed him. 'So I'll be good. I'll be very good.'

5

Mid afternoon of his second day in New York, Julian paid a visit to Vincent Corso at his home on Staten Island. They sat together in a room at the rear of the house, shutters closed, two small lamps burning.

'Bright lights everyone wants. All the lamps on and the radio turned up to make a person deaf. Not me,' Vincent said. He looked round the room. 'This is how I like it. A quiet room, not too much light. A place where a man's eyes and ears can have a rest and his brain can work. My grandson does his school-work after supper with his little radio blasting in his ear. Can a boy learn like that? I don't think so. But my daughter won't hear. To her eyes, I was born in the thirteenth century. Doesn't want to stifle the boy, she says. Better he should be stifled, I tell her, than stone-deaf from his radio. But my wife sides with her and the boy. Kindness is the answer, she says. I've got nothing against kindness. There's a place for it. I'd be the first person to make such a statement. But we're men of the world, Julian. We know that kindness by itself will never turn the wheel. Can I offer you a glass of wine? Or a glass of tea, maybe?'

Julian shook his head. 'A long lunch today. When I come to New York I have too many meetings, too many meals, too much business done in cocktail bars and restaurants.'

Corso nodded. 'My father was killed doing business in a restaurant. Adolph's on Mulberry Street. You were still in New York then. Although we never did business with you, my father had great respect for you, as I do. Many times I heard him say, "Julian behaves like a friend but he asks for nothing." And my mother, God rest her soul, never forgot your thoughtfulness at the time of my father's death.' He rang a little bell by his chair and a grey-haired woman appeared in the doorway. 'Maybe you'll bring us two glasses of tea. And some cookies also on a plate. I prefer the coconut ones.' He turned back to Julian and said, 'After a

272

large lunch and too much business talk, a bit of tea can't hurt.' He resettled himself in his chair. 'Not an hour goes by that I don't think about having a glass of wine. It was always a part of my life. My family's life. I drank wine with water in it when I was a small boy, spending many afternoons with my grandfather in Queens. He drank only Bardolino. I also developed a taste for that particular wine. My father had more refined tastes, more expensive, but for myself I always stayed with my grandfather's choice. Just there, on my desk, I always kept a handsome decanter, chilled in the summer months, of the Bardolino. I drank it for the taste, for refreshment. I've never been intoxicated in my life. I don't trust a man who's alcohol dependent. So I loved the Bardolino but did not abuse it. I had a memory of my grandfather with his great mane of white hair and his white moustache, ninety-four years old needing a cane to walk, reading with enlarging glasses and using an ear-trumpet, but still taking pleasure from his tumblers of good red wine. "That's how I'll be when I'm his age," I told myself. The years take away many of our pleasures, but that one, I believed, was permanent and reliable. When they discovered my grandfather dead in his comfortable chair by the window, he was still holding his wine glass and not a drop had spilled. A remarkable story, isn't it?'

'Yes, it is.'

'Now let me tell you the ending. Since the day my grandfather died I've been unable to drink wine. My wife said, "Don't tell me fairy-stories about some spiritual connection between you and your dead grandfather. It's a chemical problem. The doctor tells me our bodies get all changed around every seven years. You're an older man now. Younger you could drink, older you can't." Maybe she's right. But the fact is that if I drank half a glass of wine this afternoon, I'd have a restless night, my head would pound, and my vision would suffer. And although I have no history of asthma I would have asthma symptoms for forty-eight hours.'

The woman returned with the tea then and served each

of them a glass with three coconut cookies on the saucer. 'This is my speed now. A glass of tea and a cookie.' He looked up at the ceiling. 'I hope my grandfather's not watching.'

Since his nickelodeon days on the lower east side of New York, the men Julian had dealt with had been Italians, Jews, Greeks, and Hungarians, all of them immigrants or first-generation Americans. In California, particularly in the silent-film days, he'd continued to deal with the same men, men with New York roots, Budapest, Berlin, Vienna roots. He had an instinct for dealing with such men. Patience, he had learned, was his best weapon. Certain preliminaries had to be observed. Even men who had known each other for thirty years had to rekindle their relationship before any business matters could be discussed. A proposal could not simply be put forward. It had to be insinuated into the general conversation. It had to be discovered in such a way that neither man seemed to have proposed it. Thus, no matter what developed or failed to develop, neither man could fail, neither need feel rejected.

The rules were clear. No one said, 'Here's what I need from you.' No one said, 'Why are you here? What do you want?' At the end if both men said, 'That could work; let's talk about it some more', it meant an agreement had been reached or might be reached. If just one man said, 'I'll have to give that some thought. Then we'll talk again', both of them knew the bubble had burst. There might be other deals on other days but this proposition on this day was not to be.

So Julian sipped his tea, nibbled his coconut cookie, and waited. Frequently the telephone rang in another part of the house, muffled conversations were heard through the walls, and doors opened and closed, but Vincent Corso seemed not to hear. He was totally concentrated on this room, these moments, this man to whom he was speaking. 'Are you a political man, Julian? Where do the people in your business stand on the subject of Roosevelt?'

'The money people were leery about him in the beginning. A lot of panic when he closed the banks. But it's more than two years now since he took office and most of us think he's going in the right direction. The creative people have always liked him. He has a flair that appeals to them, also most of them are not conservative by nature so they supported him from the start.'

'And how about you?'

'I was a poor boy from New York, as you know. New York doesn't breed political conservatives. Most of the conservatives here either live on Park Avenue or they moved here from Ohio.'

'The papers say the film industry is full of Reds. Russkie-lovers.'

'I know. I've heard those stories. And since we've got a little bit of everything out there I expect we've got some of those as well. But they don't run the business and they never will. Just because a man disagrees with his government doesn't make him a traitor in my book.'

'Even-handed. That's the answer. Keep a steady course. My daughter gets all excited about politics. An active young woman. College graduate. Three children. Leads her husband around like a trained bear. She reads high-toned books and magazines. Eats dinner with college people. If she was a man she'd own General Motors. She keeps trying to convert me. Every month or so it's a different crusade. She tells me I have to make a statement. Stand up and be counted. But I tell her my business is business. I don't have to like whoever's running the country. Or the city. Or the police department. I have to find a way to live with them and keep my business in operation. Keep my organization together. We're like you, Julian, we provide certain services to the public. As long as nobody keeps us from providing those services I can always bring a dollar to the table. The first thing you have to know about politicians is they don't know anything except how to get elected. So you have to be patient sometimes till they settle down and figure out how things work. Certain people I know thought the world would come to an end when prohibition was repealed. They'd decided that bootlegging was the only way to make a living. But we had a meeting in the ballroom of the old Strand Hotel in Brooklyn Heights and after everybody shot off his mouth for an hour or so, my brother, Johnny's dad, stood up and said, "There was beer before prohibition, there was beer during prohibition, and there'll be beer now. More than ever. Just because it's legal don't mean we can't make our money. We don't have to be illegal to get rich." And he was right. The men who sat in that meeting now control all the beer in New York and New Jersey. And when whiskey becomes legal again they'll control that too. What goes around comes around. Patience is what I preach to my people. We got hard times right now but nobody invented that just to make *us* miserable. We get our share now and when things turn around we'll get a bigger share. Bad times keep you on your toes. Whatever business you're in. A twenty-year-old snot-nose wants to grab and scratch and make it all in six months. A few years later, if he's still around, he knows that's not the way it works.'

Julian nodded. 'In 1930, after the market crashed, people in the film business were saying, "It's all over. The business is dead. When people are broke they won't go out of their houses. They'll stay at home and listen to Amos and Andy. They can't afford to go to the movies now." It seemed to make sense but it didn't work out that way. Pretty soon we found out that movies were the only entertainment people could afford. We perfected the talkies and we started to fool around with colour film and people flocked to the theatres. We started bank nites and lotteries and raffles and give-aways and even more people showed up. Every studio in Hollywood's making a profit and the lucky ones are taking in more money than they know what to do with.'

'And from what I hear, you're one of the lucky ones.'

Julian smiled. 'It's not just luck. But we're doing all right. This will be our biggest year. Could double last year's profit. We've got a world market now for our product.'

'What happens to that world market when the war starts?'

'We're hoping it won't start.'

'It's started already, Julian. People just don't want to admit it. I get letters from Italy every week. All my family there are trying to get out. They smell war, and believe me, they know what it smells like. I have a niece who's a professor at a college in Bologna. She says the tip-off was when Hitler and Mussolini made an arrangement. She says France will fall like a leaf from a tree and the rest of Western Europe as well. And when the Germans go after England, America will come in.'

'I hope she's wrong.'

'So do I. But my wife says she's right. And I'm starting to believe my wife.' He smiled. 'Of course I don't tell her that.'

They talked for almost two hours. Twice Julian thought he saw an opportunity to say what he'd come to say, but each time Vincent slid off to another subject. Only when they stood up and were walking through the long corridor leading to the entrance where Julian's car was waiting did John Corso's name come up at last.

'Do you see my nephew out there?'

'I'm sorry to say I don't,' Julian said. 'I mean I see him. But usually we're both in a big hurry. He comes on the lot to see my brother, Sam, once in a while. He and Sam are still good friends.'

'More than that. They're friends for life, I think.'

'I think you're right,' Julian said. Then: 'I guess John must keep in touch with you.'

'Not directly. I used to get reports from his father, and my wife talks to his mother, running up the phone bills as women do. But Johnny and I don't talk much.'

'I see.'

'I'm not involved in his business out there if that's what you mean. And he's not involved with mine.'

'I didn't mean that at all. I just thought . . . I'm not sure what I thought. It doesn't matter.'

'Some people here in New York assumed that I sent John out to California, that we're partners in his operation. But that's not true. Everything he's accomplished out there he's done on his own.'

'Too bad you're not his partner,' Julian said. 'He's accomplished a great deal. And in a short time. He deals with every studio in town. We're one of his big customers.'

'I know he's moved fast. Or so his mother says.'

'No question about that. Some of the studio people think he's moved too fast but I'm sure he'll be able to work his way out of that. Those men talk big sometimes but they usually back down before they do all the things they're threatening to do.'

They walked on in silence through the house. When they came to the reception room just inside the entrance Corso said, 'Let's sit down here a moment. I don't walk much these days. When I do I get short of breath.' They sat beside each other on a small tufted couch. 'I hope you'll come again when you're in New York. If you have an evening free my wife and daughter will make you a Sicilian meal that will change your whole life. It was a treat for me to spend some time with you. I've followed your career with a lot of pride. We always saw a lot more of Sammy than we did of you but I never lost sight of what you were doing. When you know the circumstances a boy comes from it's a good feeling to watch him go to the top with no help from anybody. Just his own brains and hard work.' He patted Julian on the knee. 'A lot of people come here to see me. And I see them all, many of them people I've known for thirty or forty years, a few of them as old as I am. And I know when they come into that little room where we were sitting that they've come to ask a service. They want to pay their respects, of course, and I appreciate that. But they also need help, in every case, and they know I'll help them if I can. So while we were having our nice talk this afternoon I assumed that there was something I'd be able to do for you, that you'd come to ask me for help.'

'Not at all,' said Julian. 'I think of you often and I don't see you enough. So I thought it was time we had a talk.'

'I realize that now. And that makes your visit twice as enjoyable.' He smiled, an awkward old man's smile. 'Now I have a surprise for you. There's a service that you can do for me. You mentioned that my nephew may be in some kind of trouble.'

'I shouldn't have said that. It's none of my affair. I assumed you knew something about his operation. Since you don't I feel awkward talking about it.'

'I'm the only one who knows we're having this conversation. And no one else will know. As I said, I am not in business with Johnny. Not in any way. But he is Nick's son, so I'm concerned about him.'

'As I said, I'm sure this is something he'll be able to handle. The story in a nutshell is that he's tied up several crucial services that all the studios depend on. Most recently he's bought out the last of his rival trucking companies. That gives him a monopoly. Warner and Goldwyn and other people are worried about that. It would concern me, too, if it was anybody doing it other than Johnny. Also, there's another matter that's disturbing.' Julian lit a cigarette. 'We're a non-union industry in a non-union town. The word union scares hell out of the studios. The word is that John's having talks with a new union organization here in New York, the CIO. Have you heard of them?'

'Yes, I have.'

'If he's planning to organize his drivers and drop that whole union package on the studios, I'm afraid he'll get a big surprise.'

Corso turned slowly and looked at him. Before he could speak Julian said, 'Don't ask me to tell you what the studios plan to do because I can't do that. I'm in a bad spot here. If this turns into a war I'll be on the side of the studios. And it's a war that Johnny can't win.'

When they shook hands and said goodbye at the door Corso said, 'I know you came here in friendship and we had a good visit together. But you've also done a service for me and my family. As my father said, "Julian's a man who asks for nothing." But it's important to remember that friendship has its rewards.'

6

'From things you've said, you probably won't believe this,' Sophie said, 'but it's been agonizing for me, spending all this time at the Towers without you. First, when you were still in California, and then after you'd come home when you were down in London. That was almost worse, knowing you were so near but still not being able to see you every day, talk to you, and snuggle up in bed with you.'

They were sitting on the after-deck of the cross-channel ferry, wrapped in travel rugs on a cool but unseasonably sunny day. The deck steward had brought them steaming mugs of coffee laced with brandy.

'I wasn't alone, of course. Margaret was there, just down the corridor, and we spent a great deal of time together as we always do. But for the first time in our lives there was a strain between us. It's understandable, I suppose, when one considers everything she's gone through in a few short months. And then, of course, there was the business with Arthur that seemed to hover over us like a black bird. That really upset me. And my feeling that she was more sympathetic to Arthur's position than she was to mine made it doubly annoying. Not only was I away from you, I felt somehow estranged from my mother. So there I was, busy during the day with staff and the construction people but quite alone with my thoughts the rest of the time.' She sipped her coffee and looked back across the water toward the Normandy coast, which was still faintly visible in the clear light.

'Some people believe that even pain has its rewards,' she went on. 'I'm a dreadful coward about anything that hurts me, so I've never been able to sympathize with that viewpoint. But I do believe that isolation, as painful as it may be, can be used to one's benefit. I found myself examining all sorts of things that I've always taken for granted. I made a game of it. Looking at things and people from a different angle, forcing myself to be objective. Chekhov said – I think it was Chekhov; perhaps it was Tolstoy – at any rate somebody said that objectivity is the enemy of love, that love, by definition, is totally subjective. When it ceases to be subjective, it ceases to exist. What do you think of that?'

When he didn't answer she poked him softly with her elbow and said, 'Am I putting you to sleep?'

'No. I'm wide awake,' he said.

'No answer to my question?'

He shook his head. 'Some things make sense and some things don't. I knew that when I was eight years old.'

'So you're a lucky man. I'm still trying to figure things out.'

'No, you're not. You're trying to fix things.'

'I know you think that,' she said, 'And I know you're right. I don't like it either but I guess it's my nature. What's your nature?'

'To leave things alone.'

'You're right, of course. But I've never been able to do it. That's what I was starting to tell you. All those hours I was by myself at the Towers with crazy thoughts and anxieties bouncing about in my head, I invented a game for myself. I pretended that people I'd known all my life, Margaret and Arthur and Evan, for example, were individuals I'd just met. I tried to define and evaluate them as strangers, to see them as someone would who had know them for only a short time. At least that was my intention. But since they're all attractive and civilized and socially acceptable, I decided that almost anyone who met them or knew them only slightly would have a good opinion of them. "Seems like a nice person . . . intelligent chap . . . warm and friendly," that sort of rot. So I came up with a better scheme. Why not try to see them through the eyes of an enemy, someone who thoroughly disliked them. How did the Major feel about Margaret for example? After they broke up, how did Mary Cecil feel about Evan? And how did Evan's mother feel about Arthur?'

This game which she described quite casually to Kincaid had in fact been thoroughly formalized. 'I'll pretend that I'm a biographer preparing to write an unsympathetic biography of the person in question and requesting a candid evaluation of Margaret, Evan, and Arthur from, respectively, Major Cranston, Mary Cecil, and Amy Brock, Evan's mother.'

Attempting to put herself inside the consciousness and memory of each of these three, she wrote to herself, in effect, the following reports.

*From Amy Brock:*

Arthur Tagg is not a strong man. He tries to mask his weakness with a silence that is presented as thoughtfulness. His mind is well organized but too timid to be truly intelligent. There is nothing creative about his thinking. He is an intellectual magpie. The reticence, the kindness, the willingness to compromise, these qualities that he is so proud of are merely handmaidens of his fear, his sense of his own inadequacy. Because he is a physical coward he has the instincts of a bully. He has few men friends. He seems to be uneasy in the company of men. Ironically, although he is extremely sympathetic toward women, although they see him as friend and confidant, he sees them as inferiors. But since they're not threatening to him, he accepts them and feels at ease with them. He is not a sensual man. And even if he were, he lives by codes and rules that leave little room or no room at all for impulses that don't originate in his mind. Never in his life has he truly lost himself, in anger, in sorrow, or in passion. He never will. I'm sure he considers this his greatest strength. In fact it is a cruel weakness.

*From Major Cranston:*

As a military officer, I prided myself on my ability to assess the character of my men. The timbre of a chap's voice, his grooming, the directness of his gaze, the set of his jaw, the way he presented himself for inspection. I could spot a weakling or a bully by the line of his mouth. I had no faith in a man with soft droopy ear-lobes.

In civilian life I used the same standards of judgement. I found they applied to women as well as men. I was attracted to several young women before I met Margaret but none of them were up to the mark. Only she conformed to all my standards. She was a clean and shapely young person with a pleasant voice and a certain amount of grace in the way she carried herself. She'd had a proper education, more than enough to prepare her for marriage to a military officer but not enough so as to transform her, to make her contentious or opinionated. The day we were married I remember congratulating myself for having had the wisdom and the patience to select an ideal young woman to be Mrs William Cranston. God, what an error I made.

Early on, only months after our arrival in Delhi, I realized that she had a need to command, that inside that soft smiling exterior there was a steel component that could not be dissolved or dented. She was never angry, argumentative, or demanding, however. She triumphed by persistence, by withdrawal, by silence, by patience. Was it a characteristic she'd inherited from her mother, a famously strong-willed woman, this fanatic desire to prevail? I suspect it was. But wherever it came from, in Margaret it was indestructible.

In those early years we never had an argument. She simply encircled me, like a thousand mounted Arabs surrounding a single platoon. When she left me, taking Sophie along, to go home for her mother's burial service I knew as I put her on the ship that she wouldn't be returning to India. I was almost relieved. Whatever

283

I'd expected from marriage I had not expected that it would be an endless contest of wills, a non-violent triumph of weakness over strength.

*From Mary Cecil:*

Evan is fascinating but dangerous. He has supreme self-confidence in every area except the one that means most to him. Knowing that he could succeed in almost any field he might choose, he feels doomed to failure in the work he's best at. Nothing but playwriting will ever satisfy him but he seems strangely willing to give that up, or postpone it indefinitely, rather than risk the failure that he feels is inevitable.

He's been spoiled by women but it's made him neither vain nor cynical. He's the only man I know who truly loves women. For what they are rather than what they might be. Although he grew up without a mother he's not looking for a woman who will mother him. He's a healthy soul, in and out of bed. If he weren't intelligent and decent he would simply live moment-to-moment, love many women, and father a great tribe of children. He's a perfectly wonderful, normal man who simply can't do what he needs most to do. So perhaps he's not normal at all.

As they crossed the Channel that afternoon, Sophie summarized for Kincaid these synthetic reports she'd fabricated, carefully leaving out the part about Evan. When she finished she said, 'What do you think?'

'That's easy,' he said. 'I think you've gone round the bend.'

'Ah hah, it frightens you, doesn't it? Men don't like to splash about in the subconscious, do they? Meat and potatoes, money on the line, that sort of thing. That's where men feel at home. No suppositions, no mucking about in the unknown, no fantasies.'

'What fantasy? There's no fantasy in all that foolishness.

You just found a way to spill out your own secret thoughts and conclusions, and pretend they came from somebody else.'

'Not at all. I'm using perfectly legitimate tools. Observation, memory, and surmise.'

'You're balmy, Sophie. And by the way, what happened to Evan?'

'What do you mean?'

'Didn't you say you were sending him up as well? Intimate thoughts on the subject by Mary Cecil?'

'Abandoned,' Sophie said. 'Evan's a darling chap but there's no level of mystery there. No secrets. No subterranean passages. What you see and what he says are very much a part of what he is.'

'I'm disappointed. I was sure Mary Cecil would have some interesting things to report. I thought you were saving the best till the last. Well-kept secrets of the beach-house, champagne and sweet perversion between consenting adults. Wet towels and leather belts at work, young playwright and English actress go berserk in the surf, that sort of thing.'

'Sorry, old darling, no smut in this report. Pure scientific method. No preconceived conclusions. Allowing the facts to speak for themselves.'

'There are no facts,' he said. 'Just the fantasies of a dotty Englishwoman of a certain age, mother of two, and restless wife of a frightened husband.'

'You're frightened of nothing. I should have used the scientific method on you. A make-believe interview with some dusky maiden you seduced and abandoned in Capetown.'

'Actually it was Johannesburg as I recall.'

She had, of course, included him in her programme of character dissection, her minute examination of motive and impulse. In his case, however, she imagined no critical voice. She simply wrote down previously unexpressed views of her own.

Does he believe, does he actually tell himself, that when we're separated for a period of weeks or even months that I'm the one who brings it about? Because I respond to that primitive need he has to be alone, does he really conclude that I'm the one who seeks out empty rooms with strong locks on the door? Is it some secret he has that he believes is well kept? Did I sense it too quickly and respond too fully? Why can't he admit the whole movie business with its long shooting schedules and extended locations is perfect for him, a kind of substitute for his years on freighters, visiting dozens of different ports every year, meeting strangers, finding old friends? Is he ashamed of that gypsy strain? He must realize that it's possible to be fiercely in love with someone and still need desperately to be away from them sometimes. Does he think I don't know it? Is his insistence that I'm the one who goes off somewhere a kind of ingenuous subterfuge to conceal the fact that he's the one who goes off, who needs to go off? I never imagined he was the sort of simple one-cell creature he likes to pretend he is. But I also didn't expect to uncover great pockets of self-deception and intrigue. The irony in all this is that whatever he turns out to be, nothing can change the fact that I love him more desperately every day. I respect him, I'm proud of him, and I'm so jealous and possessive that my stomach tightens every time I look at him. I don't allow myself to consider the possibility that he's disappointed in me, that he's restless, that being married is something less splendid than he expected it to be. And God knows, I never permit myself to ask if I'm really the sort of person I insist I am, if I'm as genuinely contented as I seem to be.

A few minutes before their ferry docked she said, 'I'm so glad we went off by ourselves for a few days. Every time we do that I wonder why we don't do it more often. It never fails to bring things into focus. Important things become very important and the trivial matters have no value at all. Maybe that's our destiny, to live in isolation somewhere. In a houseboat on some lovely river. Or a stone cottage in the Orkney Islands. What do you think?'

'I don't care where we live. I'm easy to please.'

On the train from Dover to London she fell asleep, her head resting on his shoulder. 'Kent,' she said when she woke up. 'We could convert an old sheepbarn or an oasthouse and live here in solitary splendour.'

'In the next life you should be a carpenter,' Kincaid said. 'You have a great yen to refurbish the world.' When she didn't answer he said, 'As I was saying, in the next life you should be a carpenter.'

'I'm sorry. My mind wandered off. I was thinking of something else. When I was asleep just now, I dreamed you were standing in the bow of a ship, heading off somewhere. New Zealand, I expect. You weren't serious about going there, were you?'

'I wouldn't use the word serious. I felt quite good about it.'

'But you weren't really going, were you?'

'Yes, I was.'

'I'm not easy to fool, you know. I think you were just using that little story to get me back to London.'

'I don't play games, Sophie. I'd made plans to go and I intended to do it.'

'But now you've changed your mind.'

'That's right. I'll see Donleavy in the morning and tell him he's lost his passenger.'

When they arrived at their London home, Oliver and Mrs O'Haver met them in the lower hall. 'There's lovely news from your mother,' Mrs O'Haver said, 'but I'm not allowed to tell you. You'll find a message on the desk in your sitting-room.'

Sophie went straight away to the second floor, found the cable envelope on her desk and opened it.

ARTHUR AND I MARRIED THURSDAY. COULDN'T LOCATE YOU. SORRY YOU COULDN'T BE THERE. EVAN WILL GIVE

YOU DETAILS. WE'LL BE HERE IN SAN SEBASTIAN FOR
SEVERAL WEEKS. I'M VERY HAPPY. OUR LOVE TO YOU AND
KINCAID.

## 7

The following morning, as soon as Kincaid left the house,
Sophie went to Evan's flat. When he met her at the door he
said, 'I hope you've had your breakfast. There's not much
here except coffee. And a stale muffin perhaps.'

'I'm not here to eat. You know why I've come. I want to
know why I wasn't told about this wedding.'

'But you were told. When you rang me last night you said
there'd been a cable from your mother.'

'After the fact. It's humiliating. I think I can imagine why
she didn't tell me beforehand but it's unforgivable that you
didn't let me know.'

'Wait a minute. The first I knew about it was when
Margaret rang up to say she was trying to reach you but your
staff didn't know where you'd gone. I guessed that you'd
gone to Dinard but I learned long ago not to disturb you
there. It's impossible in any case. You're not listed at the
Bureau des Postes and you don't have a telephone. Also,
by the time I heard from Margaret, I barely made the
wedding myself. It was arranged for the next afternoon. I
went directly from Newcastle to Carlisle.'

'Why Carlisle, for God's sake?'

'It was a civil ceremony. Arthur insisted on doing it in
Carlisle.'

'You expect me to believe that you knew nothing about
all this until the day before the wedding?'

'Since you didn't know, why should I have been told?'

'Did they ask you to come along to the ceremony or did
you just go on your own?'

'They asked me,' he said. 'I was one of the witnesses. I
assume they wanted you for a witness as well.'

'I think not. Was Clara there?'

'Yes, she was.'

'And she was a witness along with you?'

'Yes.'

'Then they had no need for me. I was never meant to be there.'

'Nonsense, Sophie. I told you they were trying to locate you.'

'Of course they were. At the last minute.'

'As I understand it there was no chance to notify us sooner. Apparently it was a sudden decision.'

'I don't believe that for a moment and neither do you. Your father never makes sudden decisions about anything. Perhaps they did want you to be there but they certainly didn't want me. I expect that's what made things happen so suddenly. They wanted to do it before I came back.'

'Why would they do that?'

'I don't have the answer,' Sophie said. 'There are many things I don't have the answers for. In her cable Margaret said you would give me the details. So far I haven't learned anything.'

'What is there to say? A wedding's a wedding. You've been to dozens of them and so have I. People decide to get married and they do it. Sometimes it's a grand affair, sometimes it's simple, but the result's the same.'

'You're awfully cavalier about it. Is that really your attitude?'

'I don't have an attitude. It's none of my affair. When two people get married you can either applaud or get drunk or both. Nobody takes an opinion poll to help them decide whether or not they'll marry.'

'Of course they don't go to strangers but most people discuss it with their parents or, as in this case, with a son or a daughter. Are you saying that Arthur never hinted to you about what they planned to do?'

'No, he didn't. Did Margaret give you any clue?'

'None at all.'

'There you are. They decided to keep it to themselves till the last moment.'

'Doesn't that surprise you?' Sophie said. 'Doesn't it shock you?'

'I was surprised, I suppose, that it happened on such short notice. But on the other hand you and I have been talking since we were ten years old about the possibility of their getting together. As I recall, we were both keen for the idea.'

'Only because we were ten years old. If your father had come to you a month ago and told you what they were planning, if he'd asked for your reaction, if he'd simply wanted to know how you felt about it, what would you have told him?'

'I expect I would have congratulated him and told him it was a fine idea.'

'I hope not,' Sophie said. 'I hope you'd have had better sense than that.'

'All right, perhaps you're right, but let me ask you. What would you have said to Margaret under the same circumstances?'

'I know exactly what I'd have said to her. I'd have told her that she's gone through a series of traumas this past year, a particularly harrowing time in her life. You see, I'm convinced that she's not herself since Brannigan died. It's hard for me to imagine how she could have been so hopelessly devoted to a man like him, but there seems to be no doubt that she was. After the dreadful years she'd spent with the Major, perhaps it was inevitable that a man like Brannigan would turn her head and cause her to re-evaluate everything she'd believed in during her life. He mesmerized her, I think. Not in a bad way. I don't mean that. There was nothing manipulative or satanic about him. He simply showed her a way of thinking and a way of living that were new to her, and because she loved him and very much needed him just then, she put herself in his hands with the faith and optimism of a child. She opened herself up in a way that's quite unusual for a woman of her age and experience. She was in a joyful transition from what she'd always known and believed, to a whole new world of insights and freedoms. And Brannigan was her tour guide. Then suddenly, half-way through the journey, he was dead and she was adrift, somewhere in between what she'd been and what she'd started to become, vulnerable to the forces that were coming at her from both directions. She desperately needed a new route-map and she wasn't able to find one. That's what that sudden blinding hatred of the Major was all about. That was some final tribute to Brannigan, hard evidence that the direction she'd taken with him was a permanent one for her, that no tarnished monuments to the Major would be allowed to stand. She would continue to be Brannigan's woman, Brannigan's disciple, no matter what. That's where she's been, that's what she's been struggling to do through these months since he died, trying to remain as she was with him. But since Brannigan lived by no rules, no format, no credo, there was nothing he could leave her but memories of a delightful moment-to-moment experience. He had danced his way along paths that were visible only to him and she had followed. Without him she couldn't find her way. She began to feel, I'm sure, that not only had she lost him, she had lost herself, the self he had helped her to create, the woman who'd been strong enough and determined enough to free herself at last from the Major. You must know what I'm saying.'

'Of course I do. But I'm not sure how all this connects to Arthur. Are you saying she married him in desperation?'

'No. I'm saying she's a very confused woman who should not have made that sort of decision just now. Assuming it was her decision. If Arthur influenced her, if he took advantage of her vulnerability, then that's even more troubling.'

'I can't imagine Arthur influencing anyone. And I can't imagine anybody persuading Margaret to do something she didn't want to do.'

'Does that mean you approve of the marriage?'

'Approve? No one asked for my approval. They're grown-ups, for Christ's sake. They can do whatever they want to.'

'No one can do whatever he wants to.'

'Are you telling me that you sought family approval when you married Kincaid? If you had you'd never have married him. The Major was dead set against him and Margaret was something less than lukewarm.'

'This is a different situation altogether. Kincaid and I were in love with each other.'

'What does that mean? Are you saying nobody over the age of forty falls in love?'

'No. I'm saying that Margaret and Arthur may love each other in their way but they're not in love.'

'That's a distinction that only women make.'

'Nonsense. You know perfectly well what I'm talking about. I've told you that Margaret is dreadfully confused just now. She's unable to make clear decisions about things. And she's certainly in no frame of mind to make a decision about something as serious as marriage.'

Evan smiled. 'She obviously disagrees with you.'

After a moment she said, 'Did you talk to Arthur on the day of the wedding?'

'Of course. The four of us had champagne and cake after the ceremony. Then Margaret and Arthur went to the airfield to board their flight to London. They were staying all night there, in Paris then for two nights, and on to San Sebastian.'

'I mean, did you talk with him alone?'

Evan nodded. 'We spent half an hour together before the ceremony while Margaret and Clara were off somewhere discussing whatever ladies discuss before weddings.'

'How did he seem to you? What did he say?'

'He was quiet as usual. Seemed to be taking it quite seriously. Your mother on the other hand was laughing and full of fun. If you'd seen her I think you wouldn't be so disturbed.'

'Oh, God,' Sophie said, 'What a mess.'

'I don't understand why you're so bloody upset.'

'Oh, yes, you do. You may not want to understand but you understand very well. You know Margaret as well as I do. When she does something that's totally unlike her it means she's been influenced by someone.'

'Not by someone. By Arthur. Is that what you mean?'

'Of course. You see that as clearly as I do.'

'He obviously asked her to marry him. Is that what you mean by influence?'

'Of course not. I mean that someone took advantage of her present condition, her confusion and vulnerability, and persuaded her to do something she would never have done under normal circumstances.'

'But that's idiotic. If you could have seen her . . .'

'But I wasn't meant to see her. Don't you understand? Why else did they get married so quickly while I was out of the country? Arthur managed it all very well.'

'But why would he want to manipulate her like that?'

'Ahhh . . . that's the key question. He has his reasons, all right. I assure you, your father has his reasons.'

# • CHAPTER 8 •

## 1

When she left Evan's flat, Sophie went straight away to Sir Charles Tremont's office in Fetter Lane. He sat quietly at his desk listening to her. At last he said, 'It's clear that you're upset about your mother's marriage. Now I need to know whether you're talking to me as a solicitor or as a family friend?'

'As a solicitor. I'm concerned about the Wiswell estate. I'm not a legal scholar but I'm sure that a man acquires certain rights and entitlements when he marries a woman in my mother's position.'

'In certain cases, that's true. But not in all cases. There are blood rights, legal rights, marital rights. The laws on ownership are complex. I assume that ownership of assets is what concerns you.'

'Precisely. Wiswell Towers belongs to my mother, to me, and my children. As you know, my mother's brother, who has no children, signed over his rights to the Towers just after Sarah and Trevor were born.'

'You're saying that no Wiswell holdings should leave the blood-line family, that no one should be able to acquire ownership through marriage. I believe that has been the tradition, at least since I've been legal adviser to your family. When your mother divorced the Major it was clear that he had been given no ownership or property rights. And none were granted to Jack Brannigan apart from whatever changes Margaret made in her will.'

'That's what concerns me. The demands Arthur Tagg might have made. Or the assurances Margaret might have given him.'

'You understand, of course, that I can't discuss any bequests your mother has made in her will.'

'I understand that you won't discuss them.'

'I can't,' he said.

'But how do I protect my interests and those of my children?'

'As a family friend, I would say that I don't believe those interests are in jeopardy. As a solicitor, I must add that your mother controls the Wiswell estate and it's within her power to assign or re-assign portions of those holdings as she sees fit. As I recall, I saw no evidence of your concern when she was married to Mr Brannigan.'

'That was a different situation on several counts. One: I was away in California when she got married. Two: she was in much firmer control of herself and her life at that time. And three: Jack Brannigan was a different sort of man from Arthur Tagg.'

'In what way, may I ask?'

'He was in love with my mother. He didn't care if she had a hundred thousand a year or thirty shillings. Mr Tagg, on the other hand, has ambitions. In recent months he's come to believe that he's the true master of the Towers. And now he's found a way to make that come true.'

'I gather you dislike him?'

'That has nothing to do with it. I'm saying, I don't trust him.'

'But you trust your mother. Don't you think she's capable of looking after your rights and concerns?'

'Under normal circumstances . . . yes. But these are not normal circumstances. Because of what's happened to her in the past year she's in a vulnerable position and her new husband is capable of taking advantage of that vulnerability. I want to protect her. I hope you will share my concern and do what you can to protect her as well.'

Tremont smiled. 'That's my occupation. If my clients have problems and I'm unable to solve them, then soon I will have no clients.' He paused. 'Your mother is well aware, I'm sure, of the efforts I've made, and will continue to make, on her behalf. But until she tells me that she has a problem . . .'

'That's why I'm here,' Sophie said. 'I've just told you.'

'So you have. But my code of ethics does not allow me to pass your concerns along to Margaret, nor to make you aware of her concerns.'

'I understand all that. But this is not strictly a legal matter.'

'You may recall, I asked if you were consulting me as a solicitor and you said yes.'

'I should have said I was asking a friend for help in a matter that has legal implications.'

'I'm afraid the code still holds.'

'That means you won't help me.'

He shook his head. 'No, it means there's nothing I can do. Not at the moment. As I understand it, your mother was married just a week ago. I suggest you give the whole situation a second look after she and her husband have had a chance to settle in. I very much appreciate your letting me know what's on your mind. As I've said, I cannot report to you about any information I may receive from Margaret but when we do talk, she and I, the things you've told me today will certainly be on my mind.'

Late that afternoon Sophie told Kincaid about her meeting with Evan and Tremont. 'They both treated me like a child who'd run into a clean-swept room in muddy boots. Then after I came home here, I got another surprise. When I rang up the Towers, Trout told me that Arthur sent my workmen away. All the work and redecoration was halted just after I came down to London to see you.'

'Maybe your mother didn't want people in the house when you and she were both away.'

'Nonsense. I had told the builder that the work should continue and Margaret knew it. It's Arthur's doing. God knows what else he has up his sleeve. I have to go there, darling. I know I said I'd be staying here in London and I will be. But just give me a few days to sort things out and then I'll be back straightaway. But I won't move a step unless you promise me you won't go romping off somewhere. Was it New Zealand? Was that where you were going?'

Kincaid nodded. 'You're safe. The ship left yesterday.'


2


Sophie had arranged for Margaret's driver to fetch her at the Newcastle railway terminal. When he met her at the arrival gate she said, 'We'll be stopping at Wingate Fields on the way home, Alfred. I'm spending the night with Mrs Causey. We'll go on to the Towers in the morning.'

If Clara Causey had trepidations about Sophie's visit she concealed them. All through dinner she talked about the latest adventures of her daughter Nora and the accomplishments of her grand-daughter, Valerie. Clara's husband, Ned, his nose glowing a muted red in the candlelight, savoured his Nuit-St-Georges and sat quiet mostly, only occasionally blurting out a bit of county gossip or venturing an opinion about the future of wool prices if war should break out. Only when he'd excused himself after dinner and left Sophie and Clara in the drawing-room with their coffee were the two women able to discuss Margaret's wedding.

'She was dreadfully disappointed that you'd slipped off to France and she couldn't have you there with her.'

Sophie had decided to make a slow start, to hold her questions until Clara had volunteered whatever information she was willing to give. 'I'm sure of it,' she said. 'I was disappointed as well when I came home and found her cable waiting for me.'

'Fortunately, Evan was able to come up from London on short notice. And I filled in for you. It was a simple ceremony. Over in no time. Perhaps Evan has told you.'

'He did tell me a bit. But men never go into detail about such things. "A wedding's a wedding." I think that's the way he referred to it.'

'That's because he's never been married. Some little slip of a girl will bring him to heel one of these days and he'll find he has a whole new notion about the institution of marriage. I used to think he was lying in wait for you. And Nora agreed with me. But it looks as though we were mistaken. You've been married twice now but neither time to Evan.'

'I adore him,' Sophie said. 'I've always adored him. But since very few women end up adoring their husbands, I guess it's best that Evan and I have stayed as we are.'

Clara rang for more coffee then. 'And we'll have a bit of port as well.' After the maid withdrew, Clara said, 'When the ceremony ended we had champagne and cake, just the four of us. Did Evan tell you?'

Sophie nodded. 'He said Margaret was very gay.'

'All laughter and sweet foolishness. I'm sorry you couldn't have seen her. It was thrilling for me. Just a few weeks ago I was afraid I'd never see her smile again. It all seemed quite miraculous as we sat there making toasts and saying clever things to each other.'

Sophie had realized she couldn't grill Clara as she had Evan. The close connection between Clara and her mother required careful handling. As she'd come north on the train she'd sat in her compartment looking out at the fields and silently rehearsed the questions she would ask, plotted as to how she would insinuate them smoothly into the conversation. When she finally spoke up, however, it was as though she had made no preparation whatsoever. She said, 'Why didn't Margaret want me at the wedding?'

What her question lacked in subtlety it made up for in effectiveness. Clara seemed frozen in place, her cup halfway between its saucer and her lips. Sophie went on. 'You're closer to her than anyone. If you don't know the answer, no one would.'

Clara put her saucer and cup on the table beside her, touched her lips with a napkin and said, 'It was nothing like that, Sophie. I'm sure Margaret wanted you there. She tried to reach you . . .'

'I know. Evan told me that. But I told him I simply can't believe that Margaret decided to get married and two days later it was done.'

Clara smiled but it was an awkward smile. 'I'll admit, it doesn't sound like her. She doesn't rush into things, does she?'

'No.' Then: 'I know how close you two are. And you know how things have always been between Margaret and me.'

'I do indeed. I've often envied that relationship. As you know, it's something I've never experienced with Nora. We love each other, of course, but there's some competitive streak in my daughter that never allows the barriers to come down.'

'That's what I'm saying. There have never been such barriers between me and Margaret. Nothing of the sort. But in the past weeks I've sensed some change and it's been disturbing. Now there's this whole business about the wedding. I'm sure you realize I wouldn't be talking with you like this if I weren't upset. Perhaps it seems that I'm asking you to betray certain confidences that exist between you and my mother, but that's not my intention. I wouldn't have invited myself here today if I weren't quite desperate about the situation. I can't help feeling that Margaret has turned against me somehow. I'm sure you believe that she wanted me with her when she was married, she may even believe it herself, but I can't accept that. She and I have never made major decisions without consulting each other. Since I was a child I've never kept secrets from her, nor she from me. I never lied to her about Hugh. She was aware of my feelings about Toby Black as soon as I knew them myself. And even with Kincaid, in spite of the Major's shenanigans, Margaret always knew how I felt.'

'I know that.'

'She never tried to deceive me about the true relationship between her and my father. She never actually criticized him to me but on the other hand she didn't try to paint him as an admirable husband. And when she fell in love with Brannigan, I think I was the first person she told. So when I get a message from her saying, "Oh, by the way, I got married a few days ago", and when the man she's chosen is Arthur Tagg whom I've known for almost thirty years, I can have only one reaction. Why was I excluded? Not just from the wedding but from the decision. Very few days had passed from the day I left the Towers to go down to London till the day you all made the journey to Carlisle for the wedding. All that could not have been a matter of chance, Clara. I was not meant to be there and I wasn't meant to know. Now, for the first time in my life, I feel uneasy about seeing my mother. I'm angry and hurt. I don't know what I can say to her or what she might say to me.'

'I don't know how to respond. I wish I could say something to you that would . . .' Clara seemed to run out of words.

'All the way up here on the train I looked for answers. But the more I thought about it, the more confused I became.'

'I have a feeling that once you see Margaret again this will all be settled quite simply. She's as concerned about your happiness as you are about hers. If there's a misunderstanding it will clear itself up.'

'I hope you're right,' Sophie said, 'but I don't see how that can happen.' Then: 'Were you surprised when she told you she was going to marry Arthur?'

'Was I surprised?' Clara seemed cautious suddenly.

'Yes. Was it a total surprise or had she discussed it with you beforehand?'

For a long moment Clara didn't answer. At last she said, 'I adore you, Sophie. You know that. But I mustn't let myself be drawn into some sort of struggle between you and Margaret.'

'Why should there be a struggle, Clara? That's what I'm trying to find out. I ask myself if this is a problem between my mother and me or is Arthur my opponent? I assume you know there's been some tension there.'

'I sensed that. Although Margaret never gave me a detailed report. She mentioned that Arthur was slow to accept some of the changes you've been making in the house but it wasn't presented as a problem. I wouldn't have taken it seriously in any case because I remembered how keen you were to have him leave London and come back to the Towers. That was your first priority, as I recall, when you rushed back here from California.'

'Yes, it was. I thought he would bring some stability to things. It seems I was mistaken.'

'Perhaps you weren't. When Evan and I saw the two of them off from Carlisle, I felt as if I were witnessing a small miracle. I couldn't believe I was watching the same shattered woman who just a few months before was huddled here in my guest quarters afraid to go home, unwilling to see anyone. I wish you could have seen her, laughing and sipping her champagne. It was a lovely sight.'

'You didn't answer my question,' Sophie said. 'When she told you she was being married were you surprised?'

'You're relentless, aren't you?'

'I have to be. This is important to me.'

'I know it is. And I'll be as helpful as I can. Let me put it this way. I was surprised that she married so quickly once she'd made up her mind. And I did know about it a week or ten days before.'

'Before I left to go down to London?'

'Just after, I think. You see, if I was less surprised than you, it's because I'd begun to sense that Margaret's friendship with Arthur had taken a slight turn. I noticed it first, I think, when the two of them came here to stay with me at the time you were having memorial services for the Major. The change I saw was not so much in your mother as it seemed to be in Arthur. Small things. Gestures. Attitudes.

He seemed to be enjoying his food more. And the wine. And I don't believe I'd seen him smoke a cigar before. God knows, Margaret, from the beginning, has never treated him as staff. You know that. He's always been thought of as a permanent member of the household.'

'Not by the Major.'

'Of course not. But by everyone else. And now suddenly, on those days I'm mentioning, it seemed that Arthur, too, had acknowledged that he had an identity other than his work identity, that his value as estate manager was not his only value. I don't mean to say he was courting Margaret, nothing like that. I simply felt he was relating to her on a more personal level than I'd noticed before.'

'She said nothing to you?'

'Not just then. But gradually I began to pick up small clues. References to remarks he'd made, a piece of clothing he'd bought, some thoughtful thing he'd done or some compliment he'd paid her. No bright rainbows, no claps of thunder. But in a never-changing creature like Arthur, even slight modifications attract attention. Also my devotion to Margaret makes me particularly sensitive to anything that relates to her.'

'When she told you she was going to get married, did she tell you she hadn't told me and didn't plan to tell me?'

'I don't remember her saying anything about that.'

'Did she say I wouldn't be coming to the wedding?'

'No.'

'Then you didn't know till the day of the wedding that I wouldn't be there?'

'I believe she told me the day before that she hadn't been able to contact you.'

'God, it's so sickening.'

'I hope you're not over-reacting to this, Sophie. You mustn't assume it's a conspiracy of some sort.'

'But that's precisely what it was. When Arthur and Margaret decided that I wouldn't be told about the wedding . . .'

'Evan wasn't told either till the day before.'

'Of course not. They knew he'd tell me.'

'But Margaret doesn't behave like that. She never has.'

'I agree with you,' Sophie said.

'Then why would she suddenly do something so contrary to her nature?'

'There's a simple answer to that. Because someone influenced her.'

'Surely you don't believe . . .'

'Yes, I do. I believe that Arthur persuaded her to marry him and insisted that I should not be told.'

'But why on earth . . .'

'You said you'd noticed a change in him. Whatever you've observed is nothing, I'm sure, compared with what I've seen since I went to London and convinced him he must come back to the Towers. Even at the start, when we came up on the train together, I felt that something odd had come over him. He was dead silent for almost all the journey. I couldn't understand. Now I believe that was the beginning of the identity change you mentioned. Had he decided even then that he would marry Margaret? Perhaps not. But I'm sure he was aware that he would now be the dominant male in a house without a master.'

'Oh, Sophie . . .'

'I'm being candid with you. And I hope you'll be candid with me. Do you remember what your reaction was when she told you they were getting married?'

'I told her I was happy for her. I wished her the best . . .'

'I'm sure of that. But how did you feel? An hour later? A day later?'

'I was surprised. I admit that. Through the years I'd become very accustomed to Arthur's relationship with your mother, his importance to her. I felt terrible when he left and went off to London because I knew how much she depended on him. I also knew the strain she'd been under, and Arthur as well, because of the Major's accusations. It had never occurred to me that there was anything of that sort between

Margaret and Arthur. I realize there were people here in the county who assumed that under different circumstances the two of them would be married. But I did not assume that. I thought they worked well together in an atmosphere of mutual respect and affection, that it was a relationship from which each of them benefited enormously. Frankly, I believed that your mother's frustrating years with the Major had soured her on the whole notion of marriage. I couldn't imagine her ever taking that sort of risk again. Even when I knew she was seriously smitten with crazy and wonderful Brannigan, I didn't expect that it would end in marriage. But it did. And thank God for that. That was a lovely time for her. It ended sadly but all the same I'm sure she's never regretted that they had that time together. So what am I saying? Of course I was surprised when she told me about her plans with Arthur. And I had private misgivings. It's normal. Almost anyone who knows her would say she was reacting to all the sadness she went through last year. I thought the same thing. It worried me. It concerned me. But at last I decided that if there's such a thing as a safe marriage . . .'

'There isn't,' Sophie said.

'I know that. But if there were, Margaret's marrying Arthur would surely fit into that category. They've known each other for many years. They've gone through good times and bad times together. They're compatible, they're friends, they have common interests, and they're both in good health.'

'Is that a recipe for a happy marriage?'

'At my age it is. That doesn't mean there's no more fun in bed. It does mean there's somewhat less fun and it's always the same bed. Men like Jack Brannigan are hard to find.'

'What if I told you that I have a very different view of Arthur Tagg? What if I said that I think he's a self-serving man who's married my mother for personal gain?'

'I would discourage you from telling me that, I would try not to hear you if you did tell me, and if that failed I would find a way to forget what you'd said.'

Before he began to write his play, *The Fatherhouse*, while he was still writing character studies, descriptions, and making graphs of conflict and motivation, Evan wrote the following short piece in his notes.

A child can accept anything from a parent if it's consistent with the parent's previous behaviour. Surprises and changes, however, are not permitted. A father whose custom it is to wear sober cravats of maroon or grey must not discomfit his son by donning floral-print neckties or a scarlet cravat that features yellow parrots. A mother who drinks five bottles of lager between teatime and bed-time is no threat to her daughter unless she suddenly abandons beer and turns to pink gin. A father who has always worn a bowler will be criticized by his son if he changes to a tweed cap.

Although Evan was certain of neither the accuracy nor the profundity of these observations there was an apparent truth to them that fascinated him. Long after his play had opened and closed, when the characters and scenes had ceased to vibrate in his consciousness, he still remembered clearly that short preparatory paragraph he'd written. When he found himself in family situations, other people's families, he studied the parents and their offspring and tried to determine for himself which adult characteristics might be considered by the children to be permanent and unchangeable.

After Arthur's marriage, as Evan drove back to the Towers and as he rode by train to London the following day, he tried to examine the uneasiness he'd felt at the wedding and his continuing unquiet with Arthur's new marital status. Strangely, he worried the question for several hours before he admitted to himself that he was illustrating his own theorem about child/parent relations.

Once he'd ceased resisting, once he'd allowed himself to be a part of the conclusions he'd drawn about others, the facts came clear. He had been for all his life, a single-parent child. And Sophie, the other child he'd known best as he grew up, was also, for all practical purposes, in the same situation. The presence of Margaret, as fond as Evan was of her, only served to remind him that she was not his mother, just as Arthur's presence was a continuing evidence to Sophie that although she certainly had a father, he was an absentee.

By the time he was grown, at university and later in London, at an age when parents become either friends or embarrassments to their children, when he felt no need for parental love or supervision, Evan's motherless state meant little to him and his father became, in his eyes, a single man rather than a single parent. To Evan's analytical mind, Arthur's marital status came into even sharper focus when it was revealed (by Evan's mother) that technically and legally she and Arthur had never been married at all. He was a bachelor, Evan concluded, with a bachelor's habits and skills and compensations. He was master of his own movements, his meals, and his bedchamber.

When Evan had his first independent and solitary home after leaving the Towers and subsequently Oxford, he often looked round him at the books and pictures and odd bits of furniture he had assembled, and compared his flat with his father's rooms. He had made no conscious effort to duplicate that austere but carefully kept place, but even before it was called to his attention by Sophie when she first visited him there he had marked the resemblance in his own mind and had felt good about it.

When Sophie had said, 'Ah, I see it clearly. You've fashioned a monastic existence for yourself. Reading Swinburne and Shelley and isolating yourself from pleasures of the flesh,' he had replied, 'Not exactly.' As she'd proceeded to inspect his flat, had found two lady's night-dresses in the bathroom and a lacy kimono on a hook behind the bedroom door, she had said, 'I see what you mean. Not exactly monastic.'

Evan was, of course, unlike his father in almost every way. Taller, more athletic, more reckless, more iconoclastic, quicker to anger, less afraid of failure, more at ease socially, and much less influenced by public opinion. All the same, clinging to him like briars to tweed were certain conceptions and prejudices that had been part of him since pre-adolescence. Strongest of all these were his firmly held convictions about his father, what he was, who he was, and what he stood for.

Beginning with the telephone call informing him of the imminent marriage and continuing up to and through and past the ceremony itself, this monument he called father, which had been defined and identified by its flaws and debits and tarnished areas as fully as it had by its structure and polish, had slowly grown smaller, like snow sculpture in the rain. Arthur had shed his skin like an April serpent and slithered away. And Evan, in his way, felt as betrayed and abandoned as Sophie did.

In Evan's case, however, it was internal and subconscious. Whereas Sophie was both willing and able to articulate her displeasure, putting all the guilt on Arthur, Evan, sensing that it was unseemly for a man to be disturbed by his father's marriage, quickly identified with Sophie's disappointment and substituted her discomfort for his own. Thus, by changing the names, he was able to voice all his views on a sensitive subject without claiming authorship.

One late afternoon, two days after Sophie went up to Northumberland, Evan paid a visit to Kincaid, a fog shrouding Green Park, the windows steamy, and cold rain falling steadily.

'Brutal fucking weather,' Kincaid said. 'I'm surprised to see you out.'

'Had a drink, several drinks in fact, with a chap at the Savage Club. It's close by, so I decided I'd pop over to see you.'

Sophie had once said to Kincaid that for all of Evan's social grace and strong opinions on most subjects she felt he was terribly timid. 'I think that's why he makes such an effort to seem gregarious, to ask people questions about themselves, to listen so attentively to ridiculous views. It's all to cover up his shyness.'

'Maybe it's not that at all,' Kincaid said. 'Perhaps he pretends a great interest in people to cover up the fact that he doesn't give a damn about anybody.'

'What an odd idea. Whatever put that in your head? I thought you liked Evan.'

'I do.'

'Then why are you saying nasty things about him?'

'I said, he may be a closet misanthrope. There's nothing nasty about that. Some of my best friends have been misanthropes. They haven't even liked *me*.'

'You're impossible.'

Kincaid shook his head. 'Improbable perhaps but not impossible. You see, Evan had a great disadvantage. He grew up in a house of strong women and tentative men.'

'What nonsense.'

'Not at all. Margaret prevailed over both the Major and Arthur, Mrs Whitson dominates John Trout, and you rule everybody.'

'Utter nonsense.'

'Wait a minute. I'm not finished. In addition to that flaw in his upbringing, he's overeducated. I don't mean that he's learned too much. I mean, he's learned the wrong things. Evan believes that intelligence is his best weapon, and sadly enough, in his case, it's probably true. He thinks his brain can tell him where to go and what to do. If he were really smart, he'd know that the brain is only good for telling you where you've been and what you've done. All the critical decisions are made in some other part of the body.'

'The noble savage . . . I know that's your theory. But it's absolute poppycock, darling.'

'You see Evan as a civilized intellectual person, kind and

thoughtful and compassionate. I see him that way also. But I like him in spite of it.'

'You're doing it again, aren't you?'

'What's that?' he said.

'You know very well what I'm talking about. Every so often you decide to take an absolutely idiotic position and then defend it and expound on it unendingly. Pretending all the while that you believe what you're saying. And all this just to exasperate me.'

'Not true. Let's be fair about this. You choose to believe that Evan is precisely what he appears to be. Since none of us is what we appear to be why should he be the exception?'

'I'm exactly what I appear to be.'

Kincaid smiled and shook his head. 'Dead wrong. You are the exact opposite of what you think you are. But we'll go into that some day when we're in Brittany and there's plenty of time to explore it. For now I want to make one point about Evan. Then I'll get off the subject. We all like to drink and he's no exception. You get silly when you've had too much of the creature. Am I right?'

She nodded. 'And you get silent as a stone.'

'That's true. But what about Evan?'

'He holds forth.'

'Exactly. No more listening. No conversation or discussion. He lectures, makes speeches, goes on at great length. He dominates the table, the room, the scene, wherever it is. Takes charge. Takes over. He dominates. Isn't that true?'

'I wouldn't use your words, but yes, it's true.'

'Why do you suppose he does that when he's half-pissed and at no other time?'

'You tell me,' she said.

'I don't have the answer. But I think it's an interesting question.'

'I expected you to generalize and say that liquor brings out our true natures, the person we truly are or would like to be. If one expands that premise to include you and me,

309

the conclusion would be that I am at heart a silly giggling woman and you are, or long to be, a mute. How do you feel about that?'

'I think you're damned attractive and sexy when you giggle.'

The afternoon that Evan dropped in on Kincaid to discuss, as it turned out, Sophie's frame of mind, he was primed by his previous drinks at the Savage Club and determined, it seemed, to hold forth on that subject with no contribution solicited from Kincaid, who poured whisky, tended to the fire, and listened.

Evan wound down at last with a brief summation of all that had gone before. 'I have great affection and respect for Margaret, who is now my stepmother, and of course for Arthur, who is now Sophie's stepfather. And whatever my personal reservations may be about their decision to marry at this stage in their lives, I feel obligated to keep those sentiments to myself and to demonstrate my approval in every way I can. But this in no way diminishes the indignation I feel about the way Sophie was treated. I think she has a perfect right to be offended. Whatever their reasons may have been, they're indefensible. It makes me ashamed that I took part in the ceremony, and I feel guilty that when Sophie came to me I was not as supportive of her as I might have been, as I should have been. I'm sure you feel the same as I do. You must have been mad as hell when you saw how they've treated Sophie.'

'To tell you the truth I don't think you want to hear how I feel about it.'

'Of course I do.'

'One day I heard Sam Thorne talking about the art of making motion pictures, a subject that he doesn't seem to know much about. Do you agree?'

'How much money comes in and goes out, that's all Sam knows.'

'He had a formula for the kind of pictures Thornwood should make. "Happy people with happy problems." That was his idea.'

'Yeah, I've heard him say that.'

'Well, that's all I can think of when I hear you and Sophie moaning and groaning about two middle-aged people who decided to get married. If you ask me, it's not a question of who came to the wedding and who didn't, of who was told about it beforehand and who wasn't. It sounds to me as if you and Sophie, both of you, are simply pissed off because her mother and your father made up their minds to marry each other, then went ahead and did it.'

'It's not as simple as that.'

'Who says so? What's at stake? Why shouldn't they do what they want to? If they're not old enough to know what they want, when will they be old enough? Nobody has to tell them the facts of life, for Christ's sake. It's not a family matter. Everybody's not entitled to a vote. Sophie seems to think they got married for the wrong reasons. So what? If it works, it works. If it doesn't they'll either spend the rest of their lives fighting with each other or they'll split up. Everybody who's married doesn't feel good about it. Everybody who lives alone doesn't have a rotten life.'

'When you care about somebody, you hate to see them make a mistake.'

'Everybody makes mistakes. The only way to avoid mistakes is to die or go to prison. If you're born without arms or legs and you're strapped in a bed all your life, chances are you won't make many mistakes. But who the hell wants that?'

'Making light of it doesn't change anything.'

'I'm not making light of it. It is light.'

'I mean, it doesn't solve the problem.'

'There is no problem, Evan. That's what I'm saying. There is no fucking problem. You and Sophie have it in your heads that something has to be fixed. Or that something should have been fixed but wasn't. But you're whistling in the wind.'

'You're part of the family, too,' Evan said. 'I don't mean to say you're not. But it's different for us.'

'I can see that.'

'I mean, I guess we just look at things differently.'

'Yeah, I guess you do.'

Trevor's reaction when he heard about his grandmother's wedding was remarkably like Kincaid's. 'Why not? They've been friends for a long time, living in the same house. If they decided they want to get married now, why shouldn't they?'

Sarah, on the other hand, in rare agreement with her mother, was shocked and humiliated. She captured Evan for tea on one of her London days at the Royal Academy.

'Do you realize she's had three husbands in less than three years. And she's my grandmother, for God's sake. I'm surprised she hasn't been written up in the London scandal journals with photographs of the Major and Brannigan and Arthur, all side by side at the top of the front page. And a smiling photo of Margaret underneath. Sophie must be beside herself. How could she not be? And what must the staff be thinking? Thank God, I'm not still enrolled at Miss Endicott's. They'd expel me just because of my grandmother's antics. How dare she embarrass us all like this? Will Alfred the chauffeur be her next husband?'

'I know you're upset,' Evan said, 'but don't forget that Arthur is my father. No one needs to apologize for him.'

'Of course. I know that. I just feel sorry for him. She's put him in a dreadful position. Arthur's a lovely man. But surely you don't see this as an ideal marriage. I can't imagine how people in the county will react. That's not true. I know exactly what they'll think, that after years of living under the same roof, Margaret and Arthur have decided to legalize their relationship.'

'That's a rotten thing to say.'

'I don't mean that I believe that but many people will. And you know it. Why shouldn't they think that? Look at Sophie. She married an actor, for God's sake.'

'I thought you liked Kincaid.'

'I do. I'm talking about public perceptions. Not only is he an actor, he's Australian. Then Margaret divorces her husband and becomes the fourth wife of an Irishman who wanders about photographing country homes. And now with Brannigan and the Major scarcely cold in their graves, she's married her estate manager.'

'You're putting things in the worst possible light.'

'What choice do I have? What other light is there? I love my grandmother. You know that. I've always admired her and tried to pattern myself after her. But these past two or three years have sent me in circles. Since I was twelve years old I've been considered the rebel in the family. Unpredictable. Irresponsible. Liable to bring shame to the Wiswell name. Now see what's happened. Odd behaviour from the two women I'm supposed to use as models for my own conduct. Is there a lesson in that? There certainly is. The lesson is that all the words and the sermons and the strict schools and moral guidelines don't mean a thing. When the moment of decision comes you simply do as you please. Eat what tastes good. Do what feels good. And to hell with everything else. Am I supposed to feel guilty about following my own course when all round me people are doing exactly as they please? Not worrying a bit, it seems, about how it will affect other people. Am I supposed to lock myself in a room and never risk making a blunder? I don't see anyone else confining themselves like that and I don't intend to either.'

The next time she came into London, Sarah sent off a cablegram to Burt Windrow.

DID YOU THINK I'D PASSED AWAY? I HAVEN'T. BUT I'M STUCK IN LONDON. COME SEE ME.

5

Five days after Sophie left London to go to the Towers, Kincaid had a letter from her.

I will have talked to you by the time you receive this but I find it so much easier to write what I mean than to jabber away on the telephone. I detest talking on the phone, especially when it's long distance.

I stayed overnight at Wingate Fields with Clara. An awkward dinner with her and her impossible husband, Ned. Awkward because of him. He is certainly the world's most tedious and boring man. If boredom were a terminal illness, poor Clara would have been dead long since. At his present age Ned's scant intelligence and chancy information are accompanied by low energy, so he's no longer able to rattle on and be as boring as he once was. His mere presence at table, however, casts a pall over the whole exercise.

After dinner, however, Ned was ushered away and up the stairs by his man, Whiteacre, so Clara and I were left to ourselves for a nice chat. I won't go into detail about that, however, because as you can imagine our conversation centred on Margaret. Since you've heard all my views and complaints on that subject I won't parade them past you again.

Clara, as one would expect, has the instincts of a peacemaker. She was supportive, of course, and understanding, but her first and final loyalties will always be with Margaret and that, I suppose, is as it should be. I did learn, however, that the wedding plans were not the sudden last-minute affair that we had been led to believe. Quite apart from not asking me to her wedding, Margaret had obviously decided not to tell me about her decision to get married. So the excuse that I could not be reached is no excuse at all. When she made up her mind I was either still here at the Towers or I had just arrived in London before going off to France with you. So at last I know what I needed to know. All that remains now is to hear Margaret's explanation.

As soon as I arrived here I called Wilson, the construction supervisor, and told him to have his full crew, and additional men if necessary, on the job the next morning. I explained that all the work we'd planned must be finished in ten days, two weeks at the outside, before Margaret comes home.

As soon as I'd made those arrangements I called Trout and Mrs Whitson into the morning room and told them what I'd done. I explained that I was not displeased with them but I made it clear that in future, no order of mine was to be altered or countermanded by anyone. I could see that the situation made them uncomfortable but they understood what I was saying and I understood that they would do as I wished.

So that's the situation. I feel better about things now. I'll be fully occupied until Margaret comes home and then as soon as she and I have settled matters between us I'll come straightaway to London. I will be here a bit longer than I'd planned but there's nothing to be done about that. I'd love it if you'd come up but I know you won't. God, but you're a hard-headed man. I love you and I miss you and I'll be back there with you before you know it.

6

When he sat down to write a letter to his mother in California, Evan tried to remember, but could not, when he had last written to her. Nor could he remember whether she had written to him since he'd been home in England. He had a vague recollection that she'd made some reference to the Dillinger film but the letter, if she had written one, could not be found in his file drawer.

Since his days at Oxford he'd made a rule for himself that he would write to friends and family only when he was in a positive frame of mind, when he felt good about himself. From his own experience he knew that no one likes to open an envelope and have bad news tumble out.

In this instance he was writing, he assured himself, because it was an obligation. His sense of structure demanded it. Also, he felt, it was a joyous occasion. It would give Amy pleasure, he was sure, to learn that Arthur was married. She'd assumed long ago, or so she'd told Evan, that Arthur had married some woman in England. That thought had not seemed to unsettle her in any way so it certainly would cause her no pain now. On the contrary Evan believed she would feel good about it.

His letter, however, quickly took on a personality of its own. He did tell her, in the opening paragraph, that Arthur had married Margaret Wiswell, the woman in whose home he and Evan had lived since their return to England from America almost thirty years before. Beyond that he gave few details about Arthur or his new wife. He said simply that they had gone on a wedding trip to Spain and that they would continue to live at Wiswell Towers when they returned to England.

After those opening words, violating his own credo about what the tenor of a personal letter should be, Evan went into some detail about the less than buoyant state of his own mind.

I'm delighted, of course, about my father's decision. I wish him happiness and a good life. But I'm somewhat less positive just now in my thoughts about myself. I seem to be floating, in a way that's not at all pleasant.

Since I left university (some thirteen years ago) London has been home and a haven for me. My little flat here has always seemed like the centre of the universe. All the world's goods available. The culture of the centuries neatly kept in monumental buildings, each of them easily accessible. Great paintings, great music, libraries bulging with the most profound discoveries and concepts and conclusions that man has been capable of. An ideal place for a writer, I've always felt, the only place perhaps for a playwright.

But I've had another haven as well. Of a very different sort. The Wiswell home in Northumberland where I grew up. The solitude and beauty of life on the moors. Unlike London. Unlike any other place I've seen. The dales and ponds, the streams and fields. Deer and sheep and cattle, horses and house pets, dogs and cats and sweet canaries singing.

These two extremes of civilized living have always been available to me, they've anchored me, and I've felt fortunate for having them. But now somehow, and quite suddenly, neither place seems like home. When I'm in London, I have an urge to run off to the north. But as soon as I've slept for one or two nights in my rooms at the Towers, I'm anxious to board a train and return to London.

Since I've spent much of the past two years in America, in California, one might assume that I now feel rooted there. But I don't. No longing for the sunshine or the sound of the sea at night. No need for the hustle and bustle of film-making.

How can I describe the odd feeling of unquiet and dislocation that's come over me? The best analogy I can think of is this: I set something on my hall table so I'll be sure to take it with me when I go out. But when I've put on my hat and coat half an hour later and stand just inside the door, the object I'd carefully placed on the table is not there. Then comes a search of pockets and drawers and all flat surfaces, bookcases, cupboards, and under the cushions of chairs, a method-ical process at first, then more frenzied as one returns four of five times to the same place. Then comes a long pause, usually standing in the centre of the sitting room, when one calmly reviews all the movements of the past hour, tries to accomplish, by logic and calm and memory, what endless searching has failed to do. After this short period of calm, the search begins again. And again. Till at last, still wearing hat and coat, one sinks into a soft chair and accepts the fact that the object that can't be found may never be found. This is a feeling of helplessness like no other that I know. And it's the best description I'm able to give of my current state of mind.

I don't mean to upset you. You mustn't think that I'm miserably unhappy. I'm not. No one asks me what's bothering me. I don't bump into furniture or break delicate objects. I handle the daily mechanics of my life efficiently and well. People tell me how well I look. But all the while I feel like a wind-up toy, clicking and clanking its way through the day, then unwinding at last and tumbling into bed at night.

Perhaps I mentioned to you, when I was there in California, that I was seriously involved with an actress from London, a woman who had appeared in my play, *The Fatherhouse*, and who had later come to Los Angeles to be with me. She's married, I'm sorry to say, and has been for a long time, but she's been trying, since I've known her, to divorce her abusive husband.

I was very much in love with her, we were in love with each other, but things didn't work out, they couldn't work out. So we no longer see each other. Most of this happened before I left California. Except for one meeting here in London, we haven't been together for months. I admit that I miss being with her, I miss the life we had together, but if circumstances change, if it became possible for us to start again I don't think I'd be keen to do it. I realized that when I saw her here not long after I came back. Nor do I think she wants to be with me again. So, as much as I would like to find a tangible reason for the unquiet frame of mind I find myself in, I don't think I can lay the blame at Mary's door.

This letter, I suspect, is symptomatic of the condition I'm describing. Random and aimless, badly structured, stumbling about and seeming to go nowhere.

I should be able to draw some conclusions, to tell you that my head is starting to clear, but I can't do that. If you're saying to yourself, 'What has come over him?,' I can't blame you. Since I have no sensible answer to my dilemma I should at least be able to define that dilemma more clearly. But I'm unable to do that. As always, I'm moving in circles, finding myself constantly returned to the starting-point. Nothing clarified, nothing attempted, nothing accomplished. I feel guilty, dragging you into these cloudy corners but I suddenly had an impulse to see you and talk with you. Since that was impossible a letter, I felt, would be the next best thing.

Next time you hear from me I'm sure my cycle of gloom will have ended and I'll be forging ahead, laughing and dancing, with all flags flying. In the meantime don't worry about me. I will survive. I may even prevail.

7

In San Sebastian, in the Basque country of northern Spain, Margaret and Arthur stayed at the Maria Cristina: a wide beach in front of them, curved round the bay, and Mount Iqueldo behind them in the hills. They strolled the narrow streets of the old city, went for drives to Pamplona and Bilbao and Vitoria, sampled all the restaurants in the quarter where they lived, and chose at last their favourite, Casa Nicolasa. It was there, one evening during their last week in Spain, that Margaret brought up the subject she had promised herself she would avoid. 'I can't get Sophie off my mind,' she said. 'I know you and I discussed all this and tried to make a decision that would be best for everyone. But I can't help thinking I made a dreadful mistake.'

'If a mistake was made we both made it,' Arthur said. 'We may have been wrong but we weren't careless. We went over it thoroughly. It was a careful choice.'

'Careful perhaps but not kind. I don't blame you. You were trying to see it objectively from every possible angle. If we were wrong it *is* my fault, not yours. She's my daughter. I'm the only one who knows how close we've always been. It was up to me to say, "It's out of the question. I can't possibly keep this a secret from my daughter. I would never consider being married without her there."'

'Let me remind you what you said when we were discussing the matter. You said that since she hadn't been there when you married Brannigan . . .'

'That was an entirely different situation. She was in America. She and I discussed that in great detail. There was no way on earth she could have been in Letterkenny that day.'

'You also said that when she married Kincaid there was no one from the family present.'

'It's ironic, isn't it?' Margaret said. 'That I would do the same thing to her, knowing how much I was hurt when she did it to me.'

'But you got over it.'

'No, I didn't. I tried very hard, because the Major was making such a total ass of himself. I was anxious to make Sophie see that I understood why she'd gone off the way she did. And I did understand. But I didn't like it and it still bothers me. So I have a clear idea of how she's feeling just now.'

'I hate to see you torturing yourself about it. I think we should wait and see.'

'I don't have to wait. I know her. I know what's going through her mind. Sophie's a fanatic on the subject of family. All the traditions and rituals are important to her. One reason I was so upset about her running off with Kincaid the way she did was because I knew how disturbing it was to her. It's not her style. Not her way of doing things at all. She and Toby Black were married in the great hall at the Towers. Music and masses of flowers everywhere, formal dress, all the reception rooms crowded with family and friends and neighbours. That's the sort of wedding she and Kincaid would have had if the Major hadn't been such a fool. Everyone knew he was to blame in that instance. But this time I have no one to blame but myself.'

'I hate to hear you using the word *blame*. I know you feel bad but no crime has been committed.'

'Oh, I know that. And I'm sorry to be such a cry-baby, to put you in the middle. It's just . . . I don't know . . . there are so many things that bother me about it. As soon as I deal with one, another one pops up.'

'Do you want me to remind you what you said when we were discussing plans for the wedding?'

She shook her head. 'I remember it all.'

'I'm not sure you do. You were very concerned because there had been a strain between you and Sophie. We both felt it was because of me. You didn't want to risk spoiling something that was important to the two of us by causing additional friction with Sophie. You said, "There'll be plenty of time to sort things out with Sophie after we come home from Spain," and I agreed with you. I still think it was the best course. You and your daughter have been close for many years. Nothing's going to destroy that. Whatever may have been bothering her, she knows you're not her enemy. She also knows I'm not her enemy. The fact that you didn't tell her what you were planning, the fact that she wasn't present at your wedding . . . relationships don't break up on such grounds. Certainly not one as strong as yours and Sophie's.'

'My head tells me you're right. God knows I want you to be right. But why do I feel so rotten?'

8

On her way to Spain, just after she and Arthur had arrived in Paris for a two-day stop-over, Margaret had written a note to Clara.

How lovely it was to have you standing beside me during my wedding ceremony. What a sweet memory. Paris is lovely even though it's raining. Arthur and I are marvellously content. But I fret about Sophie. If you see her or hear from her, *please* write to me in San Sebastian and tell me how she is, what she's thinking, and what she's saying. I won't rest till I know how she feels about all this.

As she'd sat in her drawing-room with Sophie a few days later, Clara had been keenly aware of her responsibilities. She must listen carefully, observe closely, gather facts, and come to conclusions so she could make a full report to Margaret, an honest one, certainly, but one, if possible, that would tilt in the direction of optimism. She had no wish to be a bad messenger, no desire to spoil in any way Margaret's stay in San Sebastian.

After Sophie left Wingate Fields, just after breakfast the following day, Clara went directly to the morning-room, planning to write a letter to Margaret. But as she sat there, pen in hand, the thoughts and the words refused to come. She felt bound to tell the truth but the truth disturbed her. She decided at last that a wiser course would be to wait a day or so, give herself some time to think about the things Sophie had said and the way she'd said them. Then she could sit down and write an accurate and dispassionate letter. But the next day she postponed again. And the following day the same. At last, when her calendar reminded her that Margaret would be coming home soon she forced herself to sit down and write a report of Sophie's short visit.

How nice of you to send a card from Paris. What an enchanting place it is. I used to go there quite often with my father. But now that's all over. God knows, Ned has no interest in travel. Carlisle and Newcastle are far-away places as far as he's concerned. When I tell him about Hong Kong or San Francisco or Vienna, places I used to visit with Angus, Ned looks at me as if I'd just told him I have a deadly disease, one that might be passed along to him. My daughter, on the other hand, whose life has been studded with false starts and errors in judgement, certainly made a wise choice when she decided to live in Paris. I'm sure she'll never come back to England.

But you will, my dear. And as usual I will be eager to see you, to see if marriage has totally changed you, to hear your impressions of Spain and in particular San Sebastian. I haven't been there in years but I adored it before the war.

You asked me to let you know if I saw Sophie or talked with her. I have indeed seen her. She stopped here and stayed overnight on her way to the Towers from London. She and I stayed up late and talked the way you and I always do when you're here. After that long conversation, after Sophie had gone off the next morning, I decided I would not write to you as you'd asked me to do. I thought it was better for Sophie's thoughts and reactions to come to you directly from her once you've returned. I didn't want to risk making things worse than they are because of some inaccuracy in my reporting. I held with that conclusion until today. This morning, just after breakfast, realizing that you'll be coming home in a few days, it hit me suddenly that it wasn't fair to let you see Sophie again without some preparation for what you may be up against. So with a great deal of hesitation I will tell you, as accurately as I can, how she's feeling.

I'm sorry to report that she is bitter and bewildered and angry. She thinks she's been treated badly. It's not simply a question of her not being included in the wedding, although she certainly was hurt by that. She doesn't accept for a moment the story Evan told her, that she couldn't be reached because she was in Brittany. She believes she wasn't told about the wedding because you simply didn't want her to know.

She can't understand your making such a decision and not telling her, can't understand your taking great pains, she believes, to ensure that she wouldn't know. She sees it as a bewildering (that was her word) change in your attitude toward her. She doesn't understand it and she doesn't accept it. It seems she can only explain it to herself by believing that you were influenced, persuaded, manipulated in some way. And the villain in her scenario is Arthur. She's torn between her anger at him for engineering such a conspiracy (this, also, was her word) and anger at you for allowing him to do it.

I'm not exaggerating, Margaret. I wish I were. The fact is, I'm trying very hard not to overstate the case. As I've said, I'm trying to prepare you in some small way for what you are likely to encounter. I saw expressions on Sophie's face that I've never seen there before, heard a tone in her voice that was new to me. Unless I am mistaken, you will see and hear those same things.

I have experienced my fair share of family turbulence. The Bradshaws are no strangers to conflict. Strange mixtures of love and hatred in our blood-lines. Or so it seems. Nora versus Helen, her cousin, my mother versus my father, Angus versus Ned, Jesse versus Hugh, and many separate combinations of all those battles. But I can't remember the kind of suppressed rage I sensed in Sophie. She has turned against Arthur in a truly remarkable way. That may not surprise you but it was a surprise to me. She feels that he's competing with her, taking a stand against her. I don't understand why or how, but it seems quite clear in her mind.

I hate the thought of posting this letter. I know it will upset you. But I suspect it will not surprise you. I was aware that there were some tensions in your household. I hadn't guessed how sharp they were till my conversation with Sophie.

After such a dreary and negative letter, let me close by saying that I have no doubt that you and Sophie will find a way to get round this problem you seem to have. Nothing must be allowed to do permanent harm to the warm relationship you two have had through the years.

In Persia the king kills the messenger who brings bad news. Please spare me.

9

One early evening at the end of his work day Julian went to see Daisy Bishop in her bungalow on the Thornwood lot. Her dresser and her secretary were still there with her, and Linda, the woman the studio had engaged to look after her while the picture was shooting, was preparing dinner in the kitchen.

'You're a stranger,' Daisy said. 'I thought you'd forgotten about me.'

As soon as they saw Julian, the dresser and the secretary excused themselves and left.

'I had to make a trip to New York. I have to scurry around raising money so I can afford to treat my actresses like royalty.' He looked round the large sitting-room, fresh flowers in every corner, thick carpets on the floor, and a floor-to-ceiling cage of splendid tropical birds in the adjacent sun-room. 'Is this working out? Are you comfortable here?'

'It's wonderful,' she said. 'I don't have to think about nothing except learning my lines and doing my part.'

'That's why we wanted you to stay here on the lot all the way through the picture. We didn't want you to be distracted.'

'By Bob, you mean.'

'By anybody. Or anything. This is an important picture you're doing. You need all your concentration.'

'That's what Mr Cukor says. He says the acting's no good if you lose your concentration, even if you're not the one who's talking. He says that over and over.'

'He's right. Do you like him?'

'I love him. But I was scared to death at first. I know how good he is and how many top actresses he's worked with – I was afraid he'd yell at me or try to get me fired or something.'

'Nobody's going to fire you or yell at you when you're working for me. Besides, Cukor's crazy about you. Says you know how to take direction. He thinks you have a big future.'

'Oh, my God, that gives me goose-bumps, just to hear you say it.'

'You're good, kid. I've told you that before. And just because you don't see me every day doesn't mean I don't see you. I look at all the dailies and I like what I'm seeing. If you don't get drunk and run off to Catalina with McCrea, we'll have a dynamite picture. Eddie Roth, who's cutting it, says it's the best love-story he's ever worked on.'

'You're getting me crazy saying all those nice things.'

'Get used to it. You're a Julian Thorne discovery. You have to be good or it makes me look bad.' Then: 'How do you like McCrea?'

'You know what I think of him. I begged you to borrow him from RKO, remember?'

'I know you have a crush on him but how do you like working with him?'

'He's perfect. He's easy-going and he knows his lines and he's not on the make. But I don't have a crush on him. Not the way you mean. You know me. When I say I don't fool around, I mean it. He's just a lovable guy and he's terrific to work with.'

'That's good. It's hard to fool the camera, you know. When two actors like each other it shows. If the leading lady would rather kiss a cocker spaniel than the leading man that shows, too.'

'Listen,' she said then, 'I'm not being very polite. Do you want a cup of coffee or a whiskey or something? Linda says she can mix any kind of a drink there is. But you couldn't prove it by me. I never take a drink of anything with booze in it. Not when I'm working. And not very often even when I'm not working. But you go ahead.'

'No, thanks.' He looked at his watch. Then: 'What do you hear from Bob?'

'Not much. When he's off on location some place I usually don't hear from him. He's not a letter-writer. So I'll see him when I see him, I guess. Is he still up at Red Rock?'

Julian nodded. 'A couple more weeks. They've had bad weather, so they're five days behind schedule. As soon as that picture wraps he's due to go to Kanab. They'll be starting before he gets there, so he'll have to go direct from Red Rock.'

'He doesn't care. He likes to be busy.'

'I'm not sure he's going on to Kanab. That's why I asked if you'd heard from him.'

'Why wouldn't he go?'

'Our line producer at Red Rock is Abe Leslie. He called our production office a couple days ago and said they've been having trouble with Bob. Says he's having second thoughts about the deal he made with us.'

'He was tickled to death about it when he told me.'

'That's what our casting people thought. But now he thinks we hustled him. Promised him more money than he's getting and a more important part than he's playing. So he's been a bad boy. Doesn't want to do stunts or horse-falls and won't stage fights. Abe says he's been drinking on the job and last week he punched a prop man and broke his tooth.'

'Oh, God, he's at it again. Every time something good's about to happen for him, he finds some way to mess it up.'

'We've told Abe to try to smooth things over. So he'll be able to handle the situation if anyone can. But I wanted you to know what's happening. Our main concern is that you shouldn't be upset. So, if Bob tries to get in touch with you or if he barges in here some night to see you, at least you're forewarned.'

'I'm glad you told me. I don't even want to see him if he's

going to be drunk and crazy. I'll tell Linda to tell him I'm asleep or something if he calls up on the phone.'

Julian shook his head. 'I wouldn't go that far if I were you. Let's not turn this into a war. He understood when you started this picture that you'd be staying here on the lot till it wrapped. So there's nothing new about that. But if you won't even talk to him on the phone he'll start thinking we're ganging up on him. Then he could give us real trouble. We'll try to keep him on location for a few more weeks, but even if that blows up and he comes back to town, we'll make sure that people here on the lot will be looking after you.'

## 10

One morning, when Sarah came into London for her twice-weekly classes at the Royal Academy, she found Burt Windrow waiting just outside the building's entrance.

'Aah, there you are,' he said. He put his arms round her and kissed her on both cheeks.

'What a shock,' she said. 'You're the last person I expected to see.'

'I can't imagine why. You cabled me to come visit you in London so here I am.' He took her arm. 'Come, let's pop in here for a cup of tea and I'll tell you what I've planned for your weekend.'

'But I can't do anything. I have classes all day here at the Academy, then back to my dreary prison-school in Wimbledon for a Sunday of prayer and privation.'

'No problem, my darling. All is arranged.' He steered her to a table in the tea-shop, ordered a pot of tea and marmalade toast, and said, 'I seem to remember your saying you have an uncle named Howard.'

'A great-uncle actually. My grandmother's brother. Howard Wiswell.'

'Good, my memory hasn't failed me. While I waited for you to arrive this morning, I presented myself to the registrar of your school as your Uncle Howard, just arrived by clipper from America. Here for only two days, I said, and bloody anxious to spend some time with my niece. A family affair, actually, I told her. Gathering of the clan, so to speak, at Bath. So you're free and clear.'

'I can't believe it.'

'It's true. In the care of your uncle.'

'Only till tea-time, I'm afraid. If I'm not back in Wimbledon at five the headmistress will ring up my mum, Scotland Yard and the Archbishop of Canterbury.'

'All arranged. I explained the pressures of time to Miss Knotwood . . . isn't that the registrar's name?'

'Yes.'

'Explaining that we were in a great rush to rendezvous with the family in Bath, I asked her if she would be kind enough to ring up your headmistress, explain the situation to her, to say you'd be back for your classes first thing Monday morning. Told her your mother authorized all this, but she could not be reached because she too is on her way to Bath. Where is your mother by the way?'

'I can't keep track of her. I expect she's in Northumberland.'

'So much the better. You'll ring her there and tell her you've gone off with a school-friend to spend the weekend with her family in Canterbury, a family named Hastings.'

'But my mother will want a phone number where she can reach me.'

'And we'll give her the Hastings' number. Mrs Hastings is a dear friend of mine. An artist on the telephone. With a bit of background coaching she can handle any situation. If your mum rings up, Edith Hastings will praise your beauty and your manners and explain that you've gone off bird-watching with her daughter. Or if it's a late call she'll say you were dead tired from helping in the garden and you've gone to sleep.'

'You've made an elaborate plan then, haven't you?'

'No plan at all. I simply make it up as I go along.'

Sarah smiled. 'And where will I actually be all this time?'

'You'll be with me. If you're willing. Are you willing or have I flown half-way across the world for nothing?'

Sarah sipped her tea and looked at him across the top of her cup. 'Are you telling me you've come all the way from California to London only to see me?'

'Let me put it this way. That decision came first. But then I decided it would be an opportunity to do a bit of work in London as well. So after you've gone back to your school on Monday, I'll be doing a few interviews at the Savoy and the Garrick and picking up bits of gossip here and there before I fly back to America on Wednesday.'

'So I'm not your only priority?'

'Perhaps not. But you're my first priority.'

The reactions she'd expressed to Evan after Margaret's marriage to Arthur, her newly born conviction that the rewards in life were reserved for those who had the courage to claim them, had become more specific, if anything, since that day when she had put them for the first time into clear language. Was it the dissatisfaction she felt toward what she considered a regimented existence that caused her to feel that way, or did feeling that way create or stimulate her discontent? No matter. She made no effort, no real effort, to analyse or dissect how she felt. She only knew that she felt it more strongly with each passing day. Just as expressing her views to Evan had stimulated her to send off a cable of invitation to Windrow, so now did his appearance in London rekindle her belief that he was an ikon of opportunity, that his presence, his existence, were keys with which she could close certain doors and open new ones. Windrow would have been disappointed, angry perhaps, if he had known that this concept, this feeling of what he represented, was more exciting, more stimulating to Sarah than the prospect of a weekend alone with him.

All the same, as she lay beside him that night in an old inn on the coast road between Littlehampton and Bognor

Regis, she said, 'You're nicer than you were in California.'

'I'm always nice. Does that mean you didn't like me in California? I admit this place is an improvement over that drab motel in Culver City but I'm the same perfect person I've always been.'

'No, you're not. You're nicer now. I was frightened of you that night in California.'

'I don't believe you.'

'It's true. You were sweet to me. You could tell I was a dumb kid who didn't know anything. But something about you scared me.'

'You're not scared now, are you?'

'No.'

The inn was owned by a man named Barker, a former naval officer whom Windrow had come to know when he was living in Cape Town. Barker's wife was a slim and fierce-looking young black woman from Botswana and the chef in his kitchen was a one-eyed genius who had been renowned in Brittany for his St-Brieuc restaurant. One night, however, after a violent quarrel with his wife, a *femme de Provence* with a great black mole on one cheek, the chef, Gaillac by name, had driven to St-Malo, taken the overnight Channel boat from there to Portsmouth, and never returned to France.

Barker's clients, many of them, also came from France, to stay in the inn for a few days and gorge themselves with the cuisine of Gaillac. It was possible to spend a leisurely two or three hours in his dining-room and never hear English spoken.

'You see,' Windrow said to Sarah, 'I've brought you to a world of strangers. None of your mama's friends will see you here.'

'I don't give a damn about my mother's friends.'

'Ah, but I do. It could be dangerous for me if I'm discovered in bed with a twelve-year-old girl.'

'Don't be a bastard. I'm almost seventeen,' she said.

'Almost seventeen means you're still sixteen.'

331

'Don't you remember the first time you saw me, at my school in Ojai. You wrote in your column that you thought I was twenty years old.'

He smiled. 'I think I said nineteen. But the law doesn't concern itself with perceptions. It only looks at birth certificates.'

'Are you planning to bundle me on to a train and send me back to London? Is that what this conversation about my age is about? Do you think I'm too young for you?'

'Not at all. By the time you're twenty, I'm sure I'll think you're too old for me.'

'By the time I'm twenty perhaps I'll have forgotten I ever knew you.'

'Don't be angry. I was just joking.'

'I don't think it's funny. I'm tired of being reminded of how young I am. I'm as much a woman as I'll ever be. I'm surprised you don't know that. Perhaps you have a bad memory.'

'Not at all. I didn't come all the way from California to England to visit a child and take her to the zoo.' He took a small tissue-wrapped packet out of his jacket pocket. 'I brought you a gift. I planned to give it to you later, but since we got on this subject, and since you seem to be at odds with me, perhaps I should give it to you now.' He put it by her plate. 'Open it. I think it will please you.'

She carefully removed the paper. She was holding a passport in her hand, an American passport. When she opened it she saw her picture. On the opposite page the name: SALLY CARPENTER. Birthplace: NEW YORK CITY.

'What is this?' she said. 'Is it a joke or something?'

'Not at all. It's an official United States passport.'

'But it says I was born in 1915.'

'That's right. You're twenty years old. You want to be a grown-up woman. I just fixed it for you.'

'But it's not my name.'

'Yes, it is. When you want it to be. Whenever you have that passport in your hand, you're Sally Carpenter. I guarantee you, you can travel any place in the world with that document.'

'But it's a fake.'

'You know that and I know it. But no one else does.'

'But where did you get my picture?'

'A guy I know prints a scandal sheet in Los Angeles. He ran an interview with you and your picture in a bathing-suit. Did you see it?'

She nodded. 'Everyone saw it. That's why I had to change schools.'

'He gave me a print of the picture. I had a copy negative made, just of your head, and gave it to another acquaintance of mine who specializes in fake driver's licences, marriage licences, and passports. Do you like it?'

'I think so. But what can I do with it?'

'Whatever you want. It gives you freedom.'

'But I'm not planning a trip.'

'Maybe not. But you could. This means, you're not tied to anything, not even to your real self. It's the best identification in the world. You can go wherever you want to go and be what you want to be. You've got a secret now. You can be somebody else whenever you choose. And there's another advantage as well. If the police catch me in bed with you and want to send me to jail for sleeping with a child, I can always say I saw your passport and it proves you're twenty years old.'

'I see,' she said, 'this gift's for you then, not for me.'

He smiled. 'It's for both of us.'

# BOOK THREE

BOOK THREE

# • CHAPTER 9 •

## 1

The day after Margaret received Clara's letter, she and Arthur started their journey home, three days earlier than expected, not stopping over in Paris as planned, nor in London. When they arrived at last at the Towers it was nearly midnight of the second day. John Trout met them at the west entrance, supervised the handling of their bags, then followed them into the entrance hall. As he closed the door behind him, Margaret said, 'Isn't that Sophie's luggage just there inside the foyer?'

'Yes, it is. She asked me to have it left there.'

'Has she just come up from London?'

'No. I believe she's going to London. Early tomorrow morning.'

'Was she told that I'd be arriving tonight?'

'Mrs Whitson spoke to her about it as soon as we heard from you.'

'Ah, that's good.' She looked at the hall clock. 'I'm sure she's still awake then.'

'Actually, her maid said she retired quite early. She asked that she not be disturbed.'

Margaret had not discussed Clara's letter with Arthur. When he asked why they were returning to England sooner than planned, she said, 'I thought it would be nice to be home again.' When he didn't answer she said, 'Have you married an old lady, Arthur? Set in her ways? Longing back

337

to her dressing-table and her own soft bed?'

'Not at all,' he said. 'I'll be happy to be back home as well.'

He was not deceived, of course. The past months had taught him that when there was a certain tightness around Margaret's mouth, when she was restless but silent, when she continually picked up small objects and put them down again, when no subject seemed to hold her attention, when all or some of these symptoms were evident, the reason behind this unquiet was her daughter. Only Sophie could untrack Margaret's concentration, make her hesitate, make her forget.

Arthur was eager to believe that Sophie had been left behind when he and Margaret went to Spain. But though her name had scarcely been mentioned in San Sebastian she had been very much with them. Now, he sensed, there would be some new surprise for Margaret. And for him as well. But as he looked at Sophie's beautifully kept leather luggage martialled there in the lower hall, he had no idea what that surprise might turn out to be.

As they lay in their bed together, each of them awake but pretending to be asleep, Arthur, if he'd been granted a magic wish, would have asked for a long and peaceful night. Margaret, on the other hand, was intent on squeezing the night together, making it last only one hour if that were possible. Already, in her mind's eye, she saw herself sitting across the breakfast table from Sophie, or comfortably together with her in the morning-room, or in an upstairs sitting-room, slowly and sensibly untangling the mis-understandings they had allowed to separate them.

It was not Margaret's intention to argue her case. Or to defend herself. She was eager to capitulate. Totally. Uncon-ditional surrender. Plead guilty and subject herself to the mercy of the court. Any other solution she had considered was out of the question now. Slowly and painfully she had come to realize how much her life was intertwined with that of her daughter, how necessary it was that each of them should be always available to the other, that their lifelong connection should never be broken. She told herself that Sophie's true feelings were a perfect match for her own, that once they had talked and laughed or wept together, their differences would be swept away and the bonds that had held them together since Sophie's birth would be stronger than ever.

This is not to say that Margaret was in any way having second thoughts about her marriage. In fact, the days in San Sebastian had made her feel quiet and safe in a way that was new to her. Neither she nor Arthur had been transformed by the ceremony of marriage or the daily experience of it. They did not seem different to each other. They simply felt as though they had completed a journey that had begun years before. The final barriers between them had simply dissolved and at last they were free to touch each other.

Margaret had no intention, however, of trying to explain or describe these new feelings to Sophie. For one thing, she was acutely possessive of this new part of her life. Also, she insisted to herself that the strained relations between her and her daughter had nothing to do with Arthur. To reach this conclusion she played various tricks with her memory, readjusted certain facts, and fashioned a solid credo out of half-truths and wishful thinking. When, in weak moments, she questioned this process, she told herself that even if she was mistaken, even if Sophie did have some confusion or resentment about Arthur, it would sort itself out now that, after many years in limbo, he was a certified member of the family. Small obstacles would disappear, she told herself, when confronted by that larger truth.

These reassurances, which had been weakened and damaged by Clara's letter, came to life for Margaret again as she lay sleepless but quiet in her bed, Arthur, gone to sleep at last, beside her. Simply being in her house, in her own bedroom, surrounded by familiar things, had slowly strengthened her. Knowing that Sophie was there too, sleeping in the west wing, reassured her also. Once the two of them were able to sit down together, she told herself, still in their dressing-gowns perhaps, once they were able to talk and defer and compromise and at last agree, that ill-defined amorphous thing that had separated them would disappear. At last, feeling she had slain all her dragons, she fell asleep.

The morning sounds of the great house had begun when she woke up. Arthur was still sleeping. She slipped out of bed, put on her dressing-gown, and walked softly to her sitting-room, easing the door shut behind her. She rang for her maid then. When she came in Margaret said, 'Is my daughter up yet, Rose?'

'Oh, yes, mum. Up and had her breakfast and almost gone. I think Alfred will be bringing the car round for her at any moment now.'

'Is she still in her rooms?'

'I think not. I saw her going down the stairs, all dressed for travel. I expect she's in the drawing-room.'

'Hurry down there and tell her she mustn't leave till I've seen her. Tell her I'll be down straight away.'

A few minutes later when Margaret came down the stairway into the lower hall she saw Trout and Alfred at the entrance where Sophie's bags were being carried out. Sophie was with them. As Margaret hurried along the broad hall, Rose came up to her and said, 'I told her what you said, but she seems to be in a dreadful hurry.'

'Never mind, Rose. She sees me now.' As she came up to Sophie, Margaret said. 'It was terribly late when we came in last night. I was hoping to come to you earlier but I over-slept. Come sit with me while I have a bit of breakfast.'

'I had breakfast in my room.'

'Then we'll have some coffee together. It's dreadful having you leave like this when I've just come home.'

'Just bad timing, I'm afraid.'

Trout came back inside then and said, 'The bags are all stowed away.'

'Thank you, Trout. Tell Alfred I'll be along in a moment.' She turned back to Margaret. 'Sorry, Mother. I'm afraid I have to run.'

'No, you don't. Not this minute. Come into the music-room. We'll have some coffee brought in there.' When Sophie didn't answer she said. 'I very much need to talk to you and I won't do it standing in the hall with staff dashing back and forth.'

'I agree. We'll talk another time.'

Margaret went suddenly quite pale. 'Listen to me, Sophie. I know you're angry with me . . .'

'No, I'm not.'

'Yes, you are. I know you are.'

'Why would I be angry?'

'I don't know. Perhaps you feel you have good reasons. That's why we have to talk. Surely you're not so pressed for time that you can't spare me a half-hour.'

Sophie looked at her watch. 'I do have to be in London. I thought I'd be underway by now.'

'Please, Sophie. I want to tell you how sorry I am. I know you were upset about my wedding . . .'

'Why would I be upset? I've just ordered you a handsome gift. They promised to deliver it here in a fortnight.'

'I understand how you feel. That's what I'm trying to say. Of course you should have been at the wedding . . . I know you were hurt.'

'Not at all. I couldn't have been there in any case. Kincaid and I had gone off to Dinard. He sends you his best wishes, by the way, along with mine.' She looked at her watch again.

'Why are you doing this?'

'I'm sorry. I don't mean to be abrupt but I . . .'

'Why are you acting like this? I'm trying to tell you quite humbly that if I've done something to hurt you I'm sorrier than I can say.'

'There's no need to apologize,' Sophie said.

'There must be. If you're not angry or hurt, what possible reason could you have for treating me like a stranger?'

Sophie leaned forward suddenly and kissed the air near her mother's cheek. 'Now I really must go. I'll ring you from London first chance I get.'

Margaret stood where Sophie had left her. A freshet of air cooled her as the entrance door opened and closed. She heard the purr of the engine outside and the opening and closing of the car door. Then there was the whish of tyres on gravel as the car pulled away from the house and turned down the driveway. Margaret stood there till Trout came back inside. When he closed the door she walked back along the hall and went upstairs to her rooms.

2

'I feel as if I'm to blame,' Arthur said. It was early evening of the day Sophie had left for London. Arthur and Margaret, dressed for dinner, were having cocktails in the library.

'But you mustn't feel that way,' Margaret said. 'It's simply an ugly situation that's developed between my daughter and me, and we'll have to work it out as best we can.'

'I know you're trying to shield me but there's nothing to be gained by ignoring the facts. You know she was extremely annoyed with me even before you and I were married, so it stands to reason, in light of the way she behaved this morning, that she's included you in her feelings about me.'

'I know what you're saying. I haven't forgotten her note to you or that awkward meeting we had just afterward. But none of that explains why she's suddenly turned on me. Even if she detested you, and she doesn't of course, but even if she did, that would be no reason for her to act as she's doing toward me.'

'I don't think you should see her performance this morning as a final statement. I'm sure she'll come round in a few days.'

'I wish I had your optimism but I don't. Nor would you if you'd seen her in the lower hall this morning. There was something absolutely cold and cruel about it. She was unrecognizable. Brittle and unresponsive and determined to be on her way.'

'But that will pass. Once she's back in London, when she's had time to think about things. She'll ring you in a few days, I expect, and she'll be her old self.'

'I know you're trying to make me feel better but do you really believe what you're saying? You remember we discussed all this quite thoroughly when we decided to get married. At that time we were trying to understand why she was so out of sorts with you. I couldn't bring myself to tell her this morning that she hadn't been told about our plans because we were afraid she'd make a scene, that she wasn't invited to the wedding because we knew she wouldn't come if we did ask her.'

'So there it is, you see. Her behaviour this morning was simply a continuation of the way she was before. It seems clear that I'm the source of her discomfort.'

'But why?'

'I said this before . . . I think she resents me. She seems to have decided I'm in competition with her.'

'For what?'

'Who knows? For you perhaps. For some final authority. That note she sent me seemed to suggest that I should be more aware of the chain of command, that I should do as I'm told and not be too eager to take the initiative.'

'But that's nonsense. You've been in charge of things here for years. That's what annoyed the Major so. Why should your authority suddenly be a threat to Sophie?'

'I'm not sure. But if I was a threat to her before, I expect that threat has greatly increased now that I'm your husband.'

'I can't believe that, Arthur.'

He smiled. 'You don't want to believe it.'

'I've asked you this before but I'll ask you again. Did anything happen between the two of you that I'm not aware of? An argument. A discussion. Anything unpleasant?'

Arthur shook his head. 'Nothing of the sort you're talking about. But there was a change in our situation once I agreed to come back here. Always before Sophie had shown little interest in estate affairs, the lands, the tenants, the staff, legal and financial matters, all the things that you had put in my hands through the years. Now, all of a sudden, when she'd returned from California after Jack Brannigan's death, she seemed to feel it was her duty to take over your role without knowing exactly what that role has been. She made it clear that she wanted to be involved in estate affairs and decisions, so I worked with her. I explained all the details to her as we went along. Sophie's a bright woman. She learns quickly. But as you well know, there are some subtleties about land management, sheep and grain markets, and the buying and selling of shares that one learns only by experience. So when Sophie began to suggest ways in which she thought we might strengthen our position financially, I simply pointed out to her the courses that we'd found to be wise and others that I knew were less successful. At first she seemed amenable to my remarks but gradually she began to insist on making choices of her own. At last, to keep peace, I agreed to let her try a modest investment venture she was keen about. As I had predicted, it turned out badly. We quickly suffered a loss of just over a thousand pounds. But that lesson seemed lost on her. As one thing after another came up, I began to see that she was determined to make the point that whereas I knew the mechanics of estate management it was she who must make the critical decisions.'

'Did she say that in so many words?'

'It wasn't necessary. She made it clear by her actions. By the entire pattern of our daily discussions.'

'But there was no argument?'

'Of course not. Even when she asked my opinion of her changes in the rooms and her redecorating schemes, when I gave her my honest views in the matter, there was nothing argumentative or contentious about the discussion. It was plain to see that she didn't welcome my comments, and there was no suggestion that she would in any way alter her plans, but until she sent me that note I didn't realize she was saying that I must stay in my place and not exceed my authority.'

'It all seems so unlike Sophie,' Margaret said. 'Is it

possible that both you and I have misread this whole situation?'

Arthur shook his head. 'No, it's not possible. You read the note she sent me. It was very clear. Let me ask you something. Is it possible that your conversation with her this morning was different from what you described to me?'

'No. It was just as I said it was. But I still can't believe there's nothing to be done. I know Sophie as well as I know myself. I refuse to accept the fact that she's turned away from me because you and I decided to be married. It makes no sense, Arthur. I simply will not allow it to happen. If I've offended her or hurt her in some way, then I'm entitled to know what it is I've done. If that's not the problem, if all this is the result of some change that's come over her, then I have to find out what that is. Do you agree?'

'Of course I do. I'm just not sure how to bring all that about. I have a feeling that for now you should let matters rest.'

'That's what I can't do.'

'When she's had some time to think,' he went on, 'I'm sure she'll see things more clearly.'

Margaret shook her head. 'That won't do, Arthur. I can't just sit here hoping she'll come to her senses. The more time goes by the more difficult it will be for us to talk. I don't want to think of her as she was this morning. Nor do I want her to remember me that way. Never in my life have I been in the downstairs hall in my dressing-gown. I don't expect I ever shall be again. I trust your instincts, Arthur, I always have, but in this instance, I believe that the sooner Sophie and I can talk and say whatever needs to be said, the sooner things will be set right again.'

Before she went in to dinner she rang Sophie's home in London. 'I'm afraid she's not in,' Oliver said. 'She and Mr Kincaid have gone out to dinner.'

'Please tell her I called. And ask her to ring me in the morning.'

'Yes, of course.'

The next day, after waiting till late morning for a call, Margaret rang London again. Sophie had gone out to a luncheon. When she called that evening, she was told that Sophie was sleeping and had left instructions she was not to be disturbed. Margaret called at least once each of the next five days. She was never able to reach her daughter and her calls were not returned.

'I must go there,' she said to Arthur. 'There's no other way. Don't you agree?'

'This is between you and Sophie. You have to do what seems best to you.'

'That means you don't agree.'

'No, it doesn't. My feeling is that you have nothing to apologize for. Also, Sophie doesn't seem eager to talk to you, so until she is I think you should try to be patient.'

'Maybe I should, but I can't.'

3

When she returned Monday morning to her school in Wimbledon, Sarah went directly to the office of Wilma Fletemyer, the headmistress. 'My mother asked me to thank you for allowing me to join my family in Bath this weekend. She wanted to make sure it gave you no cause for concern.'

'Not at all. When Miss Knotwood rang me after she spoke with your uncle and explained that the Academy had excused you from your classes on Saturday we accepted her assessment of the situation.'

'If you tried to contact my mother I'm sure you discovered that she too was on her way to Bath.'

Miss Fletemyer smiled. 'Of course we have both of your mother's telephone numbers on file but I saw no need to question Miss Knotwood's explanation. Our rules are strict here, as you know, but we also try to show reasonable flexibility on special occasions, particularly for a student whose record is as exemplary as yours has been. Was it an enjoyable weekend?'

'Yes, it was. It's always a pleasure to see one's family gathered together.'

'I'm sure your uncle must have enjoyed himself.'

'Yes, I believe he did. I'm quite sure of it.'

Late that evening, in her room, Sarah took the passport Windrow had given her out of her bag and inspected it carefully, turned each page from front to back, trying to imagine the stamps that would accumulate on those pages in five years, or ten, evidence in purple ink of all the countries that would be visited by Sally Carpenter. Each time she'd seen her reflection in the bathroom mirror at the inn outside Littlehampton she had whispered, so it couldn't be heard in the bedroom, 'Hello, Sally Carpenter, *bonjour*, Mademoiselle Sallee.'

From the moment Windrow introduced her to his friend, Will Barker, as 'my fiancée, Sally Carpenter, a film actress from California', Sarah fell smoothly into that role. She wore discreet amounts of eye-shadow, mascara, and lip-rouge from a shop in Guildford, and a sleek black frock and high-heeled pumps, also purchased in Guildford, where they'd stopped on their way to the south coast. In her new clothing, in an unfamiliar place filled with strangers, and with a new identity, she called on the acting skills she had begun to develop at Ojai and at the Royal Academy, and became, as though she'd been hired for the role, a fresh new person, a composed and sparkling twenty-year-old actress. The American accent she'd used to amuse her friends at school she now used as the voice of Sally Carpenter.

As she'd told Evan when they discussed Burt Windrow, she had never been deceived by his charm, his beauty, or his extravagant accounts of his own worth. She had not of course discussed with Evan the sexual indoctrination she'd received during that long sultry night in a motel in Culver City, but that, too, as wildly new and exciting and frightening as it was, seemed almost theatrical to her, a performance, an exhibition. Her sixteen-year-old wisdom told her it was a strangely impersonal experience for him and thus it became the same for her. When it ended, when it was daylight at last and the taxi came to take her back to Kincaid's house in Malibu, although she felt light and floating and paper-thin, it seemed that no truly essential part of herself had been surrendered. Having done everything that was asked of her and everything she'd asked of herself she felt as though she'd given away nothing of real value. When she and Windrow had parted, she felt that she was unchanged and so was he. While she treasured what had happened to her she attached no deep significance to it.

This second time, however, would be totally different. She knew that from the moment she saw him standing on the pavement in front of the Royal Academy. If he had used her before, and she was certain that in his mind he had, she would use him now. Not as a sexual toy but as a symbol of something far more vital to her. She needed to demonstrate to herself that the light-hearted freedom of choice and action which, in her angry conversation with Evan, she had attributed to both Margaret and Sophie, that same carefree, don't-give-a-damn attitude was now available to her. She could risk whatever she chose to risk, ignore whatever rules threatened to inhibit her, and give herself as freely as she liked. A rite of passage, with herself in control, for her eyes only. Smashing locks, opening doors, hurdling walls.

The passport he'd brought her, the new name he'd provided, had given her the final push. By the time they arrived in Littlehampton she had become a new and marvellous person named Sally Carpenter, and he had become an adventure. No man, no situation, was a threat to Miss Carpenter, certainly not this tall and beautiful, sun-tanned and empty creature. Sally was in love with a man who was not yet available to her, so for now she would amuse herself with a handsome fool who imagined he was amusing himself with her.

It was a glorious actor's experience for her. As they walked by the sea, sat on the causeway, drank wine in a dockside pub, gorged themselves with seafood, danced to the accordion and snare-drum band at the inn, or tumbled together in the four-poster bed, she envisioned cameras following them always, shooting film from all angles, while she, Sally Carpenter, carefully sought out the lens and the light that served her best.

Her triumphant moment came, early Monday morning, still dark, as they were having coffee in bed at the inn before driving back to London. He turned her face into the lamplight and said, 'I don't recognize you. What happened to that schoolgirl I picked up in London Saturday morning?'

'She's slain. Run down by a lorry in Old Brompton Road.'

'Then who are you?'

'I'm Sally Carpenter. You invented me.'


4


The first night she was home from Northumberland, Sophie said to Kincaid, 'I want to drink great flagons of champagne and dance in my bare feet and tell you about all my triumphs. I feel like one of King Arthur's knights, blood on my lance, just returned from the land of the infidel.'

'You're in high spirits. You must have killed a lot of people.'

'I killed no one. But I firmly planted my flag. Defended my honour. Rescued myself from shame.'

They sat in the music-room then, lights dimmed, a logfire burning, and chilled bottles of champagne arriving steadily from the butler's pantry. Sophie's eyes were bright, her cheeks glowed pink from the heat of the fire, and she talked, almost without pause, for more than an hour. At last she said, 'There you are, my lord, a complete account of my victory. Since I've come from a land where I am not loved or appreciated or accepted in any way, you will recognize,

I'm sure, how eager I am to be praised and lauded before I'm carried upstairs to bed.'

'To tell you the truth, I don't think you need any praise. From me or anyone else. You seem to know your worth.'

'And for good reason. That's what you're supposed to say.'

'And for good reason,' he said.

'That's better. I'd appreciate a bit of spontaneity but if that's the best you can do . . .'

'Maybe I've had too much champagne. Why don't you pretend you're me. You praise yourself, leaving nothing out that deserves mention, and I will simply nod my head and clap my hands whenever there's a pause in the eulogy.'

'That's a fine idea. Now remember, this is you talking, telling me everything I've done and telling me how marvellous I am. It's not Sophie boasting about herself. It's Kincaid boasting about his wife, publicly giving her the credit she so well deserves. Is that right?'

'Exactly. Sophie Kincaid will now speak as if she herself was Kincaid.'

She smiled and nodded, then cleared her throat. 'Do I have to lower my voice so I'll sound more like you?'

'Not necessary. Just get on with it.'

'Very well. Here goes,' she said. 'Sophie, my precious and beautiful and valuable wife . . .'

'That's a little thick, isn't it?'

'Never mind. Please don't interrupt yourself. Because that's what you're doing, you see. When you interrupt me, since I'm speaking for you, you interrupt yourself.'

'Of course. You're absolutely right. Go on,' he said.

'Sophie, I'm here, before all these people, to praise you and salute you. On several counts. First of all, let's talk about the plot against you, the efforts made by your disloyal mother and her consort to sabotage the brilliant and far-sighted engineering and decorative work that you had conceived and planned and supervised with two unselfish purposes: to restore Wiswell Towers in its plumbing and wiring and general maintenance, and to rework and redesign the living quarters so that each member of your family would have splendid and permanent rooms for his or her private use. For reasons unknown to you, your plans met with senseless opposition. But you fought against all objections. Then, when you were out of the country with your beloved and gorgeous husband . . .'

'Wait a minute,' Kincaid said, 'you make it sound as if I'm in love with myself.'

'You are. And you should be. Let me finish,' she said. 'But then, Sophie, my darling, you showed your true character and strength of purpose. As soon as you returned to London and discovered that the work you'd started had been stopped by Mama and her consort and the workers sent away, as soon as you heard this, you reluctantly left your husband behind and hurried to Wiswell Towers to set things right again. To sum up, by hard work and self-sacrifice, you got the work started again. And by the time your mother and the man she now calls husband had returned from what we hesitate to call a honeymoon, you had completed the job right down to the last brass fixture and the last roll of carpet. No praise can be too high for such an effort. A fight against the odds.'

Kincaid applauded. 'Fantastic. I couldn't have said it better myself.'

'Just a moment,' she said. 'I'm not finished. Or I should say, you're not finished. Shall I proceed?'

'By all means.'

'You have no objection to the words I'm putting in your mouth?'

'None whatsoever,' he said. 'I've never been so articulate.'

'Very well.' She cleared her throat. 'Now . . . Sophie, my precious wife, I give you my ultimate salute for the way you've dealt with a humiliating experience. What should one do, how should a daughter react, when her mother marries an unsuitable man, when she neither consults with her daughter nor invites her to the wedding? There are many choices. An indignant telephone call, a nasty cable, a detailed letter of grievance, even an angry confrontation with the mother and her new husband. But you did none of these things. You exercised restraint and played the waiting game. You went about your business, completed your work at the Towers as mentioned in my previous tribute, and then, when your mother came to you, apologetic and wracked with guilt for having treated you badly, you neither wept nor complained. In fact you said nothing, or next to nothing. You simply cut her cold, turned and walked away, got into the car, and returned to London, leaving her standing in the downstairs hall, leaving her with something to think about. No question about that. Something to discuss with her beloved Arthur for days to come. A brilliant piece of vengeance, my darling, and I salute you for it. A twelve-gun salute. I'm proud of you.'

As Kincaid applauded, with less vigour this time, Sophie rang for another bottle of champagne.

## 5

They slept late the next morning. It was almost noon when they rang for coffee. When her maid came in with the tray, when she started to draw the draperies, Sophie said, 'Never mind, Betty. We'll leave the shades closed for the moment.'

'Shall I bring up your breakfast then?'

'No, I think not. Just another pot of coffee. And a pitcher of cold water as well.'

Kincaid came out of the dressing-room then in his robe and pyjamas and sat down on the edge of the bed. 'Don't jiggle the bed, please,' she said.

'Feeling shaky?'

'Feeling rotten. Are you as ripped as I am?'

He shook his head. 'I didn't drink as much as you did.'

'How much did I drink?'

'They're still carrying out the empty bottles.' He poured

some coffee for himself and refilled Sophie's cup. 'Did you order breakfast or is that a dirty word?'

'Don't even say it. I may never eat again, not till I come out of brain surgery.'

'I thought you never got hangovers.'

'I never did. Now I do. This one may be terminal.'

'Why don't I tuck you up and let you go back to sleep?'

'Can't sleep. Can't lie flat. All I can do is sit up in bed and drink coffee.'

'Would you like me to run a bath for you?'

'*Please.* I mean, please don't. The sound of running water would do me in. Almost any sound would do me in. I need to be in a soft cocoon with no light, no movement, no sound. Even my hair hurts.'

'Why don't I go downstairs and let you get some rest?'

'Don't leave me. I don't want to die alone like a nun.'

'You won't die. They may have to remove your head but I promise you won't die. After I'm dead of starvation you'll still be good as new.'

'How can you think about food when I'm in this condition?'

'I can't think of anything else. Not only have I not had breakfast, I had no dinner last night. As I recall we dined on champagne, a few cheese biscuits, and up to bed. My stomach thinks my throat's cut.'

'Please, darling, no cowboy images this morning. Why don't you go into the sitting-room, close the door so no smells of kippers and rashers will waft in here, and order up your bloody breakfast. Then you can come back to bed and witness my final moments on earth.'

When he came back into the bedroom almost an hour later she was still sitting up with her bed-tray in place. But her eyes were closed. He switched off the bed-lamp and started back toward the sitting-room. Before he reached the door, however, the lamp snapped on and she said, 'I'm awake. Don't run away.'

He sat down on the side of the bed again. 'I thought you couldn't go back to sleep.'

353

'I couldn't but I did. Now it's over.'

'More coffee?'

'No. Now I need sympathy and tender care. Take off your robe and slippers and slip into bed. We'll be two cripples together.'

When he was back in the bed beside her, propped up with pillows, she said, 'That's better. Isn't that better? Now that you've eaten you can doze off like an old dog. Or you can tell me stories about your early life. Shipboard adventures, fun and games in the outback, frolics with chancy ladies in low bars.'

'I think you're feeling better.'

'I wish it were true but it's not. I'm simply trying to distract myself. Get my mind off my rotten condition. Slide over this way so I can lean on you and put my head on your shoulder. Maybe you're a healer and don't know it. Maybe you'll put your cool fingertips on my temple or gently massage the back of my neck and all my aches and pains will disappear.'

He moved close to her and placed his hand on the back of her neck. 'That's better,' she said. 'That is infinitely better. My brain still has broken glass in it but at least my feet are warm.'

'Is all this going to lead to something naked and thrilling?'

'I'm afraid not,' she said. 'Any sudden movement, a rush of blood to any part of my body, and it would surely be the end of me.' She snuggled closer to him. 'You're a terribly nice chap. Have I ever told you that? That broken nose and those mean eyes are misleading. Somewhere, living inside you, there's a tender, gentle creature.'

She closed her eyes again and in a few moments, her head went heavy on his shoulder. Half an hour later she opened her eyes and said, 'Please, dear God, who looks after abandoned pets and orphaned children, forgive my sins and do something to this demon who's taken up residence in my head.'

'I'll ring for some more coffee,' Kincaid said.

'No. Water is what I need now. Great jars of cold water, most of it for drinking and the rest of it to cool my brain.'

He poured her a glass of water and she gulped it down. 'More?'

'Please, yes. It tastes wonderful.' She drank a second glass.

'Are we feeling better now?' Kincaid said.

'Only marginally. We are trying to concentrate on other things. The birds of the air and the beasts of the field.' She rested her head on his shoulder again. 'Was I dreadful last night?'

'Not at all. You were full of life. Very entertaining. What makes you think you were dreadful?'

'A slight memory loss that usually signals impending guilt. I was talking non-stop, wasn't I?'

'Not at all. You stopped every now and again to refresh yourself with a flute of champagne.'

'I have a vague recollection of some sort of charade where I was pretending I was you speaking to me.'

Kincaid nodded. 'You were playing both parts . . . the ventriloquist and the dummy.'

'And my topic was Margaret. Correct?'

'Correct. And Arthur. You dealt with both of them. At some length.'

'Was I making sense or was it champagne gibberish?'

'It certainly wasn't gibberish. And you certainly made sense. Not all the time but sometimes.'

'I don't like the sound of that.'

'No criticism intended. Have some more water.' He filled her glass again from the pitcher. She took a sip and set the glass down carefully on her table.

'You think I'm a fool, don't you?'

'Where did that come from?' he said.

'It's true, isn't it? You think I'm over-reacting. You don't understand my feelings. About the way Margaret's behaved toward me. You don't understand my attitude toward Arthur.'

'Did I say that?'

'Not in so many words. But I can tell. By a certain expression on your face. You think I'm behaving like a jackass.'

'We're not going to have a serious discussion, are we? I mean, are you asking me a serious question that I'm meant to give a serious answer to?'

'Yes. Why not?'

'Because in the first place you're in no condition for a serious discussion about anything. And in the second place I think we covered that ground thoroughly last night.'

'As I recall, I did all the talking and you did all the listening. No contribution from you. I may have been swizzled but I haven't forgotten everything. Also, you just said a moment ago that I didn't make sense last night.'

'Actually, I said you did make sense,' he said.

'But not all the time.'

'Nobody makes sense all the time.'

'Ahhh . . . I see. You're trying to wriggle out of this, aren't you?'

'What is it I'm wriggling out of?'

'You don't want to tell me what's on your mind. What was it I said that makes no sense?'

He put his hand over her mouth. 'Enough. One minute you're too weak to walk, talk, or take nourishment. Next thing I know, you're keen to take part in a great debate.'

'I have a right to know, don't I?'

'No,' he said. 'You're my chattel, my property. You have no rights.'

'I'm serious. This is important to me. You're important. What you think is important. Before I met you, the only constant in my life was Margaret. Now I have the feeling that she and I will never be close again. Not really. Not in the same way. I certainly don't feel responsible for what's happened but it's happened all the same. I don't know how I could have reacted differently than I did. If you've drawn your own conclusions, however, if you believe I've gone off half-cocked, it's important for me to know that. It's necessary.'

'No, it's not. Nor is it necessary for me to know every

thought that passes through your mind, to understand all your motivations, to approve of everything you say or do. You belong to yourself. You don't have to defend yourself to anyone. Certainly not to me.'

'I'm not defending myself. I'm just saying that it's important sometimes to feel that a particular important person is on your side.'

'I'm on your side,' he said.

'We're saying two different things. It's not enough for you to say "I'm with you. I'm behind you right or wrong." I need you to tell me I'm right.'

'You're right.'

'Damn it, Kincaid. I need you to say it and mean it.'

'Why are we having this discussion?'

'Because it's important.'

'Why now? Why this morning?'

'Because I need to know.'

'If you're sure you're right, that's what matters.'

'I'm not bloody sure. I did what I thought I had to do. I think I'm right. But I very much need you to agree with me.'

'I did. I said it.'

'That's right. You did. Like the man who comes out of the cuckoo clock to announce the time.'

Kincaid got up then, crossed the room to the bathroom, splashed cold water on his face, and dried himself with a thick white towel. When he came back, he pulled a chair up beside the bed and sat down. 'All right,' he said. 'You want to be serious . . . let's be serious. You said you need to feel that I'm on your side. I told you I am on your side. You said you need to be told you're right. I told you that as well. You weren't satisfied with those answers. If there's something else you need to know, you'll have to ask me specific questions and I will give you specific answers.'

'I can't sit here and grill you like a prisoner in the dock.'

'In that case I don't want to discuss the subject. There's no point to our having an argument when I don't know what we're arguing about.'

'We're not arguing. I don't want to quarrel with you. I just . . . I feel awful, darling. I don't like myself at all. I need you to help me. Don't just cut me off. Please.'

When he didn't answer she said, 'Nothing's more important to me than knowing what you think and how you feel. Of course I want you to agree with me and think I'm right. But I also want you to understand. And I want to understand you.' She paused. 'To start with, weren't you surprised when we found out that Margaret and Arthur were married?'

'Yes. But there's nothing you can do about it. That was your mother's decision to make. And she made it.'

'I never believe that nothing can be done,' Sophie said.

'You certainly can't tell Margaret who she should marry.'

'I realize that. But when I'm ignored and deliberately left out I can certainly make my feelings known. I assure you, there's no question in Margaret's mind as to where I stand. Since our brief encounter in the hallway the day I left, I assure you she knows she's made a serious error.'

'So you've had your vengeance. Now what happens?'

'That's up to her.'

'Do you expect her to put Arthur in the dustbin so you'll like her again?'

'You think this is amusing, don't you?'

'Not at all. I'm just trying to figure out what's going on. I assume you didn't think you and Margaret were saying goodbye for ever when you left her at the Towers.'

'Of course not. We've had differences before and we've got round them. And we'll get round this one.'

'But only if she comes to you?'

'Don't try to make me feel guilty. They played their little game with me. Now it's my turn. What I really wish we could do is get on a great ship and go away somewhere. Just the two of us. Give the two of them something to think about for a few months. I almost wish you'd tell me we have to go to America. Does that surprise you?'

'What do you think?'

'I'm sure it does. It surprises me as well. I know you have

no plans to go there just now, but it would be good enough for them, it would be proper payment for both of them, if we just disappeared for a while.'

The last evening Burt Windrow was in London he met Alec Maple for dinner at the Stafford. Maple in no way fit the description that Mary Cecil had given of him a few months before. He was as sleek in appearance as Windrow. It was as though each of them had decided to compete with the other on the field of sartorial splendour. Handsome polished boots, Trilby hats, crisp linen, and perfectly fitted suits. The moment they met in the bar and shook hands Maple said, 'Thank God, I dressed down. Knowing you've been in California with all that connotes, I deliberately rummaged through my closets for my seediest outfit. But even so, I'm sure you're embarrassed to be seen with me in that frightful ensemble. I hope you've booked a dim corner in the dining-room. Even the wine waiter will avoid us if he gets a look at that ill-fitting rag of a lounge-suit you're wearing.'

'You cheeky bastard. If you'd had any exposure to quality you'd know that my cravat alone cost more than your entire wardrobe, including whatever sad remnants you've left hanging at home.'

As soon as they'd settled into a corner of the bar and ordered two large gins, Maple said, 'Before you start lying to me about how successful you are and how many actresses with great creamy tits are waiting for you each night when you return home, before I convince you that my actual conquests far exceed your imaginary ones I suggest we square accounts. By my records I don't owe you tuppence.'

'Nor do I owe you anything,' Windrow said.

'Except admiration, respect, and non-sexual love.'

'Exactly. If I ever felt arousal with a creature like you, I would cut off my offending member and sell it to a pet-food shop.'

'I know several of your ex-lady-friends who would not consider that a great loss.'

'Sticks and stones, Maple. You're attacking an area where I feel totally secure.'

'So much for self-deception. We were settling accounts. So let's be serious for a moment. You never responded to the letter I wrote you about the American savages who attacked me in my flat.'

'Because I didn't have an answer to your questions. I don't know who they were, I don't know who sent them, and I don't know how they got your name.'

'If we're not going to be honest with each other . . .'

'It's true. I knew nothing about that whole incident till some people manoeuvred me into an office at one of the motion-picture studios and showed me the confession you'd signed admitting that you'd paid to have Tagg's car burned up and I'd found the people in Los Angeles to do the job.'

'Nasty business,' Maple said. 'Gives a man a bad conscience to put his friend in a corner. But since I assumed they'd found me through you . . . you know what I'm saying? And besides, the bloody bastards flushed my goldfish down the loo, turned my parrot loose to be eaten, I expect, by neighbourhood cats, and threatened to pop my little dog into the oven. On the other hand, you did get that bloody car destroyed and you did persuade my little Mary to come back to London, thus saving my unusual marriage. I put on a great act of suffering and destruction for her, told her that the ass-holes who abused me had said they were sent by Evan Tagg. She was so sickened by my story and by the sight of me that she severed her connection with Tagg. A masterstroke on my part.'

'But all for naught. Or so I understand. I met a chap at the Garrick bar yesterday who told me she's left you as well. Took a flat of her own.'

'That's simply a matter of convenience. A bartering point.

But wherever she gets her mail, wherever I may choose to spend the night, little Mary will be my wife till the pennies kiss my eyelids. More accurately, till they kiss her eyelids. I will surely live for ever.'

'Since you've led a saintly life, perhaps you're right. That could be a problem, however. You might be called home early to be King of the Angels.'

Maple signalled for two more drinks. 'It's a possibility,' he said.

'Now,' Windrow said, 'let's finish our book-keeping. You've told me how you suffered, through no fault of mine as it turns out, now I'll tell you what it cost me because you gave those men my name. As I began to say a moment ago, the two men who showed me your statement forced me to buy a new car to replace the one that was burned. Then they decided I should also turn over my own car, a new La Salle, to them. So I was out of pocket. Gave up the price of two automobiles as payment for doing your dirty work.'

'But that money should be credited to me in any event. Final payment to me in exchange for my withholding certain nasty stories about you.'

'That's the reply I expected,' Windrow said. 'And I'm glad to hear you say final payment. Because that's what it is, old cock. Just because we're two of a kind doesn't mean that your physical well-being won't be on the line if you try to extort either money or special services from me again. If that should happen, your little dog will be spared and you will go into the oven.'

'Shame on you. Threats from one friend to another are in extremely poor taste.'

Windrow shook his head. 'I would never threaten a man of your standing. I was merely appealing to your sense of decency.'

'Excellent. All's well that ends well.'

When they went into the dining-room of the hotel, Maple said, 'Surprised you're staying here. Good location, the Stafford, but not up to your standard, one would think.

Thought you'd be at the Ritz or Brown's or the Dorchester. Sort of a Midlands atmosphere here, wouldn't you agree? A sprinkling of commercial travellers from New York, colonials with the scent of the Tasman sea lingering about them and the odd rag-head from Calcutta bobbing along the corridor every now and then. How did you happen to book in here?'

'Two years ago, perhaps a bit longer, an item appeared in a Los Angeles paper saying that both Chaplin and Marlene Dietrich stop here when they're in London. Ever since then it's been first choice for Hollywood travellers coming to England.'

'That explains a lot, doesn't it? But why plant orchids in the city of the blind?'

'It's difficult to book in here. I was fortunate. A chap at Gaumont interceded for me. Otherwise I'd have been pigging it at Claridges.'

Maple glanced round the dining-room. 'Dreadful food, too, I expect.' He touched the menu as if it were a dead animal. '*Cuisine de Provence*, by way of Warsaw.'

'Excellent food as a matter of fact. I visited the kitchen yesterday. Not one person on the staff spoke English.'

Later in the evening when they'd finished their meal, Maple said, 'It suddenly occurred to me why you're staying in this unlikely establishment. It's just a few steps away from Kincaid's house, or I should say, his wife's house. It's in Queen's Walk. I'm surprised you're not there as a house guest.'

'Not bloody likely.'

'How's your campaign proceeding? Are you still hoping to scandalize him out of his profession?'

'It's more than a hope,' Windrow said. 'I expect to bring him down with a great clatter, probably in a matter of weeks.'

'By what device, may I ask?'

'You can ask but I can't tell you.'

'Does that mean you don't trust me?'

'Not at all. There's no one in the world I trust more than you,' Windrow said.

362

'Which is to say, there's no one in the world you trust.'

'Exactly. I will say, however, that my device as you call it, will have shock waves that go beyond Kincaid. As I carve him up like a Christmas goose I'll be able to settle a few other scores as well. I'm a powerful man now, you see. Millions of people read every word I write as they're having their morning coffee. They adopt my opinions as their own. I needn't prove what I say. The printed word is gospel in America. In a column like mine an assumption is as telling as a fact. Guilt by association can be punished as severely as real guilt. A question in print can be as destructive as a statement. I say what I like, print what I like, and suffer no consequences. The people I write about are so eager to see their names in print they object to nothing. Any abuse is accepted if the name is spelled correctly.'

'You were always a risky chap,' Maple said. 'Now it appears you're bloody dangerous.'

'Only to people like Kincaid. And those two rotten bastards who took my new car from me. They're due for a rude shock along with Kincaid.'

'A triumph in your business affairs. Power and money. But leading a lonely life. The life of a monk.'

'Exactly. You know me. Morally straight and physically clean. But women simply are not attracted to me.'

Maple shook his head. 'The truth is, you're a mean and selfish sod but women flock to you. So what's the latest? A *ménage à trois* with Lombard and Harlow, with yourself as the centre-piece?'

'Something better than that. This will amuse you, I expect. Kincaid's wife has a daughter, you know. A lovely young woman named Sarah.'

'A lovely child, I believe, would be closer to the truth. Fifteen years old, isn't she? Or is she only ten?'

'She's twenty actually. I've seen her passport.'

'Are you telling me you've invaded the castle? Is that part of your scheme against Kincaid? To seduce his step-daughter?'

363

'It didn't begin that way. The fact is I met her by chance. I was asked to observe a drama class at a school she was attending in Ojai. One thing led to another, as they say, we got on together, so now I am, as it were, a secret member of the Kincaid family.'

'How secret?'

'Completely. Sarah and I know what's going on, but no one else.'

'Until the proper moment . . .'

'I'm not sure there'll be a proper moment. I realize this might give me a certain amount of leverage in case I need it, but I don't look at her as a part of my vendetta against Kincaid. I'm quite fond of her, in fact.'

'And she is decimated by you, I expect.'

'Not at all. Perhaps that's what interests me. Oh, she's an affectionate little creature, nothing lacking there, but she seems quite unwilling to hand herself over to anyone. Gives up very little of herself. Reminds me a bit of myself when I was her age. She's an independent little hussy. Sure to be a fascinating woman one day.'

'By then, however, you'll be drinking at a fresh spring.'

'Of course,' Windrow said. 'But Sarah won't be weeping for me. I can't imagine her weeping for anyone.'

## 7

It was just before ten o'clock at night when the telephone rang in Daisy Bishop's bungalow at Thornwood Studios. Linda, her housekeeper, came into Daisy's sitting-room and said, 'It's your husband. He wants to talk to you.'

'Did you tell him I'm asleep?'

'Yes. But he said I should wake you up. He's here in Hollywood. Just outside the studio gate.'

'Oh, God. Now what?' Daisy picked up the receiver of the telephone by her chair. 'Hi, Bob. What a nice surprise. Where are you?'

'I'm at that all-night Mexican cantina just outside the studio gate. I tried to get in to see you but the guards gave me some sad line of crap and wouldn't let me in. A couple of smart-ass new guys. Never saw them before.'

'I know. I heard some stuff got stolen off the back lot so everybody's cuckoo about security. Julian says they hardly ever let anybody on the lot at night.'

'Anyway, I've got to see you. You weren't asleep, were you?'

'I was just about to go to bed. I'm in every shot in this picture. They have me in the make-up chair when the sun comes up.'

'Just put on a coat and come on out here to the cantina. You'll be back in your bungalow by eleven.'

'I don't know, Bob.'

'Stop wasting time. I haven't seen you for three or four weeks. I need to talk to you.'

'You haven't had one too many, have you?'

'Yeah, I'm dead drunk, laying underneath a parked car in Burbank.' He hung up the receiver.

Ten minutes later she came into the cantina, wearing a polo coat and smoked glasses, a uniformed guard from the studio walking with her. When she moved along to the booth where Bob was waiting, the guard sat on a stool at the bar.

'Who's that bird?' Bob said when she sat down.

'He's one of the guys who keep an eye on my bungalow. There's somebody on guard there all the time.'

'You might as well be in jail.'

'It's not like that. Julian just wants to make sure I'm safe.'

'Julian's full of crap. You ought to be sleeping at home like everybody else.'

'Julian's very good to me, Bob. You know why I'm staying here at the studio, nights and weekends and everything. We talked it over before I agreed to do it.'

'Don't kid me, honey. You agreed to do it and then we talked it over. And then, big coincidence, Sam Thorne drooled all over me and offered me work in three westerns, back-to-back. Good timing, huh? They lock you up at the studio and they ship me out of town. Keep the husband quiet. Ship him off to the hills.'

'You were tickled to death about getting all that work when you told me about it.'

'That was before I smartened up. Or before somebody smartened me up. Some dog-ass prop man got pissed off at me because I told him I needed a double-action revolver instead of a single-action. So he popped off that the only reason Thornwood hired me was to keep me out of your hair while you're working.'

'That's crazy.'

'That's what I told him. Just before I busted him a good one in the mouth.'

'I hope you're not in some kind of trouble.'

'He's the one in trouble. Not me. It's cost him a couple weeks wages to get his teeth patched together.'

'You didn't get fired or anything, did you?'

'Not me. I'm the golden boy up at Red Rock. If I've got a beef I go straight to Abe Leslie, the line producer, and he gets it all straightened out. The first week up there I told him word for word about the conversation that took place between me and Sam Thorne, and since then everything's been peaches and cream. We wrapped *Comanche Trail* at Red Rock yesterday and now I'm heading for Lone Pine for the Tim McCoy picture.'

'I thought you were going to Kanab.'

'What gave you that idea?'

'I don't know,' she said. 'I thought you told me that.'

He shook his head. 'Kanab's the last stop. Fred Veach is directing that one and Fred and me are thicker than eight in a bed. I'll coast through that job.'

'Wait a minute. I thought you were mad because you thought they'd hired you just to get you out of town. Now you're telling me everything's as smooth as syrup.'

'That's because I see what the game is now. They thought they could use me but instead I'm using them. They promised me the kind of work that was going to lead to something big but they were just jerkin' me around. So now it's my turn. I'm signed up for eighteen or twenty weeks of work, three pictures at good money. So I'm takin' their money and giving them nothing in return.'

'What do you mean?'

'I mean, I'm there but I'm not there. No stunts. No horse-falls, no putting fights together. When they look at the rushes every day, the face of Bob Sample is gonna be missing.'

'You can't do that. You can't sign a contract and then refuse to work.'

'Yes, I can, baby. Just watch me. That's what I've been doing at Red Rock ever since I got wise. And that's what I'll do at Lone Pine and Kanab. If they're willing to pay me good money to stay out of Los Angeles, then that's what I'll do. But I won't do anything else.'

'They'll fire you, Bob.'

'No, they won't. Cause if they do, I'm coming straight here to Thornwood. I'll put you under my arm and take you home. Then the two of us will pack some camping gear and go off on a long vacation. Somewhere in Oregon. Or Utah maybe.'

'But I've got eight more weeks on this picture. Ten maybe.'

'That's not my worry. I'll let Julian worry about that. You and me will catch ourselves some speckled trout.'


8


'First time I've seen you since your wedding day,' Clara Causey said. 'Just a few weeks ago but it seems like a long time. I'm accustomed to seeing you at least twice a month. I depend on it. I get cranky and start to act my age when my regular habits are disturbed.'

She was sitting with Margaret in the drawing-room at Wingate Fields. Margaret had arrived half an hour before.

'I'm glad to hear you say that,' she said. 'Cranky is a terribly good word, isn't it? Seems to match the feeling it describes. I'd begun to think I was the only person under eighty who ever felt that way. I congratulate myself every day that I haven't grown old as most of our neighbours in the county have, but then I catch a glimpse of myself in the glass or notice that I seem to be walking with unnecessary caution. Or I catch myself just before I'm about to lash out at poor Rose about some trivial household matter, such as the imperfection of my boiled egg at breakfast. Patience is the first thing to go, isn't it? Patience with oneself goes first, followed quickly by patience with everyone else. Deterioration is a hateful thing. Women colour their hair, corset their bodies, paint their faces and replace their worn-out teeth with gleaming new ones. But all the while the repairs that are needed are on the internal machinery, on perception, tolerance, sensitivity. And patience of course, as I said. Having experienced true perfection so seldom in our lives, one would think that we'd be satisfied with less. Instead we begin to discard relatives, friends, even familiar pleasures because they no longer measure up to some new set of standards we've established. It's a kind of madness, isn't it, some intimation of mortality that prompts us to discard and abandon and destroy, to try to leave nothing behind us when we go.'

'Depressing but true.'

'Doesn't apply to us, of course,' Margaret said. 'Not to you and me. We are for ever wise and young. Tending our gardens, marking the phases of the moon, enjoying marmalade and Belgian chocolate and scones with jam, venison steak and stilton, brown bread toast and sweet butter, caviar and Norwegian salmon, Sancerre and Nuit-St-Georges. Bach and Chopin, Titian and Degas, and Shelley and Browning. We're alive and breathing still, using our senses and using our minds. Am I correct or am I drowning myself in a sea of sweet pudding and self-deception?'

'You are correct in all departments. I wish I could have memorized what you've just said so I could repeat it to myself each morning before I get out of bed.'

'Ahhh, but you needn't memorize it. It's your credo. It's a built-in part of you, like the lovely little compartments in your handkerchief drawer. Am I babbling on like a demented creature? I started talking before I had both feet inside your hallway.'

'Of course you did. And if you hadn't I would have. That's why we have to meet as we do. We both know how to listen and, God knows, we both know how to talk. My father used to tell me there was no humanity or civilization in the universe till the moment when one creature spoke and another creature responded.'

Later, as they sat in the dining hall, Clara's husband having left the table early to hear a broadcast of Mahler on the wireless in his room, Clara said, 'You mustn't be annoyed with me if I say that, as eager as I was to see you, I had some trepidations about it as well. We've had telephone conversations in the past two weeks that led me to believe . . .'

'I know,' Margaret said. 'I'm sure you thought the first word that passed my lips would be *Sophie*.'

Clara nodded. 'Is no news good news in this case?'

'No, I'm afraid not. No news is simply no news.'

'You haven't talked with her?'

'Not a word since the morning she swept out of our hallway, got into the car and went back to London.'

'How strange. You must feel dreadful.'

'Numb,' Margaret said. 'After crying myself to sleep for I don't know how many nights, after writing and ringing her home for more times than I can count, I have managed to will myself into a state of numbness. Nothing solved or resolved. Everything postponed. "When there's nothing to be done, do nothing." Some folk philosopher once said that. Or perhaps I read it on a cereal box.'

'Can you simply put it out of your mind?'

'Of course not. But until some wise gypsy tells me what I can do, or unless Sophie gives some indication that she hasn't declared me dead and buried, I can't imagine what other choices I have.'

'Have you thought of going to London to see her?'

'Of course. That was my first impulse. But the truth is, I'm afraid to. As long as that possibility exists, you see, I can still harbour a bit of hope. On the other hand I can't imagine what state of mind I'd be in if I journeyed down to London, went to her house, and was unable to see her. I have nightmare visions of myself waiting downstairs in her drawing-room and being told at last that Sophie was either unable or unwilling to see me. Can you imagine me after such an experience? Alone in a train compartment rattling north to my home. That's a pain I can't subject myself to.'

## 9

'My father hates to chat on the telephone,' Evan said, 'but he called me from Northumberland last night and talked for almost an hour. He wants me to try and talk some sense into Sophie.'

'Why doesn't he talk to her himself?' Kincaid said.

'That's what I suggested. But he says there's no point to it. If Sophie won't talk to her mother she certainly won't talk to him.' They were sitting in a small and plain restaurant on King Street, mid afternoon, the lunch customers already returned to their offices, the dinner crowd not due to arrive for three or four hours. Evan went on. 'I told him I'd have a word with Sophie but I said I wanted to get the lay of the land from you first. That's why I rang you this morning. Do you think she'll talk to me?'

'Why not? She's not fighting you.'

'But do you think I can reason with her?'

'I doubt it. But you'll have to find out for yourself.'

'You don't seem much concerned about all this.'

'It's none of my business,' Kincaid said.

'Of course it is. You're part of the family.'

'Only technically. I'm a late-comer. Sophie and Margaret are two grown-up women. If they've decided they don't want to see each other, or talk, that's up to them. When they're ready to get together again, they will. If they're not ready to, I guess they won't.'

'It's not that simple. If you'd known them as I have . . . this is serious.'

'Bullshit, Evan. I've seen lots of people with serious problems in my life and I guarantee you, this isn't one of them. It's an activity for people who have no real problems. Two dogs growling over a bone.'

'You may not attach any importance to people's feelings but I do.'

'Of course you do. Because you have nothing else to do at the moment.'

For a moment Evan didn't answer. Then he said, 'Maybe you're right. Maybe it's not that important. But if I can help sort things out a bit I think it's worth the trouble. What do you think I'd have to do to persuade Sophie to meet with Margaret and talk this thing through?'

'I can't answer that. You'll have to ask Sophie.'

## 10

The following day when she met Evan for tea at Brown's, Sophie said, 'I hope you haven't come to talk about Margaret and your father.'

'Don't get high-handed with me, Sophie. Of course I want to talk about them. I didn't realize till I talked with Arthur the day before yesterday how far out of control things have got.'

'Nothing's out of control. I'm completely calm.'

'Does that mean you're satisfied with the situation between you and Margaret?'

'Not at all. But I'm resigned to it. I have no other choice. In any case I don't want to talk about it.'

'But I do. Somebody has to talk about it.'

'All this is between your father and Margaret and me. Either it will get sorted out in time or it won't.'

'That's a ridiculous thing to say. Do you mean this is a permanent condition?'

'It's permanent unless something happens to change it.'

Evan shook his head. 'Is this some new characteristic you've developed? Crisp and cool. What about Margaret? Why do you think she's been trying so hard to get in touch with you?'

'I'm sure she wants to apologize. But what good is that? It's easy to say you're sorry after the damage has been done. It's quite simple then to smile and mutter a few words of apology. But I'm not so easily taken in. Something more is required.'

'Like what for example?'

'I'm not sure. But I'll know it when I see it.'

'And until then both Margaret and Arthur are being sent to Coventry? None of this makes sense.'

'It makes sense to me,' Sophie said. 'I won't try to deceive you. I believe Arthur is primarily responsible for what's happened. But Margaret's responsible as well for allowing herself to be used.'

'Oh, for God's sake, Sophie.'

'I don't expect you to understand. Just remember what I'm saying now. Underneath Arthur's gentle exterior there is an angry, vindictive man. I think your mother must have hurt him terribly. After all these years it seems he's decided to take his vengeance on someone. And he's selected me.'

'I can't believe what I'm hearing. Where do you get these ideas? I think you're doing precisely what you're accusing Arthur of.'

'Meaning what?'

'Meaning you're substituting him for someone else you're hoping to get even with.'

Sophie laughed, a genuine laugh, one with real energy behind it. 'Who knows?' she said. 'Maybe I am doing that. Who did you have in mind?'

'Let's start with Kincaid. How are you two getting on since he came back from America?'

'Beautifully, thank you.'

372

'Why did I imagine he wanted you here in London when you were occupied with your decorators at the Towers?'

A sweet smile. 'I'm sure you didn't imagine that. I expect someone told you.' She lit a cigarette. 'I won't lie to you about it. Of course Kincaid wanted me to be here with him. So I came home, we went to Dinard for a few days, and the problem went away.'

'Don't be too sure of that. He was very sharp with me yesterday when I asked him some questions about the situation between you and Margaret. He thinks it's a great deal of fuss over nothing. An activity for idle minds. I felt he was about to hold forth about the nobility of poverty and the corruption of wealth and privilege, that sort of thing. Since you are the wealthy and privileged person he knows best, it occurred to me he might be making a statement about you.'

'Nice try, Evan, but you can't turn this around on me. We're talking about your father and my mother. Not you, not me, not my husband. Everything between Kincaid and me is flawless and lovely, thank you very much.'

# • CHAPTER 10 •

1

Ten days after he returned to Los Angeles from London, Burt Windrow received a letter from Sarah.

Are you surprised to hear from me? You shouldn't be. As you must realize by now, I'm a well-brought-up young woman. Among the other lessons I've learned from my mother and my nanny is this one: when someone has been generous or hospitable or kind, one must send along a note of appreciation. And promptly.

Unless I've misunderstood you totally, I expect you don't think of yourself as kind or generous or hospitable. But I thank you all the same.

Since our differences are more numerous and more striking than our similarities, and since we have never made nor hinted at any sort of commitment, even the most casual one, it's quite possible that we will never see each other again. If that turns out to be the case, the world will not stop turning for either of us. You have a firm grip on yourself and your life, and my life is all before me. What will unfold is still a mystery. But as young and dumb and inexperienced as I surely am, I'm old enough and smart enough to realize that the comparatively small number of hours I've spent with you have been important ones for me.

I'm not about to say that knowing you has been an

education. The fact is that I feel I know very little about you. But I know a great deal more about myself than I did a few short months ago. Before I met you that day in Ojai. That doesn't mean that I suddenly see my future laid out before me like a path of golden stones. I don't. But even though I haven't proved it yet, either to myself or to anyone else, I sense that I have more gumption and more courage now, that I'll be able to deal with things, even unpleasant things, in a way that I wasn't able to do before.

I expect all this doesn't sound so important to you. You've been independent and able to function for a long time. Perhaps it amuses you to hear that I have begun to think of myself as a grown-up. It amuses me, too. I think it's funny and surprising and quite wonderful. Since I've cried wolf for so long, since I've complained loud and long to my brother, my mother, and anyone else who would listen that I'm no longer a child, perhaps they'll be slow to see that now in fact I am what I had only hoped to be before. But now that I feel as I do, it's not nearly so important to me how other people feel.

If I seem to be saying that having you inside me and doing all sorts of strange erotic things I'd never done or even heard of before has turned me into an adult woman, then I haven't said what I meant. If I said I didn't have a jolly time with you at our inn in Little-hampton I'd be lying. But the fun of it will be less important in the long run than the fact of it. Making the decision, turning the corner, taking the risk, having a secret . . . those are the things that make me taller now. Quieter inside and enormously more confident. After I got back to school I couldn't wait to get to the Academy and my dramatic classes. I knew that the way I feel about myself now would show in my work. And it has. I also can't wait to get back to California so I can show Ethel Richmond what I'm capable of.

When will that be? God knows. Maybe when I'm as old as Sally Carpenter. And will I ring you up when I arrive? Probably not. It's lovely to have an adventure. It's folly to imagine that it's something other than that. See how smart I am.

## 2

It was two-thirty in the morning when Sam Thorne was awakened by a call from the security office at the studio. As soon as he hung up the receiver he rang Julian. 'We've got a problem,' Sam said. 'Bob Sample's been shot.'

'Where is he?'

'In Daisy's bungalow at the studio.'

'Jesus Christ. What happened?'

'Nobody knows. The security guy said Daisy's hysterical and Bob's got a bullet in his chest.'

'When did it happen?'

'A few minutes ago. An ambulance is on the way from Cedars.'

'All right, we have to move fast. Call Jack Gilder and tell him we need him at the studio as fast as he can get there.'

'I was about to call Sugarman.'

'Right now we need Gilder. I'll talk to Sugarman later. Get hold of Biggers and Leon Dart. Then call Dr Moffat and have him call Cedars. He must tell them he's Sample's doctor. He knows what he has to do. I'm leaving for the studio in five minutes. I'll see you there as soon as you can make it. Tell Security to keep everybody but the ambulance people out of Daisy's bungalow. And tell them to keep their mouths shut about all this or they'll be out on the street selling bananas.'

When he hung up the receiver Bella said, 'What's happening?'

'Nothing, I hope. Go back to sleep.'

'Doesn't sound like nothing.'

'Go back to sleep, Bella. I'll call you later.'

When Julian stopped at the studio gate he asked the guard if Sam had arrived yet. 'Yes, sir. A few minutes ago.' When he pulled up and parked outside Daisy's bungalow, Sam and Doak Hendry, the chief of security, came out to meet him. 'You got here fast, Sam,' Julian said.

'Sometimes it's handy to live close to the studio.'

'Did the ambulance come yet?'

'Came and went,' Hendry said. 'Those guys don't screw around.'

'How's he look?'

'Lost a lot of blood. And he had a big knot on his head. Must have hit something when he fell.'

'Was he conscious?'

'No. Out like a light.'

'What about Gilder?'

'He's inside on the phone. Talking to Moffat.'

Gilder hung up the receiver just as Sam and Julian came inside the bungalow. Hendry stayed outside with two of his men. When the door closed behind him he said to them, 'If anybody wants to know what happened here tonight, the answer is, "Nothing happened." I don't care who it is.'

Inside, Gilder said to Julian, 'I think we're in good shape so far.'

'Nobody called the police, did they?'

'No. Moffat will handle that. It's a gun-shot wound, so it has to be reported, but he'll stall it as long as he can. He'll have a good excuse. He's taking Sample into surgery as soon as they get him prepped.'

'Biggers and Leon Dart are on the phones next door putting the muzzle on their newspaper contacts,' Sam said. 'For now we've got things covered.'

Julian shook his head. 'We've got nothing covered till we know what happened. What's the story?'

'We don't have a story yet,' Gilder said. 'Sample was out cold, so we got nothing from him. And all the maid knows

377

is that she heard some loud talking. Then there was a shot. When she came in the room he was laid out and a revolver was on the floor beside him.'

'How the hell did he get on the lot in the middle of the night?'

'Hendry says he didn't come through the main gate or the truck gate. There's that delivery gate on Largo that most people don't even know about. They make night deliveries there sometimes. Food for the commissary, stuff for the carpenter shop. Things like that. We think he might have slipped in there,' Sam said. 'The crazy son of a bitch was supposed to be at Lone Pine.'

'Well, he wasn't.'

'What about Daisy? Has anybody talked to her?'

'She's sleeping. Dead to the world,' Gilder said. 'She was ready to run out in the street till the maid zonked her with a pill.'

'What a mess,' Julian said. He turned to Sam, 'Tell Biggers to send a message to Cukor's house. Hand-delivered. Tell him Daisy's under the weather and he'll have to shoot around her today. If he can't find a way to do it tell him we'll close down the picture till tomorrow.' He turned back to Gilder. 'Where's the gun?'

'I got here just before the ambulance did. I didn't think we wanted those guys to see it so I wrapped it in a paper towel and put it in the back of that record cabinet.'

'Is that a good idea?'

'It's not a bad idea. There was a lot of confusion here. When the time comes, if it comes, we can say we don't know who put it there. It's not wiped clean. It's just the way I found it. Or maybe it will just turn up lost. If we handle this right the police may not get involved at all. That's what we're after, isn't it?'

'I think we should have the rest of this conversation in my office,' Julian said. 'What's the maid's name?'

'Linda,' Sam said. 'Linda Morales.'

'Where is she?'

'She's back in the kitchen,' Gilder said. 'I think she's a little groggy from all the action.'

Julian walked through an archway, across the dining area, and along a short hall to the kitchen. The door was closed. He knocked lightly before he entered. Linda was sitting in a chair by the window that looked out on a walled rose garden. When she turned and saw Julian she stood up quickly and touched her hand to her hair. 'I'm sorry, sir. I was just . . .'

'Sit down, please. I'll sit here with you for a few minutes if I may.' He pulled up a chair and sat down across the table from her. The first morning light was just showing above the saw-tooth roofs of the sound stages. 'You must be tired,' he said.

'No, sir. No, I'm fine.'

'I'm going to ask one of the security men to come inside and stay in the front room. He'll be there in a few minutes. When do you expect Miss Bishop to wake up?'

'She was so frightened and crazy I thought I should give her one of her pills the doctor prescribed. When she works late she gets jumpy sometimes and can't sleep . . .'

'I understand. You did the right thing, Linda.'

She smiled, a small tentative smile. 'Most people don't say my name right. You say it the right way. Like the Mexican people . . . oh, I'm sorry.'

'*Linda*,' he said. 'It's a lovely name. It means pretty, doesn't it?' She looked confused and didn't answer. 'You were about to tell me when you think Daisy might wake up.'

She looked at the clock. 'It's more than an hour now since she took her pill. I think she won't be awake before nine. Maybe thirty minutes sooner.'

'All right. Here's what I want you to do for me. As soon as the guard comes in I want you to go into your room and lie down. You need a bit of rest. Do you have a telephone by your bed?'

'Yes.'

'Good. I'll have my secretary call you at seven-thirty. By then you'll have some rest and be able to look after Miss Bishop

379

when she wakes up. And as soon as she's awake I want you to call me so I can come down here to see her.'

'If she sleeps so long she'll be late to work.'

'Daisy won't be working today. And neither will you. Food will be sent over from the commissary.'

They both stood up then. She was a tiny young woman. When she stood facing him she had to look up. 'You're a good worker, Linda, and a loyal companion for Miss Bishop. I'm sorry you had to witness this unfortunate accident. But accidents happen, especially when there are guns in the home. People get hurt and it's nobody's fault.'

'I'm very frightened of guns. In Sonora many men carry guns. I'm also frightened of police. Will I have to see the police and tell them what happened?'

'We don't know yet. Since it was an accident perhaps the police won't be involved. But if they do question you, you simply tell them the truth. The revolver went off accidentally and Mr Sample was wounded.'

'There was so much blood. Is he dead?'

'No. They're taking care of him in the hospital now. I'm sure he'll be all right. Meanwhile, you and I have to take good care of Daisy so she can . . .'

'So she can go back to work.'

Julian smiled and put his hand on her shoulder. 'The work's not important. We just want her to feel well and not be upset.'

'But when she works again, she'll feel better.'

'Maybe you're right. You get some rest now and be sure to call me when Miss Bishop wakes up.'

Sam was on the telephone when Julian came back into the room. He hung up and said, 'That was Gilder. He's next door in a huddle with Biggers and Dart.'

'Good. Keep after them. Any word from the hospital?'

'Nothing yet. Moffat will call you as soon as he gets out of the operating-room.'

'Say a prayer. We don't want the bastard to die.'

'Maybe you don't,' Sam said. 'Personally, I don't give a damn. He's a bad apple.'

380

'Good or bad, as long as he's married to Daisy we're stuck with him. And it's a lot easier to deal with an accidental bullet wound than an accidental death.' He crossed the room and turned at the door. 'Be sure there's a security guy here before you leave. And one or two outside. Nobody comes in and nobody goes out. Drill that into their heads. If anybody screws up here it's gonna be Hendry's ass.'

'He knows that. I told him.'

'Good. I'm going to my office to shave and take a shower.' He looked at his watch. 'Bring Gilder and Biggers and Dart, and meet me there in forty-five minutes. We have to stitch this whole thing together.'

3

When the four men, Sam and Gilder and Biggers and Leon Dart, came into Julian's office they looked tired and bedraggled, still wearing the clothes they'd thrown on when Sam had summoned them to the studio. Julian, however, freshly shaved and showered, and wearing a grey bespoke suit and a crisp white shirt and blue tie, looked alert and rested.

'Moffat just called me from Cedars. He had to remove the bullet from Sample's lung but it was a clean operation and he expects no complications.'

'Did Sample talk to anyone?'

Julian shook his head. 'Before the operation he was groggy from that knock on the head. Now he's still out from the anaesthetic. Moffat put him in intensive care. No visitors. He'll be sedated while he's recovering and we'll have our security people outside his door twenty-four hours a day.'

'Will the hospital sit still for that?'

'Moffat says yes. He's king of the hill over there. I've got a clear idea of how this should play. I'll be talking to Daisy as soon as she wakes up. Then we'll know exactly what we have to do.' He turned to Biggers and Dart. 'How are we handling it with the news people?'

'Leon and I are picking up our markers all over town. Going straight to the top. Talking only to publishers and top columnists,' Biggers said.

'We told them there'd been a little accident here at the studio,' Dart said. 'Not a big problem but something that might damage one of our stars. We asked them to lay off, to alert their people not to run with any gossip or rumours they might hear.'

Biggers again. 'We said that when everything is clarified we'd give them a complete story of exactly what happened.'

'Anybody I should call?' Julian asked.

'Yes. Winchell and Justin Gold and your publisher friend at the *Times*.'

'I'll do it later this morning. No need to wake people up.'

'Can we trust these people you're talking to?' Gilder said.

'You know the game, Jack. It's a trade-off,' Biggers said. 'That's what Leon and I do. We build up credits around town. Big money for advertising. And a lot of favours thrown in. So when we have a problem they have to listen. They want to listen. They know we have to protect our people, so unless it's the Fatty Arbuckle story they'll usually sit on it.'

'Keep an eye on them,' Julian said. 'We don't want any leaks. I want this all buttoned up and swept under the rug before Sample gets out of the hospital. If he gets a shot at a little publicity, God knows what he's liable to say.'

'We can deal with Sample,' Sam said.

'What about the police?' Julian turned to Gilder. 'How do we handle that, Jack?'

'I'm having breakfast with Bruce Gillette from the DA's office in about an hour. I'll tell him we had an accident here, no crime involved, so we don't want any commotion about it from the police. He knows the name of the game. He's been a prosecutor around here for twenty years. Plays tennis with every studio head in town.'

'What about Moffat? We don't want him to look bad for not reporting a shooting.'

'That's covered. He's waiting at the hospital to hear from

382

me. After I leave Gillette, I'll call Moffat and he'll call the Hollywood police to report the accident.'

'*Accident*,' Julian said. 'That's the key word.'

'That's right,' Gilder said.

'So by the time Moffat calls, Gillette will have talked to the police commissioner about his conversation with you.'

'That's right,' Gilder said. 'He'll cool things down. But if the cops still want to talk to Daisy and her maid, we'll give them a break and let them do it. I'll be right there when it happens, and the cops will hear the same story I'll be telling Gillette. They'll hear it twice. Once from Daisy and once from the maid.'

'What do you plan to tell him?'

'A foolish accident, like I said. Here we have an important actress working in a major picture. Her husband's out of town on location for thirteen or fourteen weeks, so the studio arranges for her to stay in her bungalow on the lot. It's working fine but her husband is worried about her. So when he comes to visit her one night he brings her a small revolver to keep by her bed just in case somebody breaks in. She doesn't know anything about guns so he's showing her how it works. Most important he wants her to understand about the safety-catch. So that's what he's showing her. But the gun goes off accidentally and shoots him in the chest.'

Julian sat quietly for a long moment. Then he turned to Biggers. 'What do you think, Dale?'

'Sounds good to me. A simple story. Hard to screw up. If anybody wants to know why he was there so late it's because he drove down from Lone Pine and had to drive back again that same night.'

'What about the gun?' Dart said.

'The gun's missing.'

'What does that mean?'

Sam cut in. 'It means nobody knows where the gun is. After Julian talks to Daisy and we find out what she has to say, maybe somebody will find the gun.'

'All right,' Julian said. 'It looks as if we're in pretty fair shape. But we have to stay on top of this thing. Otherwise it could blow up in our faces. Just remember we have an actress at risk and a half-finished picture to protect. Major investments. Any publicity we get right now is bad publicity. Jack's story works, I think. A husband is concerned about his wife's safety. But in an effort to protect her he accidentally shoots himself. I don't want to see anything in the press, but at least that cockamamie story we could live with if we had to. Anything else would murder us. If the police questioned the story, if they began an investigation, if there was any hint that there was a quarrel, that Daisy and Sample weren't getting along together, that either one of them had somebody on the side.'

'Like Daisy slipping around with Kincaid,' Dart said.

'Don't even mention that. I'll drop dead on the floor,' Julian said.

'I brought it up just because it's been rumoured a few times,' Dart said. 'Items in the papers.'

'Forget you ever heard that. Or read it. We have to keep this business on the rails. We have to concentrate on our priorities. No publicity, no rumours, no investigation. Accidental shooting. Case closed. That's what we want to hear. Anything else will kill us.'

'Let's be sure we're all together on this,' Gilder said. He looked at his watch. 'I'm going to Gillette in half an hour with the accidental shooting details we just worked out. And no matter what you hear from Daisy Bishop or her maid, Julian, that's the story we're sticking with.'

'That's right,' Julian said.

'And if they're questioned, God forbid, you're confident they'll stick with that story?'

'I guarantee it.' Julian said.

4

'God, I must look awful,' Daisy said. 'Do I look awful?' She was sitting up in bed in the bedroom of her bungalow, mid morning, Julian sitting on a straight chair facing her.

'You've had a tough few hours, sweetheart, but nobody would ever know it to look at you. We could bring a camera in here and shoot close-ups just the way you are. No make-up or filters on the lens.'

'Don't try to kid me, Julian, I know how I look when I wake up. If I didn't look bad right now there'd be something wrong with me. I've never felt so rotten in my life. I hate to cry and carry on. I was never a cry-baby even when I was little. But last night I couldn't help myself. I was bawling like a kid.'

'Like I said, you had a bad experience. Did Linda tell you I called her about Bob?'

'She said they operated on him and he's going to be all right.'

Julian nodded. 'He'll be in the hospital for a while but Dr Moffat says he'll be good as new when he comes out.'

'Thank God. When I saw him laying there on the floor with blood all over him I thought sure as the world he was dead. Linda was crying, too. We were both crying our hearts out.'

'Well, it looks as if everything's going to work out fine. We just have to make sure there's no bad publicity about this. We don't want you to be hurt and we don't want to do any damage to the picture you and Joel are working so hard on.'

'Does Mr Cukor know what happened?'

Julian shook his head. 'Nobody knows anything. And we're going to keep it that way. I told George you had a touch of the flu but I thought you'd be all right tomorrow.'

'I will be. I'm sure I will be. I hate to miss work and mess up the shooting schedule.'

'Don't worry. It worked out fine. George took a crew out to Thousand Oaks today to do Joel's horseback scenes. We won't lose a minute on the schedule.'

'That's good,' she said. Then: 'Did you see Bob in the hospital?'

'Nobody's seen him except Dr Moffat and the hospital people. He's in an intensive care unit. He'll be there for several days so they can keep a close watch on him. No visitors till later. They don't want to risk somebody bringing in germs from outside. When a man has lung surgery the doctors are always afraid of pneumonia setting in.'

'When can I see him?'

'Dr Moffat says it depends on how he gets along. You may not be able to see him till they bring him home.'

'Gosh, I can't wait that long. He'll think there's something funny going on if I never go see him.'

'You have to trust me on this, Daisy. I'm juggling a lot of balls in the air.'

'I do trust you. You know that. But I don't want Bob to think I'm sore at him. Or I forgot all about him or something.'

'He won't think that. You'll send him flowers and letters every day. He'll know you're thinking about him.'

'I don't know. It makes me feel funny. I mean, I feel guilty.'

'There's nothing for you to feel guilty about.'

'Maybe not. But I feel that way anyhow.' She turned her head and looked out the window. 'Did the police come last night?'

'No.'

'Don't they know what happened?'

'They will soon. Jack Gilder is meeting right now with a man from the prosecutor's office.'

'Jack Gilder? He's that slick lawyer that people call when they're afraid they're going to jail. Ain't he the one?'

'He's a fine attorney,' Julian said. 'He knows how to get things done.'

'But how can he tell anybody what went on here last night? He wasn't here. Nobody knows what happened except me. Even Linda doesn't know. She was in her room.'

'That's the main reason I'm here. I want you to tell me exactly what took place. From the time Bob showed up here till the moment he was shot. How long was it?'

'Half an hour, I guess. Maybe forty-five minutes. He didn't beat around the bush.' She resettled herself in the bed. 'I'll try to remember everything he said and what I said, so you'll know exactly what happened. He didn't come to the front door. He knocked on the back door just next to Linda's room. She didn't want to let him in. She told him I was asleep but he barged in anyway. Bob doesn't have a quiet voice exactly, so when he and Linda were talking in the hall it woke me up. As soon as I recognized his voice, I got up and put on a robe and went into the front room. When I switched on the lights he followed me in there. And as soon as I laid eyes on him I knew he was half in the bag. His eyes get as small as peas when he's had a lot to drink. He never stumbles or staggers around, and you can't tell it by the way he talks, but those little pea eyes give him away every time. Linda's no fool. She was all ready to stay there in the room with us. She thinks that's part of her job and I guess it is, but I figured I could handle Bob better by myself. It didn't take long to find out what he was up to. He said he had his car parked outside by the delivery gate and he wanted me to throw on some clothes and come with him. He was happy as a monkey when he first came in. He said he'd told the director on the Tim McCoy picture what he thought of him and walked off the picture. Then he said a lot of nasty things about you and your brother. He said you'd lied to him, sold him a bill of goods. He said the real reason you'd signed him up for all that work was just to get him out of town. He said you want to break up our marriage but he wouldn't let you get away with it. He's a great talker when he's had a few. Like I say, he was full of beans. Proud of himself for quitting his job and for finding a way to sneak on the lot when he knew he wasn't supposed to. He's real crazy sometimes. Carries on like a wild man.' She had tears in her eyes suddenly. 'Are you sure he's all right? After the operation, I mean. You wouldn't lie to me about that, would you?'

'I told you exactly what the doctor said. He'll be fine if he stays in the hospital till he's healed up.'

'I'm sorry,' she said. 'I didn't mean to say you're a liar. I'm just so mixed up I don't know what I'm saying. Don't be mad at me.'

'I'm not angry with you, Daisy. All I want to do is help you. Try to make things easier for you. What happened then?'

'He had this crazy idea that he and I could just get in his car and start driving. Ever since I've known Bob, whenever he got into a corner, he's always said, "What do we care? Let's just get in the car and take off. Up the coast highway and to hell with everybody else." Fishing. That's what it was always about. He had all these great places to fish and he wanted me to see them. Catch fish, speckled trout he always said, fry them in a pan over the fire, and sleep in a tent in the woods, with his cowboy loop around the tent on the ground so the rattlesnakes wouldn't snuggle up in the tent with us to get warm. Well, if there's anything I hate worse than a fish flopping around it's a snake. And Bob knows that. He's always known it. But like I say, when he's on a toot or when he's not feeling too proud of himself, the first thing that comes in his head is me and him in the woods some place up in Oregon.'

'That's what he wanted last night?'

'That was part of it. When I told him I couldn't go any place because I was right in the middle of the most important picture I'd ever been in, he wouldn't listen. He kept saying, "I just told them to shove it. You can do the same thing." He said that over and over. He said, "We don't need those crappy Thorne brothers. We can work in any studio in town. We could do some pictures together. Produce them ourselves. Have control of the whole shooting match." Crazy stuff like that he kept saying. And then he'd say, "But first of all we're going fishing. Get some clothes on and let's get out of here." I just kept shaking my head and saying no, I couldn't do it. And finally he seemed to run out of gas. He just stood there with his arms hanging down at his sides and all of a sudden he started to cry. I'd never seen him cry before even when his folks died. But he was crying last night. Tears running right down his cheeks. I guess it was what they call a crying jag but I'd never seen one before. He kept saying we were going to break up, that I cared more about acting than I did about him, that being his wife wasn't enough for me. I had to be famous, had to have people running after me, catering to me, telling me how wonderful I am. Then all of a sudden, he had a gun in his hand. It scared me to death. He's always had guns around the house. I'm used to seeing all kinds of guns. But I'd never seen him carrying one before, not when he wasn't working. And I'd never seen him touch one when he's been drinking. A thousand times I've heard him say, "Drunks and guns don't mix." But there he was drunk and crying with that revolver in his hand. And he kept saying, "Maybe we'll go some place *else* together. You don't want to go to Oregon, maybe we'll grow wings like angels and fly up in the clouds. How's that sound to you? Ladies first. That's the rule. First I shoot you, then I shoot myself. How's that for a dynamite ending? I'll make you famous. They'll never forget you. You'll be bigger than Garbo. Daisy's husband killed her because he loved her too much." He kept saying nutty things like that and I was shaking like a leaf. Then all of a sudden he put the gun up to his temple and I thought, "My God, he's gonna shoot himself right in front of me." I jumped up from the couch and grabbed his arm with both hands and we twisted and turned and stumbled around, and all of a sudden the gun went off and blood spattered on me and I thought I was shot. Then Bob fell backwards and hit his head on the corner of the coffee table. I saw the blood on his chest and I knew . . . God, it was terrible. I heard myself screaming and the security man broke open the door and then I guess Linda led me into my bedroom. That's all I remember till I woke up a little while ago.'

Julian sat quiet. When he spoke at last he said, 'Are you sure you didn't leave out anything? Is that exactly the way it happened? Remember . . . this is important.'

'I know it's important. That's why I told you every little thing I remember.'

'Good. It's important for me to get it all straight.' He got up and walked over to the window. When he turned and came back to his chair he said, 'But that's not the story we're going to tell the police.'

'I thought you said the police wouldn't . . . I thought I wouldn't have to talk to anybody.'

'Maybe you won't. We hope you won't. But we have to be prepared for anything. And everyone has to tell the same story. Let's get Linda in here. She has to hear this, too.'

When Linda came into the bedroom she sat on the window seat by the head of Daisy's bed. Julian repeated to her what he'd just said to Daisy. Then he said, 'No crime's been committed here. We're not trying to protect anyone. We simply don't want things to look bad for Daisy or her husband or the studio. It was an accident and we'll say it was an accident. So if we change a few small details no one will suffer for it. We all understand that, don't we?'

'I think so,' Linda said. 'Yes, I do.'

'Good,' Julian said. 'Pay close attention now because these are the facts you must remember. *This* is what happened.' He turned to face Daisy. 'You were not surprised to see Bob last night. You knew he was coming and you were eager to see him. You knew he'd driven down from Lone Pine and had to drive back there after he left you. You were expecting him also, Linda. You were happy about it because you knew Daisy wanted very much to see him. He hadn't been drinking. The security men will say that he came through the main gate and there was no sign that he'd been drinking. Are we clear so far?'

Julian went on then to tell them the story that had been agreed on, the story that Gilder would tell Gillette. When he finished he said, 'It's a simple story. Husband concerned about his wife's safety, brings her a revolver to keep for protection. While he's showing her how to use it, it goes off and he gets shot. Now I want each one of you to tell me, in your own words, exactly what I've just told you.'

When Julian got back to his office, Jack Gilder was waiting

for him. 'You took a shave and changed your shirt,' Julian said. 'Now you look like a man who might be worth the fees you charge.'

Gilder smiled. 'No one can afford to pay me what I'm worth, Julian. You know that.'

'With your self-confidence you should have been an actor.'

Gilder shook his head. 'I've been told that many times. But I couldn't afford the cut in pay.'

'How'd it go with Gillette?'

'Smooth as silk. We should have no problem. How's your actress feeling?'

'Shaky. But she's a tough kid. She'll be all right. When she gets on the set tomorrow she'll be as clear as crystal.'

'How about the maid?'

'Smart and loyal. She understands everything. We can count on her.'

'I'm not going to ask you what really happened last night. I'd rather not know. But I don't want any big surprises either. Just tell me if it was an accident or not.'

'Let me put it this way. The story we made up is a bit simpler than what actually happened. But it was an accident. No doubt in my mind about that.'

'Good. Now let me ask you one more question. If that gun was dusted for fingerprints, whose prints do you think we'd find on it? Based on what you know.'

'Mostly Sample's. But a few of Daisy's as well.'

'So if the police got hold of the revolver you don't think it would shoot down our story.'

Julian shook his head. 'I think we'd have more of a problem if they found out the gun is missing.'

'So do I. Let me use your phone.'

Gilder dialled a number, winked at Julian, and spoke into the phone, 'This is Jack Gilder. Will you please tell Mr Gillette I'm on the wire.' A moment later he said, 'I just want you to know, Bruce, that if I'd known how much you eat for breakfast I wouldn't have offered to pick up the check.' He listened for a moment, then laughed. 'No, you bastard, I didn't promise you the waitress as well.' Another pause, another laugh. Then: 'I forgot to mention that the gun is here whenever you want it. Most of the security people here at Thornwood are ex-cops. The first one on the scene after the shooting picked it up with a towel and tucked it away so nobody would touch it. I thought somebody from your office might like to pick it up so it'll be with you in case the police need to look at it. Of course . . . that's right. Good idea. I'll see you later.'

When he replaced the receiver, Gilder said, 'Now we're heroes. I'll drop the revolver off with Gillette on the way back to my office.'

5

Just after the release of *Bushranger*, the first film Kincaid appeared in, when it was clear at once that it was a remark- able piece of work, that it would make a great deal of money for Thornwood studios, delight millions of people, and make Kincaid a widely recognized and admired actor, Evan and Sophie, meeting for one of their frequent lunches together, tried to analyse and understand the remarkable events they had been witness to and had, in some small way, helped to happen.

'It's ironic,' Sophie said, 'that such a private man should suddenly become a public figure.'

'But he must have had some impulse to be a performer. He was a busker, remember? That's how I first knew about him.'

'Ah, but that was desperation. I expect he would have tried anything just then. So he used that freakish memory and his unusual voice and found he could earn enough shillings to keep himself from starving and sleeping in doorways. But being an actor, the sort of actor one sees in the West End or in films, was surely the farthest thing from his mind. One reads in the papers that thousands of gifted people are trying to make their mark in that profession, then along comes Kincaid and it all seems to have been handed to him.'

'He still had to handle the work, however. What he did in *Bushranger* was not just luck.'

'Of course not. I meant that the ability to do the work, as well as the opportunity, seems to have been presented to him on a platter. He had no formal training, no exposure to the theatre. No education, really. Whatever he knows he's picked up along the way.'

'He's picked up a great deal, however. No one who meets him for the first time questions his intelligence.'

'But that's what I'm saying. He's all contradictions. A man who is usually silent by choice is suddenly declaiming the great soliloquies from Shakespeare on the pavement in Shaftesbury Avenue. Most of the people he meets don't interest him at all, but people are drawn to him all the same. He has no children, at least he's never raised any children, still he has instincts for dealing with Sarah and Trevor that I will never possess. When Trevor first met Kincaid he said, "I like him. He knows how to listen." Is that his secret? Someone said, "If you speak very little you'll be considered wise. If you don't speak at all, you'll be seen as a genius."'

'Poppycock,' Evan said.

'Of course. You and I were taught to speak up, to say what we know and believe, to debate it, if necessary, in a civilized way. But Kincaid's convictions and conclusions are mostly private. I've seldom seen him disagree with anyone. He simply nods his head and smiles. He's a misanthrope, you know. At heart, I think, he mistrusts everyone. Or perhaps they simply don't interest him. Most things don't interest him. He has no impulse to persuade. No desire to explain himself. He seems to have no plans or theories. One discovers what he intends to do at the moment he does it. But if that makes it sound as if he's difficult to live with, then I've said it wrong. He's an angel to live with. He's not competitive or contentious. We're alike in that respect.'

'You can't be serious,' Evan said. 'You're the most competitive animal who ever lived. You see an antagonist in every corner.'

'Not true. If you're saying that I care about a great many things, that I'm willing to state my convictions and defend the ideas that are important to me, that is true. And there, of course, is where Kincaid and I differ. He seems to care deeply about very few things. And those things, for the most part, he keeps to himself. One time I asked him, "What do you have that you could never give up?"'

'What did he say?'

'He didn't hesitate. He said, "There's nothing I couldn't give up."'

'Did that disturb you?'

'Only for a moment.'

'Then you think he doesn't mean it.'

'I believe that he thinks he means it. But I know what he's really getting at. In the last two or three years he's either earned or had handed to him almost everything any man could want. I expect his reaction to such good fortune is that it can't possibly last. So how does one guard against future loss? You simply pretend that whatever you have is of no value. You see what I'm saying? When you live with privation and hardship and neglect all your life, the fear of returning to that level causes the mind to play strange tricks.'

'There's another possibility. Perhaps the way we live is not as attractive to him as it is to us. Maybe those difficult places he came from are not as unpleasant in his memory as you imagine they are. A dozen times I've heard him say that the answer to everything is to pare your life to the bone, carve away the excess and keep it plain. I'm sure you've heard him say that.'

'Indeed I have. And it's music to my ears. No life could possibly be more simple and enjoyable than the one he has now, the life we have together. We are totally free.'

'No one is totally free.'

'We are. We have my family home in the North and our elegant house here in London. We're healthy and we love each other and we have a fine dependable staff to look after us.'

'And now he has his career as well.'

Sophie smiled. '*Career* . . . somehow I don't think that's the correct word for it. He's had a nice adventure but I expect we may have seen the end of Kincaid's acting. After all, as I said, he's not a public man, is he? I think he'll decide that privacy is as important to him as it is to me. It was a challenge to him, I think, and an opportunity to make a great deal of money. But now it's over.'

'You think the money's not important to him?'

'Not at all. He enjoyed striking a sharp deal with Julian Thorne, but apart from that, he doesn't give a damn about money. And even if he did he could always have mine.'

Evan smiled. A wicked grin. 'All of it?'

'Of course. If he wants it.'

'If I'd known you were so generous I'd have pursued you myself.'

'What a horrid thought,' she said.

'There's no need to be nasty about it.'

She laughed. 'I don't mean being pursued by you would be horrid. I meant, it must be truly horrid to discover that someone has married you for your money.'

'That's something I need never worry about.'

'Ah, but you don't need money. You have charm and talent and a noble character. You will always be loved for yourself.'

6

Trevor's reaction, or lack of reaction, to the news that his grandmother had married Arthur Tagg, was based on two factors. *One*: he shared with Kincaid the view that what people decided to do was their own damned business, and *two*: like

395

every young man of his age and class, he was primarily concerned with matters that directly affected him.

Two such matters had come to his attention at almost the same time as he had news of Margaret's marriage. A letter came from Lucy Street, beautiful and graceful as a young deer, a ballet student who had posed in his drawing classes when he was in California and had skilfully presided over his sexual initiation just before he left Los Angeles to return to England; the other letter came from Ben Quigley, a painter Trevor had met in Portugal two years before while he summered there with his mother and Sarah.

Lucy Street wrote:

I haven't been in touch with you for a while and I feel guilty about that because I really enjoyed getting all those letters you wrote and the pen-and-ink drawings you sent along. But I knew you'd understand because you, more than anybody else, know what a busy schedule I have. Then . . . how can I say this . . . something happened that I didn't expect to happen and I was very mixed-up for a few weeks. I wanted to write to you but I didn't know what to say. Then I decided it was better if I didn't write at all. Just let time go by and . . . you know, just let things sort of peter out. But I couldn't do that, especially when your letters kept coming, two or three a week. So here goes.

You've probably guessed what I'm about to say. I met a guy named Leo Mossler and I fell for him pretty hard. He's quite a bit older than me, in his thirties. He's divorced and has two sweet daughters, Hazel and Polly, who live out in the valley with their mom, a woman I never want to meet. She once threw scalding coffee on Leo. He still has an awful burn scar on the back of his hand.

I met him here at the apartment I share with my sister. She goes out with this movie cameraman and Leo is his operator. That means Leo is the fellow who actually runs those big cameras while the actors are playing the scene. So anyway he came along one evening when his boss came to see my sister. He told me later that he didn't know I was going to be there, didn't even know there was a kid sister, but I think he told me a little fib about that. Because my sister and her guy took off just a few minutes after Leo got there, leaving him there with me.

Don't get the wrong idea. Nothing happened. We just sat and talked for an hour or so and then he left. I said before that I fell for him but it didn't happen so quick. Leo's a nice-looking guy but people don't turn and look at him in the street. As soon as he left that night I got busy with some things I had to do and didn't think about him at all. But the next day he kept popping into my head. I guess it was because of those two little girls of his. His ex-wife's married again to some joker who owns a furniture store in Pacoima but Leo gets to have his daughters two weekends a month as part of the divorce agreement. He says his wife is happy to get them out of her hair. I guess she doesn't really want them but she'd die before she'd let him have them. Anyway I kept thinking about all this stuff he'd told me and it made me so sad I felt like bawling. Maybe it reminded me of how it was for my sister and me when we were little. But anyway, when Leo called me a week later and asked if I wanted to go out for some chop suey I couldn't wait to see him again. After that we started going out together any night when he wasn't working or I didn't have a class, and a month or so ago I moved in with him.

He has a sweet little house on a side-street off of Laurel Canyon. He's got a mortgage and he has to pay child support every month and he has big payments on a new Pontiac he bought after his old car got wrecked in a parking lot, so we're not going to get married for a while. But that's all right with me. As long as we're happy, what's the difference? There's plenty of time. Meanwhile I'm turning into a good cook and housekeeper. And twice a month I get to play mommy to Hazel and Polly. I'm trying to make them like me and I think I'm doing all right. It's hard sometimes because they're only four and seven and I guess they wonder why their daddy's not with their mother instead of me. Also the guy from Pacoima buys them toys and clothes that cost a lot of money, so they think he's a real hot-shot. That's all right with me but I know it makes Leo feel funny when they keep bragging about their stepfather. Saying how smart he is and everything.

I'll bet you're wondering why I haven't said a word about my dancing. My mother used to say, 'It's like God is sending you a message.' And it does seem that way. Less than two weeks after I met Leo I had a bad accident in dance class. Pulled a groin muscle and ruptured the Achilles tendon in my left leg. A special doctor who treats dancers and athletes put the cast on my ankle and he said after a year or so I should be good as new for walking and stuff. But no more dancing. If it had happened six months sooner I'd have felt like hanging myself. But since I had Leo to talk to about it, it didn't hurt so much after a while.

Naturally, I don't model for Mr Grell's art classes any more. And I miss it. But Leo would murder me if he found out I was standing up there naked in front of a bunch of strangers.

So you see, I've got a new life now, Trevor. And I feel good about it. I like looking after Leo and his little girls and we'll probably have some kids of our own when we can afford it. Like I said before, there's plenty of time for all that.

I won't be writing to you any more. I'm sorry but that's the way it has to be. I'm an old married (almost) woman now. Ha-ha.

I guess you won't want to write to me either after you get this letter. At least I hope you won't. It would just get me in trouble with Leo.

I thought a lot of you, Trevor, when you were here in LA. I really liked you. For a while there I hoped things might work out for us, that maybe we'd get together some time. But I guess God didn't send us any message.

If the letter from Lucy had the ugly effect of a door closing in Trevor's face, the note from Quigley gave promise of another door opening.

We have a proposal for you. When I know your reaction I'll write you more details and we'll make some plans.

As you know, Lenore and I have been hopping about a lot since we last saw you almost two years ago. Sicily, Malaga, Copenhagen, Senegal, Dresden, Luxembourg, and a few other places I've forgotten. Touring around, going to museums, buying a few paintings, eating well, and drinking too much. Now we've decided to wander back to Praia de Rocha, where we met you, and spend some time there, from May to October at least, and we'd like you to join us for the summer months when you're not in school. How does that sound? Since I've given up any illusions I once had about being a painter myself, you'll have the studio to yourself, well stocked with tubes of colour and great rolls of linen canvas waiting to be stretched and immortalized. So there's *that* we have to offer you, along with the splendour of our company and the brilliance of our conversation, Lenore's more brilliant than mine, of course.

If all this sounds inviting, then we'll go forward as soon as we get a nod from you. I will write a letter to Sophie and reassure her that we are as unreliable and undependable as ever, Lenore and I, but that we would truly appreciate having her son as guest and co-conspirator for as much of the summer as he can spare.

So . . . respond quickly so Lenore and I can rejoice and begin to make plans. I will not try to persuade you unduly apart from saying that if you refuse you will have lost the greatest opportunity of your young life, your entire future may be jeopardized, and neither Lenore nor I will ever mention your name again or give you coins if we find you begging in the streets.

One final note, more serious than the above. The drawings you've sent us are stunning evidence of the progress you made in your studies with Grell. I'm keen to see how your drawing skills will translate themselves into paint when you have a chance to do some sustained work.

Several times in your letters, you've mentioned your eagerness to find your way. That's an understandable, inevitable, I suppose, objective for a young painter. It can't hurt you as long as you realize that once you've found your way, you must then find another way. We'll talk about this when I see you. But meanwhile, consider the cases of men like Derain and Vlaminck and Braque. All of them did brilliant early work, then lost their way in an unbelievable fashion, forcing formulas on themselves rather than allowing the work to define itself. Even everyone's god, Cezanne, in his late paintings of blue and Indian red, made intellectual choices that seriously eroded his primitive genius.

Enough of that. You're doing fine work. All sorts of good things ahead of you. Especially this coming summer. Let us know if you can make it. If you decide to spend the summer visiting your ballerina in California, however, no one can criticize you for that choice.

Trevor answered Quigley's letter at once.

What a great idea. Do write to my mother and I will begin at once an irresistible campaign of persuasion. She likes you and Lenore, and since my Uncle Howard and Aunt Sybil will also be in residence near Portimäo, I'm sure we'll meet no serious resistance.

He included then some details about his final letter from Lucy Street. In conclusion:

I liked her a lot. I told you that before. But I'm not stupid. I know I'm a long way from being able to make permanent plans with anybody. I have a lot of work to do on myself first. I admit I thought about Lucy all the time. I certainly expected to see her again. But ten thousand miles is a great distance. And I'm still a schoolboy whether I like it or not. What I'm saying is that I'm not destroyed or surprised that she's found herself a new chap. But it makes me sick that all that talent and hard work and ambition seems to have drained out of her. She doesn't fool me. She's just using her injury as an excuse. She was an *electric* girl, Ben. Now she's fizzled out. She's going to sit in some little box house and make tuna-fish sandwiches and be a nanny for somebody else's children, and one day she'll wake up and she'll be forty years old, wondering what happened to her. Just thinking about it makes me sick as a dog.

7

Ten days after Bob Sample was operated on and placed in intensive care, Bruce Gillette rang Jack Gilder from the District Attorney's office.

'Why don't you meet me at the Roosevelt bar at four o'clock this afternoon?' Gillette said.

'Are you buying?'

'Why not? I've got an expense account.'

'It's a generous offer, Bruce, but I'll have to take a rain check. I have an appointment in Beverly Hills at four-thirty.'

'I think you'd better reschedule it. I've got some news you're not gonna like.'

'About what?'

'About the shooting at Thornwood Studios. All of a sudden we've got Otto Wirtz to deal with.'

As soon as he hung up the receiver, Gilder called Julian at the studio and told him what Gillette had said.

'Jesus,' Julian said. 'I was hoping we'd put that behind us.'

'Maybe we have. I'll have to see what Wirtz is up to.'

'I don't even like to hear Otto Wirtz's name. How did he get involved in all this?'

'He told Gillette he's representing Bob Sample.'

'Wirtz is trouble.'

'So am I,' Gilder said. 'Why don't you wait for me at the studio? I'll come to your office as soon as I leave Gillette.'

Gillette was waiting in the bar at the Roosevelt. When Gilder sat down Gillette said, 'I ordered gin fizzes for both of us. Told the waiter to put it on your tab.'

'I hope that's the worst news I'm gonna get,' Gilder said.

'It's not. Wirtz says we have to take another look at the Bob Sample business.'

'Based on what?'

'Based on his client's version of what happened. It seems that Sample has some fresh ideas about what went on. Wirtz was being cute. Wouldn't tell me the details. Wants me to put an investigator on the case so I can get all the information straight from Sample's mouth.'

'How do you mean Wirtz was *cute*?'

'Mealy-mouthed. Kissing my ass. Acting as a friend of the court. Fairness and justice . . . all that crap. Very sympathetic to Julian Thorne's problems, too. Recognizes the need for confidentiality. Wants to avoid scandal and publicity.'

'Like hell he does. He thinks publicity is what feeds the bull-dog. He wouldn't be screwing around with a sap like Bob Sample if he didn't already smell money and see his photograph in the *LA Times*. What's his angle?'

'Doesn't seem to have one. All clear-eyed and idealistic like a public defender who just passed the bar last week.'

'He must have said something to give you a hint about what he's gunning for.'

Gillette shook his head. 'Very humble. Obsequious. But just before he bowed out of my office like Charlie Chan, he gave me a bit of advice as to what the charges should be.'

'Do I want to hear this?'

'I think so. After I've finished my investigation, he thinks I'll want to go for conspiracy to commit first degree murder and assault with intent to kill.'

When he left the Roosevelt, Gilder drove to Thornwood Studios. After he'd told Julian about his meeting with Gillette, Julian said, 'How do you read the situation?'

'Hard to say. When you're up against Wirtz it's like punching pillows. He doesn't attack. He slowly smothers you to death.'

'I wish we knew what he's feeling so good about. Is there some way we can find out what Sample told him?'

'Not a chance. He won't give away anything. He wants to force the prosecutors to do an investigation. Open things up. Get it out of Gillette's office.'

'Does that mean he thinks you and Gillette are playing footsy?'

'He probably does. He thinks everybody's as devious as he is. But it doesn't matter what he thinks. There's no law that says lawyers and prosecutors can't talk to each other. It has to be that way. Saves a lot of time and useless effort. Besides, Gillette knows I wouldn't hang him out to dry. If I tell him there was an accidental shooting, one person hurt, nobody killed, he believes me. He's not about to push for a big investigation that's going to lead nowhere. He knows reputations and careers and a lot of money are involved. That doesn't mean he's dishonest, it just means he knows what's important and what isn't. He also knows he can trust me. If he caught me trying to cover up a felony, if he thought I was lying about what went on in Daisy Bishop's bungalow, he'd nail my ass to the wall in a minute.'

'Does this mean he'll be talking to Sample?'

'He has to. Or Wirtz could crucify him. Bruce will probably have one of his investigators take the testimony. But he'll sit in.'

'And you'll see a transcript?'

Gilder nodded. 'I'm Daisy's attorney. If she's indicted I'll have to defend her.'

'Don't even say that word. She's just a kid. She'd shrivel up and die if you put her on a witness stand.'

'I thought you told me how tough she was.'

'She is. About some things. But she's never been up against a sharp lawyer.'

'Have you?'

'Damned right I have. They have lawyers in New York who should be kept in cages.' Then: 'Are we going to be able to keep this out of the papers?'

'The prosecutor's office won't leak it. They have no reason to. And neither does Wirtz. Not in this case. He doesn't want to alienate Gillette. Wants him on his side. But if there's an indictment or a trial, everything's up for grabs. The papers won't look the other way and we can't expect them to.'

'All right,' Julian said. 'What's our next move? Or do we have one?'

'The next move is Gillette's. He'll talk with Sample, I expect, as soon as he's out of the hospital. I'll see the transcript and pass it along to Daisy to read, and then we'll schedule her trip to the prosecutor's office.'

'Can't they send a man here? Can't we do it in the conference room next to my office? I hate to have Daisy parading around downtown. Those court buildings are crawling with reporters.'

'That's a good point. I think Gillette will buy that. There's one other problem. When are we going to break the news to Daisy? And who's going to do it?'

'That's my job,' Julian said.

'I think you should wait till we know what's in Sample's statement to Gillette. Daisy will have to be told what she's accused of before she's interviewed herself.'

'That makes sense. I'll hold off then. No use upsetting her before it's necessary.'

'I assume she's had no contact with Sample since he went into the hospital?'

'She's sent him flowers and notes every day. She didn't expect he'd be able to contact her.'

'Well, now she's going to hear from him,' Gilder said. 'I hope she's as tough as you think.'

8

The next day, mid morning, Gilder asked his secretary to place a call to Otto Wirtz in his office. 'When he comes on the line tell him I'm on a call from New York, that I'll get back to him in a few minutes.'

'You don't want to talk with him then?'

'I do. But not just yet.'

At lunch-time Gilder met a client in the bar of the Bel Air Hotel. From his booth he could see the table in the dining-room where Wirtz had lunch every day. Wirtz always ate by himself, but was often seen to leave after his coffee with one of the sleek henna-haired ladies who seemed always to be present in the bar area.

On this day Gilder stayed on at his own table for a few minutes after his luncheon guest had left. Then he got up and walked slowly past Wirtz's table toward the front door. When he heard Wirtz's voice say, 'How are you, Counsellor?' he turned, feigned surprise, and said, 'Hello, Otto. My head was in the clouds. Sorry I didn't see you.'

'No matter. Will you join me for a cordial?'

'I'm afraid I can't. I'm behind schedule today.'

'I'm sorry we missed connections when you telephoned me this morning.'

'I don't believe I . . . did I call you?'

Wirtz nodded. 'When I came on the wire your secretary said you were tied up on a long-distance call. To New York I believe she said. Said you'd call back as soon as you rang off.'

'I'm sorry about that.' He sat down opposite Wirtz. 'I think I know what happened. I have an important client in San Francisco who has the same name as you do. *Jacob* Wirtz in his case. My secretary rings him all the time but this morning she must have got confused and called you by mistake. I'll see that it doesn't happen again.'

Wirtz, to whom chicanery and dissembling were essential survival tools, kept suspicion out of his voice but not out of his eyes. 'Ah, I see. None of us are able to find perfect secretaries, are we? To tell you the truth, however, I was half-expecting to have a call from you. Since you do so much work for Julian Thorne, I assume you also represent Daisy Bishop.'

'Oh, yes, I remember now. I had a memorandum from one of my associates saying that you're representing her husband . . . I can never remember his name.'

'Robert Sample.'

'That's right. He's a stuntman or something, isn't he?'

Wirtz smiled. A wet, underwater smile. 'I believe you'll find he has an actor's contract with Julian Thorne. A three-picture deal with options.'

'No kidding. I don't believe I knew that.'

'I assumed your friend Gillette had filled you in on all the details.'

Gilder snapped his fingers. 'That's right, now I remember that memorandum. My associate had talked with someone at the District Attorney's office.'

'With Gillette, I imagine.' An oilier smile this time.

'My wife says I have too many clients. Too much work. Says my brain's going soft. Wants me to move to Palm Springs and play tennis every day. I admit I can't keep all the details straight in my head the way I used to. Do you have that problem?'

'I can always remember the important things.'

'Somebody told me you write notes on your shirt-cuffs.'

'I've heard that story,' Wirtz said. 'It's not true.' Then: 'I know you're doing a little dance for me but let me ask you a simple question. Did your memorandum tell you that Daisy Bishop tried to kill her husband? Did it mention that I've asked for a full investigation?'

Gilder nodded. 'Now it's coming back to me. I think it slipped my mind because I couldn't believe that such a charge was being made. My understanding is that Daisy Bishop is very much in love with her husband. They have a good marriage. What reason could she have for trying to kill him? Why would she jeopardize her life and her career? She says it was an accident, her maid says it was an accident, and I've seen nothing to make me think otherwise.'

'You will. I promise you.'

'You're a married man, Otto. Look at it from Sample's viewpoint. Can you imagine putting your own wife on trial for attempted murder? It doesn't make sense. What's he after? Does he really want her to go to prison?'

'He wants justice. It's as simple as that. If your wife told you she was going to divorce you because she was in love with another man and then she shot you, wouldn't you feel entitled to some suspicions?'

'Ah, so that's it? So that's his story? I was wondering how the conspiracy charge fit in. Now I see. She's got a mystery man somewhere and she and this man conspired to have her accidentally shoot Sample with his own revolver.'

'Not accidentally, Counsellor. And the mystery man, as you call him, is in fact, a very well-known gentleman.'

When he got back to his office Gilder called Julian and told him about his meeting with Wirtz. 'Now,' he said, 'I've saved the worst for the last. Not only does Wirtz think he's dug up a motive — a lover for Daisy — he's also got a head-line. The guy he says Daisy has the hots for, the man Wirtz wants to nail on a conspiracy charge, is Roy Kincaid.'

## 9

It was nearly midnight, London time, when Julian's trunk call came through from California. Kincaid got out of bed and took the call in the sitting-room adjacent to the bedroom. The two men talked for more than half an hour. When Kincaid came back to bed Sophie, half-asleep, said, 'I wish you'd ask your lady friends to call at a civilized hour. I'm not possessive but I hate to have my sleep disturbed.' When he didn't answer she said, 'Who called?'

'Nothing important. I'll tell you about it tomorrow.'

'I don't like the sound of that. Who was it?'

'Go back to sleep.'

She switched on the lamp on her side of the bed and raised herself up on one elbow. 'Now you've aroused my curiosity, you rat. Was it really some common woman ringing up from the pub down the street?'

'It was Julian calling from California.'

'But you talked for ever. That must have been a fifty-pound telephone call. What's happening?'

He told her in detail, then, everything that Julian had told him. When he finished she said, 'I wish you'd made me go back to sleep.'

'I tried.'

'I can't believe what I've just heard.'

'You don't want to believe it. Neither do I. But there it is.'

'I'll be afraid to read the papers tomorrow,' she said.

'It's not in the papers. Not yet. And Julian says there's a good chance it never will be. At least that's what he hopes. They had the machinery all set up to protect Daisy. Now they have to protect me as well.'

'But that's a criminal charge. How can they keep that quiet? If there's to be a trial . . .'

'Julian doesn't think there'll be a trial. He thinks when the prosecutors have completed their preliminary investigations, they'll decide there's no case against Daisy.'

'But you said she shot her husband.'

'She says it was an accident and Julian believes her.'

'Julian believes whatever serves his purpose.'

'I think he's right. She had no reason to kill her husband.'

'Ah, but that's where you come in. She wanted to get rid of her husband so she could marry you. Isn't that the theory?'

'That's what her husband says. That's the charge.'

'What do you suppose she planned to do with me? Was I to be the next victim?'

'There weren't any victims. It's all hokum.'

'Is that what Julian thinks?'

'Julian's not thinking at all. He's reacting. His business feeds on publicity but it can hurt him, too. This time he's afraid of getting hurt. Even if nobody's indicted, even if there's no trial, it could make a nasty story in the papers. People like to believe the worst. It makes them feel good.'

'I don't see how they can suspect you of conspiracy. You've been here in London all the while.'

'That doesn't matter. I could have been in Bangkok . . . it's all the same. When two people cook up a scheme together, that's a conspiracy. Even if they communicate with carrier pigeons.'

Sophie put pillows behind her and sat up in bed. 'All this is gradually sinking in. And it's damned depressing.'

'I know it is. And I'm sorry. But there are crazy people in the world.'

'Not in the world,' she said. 'In Los Angeles. That's the official gathering-place for freaks and lunatics. Did she try to kill her husband or was it really an accident?'

'You asked me that before. I don't know the answer. I think I know but I can't guarantee anything.'

409

'Do you know this man . . . Daisy's husband?'

Kincaid nodded. 'I worked with him. All those weeks we were doing *Bushranger*.'

'He's an actor?'

'Not really. On the fringe. Stuntman, stand-in, dress-extra, wrangler. Sort of a handyman. Good rider, good fight man. Rugged-looking guy.'

'You liked him?'

'Didn't know him very well. We played poker together a few times, had some conversations while we were standing around, waiting for the light, or waiting for a shot to get set up.'

'Did he ever accuse you of having a frolic with his wife?'

'No. Nothing like that.'

'Wasn't that when the first items about you and Daisy started turning up in the columns?'

'I guess so. I don't pay any attention to that stuff.'

'But I'll bet he does.'

'I'm not so sure. Daisy's big news out there. People write things about her all the time. He must be used to it.'

'He's not used to you.'

'No, I guess not.'

'If he's saying you wanted her to kill him, it looks as if he has some serious suspicions.'

'You're not going to get overheated about this, are you?'

'I'm trying not to. How about you?'

'I think it's stupid. I'd hate to see Julian get burned by bad publicity and I'd hate to see Daisy's career go into a tail-spin. But as far as I'm concerned, they can say whatever they like about me. I don't give a damn.'

'But I do. This affects me as well.'

'I said before, I'm sorry about that. But that can't be helped either.'

After a moment she said, 'I'm not going to get some big surprises, am I? You haven't lied to me, have you?'

'About what?'

'About Daisy Bishop.'

410

'Didn't we discuss this a few times before?'

'I guess we did.'

'What did I say then?'

'You said there was nothing to it.'

'That's what I'm saying now. It's a lot of crap.'

'Wouldn't it be nice if everybody believed that?'

He didn't answer. At last he said, 'I don't expect you to be happy about this. I'm not either. But I can't figure out what disturbs you most. Are you afraid I'll be arrested and put on trial? Do you think I've been having a big affair with Daisy Bishop for the past two years? Or are you more concerned about what people will think if all this comes out in the papers?'

'All those things,' she said. 'All of it bothers me. I feel as if my premonitions about that crazy business and that crazy place are coming true. You know how I felt about California from the first time we went there.'

'Well, we don't have to go there now, if that's what's bothering you.'

'Of course you have to go. And I'm going with you,' she said.

Kincaid shook his head. 'Julian doesn't want me near Los Angeles. That's the main reason he called. He knows the minute I show up in Los Angeles the newspaper people will be all over me like a swarm of gnats.'

'But it's a serious charge against you. You can't just ignore it.'

'There is no charge yet. So far, it's just what Sample and his lawyer say. Julian's hoping that Daisy will never be indicted, but if she is, there'll be plenty of time for me to decide whether I want to go there voluntarily or wait to be extradited.'

'But you can't do that,' she said. 'That makes you look guilty. I think you should go there now. As soon as possible. So they don't get the idea you're hiding here in England. I'll go with you. We'll open up the house in Malibu and stay for as long as we have to.'

'I think I'd better get you a snifter of brandy. You're changing identities every time you open your mouth.' He reached over, put his arm round her, and pulled her close to him. 'Am I in bed with a stranger or is it really little Sophie Cranston?'

'The ex-Sophie Cranston, the present tortured and mistreated Madame Kincaid.'

'You're not aware of conflicting forces waging war inside you?'

'Not at all. I'm calm, self-contained, and adorable.'

'I'll be the judge of that,' he said. 'You must realize that in the space of two or three minutes you've gone from railing against everything that exists inside the state of California to insisting that we go there at once for an indefinite stay.'

'Nothing contradictory about that. I'm letting my survival instincts gain power for the moment, over my personal desires and prejudices. I don't want our relationship to be limited to jail visits. Whatever your sins and faults, Kincaid, I adore you. If I find out you've been playing house with Daisy Bishop, I'll dismember you. But until that day I am your loyal and devoted wife, willing to do anything for you or go anywhere, even to Los Angeles.'

'I appreciate the offer. But I don't want to go there and Julian doesn't want me to.'

'None the less I think you must go. We must go.'

Long after she'd gone to sleep with her head resting on his shoulder, Kincaid lay awake, trying to fit together half a dozen puzzles that seemed to have pieces missing. Homer Tony moved in and out of his consciousness. Major Cranston. Trevor and Sarah. Evan and his father. Julian and Daisy and Bob Sample. Everything gauzy and muted, overlapping, faint outlines. Only Sophie, warm and breathing beside him, seemed real. Her heart beating steadily against his arm, her body trembling once or twice from secret dreams she would never remember in the morning. He heard little snippets of sentences and words she'd said to him before she went to sleep . . . 'whatever your faults I adore you . . . your loyal

412

and devoted wife . . . do anything . . . go anywhere.'

Mixed in with these words, other phrases, unbidden, slipped into the mix, things she'd said some days or weeks before, in a wholly different context. When they'd discussed her painful new relationship with Margaret and Arthur . . . 'I've gone though hell . . . now it's my turn . . . get on a great ship and go away somewhere . . . just the two of us . . . give them something to think about . . .'

The next day, when he and Sophie were having breakfast together in the dining-room, he told himself that those two conversations that had seemed linked somehow the night before were in fact not connected at all. He truly believed it. For almost the entire morning.

# • CHAPTER 11 •

### 1

Julian and his wife, Bella, were sitting in their library continuing a conversation they'd begun at dinner. 'I considered not telling you about it. I knew it would upset you,' he said.

'It's not a question if I'm upset. It's you I worry about. All this business with poor Daisy, people firing revolvers in Thornwood bungalows, lawyers fighting with each other, Mr Cukor's nice picture in trouble maybe, because of stories that might be in the papers. I see you coming home late every evening, carrying all that on your shoulders, I feel you restless in the bed at night . . . so it's not myself I'm feeling sorry for. It's you, having to deal with all these cuckoo things and run your business at the same time. That's what worries me. And now there's this awful stuff about your brother. It's enough to drive a person crazy.'

'You're not to worry. I'll find a way to handle it.'

'I know you will,' she said. 'That's your gift, Julian. You always know how to fix things. What happens now between you and Sam is one thing. But how you feel about it afterward is something else. That's my concern. How long have you known about what's going on?'

'Since day before yesterday. As I said, at first I wasn't going to tell you.'

'We never keep secrets from each other. It's too late to start now.' She sipped from her coffee-cup. 'Two days ago . . . was that when Ethridge showed you all the financial records and bank statements?'

Julian nodded. 'We spent several hours together. You remember I was late getting home night before last.'

'Did Ethridge come to you on his own? Did he suspect there was something fishy?'

'No. I asked him to give me a breakdown of all the Thornwood deposits and pay-outs for the past eighteen months and that's what he did.'

'If there's all this funny business, why didn't Ethridge catch on sooner?'

'For one thing, Sam's his boss. Exhibitor's fees come across Sam's desk. Major expenditures are okayed by Sam. And we do get cash payments sometimes. That's not unusual. When Sam handed Ethridge an envelope full of money with a note attached saying it was from the Essaness theatres in Chicago or the Luna Amusement company in Indianapolis for such and such a picture, Ethridge had no reason to question it.'

'Did you know right away where the cash came from?'

'Not till I checked my own records that show how much each picture grossed in each market. Those cash deposits in every case were monies that didn't show on the final tally sheets. That could have meant somebody was taking those cash amounts out of the bank and pocketing the money.'

'Sam?'

Julian shook his head. 'I didn't think that. Sam is a shrewd operator but he's not a thief. Besides, it wouldn't make sense. Why deposit it all in that case? I decided those deposited amounts might have been used to pay bills that were off the books for some reason. So Ethridge went over all payments for services that Thornwood had made during those same eighteen months.'

'And . . .'

'At first I saw nothing out of line. Then I noticed that there were sizeable payments every month to two companies I'd never heard of. Acorn Services and Acme Productions. I asked Ethridge what we paid those companies for and he said the memos from Sam always noted, For Services Rendered. Neither company is listed in the telephone book and when Ethridge checked with some of our department heads and a few friends at other studios he couldn't find anybody who'd ever heard of Acme and Acorn.'

'Dummy corporations?'

Julian nodded. 'I asked Ethridge to bring up all the cheques in question. The cheques to Acme had been deposited by John Corso, the Acorn cheques by Charlie Ricci.'

'Who's Charlie Ricci?'

'He used to be in the produce business in Jersey. He worked for Sam and Corso. Now he just works for Corso.'

'How much money are you talking about?'

'Over eight hundred thousand in the past twelve months. There are also some hefty loans from Thornwood to those two companies, loans from them to us, repayment of loans, cash advances against future work, bonus payments, all sorts of tricky financial arrangements.'

'Is Thornwood being swindled?'

'That's what I was afraid of. But when we totalled the unearned cash that came into the studio through Sam and the unearned payments by cheque that we sent out, they added up like eggs in a carton. No gain. No loss. All that money just moved through Thornwood. In and out.'

'What does that mean?'

'It means that Johnny Corso has large amounts of money on hand that he's not supposed to have. So he hands it over to Sam and Sam puts it through as income to us from exhibitors. Then he gives it back to Johnny as legitimate payment for services rendered.'

'Is that against the law?' Bella said.

'It's against my law. I've known Johnny and his family all my life. I have a lot of respect for Vincent Corso. But I don't want to be in business with him. And I sure as hell don't want to be in business with Johnny. I always thought Sam was on shaky ground when the two of them were in business together in Newark. That was one of the reasons I was eager to have him come out here with me. Now it looks like he's still in business with Corso. And so is my studio, whether I like it or not. In this business nobody really trusts anyone. But I was sure I could trust Sam. Now I know I can't.'

'That's terrible, Julian. I don't even like to hear those words.'

'Neither do I.'

'What can you do?'

'I haven't decided yet.'

'You can't just cut him loose, can you?'

'I don't want to. But I can't put my company at risk either. I have to protect the studio. This isn't New York. If word gets around that Thornwood's connected to the mob we'd have to convert all our theatres to bingo parlours. I'd be as dead in this town as D.W. Griffith.'

## 2

When Otto Wirtz brought Bob Sample to the District Attorney's offices to make his statement, he expected to be met by Bruce Gillette. Instead he was shown to the office of a trim grey-haired woman in her fifties. A young man was also there, putting fresh paper into a stenotype machine.

'Good morning, Mr Wirtz, I'm Cora Faust. And this is Donald Kehoe, who'll be taking down Mr Sample's statement. We appreciate your coming in to help us in our investigation. Make yourselves comfortable and we'll get started as soon as you're ready.'

After he'd wedged himself into an armchair Wirtz said, 'I thought we'd be dealing with Mr Gillette. Are you his assistant?'

'No. I'm a deputy District Attorney, the same as Bruce Gillette.'

'Does that mean he won't be assigned to this case?'

'There is no case yet, Mr Wirtz. This is the first stage of

our investigation into the shooting incident that involved Mr Sample and his wife. We're simply trying to set down the facts. You know the process, Mr Wirtz. We will speak to all the persons involved to determine if any law has been broken and if there is evidence that might lead to an indictment.'

Sample, looking pale and sullen after his operation, twenty pounds lighter than before, spoke up suddenly. 'My wife tried to kill me. If that's not evidence, I don't know what is.'

Mrs Faust smiled. 'We don't know either, Mr Sample, not till we find out what happened.' She glanced at young Kehoe who was ready now at the stenotype, then back to Sample. 'I think the best way to proceed is for you to tell us in as much detail as possible exactly what happened at Thornwood Studios on the night in question . . .' She studied a note-pad on her desk . . . 'the night of March 27th.'

'Where do you want me to start?' Sample said.

'Let's start at the beginning. When you arrived at the studio.'

There was a long pause. Finally Sample said, 'Aren't you going to ask me some questions?'

'Only if there's something I don't understand. This is not, as I've said, a courtroom procedure. Later, when you're finished I may need to ask some questions. Until then just tell us what happened in your own words.'

'Have you talked to Daisy yet?'

'I can't tell you if she's made a statement or not. In any case it's irrelevant. Today we're only interested in what you have to say.'

'Just remember when somebody talks to her, or if it's already happened, that she's a liar and I'm not. What you're going to hear from me is the truth.'

Mrs Faust turned to Mr Wirtz, 'Please, Counsellor . . .'

'Go ahead with your story, Bob,' Wirtz said.

Sample adjusted himself in his chair like an actor searching for his key light. Then he spoke slowly and deliberately. 'I drove down from Lone Pine that afternoon. I didn't want to get to the studio till after dark because I knew I'd have to sneak in. Even though I'm under contract to Thornwood, I knew the security guys had orders not to let me in. The word had come down from Julian Thorne that I wasn't to be allowed to see my wife. You get what I'm saying? I'm her husband but they'd decided, the studio big-shots, that I wasn't supposed to see her. They were holding her there like she'd been kidnapped or something. With a guard outside her bungalow door and some Mexican dame inside to keep an eye on her.'

'Are you saying she was being kept there against her will?'

'She wasn't tied up if that's what you mean. But it sure as hell wasn't her idea. She's never made a picture before where she had to stay on the lot day and night from the first shot till they wrap. What I mean is, she was talked into it, bullied into it most people would say. Julian Thorne thinks he owns his actors, thinks they'll do anything he says. And most of them will, Daisy included. But that don't mean it's right.' He lit a cigarette, leaned forward, took an ashtray off Mrs Faust's desk, and went on. 'I made good time coming down to LA, so it was still early when I got there. I stopped at a Mexican joint on Cahuenga and had a good supper. Then I shot a few games of eight-ball at the pool hall next door. So it was late when I got to the studio. I left my car at the back of the lot on Largo Drive. Then I edged over to the delivery entrance. Not much going on there that time of night. The guard was listening to the radio and reading a paper all at the same time. I heard the phone ring then in that little shanty he sits in, and while he was yapping with somebody I sneaked past him and onto the lot. I took the dark streets and back ways to Daisy's bungalow. I know that lot like my own backyard. I went to the kitchen door where there was a light on and tapped on the glass. When the Mexican tootsie opened it a crack she said I couldn't see Daisy because she was asleep, but I said I'd raise particular hell if she didn't let me in. So in I went. As soon as Daisy came in the room she closed all the windows and pulled the shades, so I figured she was gonna start yelling at me.'

'Why did you think that?'

''Cause she's my wife. That's what wives do.'

'Why did you pick that particular night to go see her?'

''Cause I'd had enough of Thorne's crap. I knew he'd signed me to that piss-poor contract just to get me out of town. He knew I'd be raising Cain if I was living at home and he was keeping Daisy on the lot for weeks and not letting me in to see her. So after all the time I'd spent up at Red Rock, and now I was at Lone Pine with the Kanab picture coming up afterward, I decided enough was enough. That's what I told Daisy. I said, "Let's get out of here and drive all night and keep going till we hit Oregon. We'll camp out and catch some fish and have a helluva time." I meant it. I figured we were pissing our lives away. It was time for us to think a little bit about ourselves.'

'What did she say?'

'She went crazy. I mean, I've seen her steamed up before but nothing like that. She didn't yell or scream or throw things 'cause she didn't want one of those security jerks to bust in, but her face was red and her voice was hissing at me like a busted steam pipe. She said if I thought she was going to walk out on a George Cukor picture with Joel McCrea in it I was crazy as a bed-bug. The Mexican gal popped in a couple of times but the heat was too much for her, so she went back to the kitchen. I listened for a long time while Daisy reeled off my faults and shortcomings, and reminded me of every sin I've committed in all the time I've known her. Finally I got tired of listening and I said, "Cut the crap, Daisy. I'm getting out of here tonight. If you won't come willingly I'll pop you one, wrap you in a rug and carry you out of here under my arm."'

'Are you saying you threatened her?'

'No. Nothing like that. I don't beat up on women. I was just trying to shut her up. But I did intend to take her with me. I told her I loved her and being married to her was more

420

important to me than a dozen movies, Joel McCrea or not. All of a sudden her face wasn't so red and it seemed like she was really listening to me. I talked about all the good times we'd had since we met each other. From the days when we lived in a little cabin out in Sherman Oaks right up till today, when we've got a big house and two or three cars and we can do whatever we want to. Finally she sat down on the couch and told me to sit in a chair just in front of her. So I did. And she started talking to me. Real sweet. Didn't sound mad at all any more. But there was nothing sweet about what she had to say. She said she wasn't mad at me, she didn't hate me. She just didn't want to be married any more. I won't kid you none. We've had our ups and downs through the years. The battling Samples, my sister used to call us. And I'll admit that most of those battles were my fault because I used to be a two-fisted drinker.'

'Were you drinking the night you were shot?'

He shook his head. 'A couple beers maybe at the pool hall, but that's all. I was sober as a preacher. When I've got a lot of driving to do I lay off the juice. What I started to say was that in all the time we been married neither one of us ever said we wanted out. You know what I'm saying? Nobody ever said, "I've had enough" or "Get out and stay out" or anything like that. Now all of a sudden, Daisy was sitting there, looking me straight in the eye and telling me she wanted to get a divorce.'

'What did you say?'

'At first I didn't say nothing. I just sat there bug-eyed. She talked to me like I was some snot-nosed kid and she was my history teacher. She said she wasn't mad at me or anything, but sometimes people change and they don't have such a good life together any more, so the best thing they can do is go their own ways. I told her I didn't want to go my own way, that we was married and that's the way I wanted things to stay. I said the only bad thing between us was her God-damned career, and Julian Thorne telling her what to do, where to go, and what to think. I told her that's

421

why I wanted to take her off some place, get out of LA, maybe even leave California. But she just sat there looking at me as if I hadn't said anything, or like she was deaf and dumb. Finally she said she didn't want to hurt my feelings but the truth was she'd found another guy. She said she's crazy about Roy Kincaid and she wants to marry him.'

'What did you say then?'

'I don't remember exactly. I didn't know what to say. I guess I said something about Kincaid being married already, and she was married to me, and as far as I'm concerned that's the way things are going to stay.'

'Did the Mexican woman hear any of this conversation?'

'I don't know how she could. She was in a room at the back with the door shut.'

'So you told your wife you wouldn't give her a divorce?'

'That's right. I said a few other things, too. Told her what I thought of Kincaid. I was really sore by that time. I'm not sure what I said. But I didn't punch her or yell at her or anything. I just kept saying I wasn't planning to leave her and she'd better not plan to get rid of me.'

'Or what?'

'Or nothing. Like I told you I didn't try to scare her. I told her I was nuts about her and I wanted to stay married. But she just sat there looking at me like I was a bug on an apple. Cold and serious. Her mind all made up. That's the way she acted. Like she was dead set on doing things her own way no matter what I said. That was her attitude. To hell with you, Sample. But she didn't say anything. She acted like everything had been said already. Finally she got up and went into her bedroom. When she came back she had that little nickel-plated revolver of mine. Not pointing it. Just carrying it loose in her hand like it was an egg-beater or something.'

'It was your gun?'

Sample nodded. 'I've got a dozen guns. Rifles, shot-guns, revolvers, automatics . . . all of them registered and legal. When a director hires me he knows I'll show up in the right duds, carrying whatever kind of fire-arm the part calls for.'

'Does your wife know how to use a gun?'

'She's an ace. For a woman, that is. She learned it all from me when she was sixteen or seventeen years old. Ask her. She'll tell you the same thing. Her aim's not as true with a hand-gun as it is with a rifle, but she's no slouch. I saw her shoot a squirrel once with a pistol. Thirty yards away if it was a foot.'

'Why did she have a gun there at the studio?'

' 'Cause I wanted her to. When she told me she'd be living at the studio, sleeping there and everything, just when I was leaving for Red Rock, I loaded the nickel-plate job and told her to keep it by her bed.'

'You didn't think it was safe for her to be at the studio?'

'Oh, it's safe enough. But Daisy's famous now. And she's a sexy-looking kid. So you never know when some jackass might start getting ideas. You know what I'm saying? I just told her I'd feel better about it if I knew she had a gun there with her. But when I went to see her that night, I'd forgotten she had it. Then she came strolling out of the bedroom like I said, holding it in her hand. She sat down facing me again and she said, "Don't worry about the gun. I'm not going to shoot you. I just want to tell you a little story." She's always been like that, since she was a kid, her Mom said. When she wants to do a snow job on somebody, when she wants to win them over to her way of thinking, likely as not she'll say she wants to tell you a story. So that was nothing new to me. I knew there was no story she could think up that could talk me into giving her a divorce.'

'Before that evening did you have any suspicions about your wife and Kincaid?'

'Not me. But everybody else did. Ever since we all worked on *Bushranger* together there's been snotty little items in one column or another. But I never paid much attention to them. You see, when I first met Daisy she didn't know straight-up about men. She always said, "You're the only man I want."

People in the business used to talk about it. They'd say, "Daisy's a cup-cake if there ever was one, but she don't roll her eyes at nobody but Sample." And she didn't. I knew that. So I never got too excited when they printed silly stuff about her in the papers. I used to see her and Kincaid talking together once in a while on location but there was nothing cute and cuddly about it. I never gave him and Daisy a second thought till she sat there that night and told me she was crazy about him. Then I did a lot of thinking. In about thirty seconds. And nothing I thought made me feel good.'

'You said she was telling you a story.'

Sample nodded. 'Some story it turned out to be. She said, "If you don't think I'm serious, Bob, then you'd better think again. I've never been more serious than I am right now." She said she'd thought she could make me see things her way. She said, "Nobody wants to be married to someone when that person is all the time wanting to be with some-body else. At least that's how I'd feel if I was in your shoes." I told her she wasn't in my shoes and if she thought I was going to run off with my tail between my legs just so she could marry some Australian bastard, then she had another think coming. She just smiled at that, like a mink in the chicken-coop, and went on with her story. She said, "How does this sound to you? Pretend it's a movie script. A woman is desperate because she's in love with a certain man, but she can't be with him because she's already married to somebody else. When she tells her husband, he says he'll never give her a divorce. So she's stuck. She's not mad at her husband. She just knows she can't live with him any more. She can't live with anybody except this new man she's nuts about. Then one evening he's showing her how to use a gun he's given her and she says to herself, what if it went off acci-dentally and killed him? Or what if it wasn't an accident but she said it was. Or what if her husband threatened to kill himself if she didn't promise to give up this other man? What if he actually did it? Or what if he didn't do it but it was made to look like he did?"

'I asked her if she was telling me she was going to shoot me and she said no, she was just telling me a story. She got up then and walked around the end of the couch. I thought she was taking the gun back to her bedroom. Then I heard a little noise behind me, I looked over my shoulder and there she stood, with a nutsy look on her face and the revolver pointed straight at my head.'

'What happened?'

'I was on my feet and around the end of that couch like a cat. I made a grab for the gun but she shot me. She was aiming for my head but I guess I hit her arm because the bullet went into my chest. Damn near killed me. I'm lucky to be sitting here today.'

3

Cora Faust was also in charge when Daisy made her statement. This time, however, Gillette was there as well, along with Jack Gilder. The meeting took place during Daisy's lunch-break at the studio, so Cukor's shooting schedule for the day wouldn't have to be rearranged. Early that evening, after she'd finished work, she met with Gilder and Julian in Julian's office.

'There you are,' Julian said when she came in. 'Look at her, Jack. She's been up since five this morning and she looks like a bouquet of fresh flowers.'

'I don't feel like a fresh flower. I feel like an old rag.'

'Jack tells me you were upset about your interview today.'

'I wasn't upset exactly. It wasn't that. That lady . . . what's her name?'

'Cora Faust,' Gilder said.

'That's right. She was nice to me. I was expecting some hard-boiled guy like Edward G. Robinson, but she was just a regular woman. Like somebody's aunt. I mean, it's not her fault I feel rotten. I just hate to lie. I guess that sounds funny coming from an actress. That's what acting's all

425

about. Making things seem real and true when they're not. But when it's important, like this thing between Bob and me . . . I mean, I feel like a jackass when I sit there and say stuff that's not true.'

'Well, you didn't look like a jackass. They believed every word you said. And remember, you weren't that far from the truth. You told them it was an accident, and it was.'

'I still don't understand why I couldn't have told them what really happened. We weren't lovey-dovey trying to figure out how a safety-catch works on a revolver. We were having a fight. He was half-tanked and trying to get me to go away with him. He was acting crazy. I thought he was going to kill himself.'

'That's exactly the kind of story we wanted to stay away from,' Julian said. 'No crime of passion. Just an unfortunate accident. That's what you told them and Linda told them the same thing.'

'Linda wasn't even in the room that night.'

'She told them that,' Gilder said. 'But she also told them she knew he was showing you something about the revolver.'

'It's too simple,' Daisy said. 'It sounds made up.'

'Not the way you told it,' Gilder said. 'Simple is good. Simple is always better than complicated.'

'When I lie, I feel like a liar and I always think it shows.'

'It didn't show,' Gilder said. 'Even I believed you.'

'Did they ask many questions?' Julian said.

'Mrs Faust asked me how long we'd been married, and she asked if we were happy together and I said yes.'

'Then she asked if she knew of any reason why Sample would say she tried to kill him,' Gilder said.

'I told her I couldn't believe he thinks that,' Daisy said. 'All I can figure out is the medicine they're giving him is making him crazy.'

'Why is he saying that?' Julian said. 'Does anybody have a theory about it?'

'I think he's mad at the world. Trying to get even with everybody,' Gilder said.

'He's got no reason to get even with me,' Daisy said.

'He may think he does,' Gilder said. 'Don't forget . . . you're somebody and he's not.'

Daisy shook her head. 'Not possible. Bob always thinks he's somebody. He thinks he's the talented one in the family, not me. He always says, "I brought you uptown, honey. If you hadn't met me you'd still be serving coffee in some hash-house in Burbank." And you know something . . . he's right. I owe him a lot.'

'Is there any chance he believes those stories about you and Kincaid?'

She laughed. 'Not a chance in a million. We always laughed about stuff like that. Let me tell you something. My folks are Seventh Day Adventists. They raised me like a nun. I never kissed a man till I met Bob and I've never fooled around with anybody else since. And he knows it. It's a good joke, isn't it? Me playing all these racy women. Café singers and burlesque dancers and hookers, and all I know about men is what I learned from my husband. It's almost funny.'

'Not to me,' Julian said. 'There's nothing funny about it. It won't be funny till it's over. And it won't be funny then, either.'

4

Several days later Gilder met with Gillette in his office. 'We have a small problem,' Gillette said. 'Not a huge problem, maybe, but a sticky one. I've gone over these transcripts with Cora Faust, and she and I are pretty much of one mind. We don't think we could indict, bring anyone to trial, or convict with the small amount of evidence we have. But all the same I'm afraid Wirtz could screw things around and cause trouble either in court or out of it. For one simple reason. Sample's testimony, true or not, puts in a new ingredient. Motive. It's par for the course in a situation like this for the two people involved to be telling contradictory stories. You know that as well as I do. So we have to find some corroboration for either one story or the other. The maid is trying to support what Daisy says but she admits she didn't see what happened. It could have played out exactly as Sample said and the maid wouldn't have known it. She was in her room with the door closed till after the shot was fired. So whether we believe Sample's story or not, we can't prove it's untrue. And when another man is dragged into it, a famous guy like Kincaid, when Wirtz sends me copies of a dozen different newspaper clippings that hint about a romance between Kincaid and Daisy, that complicates matters. It's not hard evidence. It doesn't mean we could go forward with an indictment, but it's a case that Wirtz could try in the newspapers. And unless I misunderstand your position on this, that kind of publicity would be almost as bad as a real trial.'

'You're right. That's the problem.'

'So what we need is a third voice. And the stronger, the better.'

'But there's no such animal,' Gilder said.

'I don't mean a witness to the shooting. If I were looking at this case objectively I'd see it as an accident. But another person might read the transcript of Sample's testimony and say, "His wife had a motive." So if I were a potential defence attorney here I'd say, "Let's shoot down the motive. Let's get a statement from Kincaid."'

'Then what?'

'If we have convincing testimony from him that coincides with what Daisy told us, if I'm persuaded that there's no hanky-panky between those two, then I have no reason to believe Sample's story. I would never bring the case to trial.'

'I don't know,' Gilder said. 'I mean, I see what you're getting at but Kincaid's in London. And Julian doesn't even want him here right now.'

'He will when you explain the circumstances to him.'

'It's a long way to come. Big trip for Kincaid.'

'So much the better. Only an innocent man would make such a trip voluntarily. Friend of the court. All that crap.

Doing the right thing. If he had anything to hide he could find a hundred reasons to stay put in London. Only an innocent man would go to such trouble just to make sure that justice is done. And if we whitewash Kincaid we're doing the same for Daisy. Sample's story wouldn't be worth a nickel.'

'But would that defuse Wirtz? Couldn't he still make a splash in the newspapers?'

'He could but I don't think he will. I know Otto pretty well. He loves publicity but only if it gets him where he wants to go. If he's convinced there's going to be no indictments and no trial, then I think we'll find out what he's really after.'

## 5

Julian was having lunch in Henry French's private dining-room at Paramount. 'Jack Warner's like a woman in the last two weeks of a difficult pregnancy,' French said. 'He's having nightmares about Corso and his trucking operation. He's been talking to his people in New York and he thinks this CIO business is going to hit us overnight. Guys with beards throwing gasoline bombs at our sound stages.'

'I know,' Julian said. 'His brother Harry was complaining on the telephone to my brother a few days ago. So I told Sam to tell him I was meeting with you.'

'Good. Let's enjoy our lunch and then we'll hash it over.'

Twenty minutes later, when the Dover sole was being served, French said, 'I've got some personal matters I'd like to discuss with you. Business and personal, I guess I should say. Paramount business. I know from experience you're a man who can keep a secret, and these matters, as you'll see, are extremely secret. You may have heard some rumours that Zukor's on the way out. He doesn't like it, but the money men in New York want to make a change, so he's outvoted. He'll stay on the board and continue to rake in a lot of money but he won't be in control the way he's been for almost fifteen years. Nobody's out to get me. That's not the problem. Matter of fact, they'd like to bring me into New York, but I've made it clear, half-a-dozen times, that I'm a picture-maker and out here is where I belong, where the product's being turned out. So nothing's about to change as far as I'm concerned. They've got an idea that Lubitsch should be the production manager and I told them I have no objection to that. I'm his biggest fan. But you and I both know that Ernst won't stay off the set for very long. A year at the most and he'll be saying, "Give this office to somebody else and let me direct a Colbert picture."'

'He's too good to be stuck behind a desk.'

'Of course. Every director thinks he's a genius but Lubitsch really is one.'

They ate in silence for a few minutes. Then French said, 'Paramount's a strange operation. Starting with Hodkinson, and then with Zukor and Lasky, there was always an objective to turn out quality films. And the tie-in with UFA in Germany didn't exactly hurt us in that objective. All our pictures, even the bad ones, have had a good look. Good craftsmanship in the lighting and sets and camera-work. Many of our technicians and actors and directors came from Germany or did their early work there. For a long time De Mille was the only American director on the lot. But with all this quality the company has never had the financial stability to compete head-to-head with Metro.

'Now . . .' he went on. 'Let me tell you what's in my head. This is the confidential part. I think the day of the high-gloss super-spectacle film is fading. There will always be an audience for a De Mille picture but that classic flavour Paramount's been known for has to be tempered now by something down-to-earth, more contemporary. Not going into the ash-can, jail-house mode as much as Warner has, but giving the audience something that's closer to their own lives. You know what I'm saying?'

Julian nodded. 'I agree with you.'

'Paramount's no different from any other big company

in one respect. The motto of the top men is *status quo*. They're perfectly willing to discuss new ideas and new approaches as long as nothing gets changed. When a new Paramount picture comes to New York those men want to see the names Lubitsch or Mamoulian or Von Sternberg or De Mille on the credits. So there's my problem. I want to take what is basically a European company and turn it into an American company. I think our future's with people like Cooper and Claudette Colbert. I'd trade you Chevalier for Kincaid any day of the week.'

'Makes sense to me.' Julian said. 'Are you telling me you're getting resistance from the top?'

'Not resistance so much as inertia. You see, I'm in a good position with the board members in New York. If I'm patient, I know I'll get what I want. They don't want me to be dissatisfied and they certainly don't want me to resign. But the problem is I'm not patient. I want to get things moving.'

'You say they don't want you to resign. What if they thought you were considering it?'

French nodded. 'Something like that. I need a wedge. But it can't be done straight-on. I can't say I'm making a move if I don't get my way. When you do that you run the risk of losing even the people who support you. This would have to be a story they would hear and I could deny . . .'

'But they still might believe it,' Julian said. 'They still might say to themselves, "If we're not careful we could lose Henry French."'

'That's the way it has to play out. Something like that.'

'Do you want me to have somebody call Justin Gold or Winchell and say there's a rumour that I've asked you to come over to Thornwood?'

'You're getting warm but that wouldn't work. Everybody knows you're the boss at your studio. You make all the decisions. Nobody would believe I was giving up the top spot at Paramount to be number two man at Thornwood.'

Julian smiled. 'Tell them you're buying me out. Changing the name to Frenchwood Studios.'

'I know you're joking, but even if you weren't it wouldn't work. Too easy to check out. There's no hidden money around this town. If I were really trying to buy your studio, a dozen people in Los Angeles would know how I was planning to finance it. Also, nobody would believe you'd sell. Not unless you had something really big in mind.'

'I have a feeling you've already figured the whole thing out.'

'I'm not sure. I think I have something that might fly if you're willing to go along.'

Julian smiled again. 'If it's a good enough scheme I'll buy it and make a movie of it.'

'Like I said, it has to be big. You and I aren't sucking around looking for a job. It has to make sense but it has to be a bit mysterious as well. Since we'll deny everything we don't have to worry too much about details.' French took a sip from his wine glass. 'Here's the rumour. Julian Thorne is negotiating with a consortium of English investors who want to buy Thornwood Studios. At the same time Henry French will soon submit his resignation at Paramount Pictures . . .'

'Now we're both out of work,' Julian said.

'Wait a minute. What's going on, people will ask. What's the connection? The rumour continues: these two men, French and Thorne, will then join forces in a new organization. Thorne will retain ownership of all Thornwood theatres and both men will retain their personal contracts with a dozen major stars.'

'Then what?'

'It's only a rumour, mind you,' French said, 'but the word is that they have a new concept of film production and distribution, one that will revolutionize the business. The company will own no land and build no sound stages but they plan to release thirty major films a year.'

'What's the secret?' Julian said.

'We're not telling.' Another sip of wine. 'What do you think?'

'Interesting rumour.'

'Would it excite your curiosity if you heard it about two other studio heads, Goldwyn and Selznick for example?'

'It certainly would,' Julian said. 'And I think it would do the job for you. But I'm not sure how it would benefit me.'

'Do you think it might do you some damage?'

'I wouldn't think so. Especially if I'm going to deny it as soon as somebody asks me. But I'd have to give it some thought.'

'I want to think about it some more myself,' French said, 'but at the moment I don't see what harm it could cause either one of us. In this town it never hurts if people think you have alternatives. And, God knows, you're a king if people think you have a secret.'

After he left Paramount that afternoon, as his driver took him back to the Thornwood lot, Julian's mind quickly returned to the Daisy Bishop problem. When he was back in his office he telephoned Jack Gilder for a report on his meeting with Gillette. As soon as he hung up the receiver he placed a call to Kincaid in London.

As he lay in bed that night, Bella already asleep beside him, the meeting with Henry French eased into his mind again. There was something amusing about it. A schoolboy prank for grown-ups. Julian had known, as he and French discussed it, that though it might be useful to French in some way it was far outside Julian's normal pattern of behaviour. He was capable of being devious, but simply being devious for its own sake made him uncomfortable somehow. He also knew that French would not be surprised to hear that he had decided not to involve himself in that particular charade. For his part, if he had decided to go forward with it, he doubted very much if French, himself, when the time came for the decision, would proceed.

Julian's mother had often chided him by saying, 'Serious people don't do silly things.' As a child he had seldom thought those words were appropriate for whatever action of his was being discussed but in this case it seemed to fit.

That circuitous reminder of his mother brought his

brother to his mind, and with him the discussion about Sam he'd had with Bella a few nights before. For no other reason perhaps than the haziness of thought and concentration that precedes sleep, the discussion with French and the earlier one with Bella seemed to mist and blur together. Plus and minus. Cause and effect. He heard his voice, from some thick middle distance saying, 'I'm not sure how it would benefit me,' followed by the sound of someone laughing. Before he was able to identify the laughter he was asleep.

The next morning as soon as he came into his office he called Henry French.

'If you're still planning to have one of your shady informants plant a story that you and I are planning to forsake our studios and go into some mysterious business together, I think it's a top-notch idea.'

'I'm delighted to hear that,' French said. 'I thought you'd decided it wouldn't benefit you.'

'Maybe it won't. On the other hand it might.'


6


'Ah ha, I get my way for a change,' Sophie said. 'So we're going to California after all.' She was reclining on a *chaise-longue* in their bedroom, late at night, wearing her favourite champagne silk dressing-gown. Kincaid had just told her about his telephone conversation with Julian.

'You're an odd creature,' Kincaid said. 'Ever since I've known you, you've been waging war with me whenever I've had to make a trip to California. Now, all of a sudden when I'm not keen to go, you can't wait to take the next boat.'

'That's called reversal of roles,' she said. 'Very sophisticated and sexy. Dr Freud says it keeps love alive.'

Kincaid nodded. 'I know. I've read some of those articles. You begin to wear a starched collar, trousers, and a bowler hat, and I wear your night-dress to bed. Does that do something for you? It does nothing for me.'

'Of course not. Nor for me. But it is a bit stimulating to find yourself suddenly on the opposite side of a discussion. Our California question is an illustration of that, I expect. Besides, it's not just a whim on my part. I told you this before: I think you're obligated to be there. You're being accused of something nasty. Some sort of conspiracy. And Daisy Bishop could actually be put in prison, couldn't she? Shouldn't you go there and help set things right?'

'I don't think Julian sees it that way. He's got two actors he's trying to keep out of court. He's got a picture in the works that could capsize if there's any scandal about Daisy. He doesn't want bad publicity. In this case he doesn't want any publicity.'

'I understand all that. And I'm sure you do as well. You must have an impulse to protect his interests if you can.'

Kincaid shook his head. 'That's not my job. Julian's whole life is devoted to protecting those interests and he's good at it. He also has offices filled with people who are hired to protect his interests. If I went there, I'd be doing it to help Daisy.'

'And yourself as well, I hope. Maybe you could put to rest all those silly stories about you and her. Once and for all.' She smiled like a Siamese kitten. 'Perhaps I should testify, too. I could assure everyone that you're a loyal husband, that you never stray, are absolutely faithful to me in every way, and scarcely notice the seductive women who are always trying to attract your attention.'

'Sophie, if you were to testify, we would all be locked up.'

'That's a challenge,' she said. 'Tomorrow morning I will speak to Oliver and ask him to book us a lavish stateroom on the promenade deck of the first liner leaving Southampton for New York.'

The following day at lunch she said, 'The *Aquitania*. Sailing Thursday. Can you leave so soon?'

'I can. But you can't. I've seen your preparations for a long journey. It's like a plan to invade a hostile nation.'

'This time will be different. Just the two of us. No staff.

435

Travelling light. We'll stay at the Biltmore and live like gypsies.'

'What about Trevor and Sarah?'

'They're still at school. If we stay on in California through the summer, then perhaps Sarah can come join us. And Trevor, too, of course, if he wants to.'

After a long moment Kincaid said, 'You're not fooling me, you know. Your sudden affection for California, this willingness to go off on short notice and return to England on some unknown future date, is not what it seems. The fact is, you're still trying to shoot arrows into Margaret and Arthur. Correct?'

'Not at all. I hardly think of them at all now.'

'Of course not,' Kincaid said. 'That's some sort of vengeance in itself, isn't it?'

'Are you going to lecture me?'

Kincaid smiled. 'Not at all. I just want you to understand that I love you for your rotten self and not for what you pretend to be.'

'Did it ever occur to you that I'm going to California for your sake, so people will see us together, so they'll know that you could never be involved with a woman like Daisy Bishop. Not when you have me waiting at home.'

'A little violin music, Maestro.'

'On the other hand I might have another motive. Perhaps I want to decide for myself, once and for all, if the stories about you and little Daisy are true. One day I may even get up the courage to ask you a few direct questions.'

'Why wait?' he said. 'Do it now.'

'All right. Did you or didn't you?'

'Didn't.'

'Were you tempted or not?'

'Not,' he said.

'Are you lying or not?'

'Not.'

'So far so good,' she said. 'But I reserve the right to draw my own conclusions when I have more information. And to ask additional questions at some future time.'

'Permission granted.'

## 7

Sophie's belief that there would be no problem with Trevor and Sarah when they were told about her trip to America was accurate in Trevor's case. It gave him a perfect opening to tell her that he wanted to go to the Algarve when his school year ended, and spend the summer in Praia de Rocha with the Quigleys. Sophie told him she would answer Lenore Quigley's letter as soon as it arrived and give her acceptance of the plan.

Sarah, it turned out, presented a problem. As soon as Sophie told her about her departure plans, Sarah said, 'How perfect. I can't wait to go back there.'

'I'm afraid that won't work out, dear,' Sophie said. 'This may be a very quick trip. We're not opening up the house.' She told her about their decision to stay at the Biltmore and then, searching for a diversion, she mentioned Trevor's plans for the summer.'

'I don't give a damn what Trevor does. I have my own ideas. And I won't be left behind in dreary London all summer long.'

'But Los Angeles is no great joy in summer. And besides, as I've told you . . .'

'But I shan't be in Los Angeles. I'll stay with Ethel Richmond in Ojai. I've had a number of letters from her and I know I'll be welcome. I'm eager to tell her all I've learned at the Royal Academy. And she says I can take classes there at the school even though I'm not a full-time pupil as I was before.'

'I'm afraid not, Sarah. It just won't do.'

'Of course it will. I was going to ask you to send me there this summer even if you and Kincaid were not going.'

'It's not fair to you, dear. What if Kincaid's business is

settled quickly and we come back to England straight away? I'd hate to have to tear you away . . .'

'You wouldn't have to. I could stay on till it's time to come back here for next term. My final year in school, thank God.'

'Kincaid had a good idea,' Sophie said. 'He thought you might like to stay on here in London and take summer classes at the Academy.'

Sarah shook her head. 'I don't want to be stuck in London all summer.'

'But you wouldn't be alone. Oliver and Mrs O'Haver and the full staff will be here.'

'Can you see me having a riotous summer with Oliver and Mrs O'Haver?'

'I'm sure we could find a suitable young companion for you. A Scandinavian girl perhaps. I'll speak to your Uncle Howard. He has friends at the Swedish embassy.'

'I don't want a bloody Swedish companion from the bloody Swedish embassy. I want to go to California and that's what I intend to do.'

'You won't get far using that sort of tone with me, Sarah.'

'And you won't get far treating me as if I'm a ten-year-old with braces on her teeth and her hair in braids. I'm a sensible young woman now and you mustn't be the last person on earth to realize that. I must be allowed to make some decisions on my own.'

'Of course you must. In this particular case, however, I'm afraid there's nothing to be done.'

'But this particular case is the one we're talking about.'

Sophie smiled. 'I'm sure I once spoke to Margaret exactly as you're speaking to me now. I'm sure every girl your age . . .'

'Please, Mother. I'm not interested in every girl my age. I've heard all the stories about mother-daughter relationships. I'm not trying to understand you or make you understand me. I just don't want to be an appendage any longer. You mustn't expect me to be content with that.'

'Let's not let this get out of hand. You and I don't have

a troubled relationship. We don't need counselling. We're simply trying to make plans for your summer.'

'No, we're not. You've already made a plan and I don't accept it. I've told you I want to go with you Thursday on the *Aquitania*.'

'And I've told you that's impossible.'

'Then there's nothing more to talk about, is there?'

'I'm not sure I like the sound of that,' Sophie said.

'Why not? You sail away as planned and I stay here. That's what you want, isn't it?'

'Not just that. I want to feel that you're happy with the situation as well.'

'I am,' Sarah said. 'I'm delighted with my plans. After you leave, I'll be on the next ship to New York. It's the *Mauretania*, I believe. Leaves Southampton a week from tomorrow.'

'You're not serious. You can't do that.'

'Why not?'

'You can't just travel on your own.'

'Of course I can. I have money.'

'I realize that. But all the same . . .'

'I also have a passport.'

'Actually, your passport's in the wall-safe in my sitting-room.'

Sarah shook her head. 'I have another passport. An American passport. Under another name but with my photograph in it. According to my date of birth on the first page I'm twenty years old.'

'Why are you telling me this fairy-story?'

'Think what you like. It's the truth. And I assure you, I'll either go along with you to California or I'll arrive there a week or so later on my own.'

That evening, when she told Kincaid about her talk with Sarah, Sophie said, 'As I drove back from Wimbledon I couldn't help wondering if I was as great a mystery to my mother as Sarah is to me. I know she was lying to me about the passport but I can't imagine what she hoped to gain by it.'

439

'That's pretty obvious,' Kincaid said, 'if you think she's going to America whether you take her or not, then she must believe that you'll relent and take her. I tend to believe that myself.'

'Then you're both mistaken. Surely she doesn't imagine I'm taken in by such a story.'

'Did it occur to you that she might be telling the truth?'

'About the passport? Of course not. It's impossible for someone like Sarah . . .'

'No, it's not. I bought a fake passport for Homer Tony.'

'But all the same . . .'

'Nothing's impossible if you have determination and a bit of money.'

'You're no help, Kincaid. Now I don't know what to do.'

'Trust your instincts. If you think she's bluffing, call her bluff. I'll make arrangements for her to attend the Royal Academy this summer and she'll live here in the house as you planned.'

'But what if it's not a bluff?'

'Then she'll either run off somewhere as she did before or she'll book a stateroom for herself on the *Mauretania*.'

'Can you imagine Sarah turned loose on an ocean liner?'

'Of course I can. She'd have the time of her life,' Kincaid said.

'That's what I'm afraid of.'

The following morning, Sophie asked Oliver to book a single stateroom for Sarah on the *Aquitania*.

8

'Why would you ask a question like that?' Julian said.

'Because I want to hear your answer,' Sam said. 'Little by little I'm starting to feel I'm not a member of this company any more. What's going on?'

They were sitting in Julian's office, nearly dark outside, the lot quiet and almost deserted now, the car-park empty, the sound stages locked up for the night. 'I've been busy as hell, Sam. A lot on my mind. You know what's going on around here.'

'As a matter of fact I don't. That's what I'm talking about. And whatever I do know hasn't come from you. It's been three weeks or a month since you and I sat down and talked together. And don't tell me it's because you're busy. You're always busy. But we used to have our morning meeting anyway, regular as clockwork. Going over reports from the exchanges and the exhibitors, checking the grosses. Now all of a sudden . . .'

'We talked about this before, Sam. The morning's become a real crunch for me. All our production problems seem to come up first thing in the morning. And any phone calls I have to make to New York have to be done before lunch. When it's two in the afternoon here all those New York sharp-shooters are either half in the bag or they've gone home for the day. So it works out better for me to check the distrib-ution sheets late in the afternoon, when everybody's gone home and the phones stop ringing.'

'But you do it by yourself now.'

Julian smiled. 'If I can't read those figures by now I should turn over my job to somebody else.'

'That's another thing. Maybe you're thinking of doing that.'

'Not me, Sam. I've got the best job in the world. I can't be fired.'

'Did you see Justin Gold's column this morning? He says there's a report floating around that you're planning to sell the studio and go into business with Henry French.'

'Justin's slipping. He shouldn't print silly stories like that.'

'Maybe not. But a lot of people seem to think there's some-thing to it. I must have had a dozen phone calls before ten o'clock. That's why I wanted to see you this morning.'

'You should have told me that's what you wanted to talk about.'

'Since when do I have to have a reason to come to your

office? Since when do I have to explain away rumours about you selling the studio when you've never even mentioned it to me?'

'Things happen fast, Sam. Sometimes I can't tag all the bases.'

'Don't give me that, Julie. Not long ago I was first base. There was nothing in the works, nothing in your head, that I didn't know about. Now all of a sudden I'm getting nothing but surprises. People tell me stuff I should have already known. I get asked questions I don't have answers for. It didn't used to be that way. I was on top of everything.'

'It can't be helped, Sam. There are just so many hours in the day. I'm sure there are all sorts of things crossing your desk that you don't report to me. It's the same here. But there's nothing sinister about it. I'm not keeping things from you.'

'Maybe not. But it looks that way to other people.'

'What other people?' Julian asked.

'All right, I'll give you an example. John Corso comes to me all hot and bothered and wants to know why you flew to New York to see his Uncle Vinnie.'

'I didn't go to New York to see Vinnie. But while I was there I paid him a visit. Is that something I should have discussed with you? Is that what you're saying?'

'I'm just telling you what John said. He thought it was funny that he knew about it and I didn't.'

'Did Vinnie tell him I was there?'

'He didn't have to,' Sam said. 'Johnny has people who report to him from New York. He likes to know what's going on.'

'Maybe he does. But it's none of his business what I do.'

'He don't see it that way. He's got some idea that you and Vinnie were talking about him. He says Vinnie rang him up a day or so after you were there and offered some advice about Johnny's trucking business out here. He told him to lay off the CIO connection.'

'I think that's good advice but it didn't come from me.'

'Johnny thinks different. He was riding me about it.

Thought I knew what you were up to.'

'You can tell John for me that I wasn't up to anything. I just had a nice cup of tea with Vinnie.'

'I'm not telling him anything. He really gets hot when this union thing comes up. Those guys really have their hooks in him.'

'Johnny should listen to his uncle. If he pushes too hard with these studio people he'll end up with nothing.'

'What do you mean by that?' Sam said. Then: 'I'm not asking for Johnny's benefit. I don't pass things along to him. I just want to know for myself.'

'I don't know the specifics. I'm sure Sam Goldwyn and Mayer will be the tough nuts to crack. And those two don't tell me what they're talking about.'

'Where do we stand? The studio, I mean.'

'You know the answer to that as well as I do. If Johnny outmanoeuvres the studios then we fall in line with everybody else. But if they find a way to beat him, then we'll be against him, too. Thornwood's not calling the tune here. We're playing follow the leader. Whoever ends up with the trucking business, that's who we'll deal with.'

'Johnny won't sell out to anybody. I promise you that.'

'That's what everybody says. Just before they sign the sales contract.'

'I think you know something you're not telling me.'

'I don't know anything, Sam. I'm just blowing smoke.'

When Sam went back to his own office he found Ellie Rawson waiting there. 'The man at the gate said your car hadn't left, so I decided to wait for you,' she said.

'I'm glad you did. What's happening?'

'Nothing written down that I can bring you. Not yet. But Windrow's all steamed up about something. Spending more time than usual on the phone. Calling all over the country. New York, Chicago, Kansas City. He hasn't turned anything over to me yet but I looked at the note-pad he keeps by his phone and he'd written down your name and Julian's. And the name Corso several times.'

'John Corso?'

She nodded. 'And Vincent Corso, too.'

Before she left his office Sam said, 'My brother is buried in work right now, so I won't be passing this information along to him till I think the time is right. You understand?'

'Of course, Sam.'

She sat in her car in the car-park till she saw Sam drive away. Then she walked back to the executive office building and spent ten minutes with Julian in his office.

As soon as Sam got home he closed the door of his den and called John Corso. Ten minutes earlier Julian had placed a call to Vincent Corso's home in New York.

## 9

The day after Kincaid and Sophie arrived in Los Angeles, Sophie, having spoken on the telephone with Ethel Richmond and having satisfied herself that Sarah was indeed welcome there as a house guest and special student, drove up the coast to leave her daughter at the school in Ojai. Kincaid stayed behind in Los Angeles to meet with Julian in his office.

'I know there was a great deal of sadness in your wife's family last fall,' Julian said. 'And I feel guilty that there was nothing I could do to lighten the burden. As you know, better than anyone, we were scrambling to get the Dillinger picture ready for a Christmas release so a great many other things weren't attended to.'

'I'll tell Sophie what you just said. She'll appreciate it.'

'I've been remiss in other areas as well. I can't decide if I'm taking on more work each year or if I'm less able to handle my regular load. But in any case I seem to be struggling always to finish Wednesday's work by the following Friday. I've had my people send you all sorts of press-cuttings about *Dillinger*, so you know how successful it's been and continues to be.

When all the returns are in we expect it will do as well as *Bushranger*. Maybe better. Although *Bushranger*'s found a whole new life since *Dillinger* came out. When I looked at my calendar this morning I couldn't believe that almost six months have gone by since we sat down like this and had a proper chat. Do you realize . . . of course you do . . . that I haven't set foot in London for almost a year now?'

'If I hadn't realized it, Rosamund Barwick would have reminded me. She's out of sorts with you. Thinks you've dropped her.'

'No one ever drops Rosamund.'

'I explained to her how busy you are, great demands on your time, but she was having none of it. She said, "Business takes preference over gossip only in decadent societies."'

'That sounds like her. But Hollywood, sad to say, is not London. That's why I'm keen to go there as soon as I can. Perhaps I'll book passage to England when you and Sophie return.' Julian smiled. 'If Rosamund is truly cross with me I'm in serious trouble.'

'I'm sure she'll forgive you. She can't afford to lose friends these days. Or so she says. Every time I see her she gives me a listing of all her famous chums who have died in the past few months.'

There was a light tap on Julian's office door then and his secretary stepped in. 'Excuse me. I know you said you'd be taking no calls while Mr Kincaid is here, but it's Mr Sugarman and I thought perhaps . . .'

'Yes, I do want to talk to Ralph. Thank you, Frieda.'

She smiled and withdrew, and Julian picked up the call. He talked softly and briskly for a few minutes. When he replaced the receiver he said, 'Ralph sends his best to you. He'll be with you tomorrow when you have your meeting at the District Attorney's office. Jack Gilder will be there as well. He's representing our interests in this matter. And he'll be defending Daisy if, God forbid, there's a trial. He tells me that Bruce Gillette and a woman named Cora Faust will be there to represent the District Attorney. Mrs Faust will take your statement.'

'I'm not going there with a dog and pony act,' Kincaid said. 'I'll answer questions if they make sense but I'm not planning to tell the story of my life.'

'No one's going to manhandle you. Sugarman will see to that. I think they're impressed that you've come all this way to be helpful.'

'I certainly want to help Daisy if I can. Bob Sample's an ass-hole. I'm surprised somebody didn't shoot him a long time ago.'

'Nobody shot him,' Julian said. 'It was an accident.'

Kincaid smiled. 'I've seen that look on your face before when I was answering questions from reporters. Don't worry, Julian. I'll be a good boy. When they ask me if I'm sweet on Daisy, I'll say she's too old for me. Or too fat or too ugly. Or she has hairy legs. I promise you no one will think we've been snuggling up together.'

10

The following afternoon just after Cora Faust had introduced herself and Bruce Gillette to Kincaid, Ralph Sugarman said, 'With permission I'd like to say a few words and ask that they be included in the written record of this session.'

'Please proceed,' Gillette said.

'It should be made clear that Mr Kincaid's presence here is in no way a response to accusations or charges which have been made by Robert Sample or anyone else. No subpoena has been issued to Kincaid. No invitation or request has come to him from the prosecutor's office or from any other legal entity. He appears here voluntarily, in the name of justice, as a man who may or may not have knowledge or insight that can help to clarify the facts in this matter. He presents himself in the interest of truth and will respond to reason-able and pertinent questions. But he is under no obligation to answer questions that either he or I, as his legal representative, may feel are inappropriate or offensive. If Mrs Faust and Mr Gillette agree with these stipulations I will allow Mr Kincaid to proceed.'

Gillette and Faust looked at each other and nodded. Cora Faust said, 'We agree.' She turned to Kincaid then and said, 'We do understand that you've come here voluntarily and at your own expense and we appreciate it. There will be no set pattern to this meeting. We do not think of it as an interrogation but if you would prefer a question and answer format we can do that. How much have you been told about the shooting incident that involved Robert Sample and his wife, Daisy Bishop?'

'Not a great deal. I know he was shot in the chest when he was in her bungalow on the Thornwood lot. I believe she says it was an accident, and he says she tried to kill him because she's in love with me. And did he also say that I was in on it, that Daisy and I had planned the whole thing?'

Cora Faust nodded. 'That's what he told us. Conspiracy to commit first degree murder.'

'But he's not dead, is he?'

'No, he isn't. So it becomes conspiracy to attempt first degree murder.'

'Well, as Mr Sugarman said, I'm not here to defend myself. But I'll be happy to tell you what I think of Bob Sample. He's a crumb. From what I've seen of him and from what I've been told by other people, he only has one accomplishment to his credit. He managed to marry Daisy Bishop.'

'How would you describe your relationship with Sample? Does he have any reason to want to damage you?'

'We don't have a relationship. He was a stuntman and a wrangler on a picture I did. I've been in poker games with him on location when we were killing time between takes, and I've heard his endless line of crap about what a great hand he is with women. Everybody's heard that. But that's about the size of it. As far as his wanting to get me in some kind of trouble, you'll have to ask him about that.'

'Let's talk about Daisy for a moment. What's your impression of her?'

'Don't know her very well except as an actress. We've done two pictures together. I think she's good at what she does and she's easy to work with. I have a lot of respect for her work and she seems like a first-class woman. Knows how to handle herself. She learns her lines, she shows up on time, and everybody likes her. Even other actresses like her, and that's saying something. Nobody knows what she sees in Sample but she knows, I guess. People tell me she never has a bad word to say about him.'

'You say you've appeared in two films with her. Could that be the reason Sample's making these accusations? What sort of scenes did you and Miss Bishop play together?'

'They weren't love scenes if that's what you mean. I never play love scenes. I shoot a lot of people, then somebody shoots me and that's the story. She played my girlfriend in both the pictures I've done but there were no scenes your ten-year-old daughter couldn't watch.'

'Mr Sample's attorney has given us copies of a considerable number of press-cuttings, newspaper and magazine columns that refer to some sort of off-screen romance between you and Miss Bishop. Are you aware of those stories?'

'I've heard about them but I don't read that junk.'

'You have no idea why reporters and columnists would write such things?'

'I know exactly why they write them. With nine out of ten films the same thing happens. Some publicist or press agent who's hired to plant items about the studio, the picture, or the actors in the picture, drops a hint in some columnist's ear about the leading man and the leading lady continuing to play their love scenes after the day's work is finished. The next day it's in the paper and from that moment it's considered a fact, a piece of history, something for a writer to put in his gossip file and pull out whenever he needs an extra line in his column. Nobody pays any attention to it except the people who write that crap and the dime-store clerks who memorize it every day.'

'When you were working with Mr Sample did he ever speak to you about these gossip items linking you with his wife?'

Kincaid smiled. 'No. I wish he had.'

'Why do you say that?'

'I just mean it would have given me a chance to explain the situation to him.'

'Mr Sample has told us in great detail about the conversation between himself and his wife on the night of the shooting. He says she told him she planned to divorce him, that she was in love with you and wanted to marry you. How do you feel about that?'

'It's a stupid story.'

'You think it's impossible that she could have said those things?'

'It's not impossible, I guess. But it's hard to imagine. On the other hand I don't know what's going on between Daisy and Sample. Maybe she does want to divorce him.'

'Is it possible that she's in love with you and you don't know it?'

'Anything's possible, I suppose. I've heard that under certain conditions a mouse can kill a tiger. And eat him. But I've never seen it happen. If Daisy Bishop has decided she's in love with me, she's never told me about it. Equally important . . . no one's ever told my wife.'

'One final question. If, after we finish this informal investigation, the prosecutor should decide to bring this case to trial, if you were formally charged with conspiring to do some injury to Sample, how would you defend yourself?'

'I wouldn't. Bob Sample's either lying or dreaming. There's nothing between me and Daisy and there never has been. Sample knows that and so would anybody else who's paying attention to the facts.'

A bit later, when they were walking together toward the car-park, Ralph Sugarman said, 'I don't know what I'm going to do about you, Kincaid. Somehow you have to cure yourself of being a shrinking violet. You have to learn to

449

assert yourself, to say what you mean.'

Kincaid grinned. 'I'm a timid soul, Ralph. Always have been. I expect there's no cure for it.'

11

After he left Sugarman, Kincaid drove across Court Street to Figueroa, then down to Olympic Boulevard. He turned west then and headed for the ocean. When he came to the coast highway he turned right and headed north. The sky was grey and overcast, and traffic was light. He passed Malibu and Trancas and continued farther north till he turned off the road at the entrance to his own property, a security car parked just inside the gate.

When he pulled up and stopped in front of his house, another security guard got out of his car and walked over to meet him. 'I'm Mark Winsey, Mr Kincaid. I was here last winter when you closed up the house.'

'Good to see you. How's the place holding up?'

'Like a fort. We walk through it twice a day, check the water and the heat, look for leaks and so forth. I think you'll find it's just like you left it. We had a mild winter out here. Not much rain to speak of. No wind storms.' He took a ring of keys out of his pocket. 'I guess you want to go inside and check it out.'

'No, I don't think so. Not right away. I think I'll walk around the grounds a little.' He looked out past the stables to the cottage where Homer Tony had lived. 'Is the cottage open?'

'Yes, sir. Since the police came and took their locks off our people have used the kitchen out there to make coffee. We thought that was better than tracking into the kitchen of the main house. I hope that's all right with you.'

'That's fine.'

'If you want to go in the cottage, you'll find it's spic and span. We clean up good whenever we use it. If you look in

450

that storeroom behind the kitchen you'll see a couple big cans of gasoline. The grounds-keeper wanted to keep some there for his tractor and I told him I thought that would be all right. We'll move it on up to the garage if you'd like that better.'

Kincaid shook his head. 'No problem.' He walked away from the house then, past the stables and the corrals and the cottage, then on across the wide meadow to the far end of the property. He followed the wall to the ocean side, then followed the rim of the sea-cliff back north in the direction of the house. The on-shore breeze had picked up. It ruffled his hair as he walked beside the waist-high stone wall. When he came to the spot in the wall where a ten-foot-wide opening had once been, he sat on the stones, his back to the house, and looked out at the ocean. He stayed there for a long time, silent and inert, watching the sun sink slowly toward the horizon line. When he stood up at last he walked across the grass to the cottage.

The interior was unchanged since the last time he'd been there. He walked through the kitchen and the three other good-sized rooms, everything just as HT had left it the night he was taken to jail. His clothes on pegs and hangers, books and magazines and maps in neat piles on tables and shelves, one of the *Bushranger* posters, featuring a ferocious portrait of HT, tacked on the wall and countless drawings of him that Trevor had made stuck up in all the rooms. In the store-room behind the kitchen, his canvas jacket and work clothes still hung on brass hooks, his boots sat in the corner. And his tools were there as well. Axe, saws, hammers and mallets and sledges, bolt-cutters and post-hole diggers. And the cans of petrol for the gardener's tractor.

Kincaid switched on the lights and sat down in the rocker by the cold fireplace. He leaned his head against the chair-back and closed his eyes. When he opened them again he focused on the *Bushranger* poster, just over the mantel, Homer Tony's jungle-dark eyes staring back at him. Kincaid got up then and studied that face more closely, the

451

close-cropped tangle of hair, the wide mouth and sunken cheeks, and the intricate grid of tribal scar-welts on the cheek-bones and forehead and the bridge of the nose. It had seemed to Kincaid that Homer Tony's fingertips were irresistibly drawn to that coming-of-age pattern of scar tissue. When he read or listened to the wireless he silently traced that beautiful ugliness. As though he was reading hieroglyphics that would make old mysteries clear to him. Many times, as he watched his friend's hands touching and exploring the tortured map of his face, Kincaid's hands had lifted to the hard smoothness of his own cheek-bones. He did it again now as he stood at the fireplace studying the fierce poster, the dark settling in outside the shuttered windows and the wind rattling the door of the tack-room up the slope.

# • CHAPTER 12 •

1

When Sophie came back to Los Angeles from Ojai, after leaving Sarah with Ethel Richmond, she said to Kincaid, 'I have a feeling I've just done something stupid. I hope I'm wrong but I'm sure I've made a mistake.'

'How do you mean?'

'With Sarah. I'm so accustomed to her fighting and resisting every step of the way. So when she's deliriously happy about something it makes me uneasy.'

'That doesn't make sense.'

'I know it doesn't. But the feeling persists.'

'She liked that school when we were here last year,' Kincaid said. 'So why are you surprised that she's glad to be back there?'

'I can't tell you. It just seems different somehow. Last year she was enrolled as a pupil. I felt the school was responsible for her. Now it seems she'll be a sort of drop-in student and a house guest. She and Ethel Richmond threw their arms round each other like old school chums. I felt like an outsider.'

From their first meeting Ethel Richmond had been fond of Sarah. And she understood why. This gifted and ambitious youngster seemed to Ethel a mirror image of herself fifty years earlier. As she talked with Sarah about her dreams and disappointments, as she watched her work in class, saw her grow as an actress, Ethel had sharp, sometimes painful memories of her own beginnings in the theatre.

There was nothing parental in her affection for Sarah. Ethel had no latent desire for motherhood. 'All actors are children,' she had once said in an interview for a New York paper, 'and I am no exception. My work demands that quality. I must live with make-believe as freely as a child does. Illusion and games must have reality for me. Otherwise how can I make an audience accept a world of shadows and imagination? The role of a parent, however, is a different matter. A mother must teach her child the difference between reality and fantasy. I could never do that because I don't recognize the difference.'

To the young women in her classes she often said, 'I am your teacher. You are my students. That is our connection. I am not a mother-substitute. Your feelings for your parents, good or bad, positive or negative, are not to be visited on me. Some of you, by the time you leave St Hilda's, will have become my friends. But we will never be relatives. You must find the pleasures and the pain of family life elsewhere.'

Although she had, from the start, a strong personal connection with Sarah, those other teacher-pupil guidelines still applied. The additional element, in Sarah's case, was that Ethel looked on her not as a pupil, but as an actress like herself. In spite of the great difference in their ages and experience they were in a sense, comrades, two women in the same profession with similar tastes and antipathies and insecurities. It was not surprising, then, that she felt no impulse to regard herself as either guardian or chaperone to Sarah.

There was another ingredient, as well, in the brew. On the four or five occasions when Sophie had visited the school, when Ethel had seen mother and daughter together, she had been stunned by Sophie's inability or unwillingness to see Sarah as the gifted young woman she was. In a darkened room one might have concluded that Sophie was speaking to a ten-year-old child. And Sarah's nature and bearing did indeed seem to regress when she was in the presence of her mother. She became, as if on demand, a younger, more malleable creature. Was it a kind of tropism stimulated by Sophie's presence? Or had Sarah learned to simulate a certain behaviour pattern because she realized it was expected of her? Either answer was horrifying to Ethel who believed it was a woman's right and obligation to define herself as she saw fit, accepting no one else's formulas or structural schemes.

It was not surprising then, that when Sarah returned to Ojai, not as a ward of St Hilda's but as a friend and house guest of Ethel Richmond, she was treated as a responsible, self-propelled adult, one who could make her own choices, plan her own schedule, and keep her own hours. Any impulse that might have involved placing limitations on Sarah or limiting her choices was quickly quelled by Ethel's reminding herself that she must not become a clone of Sophie, not even in the smallest particular.

If an impression has been given that Sarah was turned loose and allowed or encouraged to run free like a beach-child, then further information is necessary. Sarah, because she treasured the freedom of movement she had suddenly discovered, was careful not to abuse it. Most of her evenings were spent with other students, in school activities, or at home in Miss Richmond's house. When she wanted to be away, she explained that she was going by bus to Ventura or Santa Barbara and specified the precise arrival time of the bus that would bring her back to Ojai. And she religiously stuck with whatever schedule she had laid out. On occasions when she planned to spend the night with Windrow in Los Angeles she told Ethel she'd be with her mother at the Biltmore. And wherever she went, her Sally Carpenter passport was in her pocket or her purse.

2

Twenty-five days after Kincaid gave his deposition in Bruce Gillette's office, Gillette sent a message to Otto Wirtz.

This office has reviewed all the existing facts and

circumstances relative to the shooting that took place in Daisy Bishop's bungalow at Thornwood Studios. We have also reviewed, along with the District Attorney, the testimonies of Daisy Bishop, Robert Sample, Linda Morales, and Roy Kincaid. Please be present in my office at 3 p.m. May 15th to hear our conclusions. Along with my associate, Cora Faust, and myself, the following persons, and only those persons, will be present: Otto Wirtz, Jack Gilder, and Ralph Sugarman.

The day of the meeting Sugarman and Gilder met for lunch at Perino's.

'Have you talked to Gillette since he set the meeting?' Gilder said.

'Just to tell him I'd be there. How about you?'

'Same here. I don't mean I haven't talked to him but I've stayed away from the Daisy Bishop business. I made my points at the beginning. He knows where I stand and he knows what's at stake for the studio.'

'But you don't know what he's decided? What the office has decided?'

'He hasn't told me,' Gilder said. 'But I think I know. So do you.'

Sugarman nodded. 'There's no case here. And if it did come to trial by some miracle, I'd love to be the defence attorney. I'd put the prosecution away with my opening statement.'

Gilder nodded. 'That's right. But by the time Daisy and Kincaid were acquitted, Julian would be bleeding from every pore.'

'Wirtz is an ass-hole, but he's not stupid. He knows he's got no case. So what's he after? You think he just wants to damage Julian and the studio?'

'Not a chance. There's no money in that for Wirtz. Somewhere there has to be a pay-off.'

'You think he's angling for a civil suit?'

'I thought that as soon as I heard he was on the case. But

456

I expected he'd drop a hint by now. I can't figure out his angle. And I can't figure out Sample's angle.'

'Maybe after this meeting we'll know the answers.'

'If we were dealing with anybody but Wirtz you'd probably be right. But he's an odd bird. I don't like the smell of this thing. I think he's pushing for a trial even if he thinks he'll lose.'

'So anything we get out of him today we'll have to squeeze out. Is that what you're saying?'

Gilder nodded. 'That's the way I see it. That's why I thought it would be a good idea for us to have lunch. One of us might have a bright idea.'

'If you and I can't squeeze him, Jack, nobody can.'


3


The five lawyers were gathered round an oblong table in the small conference room adjoining Gillette's office, Gillette and Cora Faust on one side, Wirtz facing them, Gilder and Sugarman at opposite ends. And a young woman with a steno-type machine. Mrs Faust, with two thick folders of notes, transcripts, and photocopies on the table in front of her, had been reviewing the pertinent facts of the Sample shooting for more than twenty minutes.

'We're all officers of the court,' she said at last. 'And we're reminded every day that law and justice are not finite sciences. This case we're dealing with is another example of that. A man has been shot. There were no witnesses. The victim says his wife intended to murder him because she's in love with another man. His wife has told us she loves her husband and the shooting was accidental. Each of them had had previous access to the weapon and the fingerprint evidence indeed proves that each of them at some time had handled the gun. There was also residual evidence of nitrate on her hands as well as his. Here, too, this would be possible no matter which story we chose to believe. The maid, Linda

Morales, who was the only other person present in the cottage at the time of the shooting, testifies that she heard no loud voices or other commotion that might indicate an argument was going on between Bishop and Sample. Her statement would seem to contradict, at least in that respect, Sample's version of the shooting. Regarding the motive that may have prompted Bishop to shoot her husband, she denies Sample's charge that she wanted to leave him and be free to marry Roy Kincaid. Her statement and that of Kincaid are identical. Each of them swears that there is not now nor has there ever been a romantic and/or sexual relationship between them. Our investigation has found no independent evidence that contradicts their statements. We are aware that public figures are involved here but that circumstance has in no way influenced our weighing of the facts. We find no evidence of conspiracy, no known motive for a premeditated assault with a deadly weapon. In short, apart from the victim's description of the shooting, we find no evidence that a crime has been committed. In light of these conclusions, the District Attorney believes there are no grounds for prosecution, no reason for further investigation or indictment.'

After a long moment, Wirtz said, 'May I speak freely without prejudice?'

'By all means,' Gillette said. 'Mr Gilder and Mr Sugarman may also have points they wish to make.'

'Thank you,' Wirtz said. 'I appreciate your co-operation.' He repositioned himself in his chair, smoothed his thin hair with one hand, and continued. 'I've found that hard physical evidence and unchallenged testimony by concerned parties are quite often not the determining factors in a decision to prosecute. I am disturbed, for example, by the fact that the police were not notified until the victim was removed from the scene and taken to the hospital.'

'May I comment on that?' Gilder said. 'This is something that concerns all of us. My first knowledge of the incident was when I received a call from Sam Thorne telling me there'd been a shooting. I asked him at once if the police had been called and he said yes, the security people had called them. He believed that was true. So did I. Only when Dr Moffat made his required medical report to the police did we learn that they had not been informed previously. I immediately called Mr Gillette to inform him and I believe he also talked to the police.'

'That's correct,' Gillette said.

Wirtz smiled his ice-cream smile. 'I find that account completely persuasive,' he said to Gilder, 'because I've known you for years and you're an honest man. But if I were lecturing a group of law students I would advise them to accept no story until it's tested by sworn testimony and cross-examination.'

'That's certainly true,' Gillette said, 'once a case is brought to trial. But I'm sure you're not suggesting that a trial should be held any time a complaint or an accusation is made.'

'Of course not. But when an attempt has been made on a man's life, extra scrutiny is justified. Just because I'm the only person in this room who believes Daisy Bishop should be tried in criminal court doesn't mean I'm wrong.'

'You're mistaken about one thing,' Sugarman said. 'I represent Mr Kincaid, and both he and I would be delighted to present his answer to Mr Sample's accusation before a grand jury, in court, or in any other forum. Mr Gilder and I haven't discussed this but I suspect he's as convinced of his client's innocence as I am of mine.'

'I have no quarrel with the District Attorney's decision not to bring this case to trial,' Gilder said, 'but what a pleasure it would have been to defend it. I can't remember a case where there was less evidence against an accused person.'

'I'm sorry we can't accommodate you, gentlemen,' Cora Faust said, 'but we are obliged to save the state's money for the many cases that demand prosecution.'

'This is such a convincing display of logic and reason,' Wirtz said, 'that it almost seems rehearsed.' He quickly held up his hand. 'Strike that remark. No suspicion of collusion intended.'

He paused. 'I would be less than candid with you, however, if I didn't tell you that my client, Mr Sample, will be less sanguine about this decision than I am. I am bound by the ethics and tradition of legal procedure but he is not. He's an angry man. He's been injured, physically and emotionally, and he resents it. A felonious assault has been committed and he believes someone should be brought to justice for that act. I agree with him and I've told him that. Without questioning the integrity of this investigation, I must say that I believe mistakes and oversights have been made. I beseech you on Sample's behalf to re-examine the evidence and testimony you already have before you. My confidence is just as strong as that of my fellow counsellors here. When the truth about this crime is presented to an objective jury, I am convinced that both Daisy Bishop and Roy Kincaid will be sent to prison. That opinion, I realize, has no weight here. As I've said, I accept your decision. But my client will not. That I'm sure of. Because of his profession and that of his wife he has access to the media and I assure you, once I've told him your decision, he will make full use of that access. Adultery and attempted murder and perjury don't go down well with the public.'

Directing his remarks to Bruce Gillette, Sugarman said, 'Since I came into this situation a bit later than everyone else, since my client, Mr Kincaid, is only tangentially involved, perhaps I can see these events from a slightly different viewpoint, not a strictly legal one. Might I be allowed to make a few relevant observations which would not be intended to influence in any way the decision of the prosecutor's office but which might help to dissipate whatever bad feelings seem to remain?'

A glance between Faust and Gillette, then: 'I said at the beginning that we'd be following no strict rules of procedure here, so within reasonable time limitations any remarks that won't lead to fisticuffs are welcome. When we adjourn we'd like each of you to feel that you've made your points and expressed your concerns.'

'Thank you,' Sugarman said. He turned toward Wirtz. 'You said something a few minutes ago that caught my attention. You referred to the physical and emotional damage that have been done to Mr Sample. Let's think about that for a moment. Even if we conclude, as the District Attorney has, that no felonious act has occurred, that there is no criminal evidence to justify a trial, isn't it possible, as I've said, that we might pull back from the strictly legal aspects of all this and look at it from a more subjective and humane point of view?'

'Are you suggesting that a civil action might be in order?' Gilder said. 'Because if you are . . .'

'Not at all,' Sugarman said. 'It would not be appropriate for me to propose that in any case. I'm simply trying to say, and saying it badly, I'm afraid, that I would be interested in exploring a bit further, Mr Wirtz's comment about the emotional damage that's been suffered by his client. We know the facts about his gun-shot wound. Perhaps Mr Wirtz would be willing to give us more information about these other wounds.'

Gillette turned to Wirtz. 'Do you have any response to that, Counsellor?'

'I must say I'm impressed by Mr Sugarman's benevolence. It's a quality he doesn't often display in court.'

'I accept that as a compliment,' Sugarman said.

'Of course I believe that the emotional damage Mr Sample suffered is a critical part of the case we hope to bring to trial and I welcome the opportunity to discuss that damage. But I want to be very clear on one point. We believe this is a criminal case and should have criminal prosecution. There may indeed be grounds for a civil complaint but that's another matter altogether. Mr Sample simply wants to see justice done and so do I. If he decides to air all the facts in the newspapers it will be for one purpose only, to force you people in the District Attorney's office to rethink the decision you've just told us about and bring Daisy Bishop and Kincaid to trial.'

461

'What you're saying,' Gilder said, 'is that if Sample's wife is indicted and tried, he will feel that justice has been done and both his physical and emotional damage will have been repaired.'

Wirtz nodded. 'That's how the process works, isn't it?'

'Not necessarily,' Cora Faust said. 'His physical damage is in the hands of the doctors. And as I understand it that healing process is coming along nicely.'

'Yes, it is.'

'So if you were able to force a criminal prosecution by whatever means it would be your client's emotional wounds that would benefit.'

'I suppose you could say that. But more important, justice would have been done.'

'If the trial came to pass,' Gillette said, 'and both Bishop and Kincaid were acquitted would you and your client be satisfied that justice had been done?'

Wirtz smiled. 'I would only believe that one battle had been lost. My client, I'm sure, would feel betrayed.'

'So a civil suit might be the next step.'

'To me this is a criminal matter. Since accepting this case I have never mentioned a civil solution and I'm not mentioning it now.'

'Your client wants justice to be done,' Sugarman said. 'All of us do. But in this case, if a trial occurred, and if the jury found in his favour, his wife could be sent to prison for a long time. I'm sure he realizes that.'

'Of course.'

'Daisy Bishop says she loves Sample and always has. No one who knows her questions that. How do you think he feels about her?'

'I haven't asked him directly. But I know he wants her to be convicted, so I can only assume . . .'

'Would you say he hates her?'

'I don't know. You'll have to ask him that question.'

'I'm simply asking your opinion. In your experience, doesn't an intense desire on the part of a witness to convict

462

someone take on certain characteristics of hatred?'

'I wouldn't call it hatred. She did a terrible thing to him. She's done a great many damaging things. I expect he wants to get even. It's human nature.'

'Would he lie to get even?' Faust said.

'He wouldn't shoot himself in the chest if that's what you mean. I'm starting to feel that I'm in the witness chair.'

'We can close this discussion any time you like,' Gillette said.

'I'm sorry,' Sugarman said to Wirtz. 'This started out as an attempt to be helpful to your client. From my standpoint that still is the intention. You said Daisy Bishop has done a number of damaging things to him. Can you enlarge on that a bit?'

'You people have been around the edges of the motion picture business as long as I have. Everything repeats itself out here. Most of the lives people live read like bad scripts. The head of a studio doesn't drink or smoke or swear but he likes eight-year-old girls, the ex-lifeguard who gets hundreds of letters a week from love-struck women is in love with his make-up man. Then there's the actress who makes ten thousand dollars a week but her husband can't get a job. Daisy Bishop and Sample fit somewhere in the last category.'

'He holds it against her because she's doing well and he's not?'

'He thinks she holds it against *him*. Maybe she does and maybe she doesn't but that's how it appears to him. When the phone rings it's for her. When the cheques come in the mail they're made out to her. She gets interviewed. She gets photographed. She used to be his wife. Now he's her husband. She never stops working, so she has to get up at five in the morning. That means she's in bed by nine. So if he wants to drink and bounce around the Strip at night, he does it by himself.'

'I don't think I understand,' Gilder said. 'We've been talking about a man who hates his wife so much he wants her to rot in prison. The man you're describing is disappointed because he can't spend more time with his wife. Which is it?'

'I didn't say he hated her. You did. But if he does hate her it's just since she tried to kill him.'

'Has he talked to her since the night he was shot?' Sugarman said.

'No. He doesn't want to see her. But she wrote to him while he was in the hospital.'

'Does he know what she told us,' Cora Faust said, 'that she loves him, has always loved him, and doesn't want their marriage to end?'

Wirtz nodded. 'He knows it but he doesn't believe her. She said that in the notes she wrote him, but he thinks that was just Julian Thorne's hand on the fountain-pen. You see, that's the problem. Sample has reached a point where he can't separate his wife from the studio. He thinks she's changed and he blames the studio for it. He thinks Thorne runs her life. Thornwood comes first for her and Sample comes last. He has no dignity. No identity. He has no career. No money of his own. He's a desperate man. And now she wants to leave him for another man, someone who makes even more money than she does. And to make it worse, Kincaid's another Thornwood product. So when you ask me why Sample's vengeful and bitter, I say it's based on a lot of things. The shooting just brought it all into focus.'

Gilder and Sugarman exchanged a look. When Gilder looked back at Wirtz he said, 'Something doesn't add up here. It sounds as if Julian Thorne's the one he's sore at, not his wife. Sample doesn't sound like a man who wants to see his wife in jail.'

Gillette was called to his office then. 'Five minutes,' he said as he closed the conference room door behind him. Gilder and Sugarman excused themselves and went to the men's room just down the corridor from Gillette's office. 'I'll make this fast,' Gilder said as soon as they were inside the lavatory. 'Julian didn't want anybody to know this story but himself and me. The shooting was an accident but in a different way than we've described it to Gillette. The way Daisy told it to us was that Sample was threatening to kill himself. When he put the revolver up to his head, Daisy tried to stop him but the gun went off and shot him in the chest. The maid didn't see it happen but she heard him threatening to do it through the door. Julian wanted to stay away from any hint of a marital squabble, so we went with one lie and Sample made up another one.'

'You think Daisy told you the truth?'

'I'll bet on it. She's got no reason to want Sample dead. She's crazy about him.'

'You think Wirtz knows this story?'

'I don't know. But if we find a way to hit him with it maybe we'll find out.'

On the way back to the conference room they stopped in Gillette's office. He was just coming off a phone call. 'Give us twenty more minutes, Bruce,' Gilder said, 'a half hour at the most, and I think we can bury this thing.'

'Just don't put my tail in a crack. I'll be with you in a minute.'

As soon as Gillette rejoined them all in the conference room, Sugarman said to Wirtz, 'I can't speak for the other people here but for my part I'm very appreciative of the way you've filled in some of the open spaces in this situation. It looked pretty black and white to me before, but now I see there are many shades of grey. I'm sure we haven't heard the last of this, because if your client's as determined to go public with all the details as you say he is, God knows where it could end. I know you're a skilful attorney but in this case I certainly don't envy you your job. When I was a young lawyer I had a friend on the police force in Cleveland who told me the trickiest calls they got were domestic disputes. He said, just when you were about to collar a drunk who'd been slapping his wife around, the wife would sneak up behind you and crown you with a skillet. I agree with what Mr Gilder said. It sounds as if Sample is more angry with Julian Thorne than he is with his wife. You could get back-doored all round, Mr Wirtz. While you're trying to make the case for bringing Daisy to trial she and Sample could spend a few hours together and decide to go on a second honeymoon. People suddenly get amnesia or they start to remember things they'd forgotten before. All at once you find new stories flying at you. Like the story I just told you. The wife cold-cocks a cop who's arresting her husband for beating up on her.'

'You'll be able to handle it. I'm sure of that,' Gilder added, 'but when you're dealing with actors, trying to get the same story twice, you can go crazy. As I understand it, Daisy and Sample still have the same home address. If those two get lovey-dovey again, the game's off. Say, for example, you've made your case with the papers and the public and Gillette here has changed his mind as well. Everything's set for the indictment, and all of a sudden Sample has a flash of memory and a whole new story appears.'

'Maybe he'll discover he's been in a state of shock ever since the shooting,' Sugarman said, 'but now he remembers that he was drunk when he went to her bungalow that night. He wanted her to go away with him, get away from everything for a few weeks. She said she couldn't because she had to finish the picture she's on. So he showed her the revolver and said if she didn't go with him he'd kill himself. She thought he meant it, and grabbed for the gun. It went off and he got shot. Bingo. There goes your case. The chances of that happening are one in a million, I guess, if Sample's as angry as you say he is. But all the same, when you've got a family situation you never know what to expect.'

'I've been practising law for a long time,' Wirtz said. 'I've had all sorts of surprises.'

'Of course you have. That's why you know what I'm saying is true,' Gilder said.

'Did someone tell you that suicide story?' Wirtz said.

'No. I just made it up. Did somebody tell it to you?'

Wirtz shook his head.

'Here's another possibility,' Gilder said. 'When Julian

466

Thorne realizes he's the one Sample's steamed at, I guarantee you, he'll try to make amends in some way. Julian wants people to like him. And, God knows, he's generous with his money. What would you say, for example, if Sample came to you and said Julian had offered him an executive position at the studio. Let's say production supervisor on all of Thornwood's western films. Fifty thousand a year, a ten-year contract, a big office, and the use of a studio limousine. I'm sure Julian would also agree to take care of whatever legal fees Sample owes you.'

'Are you making an offer for me to take to my client?'

'Of course not. Since there's no prosecution scheduled, there's no reason for any offer to be made. We were just sketching out a possible scenario for the future, when you've persuaded the prosecutor to prosecute and your client decides that his original testimony was false. When you take that news to Mr Gillette or one of his associates, no mention will be made of the sudden remarkable improvement in Mr Sample's financial circumstances but I'm sure someone would bring those facts to Mr Gillette's attention. Do you begin to get a whiff of trouble on the horizon, Mr Wirtz?' When there was no answer, Gilder said, 'How about you, Mrs Faust? Any comment from the prosecution point of view?'

'When money or other gifts are solicited or accepted for the purpose of blocking or aborting an upcoming prosecution, that act itself is a felony.'

'And in the circumstances I've described, who would be liable?'

'Both the lawyer and his client.'

4

Ellie Rawson telephoned Sam at his home at seven in the morning. 'I wanted to catch you before you went to the studio. I'm calling from my house.'

'Are you all right? Your sister's all right?'

'We're fine. But the situation we discussed before is starting to percolate. There's a Windrow column that's scheduled for next Tuesday. I just sent a copy of it by messenger to your house. And he's working on a much longer piece on the same subject. Scheduled for the *Kansas City Journal* a week from Sunday. This is dynamite stuff, Sam. You'll see when you read it. But don't call me at Windrow's offices. I'll ring you from a pay phone when I take my lunch break.'

Marie had got out of bed and put on a robe while Sam was on the phone. When he hung up she said, 'Before breakfast you're getting calls in the bedroom. Who was that?'

'Ellie Rawson.'

'Ellie, Ellie . . . sweet woman. You should have let me say hello. How's her sister?'

'Mona's fine. Everybody's fine.'

'She called you at the crack of dawn to tell you she's fine? Later in the day she gets sick maybe? Too weak to pick up the phone?'

'She wanted to catch me before I went to the studio.'

'She caught you before you went to the bathroom even. What's so urgent it can't wait till office hours?'

'Give it a rest, Marie. She wanted to tell me she sent something by messenger.'

'To our house?'

'To our house. It should be here any minute.'

'So what is it?'

'It's a bomb. When you untie the ribbon and open the box your entire neighbourhood explodes.'

'No bomb jokes, please. Such things happen, you know. California has its share of loonies and moon-walkers. Radicals and Reds and rag-heads every place you look. Can't wait to get to America, those people, and the next thing you know, they want to blow it up. You've got a sick sense of what's funny, Sam. Just since we came to California. I like a good joke as well as the next person but any joke about a bomb blowing up in my face is not funny.'

468

'Then don't laugh, for God's sake. Am I supposed to have my feelings hurt, break into tears maybe, because you don't think I'm funny?'

'Don't start up with me. I haven't even brushed my teeth with Ipana yet. A woman asks her husband a simple question, she's got the right to a decent answer. True or false?'

'All right, already. Ellie's got a friend who thinks she's got an idea for a movie. It's probably a piece of crap but she asked me if I'd read it and I said I would. So she's sending it over.'

'You're a business person, Sam. You've told me so yourself. A thousand times. Money and contracts. Buying equipment and firing people. So now you've decided you're an expert on making movies as well.' She walked toward the door. 'Tea or coffee you're having this morning?'

'Whatever you're having.'

'I'm making a nice pot of Orange Pekoe for myself.'

'Then I'll have tea.'

'And a piece of crumb cake.'

'Whatever you say.'

The messenger arrived when they were at the breakfast table. When Sam came back to the kitchen Marie said, 'A man comes to the door when we're still in bed practically and you come back empty-handed. Where is it, whatever she sent?'

'I put it in my briefcase. I'll read it when I get to the office.'

'I had it in my mind while I was waiting for you to come back, my tea getting cold in my cup, that you'd read it to me out loud and maybe we'd have a good laugh. Or maybe I could get to be an expert on making movies like you are. Then there'd be two of us in the house.'

As soon as he was inside his car, while the engine was idling, he tore open the envelope the messenger had brought and studied the typewritten page Ellie had sent along. When he finished reading it he said, 'Jesus Christ.'

An hour later he met John Corso in a coffee shop at the corner of Vermont and Franklin. They sat down in a booth in the back corner and Corso said, 'I left my glasses in the car. Read it to me.'

'This is hot stuff, Johnny. I'm not gonna blurt it out in some dime-a-dozen coffee-shop.'

'Who said blurt it out? Talk soft. I'll hear you. It's my eyes that ain't worth a shit. There's nothing wrong with my ears.'

Sam looked round him, satisfied himself that there was no one seated nearby, and began to read in a husky whisper. 'Big news coming in Los Angeles. Now that prohibition's over and the illegal booze money has dried up, are the crime families from New York and Chicago moving into the motion-picture business?'

'That son of a bitch,' Corso said.

'It gets worse,' Sam said. 'Is it a coincidence that John Corso (Johnny Cello to his New York friends) . . .'

'He's got the balls to mention my name?'

Sam read on . . . 'John Corso and Sam Thorne, the number two man at Thornwood Studios, were business partners for years in New Jersey? And how does Roy Kincaid, Thornwood's hot new box-office star, fit into the picture? He admits that he's spent several years of his life in various prisons. And when his friend, Homer Tony, under indictment for rape and assault, jumped bail and left the country, there is evidence that Kincaid, who guaranteed his bond, may have engineered that escape. Rumours persist also that his employers, Sam and Julian Thorne, along with Corso, may have had a hand in that manoeuvre.'

'This ass-hole's crazy,' Corso said. 'Where does he get his information?'

'There's more,' Sam said. 'Against the background of Kincaid's apparent disregard for all laws and Corso's newly acquired power over the movie industry through his trucking monopoly, one can't help wonder what's going on. When we contacted the Los Angeles police they seemed strangely disinterested. But not the West Coast office of the Federal Bureau of Investigation. They hinted that J. Edgar Hoover may be sending a squad of agents to Los Angeles to take a close look at the situation. This is a development we should all support. Having fought a courageous battle against radicals and trade unionists, it would be tragic if our industry allowed itself to be taken over by organized crime. Let's lock the barn door before the mob steals our horses.'

'Is that it?' Corso said.

'More to come. Ellie says this is the first of a series. He's doing a long story for the *Kansas City Journal* a week from Sunday.'

'He can write till he's blue in the face. Getting it printed is something else again. One phone call and we shut off his water in Kansas City. He won't get this story printed or any other story. He won't be syndicated. He won't be working there. Just because he can talk on the telephone and use a typewriter cuts no ice with me. My ten-year-old kid can do that. I didn't like that Limey bastard the first time I laid eyes on him in your office. But we tied his pecker in a knot then and we'll do it again.'

'It might not be so easy this time. He's got a reputation now. Some other syndicate would probably take him on.' Sam folded the sheet of paper and put it in his jacket pocket. 'A hot story like this, he can always find somebody to print it.'

'You're right. But he hasn't started looking for anybody else yet. Before he does that I'll send someone to have a talk with him.'

'That's dangerous, Johnny.'

'Everything's dangerous. You think that crap he's writing ain't dangerous?'

'But if somebody leans on him this whole thing could . . .'

'Nobody's gonna lean on him, Sam. If I was gonna do something tricky I'd have done it when we had him dead to rights on the car-burning. I just think he has to talk to my legal adviser so he understands what he could be up against.'

'Do me a favour. Let me talk to him first. Sort of slide into it. Then if he tries to hard-nose me, we'll let your *consigliere* take over.'

471

'Is that your idea or Julian's?'

'What do you mean?'

'Just what I said.'

'Julian doesn't know I'm talking to you. He doesn't know anything about this story. I called you as soon as I got it this morning.'

'Stop jerking yourself around, Sam. You think you got information that Julian ain't got? You think this dame that's reporting to you ain't giving the same information to Julian?'

'Why would she do that? She's my contact. She used to be my secretary.'

'And before that she worked for Julian, didn't she? Use your head. Julian's the boss. He's got lines out all over town. Three weeks ago you told me he was sloughing you off. Isn't that what you said? Leaving you out of meetings. Too busy to talk. One thing and another. If that's going on you can mark my word . . . you ain't his primary source for nothing.'

'I'm the number two man at Thornwood. Everybody knows that.'

'Bullshit, Sam. If number one is putting the freeze on you you're number zero. Let me ask you a question. Do you think there's a chance that Julian knows you've been juggling his money?'

'I never took a nickel of Julian's money.'

'Maybe not. But you made some financial adjustments that benefited me. And in exchange for those favours you benefited pretty good yourself. Am I right?'

Sam nodded. 'We helped each other out.'

'That's right. Like we've always done. Two old pals. But it wouldn't look that way to Julian. I'm asking you if he's wise to what we've been doing?'

'Not a chance. He leaves the books to me. And all those transactions are covered. Everything's on the up and up.'

Corso smiled. 'Just asking.'

Sam drained his coffeecup. Finally he said, 'So how do you want to handle Windrow? Will you let me talk to him first? I won't threaten him. I think I can convince him that this stuff he's writing is bad for the whole industry. What do you think?'

'It looks to me like you and Julian got something big at stake. So do I. But they may not be the same things. You know what I mean? So let's leave it like this. I'll decide what's in my best interest and you look out for yourself. If I decide to talk to Windrow or take some other action I'll do it. Whatever you decide, you do that. You don't have to tell me what you're up to and I won't tell you. That way we're both protected.'

'From Windrow or from each other?'

'We've never had to worry about each other, Sammy.'

'I know it. That's what I'm talking about.'

'We still don't. You trust me and I trust you.'


5


It was mid morning when Sam drove his car on the Thorn-wood lot. Before going to his own office he went to see Julian. As he passed Frieda's desk on the way to Julian's office door she said, 'He's not here, Sam.'

'Is he on the lot?'

She shook her head. 'He didn't come in at all this morning.'

'Is he sick?'

'No. He's flying to New York this morning. He didn't tell me the exact time. He may have taken off by now. Didn't he tell you he was going?'

'I left early yesterday afternoon and I was late getting in this morning. Haven't been to my own office yet. He must have left a message there with Norma.'

When he sat down behind his desk a few minutes later there were half a dozen telephone messages but none from Julian. He buzzed his secretary on the intercom.

'Are these all my messages?'

'Yes, sir,' Norma said.

'Julian didn't call me?'

'No. Frieda says he won't be in today.'

'I know that, damn it. I just want to know if he called.'

'No, sir.'

'All right. Get me Ellie Rawson in Burt Windrow's office.'

A few minutes later Norma tapped on his door and came in.

'What happened to the call?' Sam said.

'Something odd going on. When she came on the phone I said, "It's Sam Thorne for you, Ellie", and she said, "Mr Windrow's not in his office just now. I suggest you call back this afternoon." When the line went dead I called again and the same thing happened.'

'Jesus Christ, what's the matter with her? Give me the number. I'll call myself.'

As soon as he heard Ellie's voice he said, 'It's Sam Thorne, Ellie, and I need to talk to you.' No answer. The line went dead. When he dialled again another woman's voice said, 'Miss Rawson's gone for the day.'

Half an hour later she called him. 'You're going to get me in a hell of a mess, Sam. I told you not to call me at Windrow's office.'

'Where are you now?'

'In a telephone booth. Did you get the envelope I sent you this morning?'

'I got it all right. But now I can't locate Julian. Did you send it to him as well?'

'Did you want me to?'

'No, I didn't. But I thought . . .'

'I sent it to you, Sam. I thought you'd want to decide whether to tell Julian or not. Did I do the wrong thing?'

'No, you did what I wanted. Frieda says he's taking a plane to New York this morning. Probably on his way by now.'

'I don't think so,' she said.

'What do you mean?'

'One of Windrow's spies at Metro checked in an hour or

so ago. She said there's a big meeting in Mayer's office this morning. Every studio head in town is there. She rattled off all the names on the phone. Julian's there, too. Or at least he was there.'

'What's going on?'

'That's what Windrow's trying to find out. But nobody knows.'

'Thanks for the tip.'

'Don't hang up for a second,' she said. 'I hope you've got that job cleared for me at Thornwood, Sam. It's time for me to get out of this place. I told Windrow I'd be leaving next week.'

'I understand,' Sam said. 'Everything's in order here. Your office is ready whenever you are.'

As soon as he hung up he called Metro. He was passed along by three secretarial voices before a woman with a rich Hungarian accent said, 'Yes, Mr Thorne, I am Mr Mayer's assistant. What may I do for you?'

'My brother told me he'd be in a meeting there and it's quite urgent that I speak with him.'

'I'm terribly sorry but the meeting ended almost an hour ago. Your brother and Henry French left together as soon as it was over.'

6

'Who is this man Windrow?' Vincent Corso said. He had just finished reading the typewritten page Julian had given him.

'He's an Englishman. Used to be an actor. Then he got an opportunity to take over a syndicated gossip column that someone else had been writing and he seems to have made a success of it.'

'I don't read that trash but I seem to remember his name.'

'There was an incident some time ago. Someone poured

475

gasoline on one of our studio cars and torched it. It turned out that Windrow was involved.'

'But I wouldn't have known about that,' Corso said.

'I wouldn't think so. But there was a time when Sam needed to make some contacts in London and I believe John may have helped him out with that.'

Vincent shook his head. 'Maybe I heard the name from John but I don't think so. He keeps things to himself. Just as I've always done. The young men have all the answers, don't they?' He sipped from his teacup. When he set it down he touched the typewritten sheet on the low table. 'I'm not sure why you brought this to my attention. As I think we discussed the last time I saw you, I'm not an active man any longer. I still have my health, thank God, and my old age is provided for, but other people have taken over the details. You know what I mean? Sometimes I'm asked for my opinion but not very often. I was never blessed with a son but I have three fine nephews, John and his brothers, and all of them seem to have a gift for business. I've heard that old friends in New Orleans and Chicago have made some investments in California and it's an obvious fact that John has done well with his trucks and his other operations, but when I read something like this that Mr Windrow has written it has no reality for me. I can't imagine that anyone would take it seriously. From what I see in the papers, Mr Hoover has his hands full with those farm-boys robbing banks and shooting policemen in the Midwest. I don't think he'll waste time trying to connect John's business with people who are breaking our country's laws.'

'You're right,' Julian said. 'I agree with you. But as we discussed when I was here before, the studio people are very nervous about one man getting a lock on some service they depend on to make movies. I convinced them that the CIO business didn't have to be a menace. And I believe John indicated he might be willing to back away from that. At least for now. So things had begun to calm down a bit. Then the word got out that Windrow was about to do a series of columns about organized crime muscling into the studios and somebody got hold of a copy of this story I just showed you, linking John to certain crime organizations here in the East.'

Corso smiled. 'This man Windrow's right about one thing. Prohibition's over. People are legitimate now.'

'I agree with you. But Hollywood's a small town. Men in my business don't read much but when they see something in print they believe it. As soon as word got out about this article, all the studio heads got together like a bunch of army generals to decide what they're going to do.'

'When did this happen?'

'Yesterday morning. Before I flew to New York.'

Suddenly Vincent seemed to choose his words carefully. 'You were in this meeting, of course.'

Julian nodded. 'As I said, it was the top man from every studio in town.'

'And did they reach a decision?'

'Yes, they did. And it's not good news for John, I'm afraid.'

After a moment Vincent said, 'I told you the last time you came to visit me how much I respect you. But I want to be very clear about this. I am interested, of course, in anything that affects my nephews and their families but I have no position at all in their various commercial affairs. I'm only their uncle. I'm not a business associate. I know none of the details of John's operation in Los Angeles. When he's successful, I celebrate. When he has problems, I sympathize. Beyond that . . . nothing.'

'I understand that. And it's in that spirit that I'm talking to you. Not as John's associate but as his uncle. Business is one thing. Family is something else.'

'Exactly.'

They sat quietly then with their teacups, only faint sounds from the kitchen easing into the room. At last Vincent said, 'You say they reached a decision. What is it?'

Three days after Julian returned to Los Angeles from New York, Burt Windrow was killed in an automobile accident. He had been driving, just past midnight, from Ventura Boulevard toward the ocean on the Malibu Canyon road. His car had gone off the road at its highest point and had crashed on the floor of the canyon five hundred feet below. Since there were no witnesses and no skid marks the police concluded that he'd been travelling too fast to negotiate the curve where his car went out of control.

When the police were bringing his body up the steep slope to the road they discovered, two hundred feet from the top, the body of a young woman. She had been thrown from the car as it hurtled and bounced its way to the foot of the canyon. In the pocket of her jacket was a passport. The newspaper reports of Windrow's death named Sally Carpenter as his companion in the car. Only after Ethel Richmond called the Biltmore to see if Sarah was with her mother, only then, when she'd been reported missing to the police, was the link made. Tentatively at first, when Kincaid was shown the passport, and conclusively, when he viewed her body in the morgue.

For many months afterward, for years in some cases, when people who knew him personally, as well as thousands of people who had known him only from his two films, were trying to unravel the enigma of Roy Kincaid, the people who knew him best, those who had seen him during those last weeks he spent in California, tried to remember things he'd done or said that would have given some clue to the events that came later.

No one, however, was able to point out anything significant, any signpost that might have led an alert person to predict all or part of what was to unfold. No one could remember any revealing thing he had said during that time. Without being sullen or reclusive, he had been, they concluded, remarkably silent. So, they asked themselves, was that the missing puzzle-piece, that silence? Should that have made people aware that some thundering sea change was taking place?

Sophie believed, at least she professed the belief, that Sarah's death had affected him in some way that no one could have predicted. It was a conclusion that calmed her, somehow, and freed her in her own mind of any guilt.

Grief, however, is an elusive rationale. No one can guarantee what its effect will be. Grief or unrequited love can motivate almost any reaction, or so we believe. So when Sophie labelled Sarah's death as the stimulus for Kincaid's behaviour, no one contradicted her. Any other theory, her family concluded, would have been needlessly cruel, if expressed, to Sophie.

But all this came later, when her own grief about Sarah had diminished, and when any death, tragic as it might be, seemed logical and inevitable when measured alongside the puzzle of Kincaid. Only then did Sophie feel the need to serve herself, to touch up her own self-portrait, to anoint herself with the loving attention she had previously given to Sarah and Kincaid. She was, after all, the survivor. And at last the dead must bury the dead.

These after-the-fact adjustments and rationalizations, however, must not be allowed to overshadow the true shock and sadness she felt when Kincaid told her the final truth about Sarah. Sophie trembled and was unable to speak. She tried to stand but could not. Her limbs ached and her eyes, and painful moans came out of her throat in a regular rhythm like water crashing on rocks. After she was sedated, lying heavy in her bed, those sounds, muffled now, maintained their steady rhythm, like the growls of a gut-shot animal.

Nurses were brought in to stay with her and Kincaid sat beside her bed except for the hours when he was doing the housekeeping of death. Sending cables, making trunk calls, supervising the details of shipping Sarah's body to England. But busy as he was, the hours crawled by. He had no appetite and except for fitful naps in chairs, he couldn't sleep.

When he sat in Sophie's room she lay for hours with her eyes closed. When her eyes opened she looked at him with no expression. There seemed to be nothing she could say to him. And nothing he could say to her.

## 8

Two days after Windrow's death John Corso had a call from his father in New York. 'Your Uncle Vinnie wants to see you.'

'What's he want from me?'

'Don't ask me. He's taking the train to Chicago tomorrow and he wants you to meet him there on Thursday.'

'I can't just jump on a plane and fly to Chicago.'

'Suit yourself. I'll give Vinnie your message.'

'Wait a minute, Papa. Look, if Vinnie wants to see me I'll go meet him. Where's he staying in Chicago?'

'The Bismarck.'

'That's a dump.'

'So sleep in the streets. It ain't a honeymoon, Johnny. You're just gonna visit with your uncle. Be nice to him. Maybe he'll send you a fruit-cake for Christmas.'

John's plane battled a storm all the way to Chicago. On his way from the airport to the Loop hailstones hammered on the roof of his taxi-cab. And all through the night the wind and rain beat against the window of his hotel room.

The next morning he sat with his uncle in Vincent's single room at the Bismarck. 'This ain't much of a room, Uncle Vinnie.'

'You don't like it?'

'It's a great room for a midget.'

'It's a place to sleep. I've got a decent bed, a couple of chairs, and a toilet where I can take a leak.'

'I'd go nuts in a room this size. I need to spread out. I got myself a nice suite at the Palmer House.'

'When you're my age you won't need so much room.'

'I guess not.' He took out a cigar case. 'You want a nice cigar? A guy makes 'em for me. Some nutsy Cuban.'

'Don't smoke please. It gives me a headache and my sinuses dry up. Now . . .' he resettled himself in his chair. 'Now we'll talk some business.'

John smiled. 'Your business or mine?'

'My business. I don't concern myself with other people's business.'

'Last time we talked you told me you was about to retire.'

'That's because you were asking for something I didn't want to give you.' He opened a small bottle that had been sitting on the table beside him and popped a pill into his mouth.

'You taking pills now, Uncle Vinnie?'

'Over-the-counter only. I don't believe in dumping a lot of chemicals in my body. A little antacid is all. I get gas when I travel on a train.' He screwed the cap on the pill bottle and carefully placed it on the table. 'Now let me tell you why I wanted to see you. And by the way, I want you to know I appreciate your flying all this way to meet me. I myself have never been inside an airplane.'

'You're lucky. I thought I'd be dead before I got here.'

'So you're here,' Vincent said. 'That's what counts.' His eyes drifted off then, as if he'd lost his train of thought.

'You were about to tell me why you wanted to see me.'

The old man snapped back into focus. 'Important changes are starting to happen. There was a time when we and our friends thought the only way to bring a dollar to the table was to be in New York or Philadelphia or Miami. Chicago was big, too. But Kansas City was as far as anybody wanted to go to do business. Now the picture's changing. We're making plans for the west.'

'Isn't that what I've been telling you and Papa? Los Angeles is the place. Why do you think I . . .'

Vincent held up his hand. 'Wait a while. Let me finish. I'm talking about the state of Nevada. We've got a foothold there. We've made friends, bought a certain amount of land,

and now we're ready to make our move. It's four years now since they legalized gambling in that state. So that's the door-opener. Reno's already in place just waiting to be developed. And Nevada City. And there's a little place nobody ever heard of called Las Vegas. Hundreds of acres we own there. We're going to turn that town into the gambling centre of the world. Clean and legal. Casinos, hotels, entertainment, recreation of all types. A place to take your family.'

'But we could have all that in Los Angeles. And I'm already set up there.'

Vincent shook his head. 'No gambling there, Johnny. If Los Angeles was a gambling town we'd have gone in there years ago. But it won't work. Out there you've got crusaders, policemen, dumb politicians, religious nuts, and a lot of poor people. Mexicans and blacks and dirt farmers looking for a relief cheque. Sure, there are some well-off movie people but that won't ring the bell for us. Besides, when we're set up in Nevada, we'll get those people we want from Los Angeles. And Denver and San Francisco and every place else as well. People that want to gamble and get laid and have a good time will come to us. And they'll keep coming. We don't need to squeeze into somebody else's town. This will be our town. We won't have to pay off every politician with his hand out. We'll have our own politicians. In ten years we'll pick the Governor. It's a new world, Johnny. A big plan, a big investment, and a pay-off such as you can't imagine. And you'll be a part of it. You and your brothers. Up to now all this has been worked out by your father and me and our friends. Now we want to bring in you and Nello and Frankie. Your dad's talking to your brothers today, and as soon as you and I get back to New York we'll all sit down with the lawyers and the accountants and put together an operational plan.'

'What do you mean, New York? I got my hands full in Los Angeles. I have to get back there.'

'I know a little bit about your problems out there.'

'I didn't say anything about any problems.'

'I know you didn't,' Vincent said. 'But we'll get into that later. We've got bedrooms on the train back to New York tonight. We'll have a nice meal in the dining-car. Then we'll go into the California business in detail.'

'I mean it, I have to get back to Los Angeles. I mean, I'd go to New York with you if I could but I just can't do it.'

'Sure you can, Johnny. It'll work out fine. You'll see.'

## 9

'Do you feel guilty about Sarah?' Sophie said. It was the first day she'd been out of bed and off medication. Her maid had called the service desk of the Biltmore and arranged to have a masseuse, a hairdresser, a manicurist, and the Chinese woman who did facials come, one by one, to the bungalow. By mid afternoon Sophie was downstairs, beautifully dressed, sitting in the garden-room with Kincaid.

'No,' he said. 'I feel rotten about it but I don't feel guilty.'

'I feel so guilty I think I'm about to wither up and die. I keep telling myself if I hadn't brought her here a few weeks ago she'd be alive now. I feel as if I never should have brought her and Trevor when we came here before. Remember, I told you I thought I was making a dreadful mistake when I agreed to let her stay with Ethel Richmond. How right I was. How foolish I was not to follow my instincts. I don't know how she met that fool Windrow but I can't help thinking there must have been some connection with the way he feels about you. I have a thousand questions I want to ask Ethel Richmond but I don't trust myself to be in the same room with her. Why was Sarah allowed to roam free? How well did she know Windrow? Was she living with him? And what about that passport with her picture in it but someone else's name? She told me she had such a passport . . . you remember that . . . but I didn't believe her. I still can't believe that a child like Sarah . . .'

'She wasn't a child, Sophie.'

'She was my child. And I can't imagine what prompted her to deceive me the way she did, in such a systematic way. Did I do something terrible to her that I wasn't aware of?'

'I know how upset you are, Sophie, but you're talking as though Sarah had something to do with her own death. It wasn't something she did to make you feel bad. She was killed in an automobile accident.'

She shook her head. 'We always put labels on things, so people won't ask questions, but I don't think anything is an accident. There's always something or somebody behind whatever happens. When a great number of unhappy things flood over you all at once, you can be sure it's more than coincidence.'

'I don't have an answer for that. I don't know what you're talking about.'

'Survival. That's what I'm talking about.'

Later that afternoon a note came in the mail from Ethel Richmond.

> There's no way I can say how sorry I am about Sarah. I knew her for just a short time but she was very dear to me. She was a wonderfully gifted young woman and I know how much you'll miss her. Please accept this heart-felt expression of my sympathy.
>
> There are a number of her things still here in my home. I assume you will want to have them. Please telephone me at the school so we can make arrangements for you to come and collect them.

'What gall that woman has. How dare she send me a sympathy note. Is it possible she doesn't know how I feel about her? I'm tempted to drive up there myself. She deserves to be publicly humiliated.'

Kincaid didn't answer. He folded the note and slipped it back into the envelope. Sophie took it from his hand, tore it in four pieces and dropped it on the carpet.

'I'll drive up tomorrow and pick up Sarah's things,' he said.

Sophie shook her head. 'Then you'll have to go alone.'

'I wouldn't let you come with me.'

'Thank God someone understands how I feel.'

'I don't understand at all. I know you feel something but I can't figure out what it is.'

'My God, are you going to turn on me, too?'

'Not me,' he said. 'I just hate to see you in a battle with yourself.'

She had dinner alone in her bedroom. When Kincaid went in to say good-night she said, 'Did you hear my jabbering on the telephone late this afternoon? I had all sorts of odds and ends to clear up. Things I ordered in shops, that sort of thing. Now I'm going to try to sleep without pills for the first night since. . . please put your arms around me.'

He sat on the edge of her bed and held her close to him. 'What a good feeling,' she said. 'You always make me feel safe. We never should have left our little cottage in Dinard. You know that? What a wonderful place to escape. Sometimes it seems that's all I've ever thought of. Escaping. When my mother and I left India to come back to England, I remember standing at the boat rail and saying to myself, "I'm escaping." It's a wonderful word, isn't it? Till I met you, it seemed I was always running from something. It's still my strongest instinct. Except now I want you to escape with me.'

When he kissed her good-night she said, 'Pretty soon you must come back to my bed. I promise I won't be all jumpy and red-eyed and hysterical. I hate to sleep alone.'

He turned off her bed-lamp then. As he crossed the room to the door she said, 'I have a good idea. Don't go to Ojai tomorrow. Go Wednesday. Take me for a long drive tomorrow. We'll race out across the desert with the top down and the wind blowing our hair. We'll smell the orange groves and eat a truck-driver's lunch and pretend we're never coming back.'

485

'What am I, a stranger or something?' Marie Thorne said.
'Just answer one question. Do I pry into your business? Do
I lift up the phone when you're talking to find out who it is
you're talking to? Some women do that, you know, but I'm
not one of them. Leave the men to their business, my mama
always said. And I've followed her advice. Bella agrees with
me. She doesn't nose into Julian's business at the studio any
more than I nose into yours.'

'I don't know what the hell you're talking about.' It was
early evening. Sam had just come home from the studio.

'I'm talking about consideration. Common courtesy. You
can have all the secrets you want at work. I don't even want
to hear about those nutsy actors and all the financial shenanigans you and Julian are up to every day. But when it's
something that concerns our close friends, yours and mine,
two people we've known since we were little kids, people
who we're over to their house once a week or they're at ours,
then I say, what's got into your head that you wouldn't tell
me . . .'

'Tell you what? I don't know who you're talking about!'

'Are you dumb all of a sudden? Who do you think I'd be
talking about? Arloa and John. The Corsos.'

'All right,' he said. 'The Corsos. What about them?'

'I can't believe my ears. You're still not going to tell me.'

'You're making me crazy, Marie. What am I supposed to
tell you?'

'So that's it. You're pretending you don't know anything.
All right. So let me ask you a question. When did you talk
to Johnny last? You two talk to each other twenty times a
day. When was the last time?'

'Right before he went to Chicago to see his uncle. Haven't
heard from him since. The people in his office said he's not
back yet.'

'You mean, you haven't talked to him since he left? He
hasn't called you from New York?'

'Chicago, Marie, not New York. I just told you he went to Chicago.'

'Don't get smart with me. It looks like maybe I know something you don't know for once. Arloa called me this afternoon. Called me from the railroad station downtown. She told me she was taking the train to New York. That's where John is. Not Chicago. New York. They're moving back east.'

'You're crazy.'

'I may be crazy but I'm not deaf. The truck came this morning for their furniture, they put their house on the market, and they're gone. Arloa's tickled to death. She always hated this meshuggenah place out here.'

'John's got a business here. He can't live in New York.'

'That's what I said but Arloa just laughed. She said, "No business. No more business. He sold it."'

Half an hour later Sam was sitting with his brother in the library of Julian's home. 'What the hell is going on?' Sam said. 'Since when do I get the latest news from my wife? She tells me Corso unloaded his business and he's moving back to New York. Did you know that?'

'I knew it was in the works.'

'What's the big secret? Why didn't I know it?'

'I didn't tell anybody, Sam. Why didn't Corso tell you?'

'That's the other thing. That's why I don't believe it. Why would he get rid of everything he's built up out here?'

'He sold it, Sam. The whole works. Marie had it straight. The papers were signed yesterday and the money was transferred. In New York.'

'You seem to know all about it.'

Julian nodded. 'I put the deal together.'

'You bought him out?'

'No. I just made the deal.'

'Why?'

'Because somebody had to do it.'

'Are you telling me you actually talked Corso into selling just when he was sure he had the world by the ass?'

'I didn't talk to him at all. I dealt with his uncle.'

'You mean Vinnie sold him out?'

'No. Vinnie did him a favour. I told him if John didn't sell at a fair price he'd be stuck with a business that wasn't worth a nickel.'

'And Vinnie believed that?'

'It was the truth and he knew it. The studio people had decided to go it alone. Set up their own operation. Trucking, catering, dry-cleaning, the whole works. The day after John flew to Chicago every contract he had with every studio was cancelled as of next month. By then we could have put together a temporary truck fleet that would have serviced the studios till we could find a management team and buy our own equipment.'

'Jesus. I didn't think anybody could put the screws on Johnny.'

'Nobody put the screws on him. He didn't have to sell.'

'The hell he didn't. The way you tell it, he'd have ended up with a parking lot full of empty trucks.'

'That's the way Vinnie looked at it. So the studios set up a corporation, took over Corso's equipment, and paid him a fair price.'

'How much?'

'Both parties agreed not to talk about the price.'

'You can tell me.'

'Sorry, Sam. I can't tell anybody. But the studios thought it was fair and so did Vinnie.'

'But what did Johnny think?'

'I guess Vinnie's the only one who can answer that.'

'Johnny may have the last laugh after all. He was the brains of that operation, you know. He kept things moving. You'll have a tough time finding a man who can do what he did.'

'We've already found one. He knows about trucks, he's an experienced executive, and he knows the ins and outs of the movie business.'

'A local guy?'

'He's local now. But he came out here from New York.'

'Do I know him?'

Julian smiled. 'As well as you know yourself.'

'What does that mean?'

'It means, we want you to take the job.'

'You're kidding me.'

'No, I'm not. You're the first choice. And before you answer, let me tell you we're talking about big money. Bonuses. Profit-sharing. The whole works. The studios just want service and continuity, a dependable, non-union outfit. You'll have the same operation Corso had. We're handing it to you on a silver platter.'

Sam shook his head. 'Not me, Julian. I've got a job and I like it.'

'But this is a chance to run a company. You'd be the boss. Why don't you think it over for a few days and then we'll talk again?'

'I don't have to think it over, Julian. I'm staying with you. I like it where I am.'

After a long moment Julian said, 'I was hoping we could do this the easy way but I guess we can't. What if I told you that Ethridge did a detailed examination of the studio finances for last year? Then after we looked at what he found he did the same thing for the past five years.'

'You don't need Ethridge to give you that kind of information. That's what I'm for.'

'Let's not kid each other, Sam. You've been working some kind of a hustle. Corso's money and Thornwood money. In and out. Here and there.'

'I don't know what you're talking about. Corso's company sends us legitimate bills for services and we pay them.'

Julian shook his head. 'It's no good, Sam. It won't wash. I'm not asking for an explanation. I know all I need to know. For some reason Corso needed to hide money and we were hiding it for him.'

'If you think I had my hand in the till . . .'

'I don't think that. I didn't say that. But if Corso wasn't paying you off he should have been. That's not the point.

Whether you were pocketing money on the deal or not you were putting the make on me and my studio.'

'You're wrong, Julie. I've been straight with you.'

'Don't try to hondle me, Sam. I know what I'm talking about and so do you.'

'Corso's my friend, Julian. You know that. What's wrong with doing a favour for a friend?'

'That's the problem. You think there's nothing wrong with it. We're in business, Sam. Big business. You can't make decisions that affect me without telling me what you're doing.'

'Are you saying that if I'd told you what I was doing for Corso you'd have told me to go ahead?'

'That's a good question. Since you didn't tell me you must know the answer.'

'I don't see who got hurt.'

'I know you don't. As I said, that's the problem. Let me ask you another question. And I warn you, I already know the answer. When Ellie Rawson sent you that column Windrow was about to publish, did you show it to Corso?'

'Sure I did. His ass was on the line.'

'So was mine. Why didn't you show it to me?'

'I figured Ellie sent it to you at the same time she sent it to me.'

'She did. But you didn't know that. You told her not to send it to me. You didn't want me to see it.'

'Who told you that?'

'Ellie told me.'

'She's crazy. I was going to bring it to you myself.'

'When?'

'That same day.'

'But you didn't.'

'I couldn't. You went off to New York.'

'What time was it when Ellie sent that envelope to your house?'

'Early morning. Seven-thirty maybe.'

'Where do you think I was then?'

'At your house, I guess.'

490

'But you went to Corso's house.'

'I guess you're saying I should have gone to you first.'

'It seems reasonable to me.' Then: 'What did Corso say when he saw what Windrow had written?'

'He was sore as hell.'

'I'll bet he was. So was I. Did he have any ideas about what should be done?'

'He said he'd contact people in Kansas City to see that Windrow's stuff wouldn't be printed. And he said he'd send someone to have a talk with Windrow.'

'Did he do that?'

'I don't know. I told him to hold off till I'd had a chance to talk to Windrow myself.'

'Did you talk to him?'

'No. I changed my mind.'

'Did Corso get to him?'

'I don't know. Next thing I knew Windrow was dead and John was in Chicago.'

'Do you think Windrow's car went off that cliff by itself?'

'What do you mean?'

'I mean, when you heard about it did you think it was an accident?'

'That's what the papers said. So I guess they're right.'

'I hope so. I'd hate to think that girl was killed because somebody decided to kiss Windrow goodbye.'

'It was an accident, Julian. What can you do?'

The following morning in Julian's office, Sam and Julian sat facing each other. At last Sam said, 'I never thought it would come to this.'

'Neither did I.'

'When I came out here, when you talked me into it, I thought we'd stick it out together.'

'So did I, Sam.'

'I guess Marie would be just as happy if we packed up and went back to New York, the way Johnny and Arloa did.'

'You could always do that, but I hope you won't. I want you to take over the trucking operation. I told you that.'

491

'Is everybody in town gonna know you dumped me?'

Julian shook his head. 'Nobody knows anything except you and me.'

Sam put a cigarette in his mouth and lit it. 'Look, Julian, I'm not perfect. I never said I was. Maybe I made some mistakes. But I was never out to get you. We're brothers, for Christ's sake.'

'That's right, Sam. That's what makes it tough.'

11

Kincaid got up early the morning he drove to Ojai. Sophie was still asleep but he left a note on her dressing-table.

I should be back by mid afternoon. I'll see you then. If I'm a little late don't fret.

It was clear and cool outside, a blue and gold morning. Traffic was light as he stayed on Wilshire Boulevard all the way west through Hollywood, Beverly Hills, and Westwood to Sepulveda. There he angled off on San Vicente to the coast highway. At Topanga Canyon he pulled into the car-park in front of a one-storey building with a sign reading *Malibu Security Systems* on the roof. Inside there was a grey-haired man at the desk. Kincaid identified himself and gave instructions that the guards and security people at his house above Trancas should vacate the property as of noon that day. 'Is this a permanent cancellation of service?' the man behind the desk asked.

'I'm not sure. I'll notify you when I've worked out my plans.'

On up the coast, at Point Dume, Kincaid parked his car and climbed down the rocky path to the beach. He walked south on the hard-packed sand just above the water's edge till he came to the cove where the brown seals barked and swam and sunned themselves on the rocks. He turned

492

around then and walked back to his car.

In Oxnard he had breakfast in a Mexican coffee-shop just off the highway. Huevos rancheros, sausage and fried potatoes, and two mugs of black coffee. It was past eleven when he pulled up in front of Ethel Richmond's house. As he got out of his car a young girl came out of the house and down the steps to meet him.

'I'm Rosemary,' she said. 'Miss Richmond has a class this morning. If you can wait she said to tell you she'll be home at twelve-thirty.'

'I'm sorry,' he said. 'I have to get back to Los Angeles.'

She showed him where Sarah's things were, just inside the front door. Several pieces of luggage and two cardboard boxes sealed with paper tape. The girl helped him carry the things out and put them in the car. When they were finished she said, 'Are you Sarah's father?'

'I'm her stepfather.'

'All the girls here felt awful when we heard what happened to her. Miss Richmond was so upset she couldn't do her classes for several days. One day she broke down, and cried right in the middle of her lecture.'

It was early afternoon when Kincaid turned off the coast highway on the road leading to his house. There was no guard at the gate. And no security people at the house when he got there.

He left his car in the driveway beside the house, took off his jacket and left it on the front seat. Then he walked across the lawns, past the stables, to Homer Tony's cottage, opened the tool-shed in the back, and took out a crow-bar and a heavy sledge-hammer. Carrying those tools he walked across the pasture toward the spot where the land fell away sharply to the sea below. He located the spot in the wall that had once been open, where, when he and Sophie first saw the property, there had been a gap in the old stone wall that edged the top of the cliff. That mysterious gateway leading nowhere had disturbed Sophie. When he'd started construction on the house Kincaid had specified that the space should

493

be filled, that the stone wall should be restored and made continuous and complete.

As he stood now, looking at the wall, it was not easy to tell where the new stones and mortar had been put in. But Kincaid had studied the wall many times, had admired it and inspected it with Homer Tony. He knew precisely where the original opening had been.

There was an easy on-shore breeze across the high meadow but the sun was high now and warm. Kincaid took off his shirt, picked up the sledge, and began to demolish the new section of the wall, dislodging the stones one by one and rolling them down the cliff to the rocks below.

## 12

It was late afternoon when Kincaid came back to their bungalow in the Biltmore gardens. As soon as he opened the door and went inside, even before he found Sophie's letter, he knew she was gone. It wasn't necessary to open closets or count pieces of luggage. There was a neat emptiness to the rooms that gave a clear message. Her letter, in its blue envelope, was stuck with tape to the mirror in his bathroom.

Don't be angry. I'm not a crazy woman. I just feel a maddening need to do something, to get outside myself somehow. I'm not running from you. It's not that. I'm running from myself. And from a place where every palm tree, every flower scent, the sound of every automobile horn, reminds me of Sarah.

I'm taking the noon train to New York. I'll be staying at the Commodore. I'll ring you from there as soon as I arrive. After all those hours on the train I hope my head will be clearer and I'll be able to make more sense than I'm making now.

I regret that we had that conversation about escaping

from things. I don't want you to think that's what I'm doing now. I'm not. I'm simply trying to work myself out of the dreadful muddle I've been in, trying to know what I've done to deserve all the agony that's been heaped on me during these past months.

I know I'm too sensitive. I've always been. But I've made great efforts, since I was a child, to conceal that weakness from other people. Why have I done that? Why should I have to do that? I don't know. That's one of the questions I need to answer for myself.

I know this sort of soul-searching can be boring to someone who's forced to watch the process. That's the principal reason I'm going off. I don't want you to think of me as tiresome and childish. Or vengeful. Because I'm not. But all the same I have violent impulses sometimes. I feel as if I'm at war, defending myself against all sorts of people, people I once loved and depended on. It's a lonely feeling when you realize there's no one, or almost no one, you can count on. Apart from you I have nobody. I'm slowly coming to realize that. So I thank God for you. But what has become of all the other people I've loved and befriended and catered to through the years? Why have they turned against me? What possible reasons could they have?

I had a frightening dream a few nights ago. I dreamed about Sarah. I've dreamed about her almost every night since we found out she was dead. But this was different. It was as though she was contacting me directly from wherever it is she's gone to. And she was laughing at me. A cruel and ugly sort of laugh. As though her death had been in some way a triumph over me, a way of getting even. I was trembling when I woke up. I lay awake for a long time. Then a peculiar thing happened. When at last I was able to go to sleep again, I had the same dream. But this time, instead of laughing, Sarah was screaming obscenities at me. I'll never forget it. It's etched on my memory like a tattoo.

Does Trevor's decision to go off for a summer with the Quigleys signal that he, too, is making plans to abandon me? A few months ago such a thought would have been laughable, but now that I'm beginning to see people for what they really are, all my foundation-stones are tumbling.

Consider Clara Causey for example. All my life she's been a second mother to me. She's often said that she feels closer to me than she does to Nora, her own daughter. And I have always relied on her. Loved her and trusted her and confided in her. But the last time I saw her, after Margaret's marriage, when I stopped off to spend the night at her home on my way to the Towers, I realized when I left the next day that she, too, had undergone some change. Some nasty reversal. As we'd talked the night before, I could see she was choosing sides. For all her sympathetic manner and her apparent appreciation of my feelings about Margaret's sudden marriage, it was clear that she was listening to me but not hearing, that she was fully and permanently in support of my mother, and that nothing I might feel or say would change that. It was a painful, disheartening moment for me. I suddenly felt like a leper, an abandoned person. It's a feeling I have very often now. It bewilders me and frightens me. Do I have a bell round my neck whose warning sound is heard by everyone but me?

All these thoughts I'm pouring out to you are sharply focused just now because I know that in a short time you and I will be on a ship to England. Heading home for Sarah's memorial service. So there I'll be, surrounded by people who will pretend to sympathize with me and wish me well, but who in fact will be judging me, assessing my guilt, and secretly listing my shortcomings.

Strangely enough, this prospect doesn't frighten me. The truth is I'm looking forward to it. If Margaret and Arthur imagine that the tragedy of Sarah's death will in any way soften my feelings toward them, they're in for a surprise. I am no longer keen to turn the other cheek. On the surface I will be docile and civilized and familial but I plan to make them suffer for the way they've treated me. People who have seen me as a victim will discover that I'm well able to protect myself and my interests.

Sad as I am about Sarah's death, I feel a kind of exhilaration about the future. No one (except you, of course) will ever own me again. No one will be allowed to hurt me.

Then there's the question of Trevor. Losing my daughter has made me determined not to lose my son. I'll see to it that he has absolutely everything a boy could want. You and I will take a long beautiful journey this summer and he'll come along. Maybe the three of us will roam the world for a few years. All those other fools who thought they could abandon me will find that I've turned the tables on them.

Please try to understand this childish need I have to spend some days alone. To wrestle with my own problems. Please clear up whatever loose ends you have in California so you can proceed to New York in a week or ten days. I will welcome you there, we'll drink lovely champagne and make elaborate plans for the future. We'll leave our enemies behind and make a private world for ourselves.

Kincaid had read her letter in his bathroom where she'd left it. When he came to the end, he looked up slowly and saw his own reflection in the glass. His expression was that of a man who'd just witnessed the fall of a child from a high window. 'Good *God*,' he said.

13

The following night, very late, almost three in the morning, Kincaid's house by the ocean exploded in flames. Fire-trucks came from Santa Monica, Oxnard, and Malibu. By the time they arrived, however, the garages, the stables and barn, Homer Tony's cottage, and the main house were burning like torches. The firemen could only water down the surrounding fields, prevent the fire from spreading, and watch the great house crackle and roar and slowly turn to a blackened shell.

When the sun came up, Kincaid's car was found among the rocks at the foot of the cliff, directly below the opening in the stone wall. There was no one inside it and there were no bloodstains or other evidence to indicate that any-one had been behind the wheel when it crashed on the rocks.

Later that day when the ashes had cooled, the firemen walked through the ruins of the house. There was a strong smell of gasoline and two charred and twisted gasoline cans were found among the ashes and rubble. But after close inspection the county police and firemen concluded that no one had been inside the house or any of the other buildings when they burned.

Sophie learned about the fire two days later when her train reached New York. When she was informed that Kincaid had not been seen since the fire she told the authorities that he often went off by himself for days at a time. That was surely what he had done in this instance. This matter-of-fact explanation, however, was in no way a reflection of her true feelings. She secretly believed he was dead and she was stunned by grief. Once again she was being punished.

When she returned to England, when people were whispering and newspapers were printing their speculations that Kincaid was still alive but had chosen, for reasons of his own, to disappear, Sophie made a public statement that she now believed her husband was dead. Either he had perished in the fire or had been killed by the people who set the fire. 'If Kincaid were alive,' she said, 'he would be back with me by now. Nothing could have kept him away.'

14

The chronicle of any man's life can not be brought to a proper conclusion until that life ends. In the months following

Kincaid's disappearance scarcely a week passed without some new evidence being produced or some rumour being publicized. He had been seen in San Francisco, in New Orleans, in half the cities and towns in southern California, in London, of course, in Berlin and Buenos Aires and Toronto. Because it was generally known that he was Australian, multiple sightings were reported there. Newspaper people scoured Tasmania, every corner where he was known to have worked as a young man. Regular visits were paid to seamen's hotels, and to the cattle run where he'd worked in Glenrowan. All sightings and hare-brained theories were checked out by someone or other. And always it was done with a spirit of optimism. People truly believed he would turn up at last, return to California, and resume his career there. That theory appealed to them, so they believed it. Then suddenly they stopped believing. Or so it seemed. And the newspapers, for the most part, stopped publishing the rumours, the sightings, and the theories. Wireless comics, who had made frequent references to him, stopped doing so. People stopped saying, when someone didn't show up as planned, that he'd 'done a Kincaid,' and the showings of *Bushranger* and *Dillinger* became less frequent in theatres round the world.

In Launceston, however, in northern Tasmania, there was a retired mathematics teacher named Lester Rigby who wrote occasional features for the local newspaper and had once had three short articles accepted by the *Melbourne Press*. Since the first articles about Kincaid's career had appeared in Australian papers and magazines, Rigby had read and digested and catalogued every piece of available information. He considered himself a man who might one day write the definitive biography of Roy Kincaid.

Disturbed by Kincaid's disappearance, Rigby told his brother Abel, with whom he lived, that sooner of later, he would solve that mystery. Abel, a stone-cutter, also retired, who was able to drink as much stout in one evening as his brother, nodded his head each time he heard Lester's prediction and said, 'I've full confidence in you. You're the man for the job, all right. I think you might pull it off.'

It was Abel, five years after Kincaid's disappearance, who carried home the information that sent his brother to Flinders Island. After pub-closing one night he came home and said, 'Maybe I've located Kincaid for you.' He'd met a chap in Boylston's public house who'd just returned from a journey to Whitemark on Flinders Island. 'He goes there to buy sheepskins from the Aborigines. They have a wee settlement there,' Abel said. 'He was a pleasant bloke. A good talker. He was telling me stories about those people and the way they live, just minding their sheep and keeping to themselves except when they come into Whitemark on market day and get pissed in the pubs. He said there's one of them there, a fierce-looking bugger, who has his own little sheep station and lives in a cabin off in the hills, just him and his dogs. But every now and again he shows up in Whitemark, this fellow, and sits in a corner of the pub, all alone and silent. He speaks no English, nor does he seem to understand it. Speaks a tribe dialect from Queensland where he says he comes from. But on certain occasions, this chap told me, he's been known to stand up on his two feet, drunk as a lord, and rattle off speeches from Shakespeare like a proper trained actor. The Aborigines don't know what he's saying but the publican does, and he doesn't know what to make of it. I remember you told me once that Kincaid used to stand on the pavement in London and spout off long passages from Shakespeare, so I thought there might be some connection.'

The following week Rigby crossed Bass Strait on the mailboat that went each Thursday from Devonport to Flinders. When he returned six days later, his brother drove to Devonport to pick him up. As soon as they met at the foot of the gangway, Rigby said, 'A bloody wasted trip, Abel.'

'You don't mean it. Couldn't you locate him?'

'I found the fellow you heard about. But it's not Roy Kincaid. The man's like a picture out of a child's book about Aborigines. Long hair and a beard, his skin turned to leather by the sun and the wind.'

'Could you talk to him?'

'Not a word. The chap who took me into the hills to the sheep station knows a few words of the dialect the fellow speaks, but all the same they didn't seem able to communicate much. It didn't matter, however, because as soon as he said a few words I knew it wasn't Kincaid. He spoke in a sort of husky whisper. Sounded nothing at all like Kincaid's voice.'

'He's an actor, you know,' Abel said. 'Maybe he was putting one over on you. Remember what the publican said? That he rattled off those speeches in perfect English.'

'I know. He told me the same thing when I talked to him. But I don't believe it. I think he's made it up. It doesn't matter anyway. If the chap I saw spoke English like a rector he couldn't be Kincaid.'

'How's that?'

'Remember the old Aborigines we used to see when we were small lads, when some of the tribes still lived here in Tasmania? Remember the scar-welts on the men's faces? That pattern of scars they'd cut with a knife across their cheek-bones and foreheads?'

Abel nodded. 'Always scared me half to death. I remember that. I used to run like a goat when I saw them coming.'

'Well, that's the kind of face I saw over there on Flinders Island. Tangled hair and scars on his cheeks. He's surely a man from the Queensland tribes. That lot is locked into another century, cut off from everybody. But whoever he is, he's not Roy Kincaid. He's not anybody. He's just a poor solitary bastard with two dogs and a herd of sheep.'

15

The predictions about her future that Sophie had made to Kincaid didn't turn out as she had expected. If the deaths of Brannigan and the Major had seemed to wrench Margaret's family apart, Sarah's death and Kincaid's disappearance had the opposite effect. From the day Sophie returned to the

Towers she found a tender climate there. Solicitude and kindness. One sensed an unfamiliar but warm silence in the corridors and reception rooms, something almost serene.

There was no explanation for it. The sadness about Sarah's death was evident, of course, but there was no element of performance in the grief, no subtle competition to determine which family member was most deeply affected.

After the memorial ceremony, during the following days, the great house slipped smoothly into familiar routines. There seemed to be no contrary positions. All judgements and opinions appeared to be acceptable. No one frowned or bit his lip. No challenges were heard. No questions were raised as to when Sophie would return to London. Long before she decided to sell the London house there was an unspoken assumption at the Towers that she had come home to stay. If this realization was unsettling in any way to Margaret and Arthur their discomfort was not visible. Soon after Sophie's return it became apparent that she was accepted now as the central figure in the household, free to plan, to manage, to choose, as she saw fit. With Evan counselling her, just as his father had counselled Margaret for so many years. One morning when John Trout and Mrs Whitson were having tea together in the kitchen she said, 'How lovely it is now. For years we all looked after the young people. Now the young people are looking out for us.'

Evan didn't abandon his writing, of course. He spent at least an hour every day in the handsome study Sophie had fitted out for him, going over his notes and making plans to begin a new play. Sophie encouraged him. They spent hours together, discussing various projects, weighing their possibilities, searching for a concept that would be truly significant. For nearly two years Evan worked on revisions of a play he'd written while he was still at Oxford. At last, however, he decided it should be abandoned. Sophie agreed with him. But she continued to advise him about his future work.

There was an easy fluid movement now to days at the

Towers, a sense of completion. The hunter come home.

The four of them, Margaret and Sophie and Arthur and Evan, dressed each night for dinner. They played bridge together, listened to the wireless, and the men played billiards. When they said good-night, Margaret and Arthur turned toward the east wing, Sophie and Evan toward the west.

The four of them discussed everything together except for certain matters that were never discussed. A few of their neighbours in the county were astonished when they realized at last how things were between Evan and Sophie but most of the people who had known them since they were children together were not surprised at all. Mrs Whitson, although she pretended not to notice the living arrangements in the west wing, gave full approval to their frequent journeys to Dinard. 'How nice for the young people to have a bit of a holiday in France.'

Although Kincaid was not a forbidden subject his name was seldom mentioned. Both Sophie and Arthur were convinced that he was dead. Evan and Margaret, by their silence, seemed to agree. But Trevor, who had never doubted that Kincaid was still alive somewhere in the world, expected that one day he would see him again.

# A selection of bestsellers from Headline

**FICTION**

| | | |
|---|---|---|
| STUDPOKER | John Francome | £4.99 ☐ |
| DANGEROUS LADY | Martina Cole | £4.99 ☐ |
| TIME OFF FROM GOOD BEHAVIOUR | Susan Sussman | £4.99 ☐ |
| THE KEY TO MIDNIGHT | Dean Koontz | £4.99 ☐ |
| LEGAL TENDER | Richard Smitten | £5.99 ☐ |
| BLESSINGS AND SORROWS | Christine Thomas | £4.99 ☐ |
| VAGABONDS | Josephine Cox | £4.99 ☐ |
| DAUGHTER OF TINTAGEL | Fay Sampson | £5.99 ☐ |
| HAPPY ENDINGS | Sally Quinn | £5.99 ☐ |
| BLOOD GAMES | Richard Laymon | £4.99 ☐ |
| EXCEPTIONAL CLEARANCE | William J Caunitz | £4.99 ☐ |
| QUILLER BAMBOO | Adam Hall | £4.99 ☐ |

**NON-FICTION**

| | | |
|---|---|---|
| RICHARD BRANSON: The Inside Story | Mick Brown | £6.99 ☐ |
| PLAYFAIR FOOTBALL ANNUAL 1992-93 | Jack Rollin | £3.99 ☐ |
| DEBRETT'S ETIQUETTE & MODERN MANNERS | Elsie Burch Donald | £7.99 ☐ |
| PLAYFIELD NON-LEAGUE FOOTBALL ANNUAL 1992-93 | Bruce Smith | £3.99 ☐ |

**SCIENCE FICTION AND FANTASY**

| | | |
|---|---|---|
| THE CINEVERSE CYCLE OMNIBUS | Craig Shaw Gardner | £5.99 ☐ |
| BURYING THE SHADOW | Storm Constantine | £4.99 ☐ |
| THE LOST PRINCE | Bridget Wood | £5.99 ☐ |
| KING OF THE DEAD | R A MacAvoy | £4.50 ☐ |
| THE ULTIMATE WEREWOLF | Byron Preiss | £4.99 ☐ |

*All Headline books are available at your local bookshop or newsagent, or can be ordered direct from the publisher. Just tick the titles you want and fill in the form below. Prices and availability subject to change without notice.*

Headline Book Publishing PLC, Cash Sales Department, PO Box 11, Falmouth, Cornwall, TR10 9EN, England.

Please enclose a cheque or postal order to the value of the cover price and allow the following for postage and packing:
UK & BFPO: £1.00 for the first book, 50p for the second book and 30p for each additional book ordered up to a maximum charge of £3.00.
OVERSEAS & EIRE: £2.00 for the first book, £1.00 for the second book and 50p for each additional book.

Name ...................................................................................

Address ...............................................................................

...........................................................................................